EAST OF THE SUN, WEST OF THE MOON

EAST OF THE SUN, WEST OF THE MOON

JOHN RINGO

EAST OF THE SUN, WEST OF THE MOON

A Baen Books Original

Baen Publishing Enterprises
P.O. Box 1403
Riverdale, NY 10471
www.baen.com

ISBN 10: 1-4165-2059-7
ISBN 13: 978-1-4165-2059-7

Cover art by Kurt Miller

First printing, May 2006

Distributed by Simon & Schuster
1230 Avenue of the Americas
New York, NY 10020

Library of Congress Cataloging-in-Publication Data

Ringo, John, 1963–
   East of the sun, west of the moon / John Ringo.
       p. cm.
   "A Baen Books original."
   ISBN-13: 978-1-4165-2059-7
   ISBN-10: 1-4165-2059-7
   1. Space warfare—Fiction. 2. Power resources—Fiction. 3. Human-computer interaction—Fiction. 4. Human-alien encounters—Fiction. I. Title.

   PS3568.I577E37 2006
   813'.6—dc22

                                            2006003143

10 9 8 7 6 5 4 3 2 1

Pages by Joy Freeman (www.pagesbyjoy.com)
Printed in the United States of America

To Miriam.
For reminding me how to laugh.

And, as always, for Captain Tammara Long.
You fly with the angels now.

ACKNOWLEDGEMENTS

I'd like to thank, as usual, Travis (Doc Travis) Taylor for help in technical aspects of this book. Notably, for straightening me out on some fairly simple aspects of orbital mechanics and reentry. I'd also like to thank Timothy (Uncle Timmy) Bolgeo for correcting my numerous mistakes in electrical design. I'd also like to thank Patrick Vanner for saving me from making various technical mistakes as well as for the suggestion to use shuttles. As usual, any mistakes that are left are mine and not theirs.

I'd also like to thank Linda Donohue for a great outfit and the girls at the San Diego Hooters, Downtown, for providing me with about half the minor characters on Team Icarus. Inspirational ladies all.

PROLOGUE

Orc Private Tur-uck was having a bad day. It had started by being left in the camp to guard the baggage and had only gotten worse when the humans counterattacked and took the portals. He slammed his shield into the human pussy and drove him back, striking hard with his broad, curved sword. The blow slipped past the human's defenses and blood flew from a deep gash that gaped like a bloody grin. Then the orc stabbed back in a blinding reverse and drove the sword into the human's throat, ripping it out in a welter of gore.

"The doors!" Sub-leader Grath bellowed. "Forget the humans! Get the doors up!"

Tur-uck sheathed his sword and dropped his shield, sliding his fingers under the edge of the fallen doorway. The portals, until the humans had taken them, had been spilling out the victorious hordes of the Masters. None could stop the Horde; it was victorious in every battle. Except, a quiet voice suggested, this one. The humans had appeared from their own doorways and were knocking down the doors of the Masters, and the Horde, blindly obeying orders, was dashing out of the camp, leaving it to the human invaders.

The doorway was heavy and the attack had cost Grath's group many lives. Lives were nothing; they were to be spilled for the Masters. But they had barely enough to lift the portal to the level of Grath's knees, much less set it back upright. It was heavy metal with a concrete base and no matter how they struggled they could not get it more than a meter off the ground.

Tur-uck suddenly let go and dropped to his hands and knees, scuttling under the doorway.

"Come back here, you coward!" Grath shouted, his voice made guttural by the Changes to his throat and the large canine tusks in his mouth.

"I'm going to get help!" Tur-uck shouted, but he knew he was too late. Already more of the humans were charging Grath's remaining orcs and from the far side there would be no way to raise the doorway.

Tur-uck jumped upward, exiting the portal near its top and falling through the air without a cry to thump to the ground on the far side. His ears were immediately assaulted by the blessed sound of thousands of orcs, angrily balked by the fallen doorways. One of them kicked him as he rolled across the ground, but that was more in the way of a greeting than in anger. It was simple courtesy to kick someone when they were down.

"You!" one of the Lesser Masters shouted, striding forward and waving back the orcs that were gathered around the mirrorlike portal. "Where did you come from? What in the hell is happening?"

"Master!" Tur-uck groveled, rolling to his hands and knees and bowing his head. "The humans have taken the portals and tipped them over! We tried to right them but we were about to be overwhelmed. I returned to bring word, Master!"

"How the hell did that happen?" the Lesser Master shouted.

"What the hell is happening?" another voice bellowed and the orcs fell silent, falling to their knees and bowing as a True Master approached.

"Lord Chansa," the Lesser Master said, bowing so that his robes swished back and forth nervously. "This one has returned through the portal. He says that the humans have taken the camp on the far side and are turning the portals face down. We can't push through that."

"Damn!" Chansa shouted. "Damn and damn and damn again!"

Chansa Mulengela was a huge "natural" human. He was nearly three meters tall, broad and thick in proportion, designed right at the limits of what a normal human could support. Huge, dark and fearsome, he appeared like nothing but a human juggernaut, especially when, as now, he let loose his volcanic temper.

Tur-uck had assumed the full prostration, nose in the dirt, arms and legs spread, as the True Master approached. At the sight of the Master's anger, many of the gathered orcs had followed his example.

"You!" Chansa said, tapping him on the side. "Get up. Tell me what you know."

"Master!" Tur-uck said, almost overjoyed to be actually addressed by a Master but well aware that it might be the last conversation he ever had on earth. He stumbled to his knees and bowed his head, hands clasped in front of him. "I was part of Sub-leader Grath's group. We were assigned to provide internal security to the southeast portion of the camp. The camp was attacked by dragons as the portals opened. We reacted to the landed dragons then saw many human soldiers pouring out of other portals. They were pushing the portals of the Masters over so we went to stop them. There were only four on the portal that we attacked, but they killed eight of my leader's group. We took the portal and the remainder of us tried to raise it, but it was too heavy. So I came through to bring word. Master, spare me!"

"Stand up, orc," Chansa growled. "Let me look at you. Did your sub-leader order you to return?"

"No, Master," Tur-uck admitted, getting to his feet and standing to attention. The build of his body did not permit him to stand fully erect and his long arms dangled almost to his bowed knees. "He ordered me *not* to return."

"So, why did you?" Chansa asked, mildly.

"I . . ." Tur-uck started to reply then stopped. "Masters needed to know. There was not time to explain, Master. I beg your forgiveness! I was not fleeing battle, Master! I am brave and willing to die. My life is yours, Master! But the Masters needed to be told!"

"My God," Chansa muttered. "Celine finally screwed up and produced an orc with initiative."

Tur-uck didn't know what that meant so he remained mute.

"Did you challenge Sub-leader Grath for his position?" Chansa asked, walking around the orc and looking him up and down. "You are a prime specimen. You might have won."

"I did not, Master," Tur-uck admitted.

"Why not?" Chansa asked.

"Sub-leader Grath was a good leader, Master," Tur-uck said, nodding in nervousness. "He kept us fed and told us of good ways to fight, to kill the humans. I . . . I did not wish to challenge him until he had taught me all I might learn from him."

"And one with patience?" Chansa laughed. "So all the portals are down?"

"They appear to be, Marshal," the Lesser Master interjected.

"I wasn't talking to you," Chansa snapped. "Orc, what is your name?"

"Tur-uck, Master."

"All the portals are down, Tur-uck?"

"Yes, Master," the orc admitted. "The west side was commanded by a Greater Dragon and none could defeat her. Many human soldiers had also attacked and there appeared to be an attack on the south gate. Most of the Horde had left by the north gate by the time I came through."

"The human soldiers, you fought them?"

"Yes, Master."

"How was their armor marked? Their shields?"

"The shields were marked with words and a sword, Master," Tur-uck said. "I do not know the words. Their armor had a device of an eagle, here," he said, indicating the left breast.

"Blood Lords," Chansa snarled. "Very well. Tur-uck, you are made a sub-leader as of now. Of course, you must fight to retain your position, but you have it. Good job coming back; I'm willing to accept that it was not for lack of courage."

With that the True Master strode away and Tur-uck sagged in relief.

"I would have had your head off for disobeying orders," the Lesser Master snarled.

"I live to serve, Master," Tur-uck said, falling to hands and knees. "My neck is yours to strike."

"Get up," the Lesser Master said. "Your life is Marshal Chansa's to take and his decisions I don't question. I'll assign you a sub-group. Don't fisk up or I *will* have your head."

"Yes, Master," Sub-leader Tur-uck replied, rising to his feet and admitting that maybe he wasn't having such a bad day after all.

CHAPTER ONE

As the axe clanged off his shield, Herzer knew he was having a bad day.

His opponent was as fast as he was and darned near as tall and strong. Furthermore, Herzer had never in his life fought someone who used an axe with such effectiveness. The weapon had a meter and a half metal-covered shaft and his opponent used it as a combination of quarterstaff and axe to great effect.

Herzer Herrick was a young man just nearing his twenty-fifth birthday, a shade over two meters tall and broad in proportion, with black hair and dark green eyes that, as now, slitted into fiery intensity when he was in combat. His face had a long scar on the cheek and more scars crisscrossed his unguarded forearms, visible proof of his many battles.

Herzer flickered the tip of his longsword forward and was rewarded with another one of those nasty spin and catches, the haft of the axe clanging into his blade then the head sliding down to trap it. Before he knew it, the butt of the axe was hammering into his shield and he leapt back, disengaging his blade with difficulty.

"Think you're tricky?" Herzer panted.

"Very," the man said. He began spinning the axe overhead, clockwise, moving back and forth lightly on his feet. "Trickier than you, Major. As you'll learn when I kill you."

Herzer knew there was a reason to the motion but he couldn't divine it. The axe could slam down but with all that momentum

5

there was no way that his opponent could use it for an effective block. Especially if he came in low. He circled to the left, then lunged forward in a shield bash, his sword held low at his side, point angling upward to slip through chinks in his opponent's armor.

It took him a moment to realize what was happening as the axeman brought the spinning circle of steel downwards and neatly kicked the sword out of midline. The axeman rode the shield bash backwards, actually loosing contact with his axe as it spun around the fulcrum of Herzer's useless sword. Then his shield was wrenched outwards as a tremendous blow struck him on his chest armor.

"Kill point," the judge said. "Break."

"Kill point?" Herzer protested, looking down at the blue mark. The axeman had first pulled his shield outward, then used his own energy to hammer the reverse point of the training axe into his armor. He supposed it would have punctured the armor and given him a wound. But he'd had, and fought with, far worse.

"In space," Colonel Carson said, pulling off his helmet, "that would have opened up your armor and vented your atmosphere. It's a kill. Trust me."

"Well, it's a good thing I'm not going along on your mission, then," Herzer said, grinning. "On the other hand, I can think of two or three counters to that move. All of which would leave you disarmed, or dead, or both. How many do you have in your bag of tricks?"

"Hopefully enough," Carson said with a grin. "We've been training for this mission for two years and from what Miss Travante tells us, New Destiny had yet to even begin to plan when she . . . errr . . ."

"Megan generally uses the term 'escaped,'" Herzer said with a grin. "I generally say something like 'blew that popsicle stand.' Sometimes she doesn't get the humor."

"I see," Colonel Carson said, somewhat uneasily. While it was true that he outranked Major Herrick, there was no one in the army of the United Free States, with the possible exception of Duke Edmund Talbot, who was more famous. And with his engagement to the new Key-holder, Countess Megan Travante, Herrick's career was presumably unlimited. Carson was well aware that he was probably dueling with a future boss and certainly someone with the ear of some very important people so he chose his words carefully. "I don't say it will be a cakewalk, unless they intend to just let us steal all the fuel and do nothing about it. But we should be able to handle anything they throw at us."

Herzer grimaced despite the careful phrasing and shrugged.

"Colonel, with all due respect," he said, carefully, "I would strongly suggest that you not even think that. New Destiny is, in many ways, better at this war than we are. They are better at intelligence gathering, they are better at . . . call it 'special systems' development and they are not stupid when it comes to tactics. I've taken that attitude before and it bit me in the ass. So has Duke Edmund and it bit *him* in the ass. I would strongly suggest that you assume New Destiny is going to throw something you've never seen at you, that is game winning, and plan for it. Otherwise, it's going to bite you in the ass. And there won't be a second shot at this mission, sir."

Carson sighed. "So I'm aware."

"Big pressure, sir," Herzer said, nodding. "Welcome to the world-saver's club. Admission is hard. Staying in is harder," he added with a grin, holding up one arm that terminated in a complex prosthetic.

"You haven't had that replaced, I notice," Carson said, walking over to the racks and putting up his armor and weapons.

"Well, Megan has access to the power," Herzer admitted. "And Mistress Daneh, or even her daughter Rachel, is more than capable of doing the regeneration. But . . ." He looked at the device and clicked it thoughtfully. "It has some things it does better than a hand and, in general, I've found that those are useful. Maybe if we ever win this damned war I'll have it replaced. Until then, I think I'll keep it. Great for opening beer bottles."

"And speaking of Lady Megan," Carson said, smiling. "Where is your fiancée?"

"Getting ready for the Foundation Ball, sir." Herzer grimaced, looking up at the wall mounted chronometer. "Which I'm also supposed to attend."

"Hanging out with the nobs, eh?" Carson said, smiling. "Why don't you look happy? Plenty of majors would like an opportunity to bend the ear of the Army commander, for example."

"Well, honestly, I can bend Duke Edmund's ear any time I'd like, sir," Herzer said, shrugging. "And if he thinks it's worthwhile he'll bring it to Minister Spehar, which carries more weight than a major doing it. But, honestly, sir, it's four hours of standing around making polite conversation with people who will take your words and use them as a knife in your back. Then there are the after-dinner speeches. I don't even get to sit with Megan since she's *real* high society and I'm just her . . . fiancé. I'll be down in the peanut gallery with the lowlifes like . . . well . . . colonels and select members of the House of Commons."

"Sounds idyllic," Carson said with a chuckle.

"Thanks," Herzer replied, putting away the last piece of armor. "I hope to see you again before your mission, sir."

"I'm sure we'll meet again, Herzer," Carson said, holding out his hand. "Try to enjoy yourself at the ball. I understand that the cream of Washan's lovelier ladies will be there as well."

"I've already got the loveliest girl at the ball," Herzer replied with a grin.

"You look absolutely lovely, Megan," Mirta said, taking a last tuck in the councilwoman's dress.

Megan frowned at the mirror and opened her mouth, then cut off the comment. She couldn't say she hated the dress because Mirta had made it and, honestly, it was beautiful. And she couldn't comment on her hair with Shanea putting the final touches on it. Finally she grimaced and shook her head, lightly.

"I've got a spot developing on my nose," she snapped.

"It's *impossible* to see," Mirta replied sharply. "Take a deep breath. You killed Paul; facing these people is a minor inconvenience. Your dress is lovely and beyond the height of fashion. It's going to *set* the fashion for at least the next year. Your hair is lovely and *it's* going to set a fashion. Your makeup is lovely. You are lovely. Meredith is fully dialed in on everything you're going to *achieve* this evening and *she* is lovely but just a shade less lovely than you. You are absolutely going to slay them. Don't you always?"

"I think this will hold even in the humidity," Shanea said, teasing Megan's hair up and spraying a stray strand into place. "You'll look great at the ball. I wish *I* was going instead of Meredith."

"There will be other balls, Shanea," Megan said, smiling. Shanea was a dear but she had the brains of a gnat, and the Foundation Ball would be attended by all the highest of society. Which meant that more deals would be made and more bills finalized than in all the committee meetings in the next month. Which in turn meant that it would be a vicious political dogfight taking place over cakes and champagne. Taking Shanea into that was out of the question.

Megan stood up and allowed Shanea and Mirta to help her into the dress. She could easily do it herself and would have preferred to, but the two, along with a few others, had attached themselves to her like limpets and, honestly, they were far more capable of this sort of thing than she was. She nodded as Meredith came into the vanity room and smiled.

"You look like Athena, Meredith," Megan said.

"Thank you." Meredith Amado Tillou was a tall, exquisite brunette dressed, like Megan, in a dress that was backless with a high collar and cut low at the front. Hers was not cut quite as low as Megan's and it lacked the slits on the side that teasingly revealed long legs. She was not going to the ball to be noticed. Quite the opposite. If she had a choice in her manner of dress it would be a full coverage dress and a hooded cloak.

Her expression was much the same as it had been for four years in Paul Bowman's harem, blank. But the eyes were different. While in the harem she had participated in one of the two revolts against Paul's bondage and, when unsuccessful, she had been brain locked and kept as an imbecilic brood mare for Paul's "breeding group." When Megan killed Paul it released the bond, and the memories of four years of unwilling bondage, of the things that had been done to her and of the things she did. Now she viewed the world through eyes that were as cold as an iceberg and for all the world as deadly.

As Megan had quickly learned, the mind that had been released was at least as good as her own. Behind that blank mask was a brain like a computer with a virtually perfect memory and a phenomenal ability to synthesize information, making connections where others did not see them. For all that she had, apparently, no ambitions for greater power. She had become Megan's political aide and would be attending the ball in that position.

As Mirta was fastening the last catch, Ashly walked in the room, frowning.

"Megan, there's been a change," she said, unhappily. "You were supposed to go to a late meeting with Duke Dehnavi and his wife after the ball. I just got word that he's planning on bringing . . . someone other than his wife."

"Cancel it," Megan snapped. "I'm not going to be seen in public with him and his latest doxie!"

"He's a key vote in the Intelligence Joint Subcommittee," Meredith said, evenly. "Your father will need his support for the new funding bill. Especially if he wants to increase the size of the agent training program. The meeting will not cinch it but canceling it would inevitably cause him to view anything brought up by a Travante through a negative light. He has openly boasted of having managed to arrange it. He is also involved in the Agriculture Committee which will be looking at bills related to military food support over the next six months. Various other political items come to mind since he is a quiet power in the Corporate Party. Which is why Ashly arranged the meeting."

Megan sighed and grimaced.

"Careful," Mirta said, "don't break the makeup."

"Mirta, analysis, please?"

"Okay," the older woman said, sighing. Mirta looked as if she was in her late teens, one of the reasons Paul Bowman had picked her up along with the others. In fact she was well over a hundred and besides being Megan's seamstress acted in the role of socio-political advisor. Ashly handled the social planning but Mirta advised on who could and should be graced with the presence of the newest, and youngest, and prettiest, Key-holder in the increasingly political climate of the United Free States capital.

"Short term, you gain," Mirta said. "You need the vote to get the bill out of committee without having it gutted. Long term . . . you're giving support to the cookie eaters. That means all the wives will *really* get their knives out for you. If you were married to Herzer, he wouldn't dare try this. But he thinks since Herzer's your fiancé, and you're assumed to be . . ."

"Carrying on relations," Meredith continued for her.

"Yes. That. Since you're carrying on regardless, he thinks he can score points and make it more acceptable for him to trot out his cookies. Since his wife is a rhino, politically, it's actually better for him to attend with his cookies, believe it or not. But . . ."

"Herzer won't want to come, anyway," Megan muttered. "Ashly: Send a message to the duke telling him that I will be unattended by my . . . fiancé . . . and since it would be imbalanced, etc."

"Good call," Ashly said, relieved.

"*Public*, Ashly," Megan snapped. "Very much *public*. A male aide, fine. I'll have Meredith with me. A doxie, *no*."

"Will do," Ashly muttered. "De Funcha. Very new, very hip, brightly lit, I know the maitre d' so getting you a *good* table at the last moment won't be a problem, not that it ever is—"

"Handle it," Megan said. "Meredith, let's go."

"The Honorable Jasper Thornton!" the majordomo at the top of the steps cried over the buzz of voices in the ballroom. "Mrs. Jasper Thornton."

"Her name is Amelia, for God's sake," Megan muttered angrily.

"Smile for the cameras," Herzer muttered as they stepped forward. "Although, I really hope he doesn't screw up and call me 'Mr. Megan Travante.'"

"Countess Megan Samantha Travante!" the functionary said without a glance at the card Herzer handed him. "Major Herzer Herrick!"

The low buzz of conversation stopped and the group broke into apparently spontaneous applause as a chemical flash caught the couple standing hand in hand. It would probably make the morning edition of the *Washan Times*, society page if not the front, and be in Lasang in no more than two weeks by courier.

Megan waved in appreciation of the applause as, shadowed by Meredith, they stepped down the stairs to the floor of the large room. The room was not filled to overflowing, by any stretch of the imagination, but Washan in summertime was hot and the candles and lamps that lit the room added to the heat of the pressed bodies, turning it into a sauna. Megan was afraid she could already feel her hairdo wilting.

"Remember, the slave said," Herzer said, leaning over to whisper in Megan's ear, "you too are mortal." He was dressed in the most formal uniform of the UFS, a tight coat worn short, open at the front in deference to the heat, with a blinding white undertunic on which his Eagle hung from a thick scarlet ribbon. The coat was gray, the newly chosen color of the UFS Army uniform, with light blue lining to denote his branch of infantry. The gray pants had a blue stripe down the side as well. It was topped by a light blue beret. The coat was heavy with his medals and qualification badges; two silver eagles to match the gold, the now defunct aurea victorous, wound badges, dragon qualification, maritime aviation badge, air combat medal. Megan had insisted that he wear all of them. There were a few with more medals in the room, the UFS Army was already getting medal happy. But there were none with more medals for valor in combat.

Megan snorted softly and took the first hand that was outstretched to her.

"Duke Okyay, a pleasure to see you this evening . . ."

Herzer detached himself as soon as Megan began politicking, grabbed a glass of sarsaparilla and a plate of munchies and worked his way over to the corner where Edmund and the Army commander were ensconced.

"Duke Edmund," he said, pushing past an aide. Most of the flunkies were staying well back from the great men and surreptitiously acting as a filter. The Army commander's new aide had apparently not recognized the unknown major.

"Hey, Herzer," Edmund said grumpily. "Welcome to the jungle."

Herzer grinned slightly when he saw the turning aide grimace and face back to watch the goings-on.

"I'm afraid I'm going to be spending far too much time, here," Herzer said, frowning. "Megan's taken to it like a duck to water."

"Don't be too sure," Edmund replied. The duke was noticeably older every year as the weight of being the preeminent field commander of the UFS forces bore down on his shoulders. What little hair he had left was entirely gray and was shorn close to his scalp. But he still retained his salt and pepper beard and an almost alarming presence. Next to him General Galbreath, ostensibly the commander of all UFS ground forces, was a pale, thin shadow. Effectively Edmund let Galbreath get on with the politicking and administration while Edmund got on with winning the war.

Barely seven years before, the world had been a virtual utopia with unlimited power and technology so advanced it approached magic. Disease and want had been eliminated and a worldwide network of teleportation and replication permitted humans to live as gods, their bodies and lives playthings in a continuous life of merriment.

In a moment it ended as the Council of Key-holders that controlled the network fell out in what amounted to a worldwide civil war. Now the majority of the power from the twelve remaining fusion power plants was devoted to energy attacks between the two factions of Key-holders and armies were forming on both sides. The Freedom Coalition, those who fought on the side of Queen Sheida and her allies, used unChanged humans for their forces while the New Destiny coalition modified the bodies of their soldiers, and increasingly their support forces, into bestial creatures that were almost incredibly tough and strong while being loyal to the point of suicide. Already, the United Free States, the portion of the Freedom Coalition that held Norau, had beaten off major attacks from the orcs of New Destiny. It was time for some payback.

Edmund Talbot had been a reenactor before the Fall, a person who spent his time creating a very close approximation of a time "when." He'd lived in a stone house, crafted swords and armor, and generally lived a comfortable life as a feudal lord with extra amenities such as antique flush toilets. After the Fall it had been revealed that he was one of the few legends of the pre-Fall period, Charles "The Hammer," a man who had gone into Anarchia and tamed it in a few short years, disappearing thereafter, as mysteriously as he had appeared, but leaving in his wake a stable government that, as far as anyone knew, still existed.

Since the Fall he had been the UFS' preeminent general, winning battle after battle against New Destiny.

The brand new Key hanging from a ribbon around Duke Edmund's neck, the one recovered from Elnora Still after her assassination by New Destiny, showed just who had *true* precedence between the two.

"Your reputation precedes you, Major," Galbreath said, sticking out his hand. "I think that what the duke meant was that, given the planned counterattack on Ropasa, it would be . . . difficult for the Army to lose one of its brighter field lights to politic in Washan."

"I've got a dozen posts I need you at *now*," Edmund growled. "Professor at the War College comes to mind. So does a battalion command. Hell, command of the new legion we're trying to raise. Get married, go on your honeymoon, get your tubes cleaned and then pack your bags."

"Hell of a choice, sir," Herzer said, grumpily. "With Megan, who I love and want in a the worst *possible* way, in the capital, doing *this*," he said, with a dismissive wave at the height of Washan society, "or eating cold monkey on a stick in Ropasa."

Edmund chuckled. "Let me guess which way you'd hop."

"Cold monkey," Herzer admitted. "Although, if I was at the War College Megan would at least be no more than a day away."

"Once we have control of a significant portion of Ropasa," Edmund reminded him, "we can set up portals. Then she's just a jump away."

"You're going for a direct invasion of the mainland?" Herzer asked. "Megan supports an invasion through Gael and the retaking of Breton first."

"Is that an unofficial message from a fellow council member?" Edmund asked, raising one eyebrow. "That is, after all, what parties like this are really for."

"No, of course not," Herzer said, testily. "But you know she supports the Gael. Don't you?"

"I'm well aware of it," Edmund said. "But with an invasion force on his home coast, Chansa will be forced to recall the units that are attacking the Gael. Then they can *have* Breton for all I care."

"There's that," Herzer said, frowning. "I suppose you're correct."

"Penny for your thoughts?" Edmund grinned.

"Your mind is a bog, boss," Herzer admitted after a moment. "But Chansa is anticipating a direct attack on the coast and from what I've seen he's building up significant forces around fortified positions. From the reports I've seen he appears to *already* be pulling back forces from Breton. Even if we get a beachhead, we'll be stuck butting our head against division after division of his orcs, many of them in fortresses. Even if we *get* the new legion, which is a real hot topic right now, the parity of forces will be extreme. And if we don't take the fortresses, they'll be in our rear. All of the ports are heavily defended so support will have to come over the beach. And it means shuttling all our forces across the Atlantis until we can take and hold a large enough area that Mother will consider it to be held by force majeure and we can set up portals."

"Teaching me to suck eggs, Herzer?" Edmund said, smiling faintly.

"No, just wondering what you're *really* planning," Herzer admitted. He'd never been able to guess, but . . . it didn't keep him from trying.

"With any luck at all, it will all be moot," General Galbreath noted. "If Colonel Carson succeeds, the war will be over."

"And he is training well," Edmund said, distantly. "Herzer, have you taken a look at the Icarus force?"

"Not in depth," Herzer admitted. "Among other things, I'm not cleared for full information. But I was sparring with the colonel earlier today and he's a formidable fighter. If many of his men are like him, they're going to do well."

"And if we have the fuel tanker . . ." Galbreath said, breathlessly.

"That's it," Herzer said, nodding. "We keep the fuel and as soon as the New Destiny reactors run out, only Sheida and the rest will have power."

"And then we'll be able to stop this bloody war in its tracks," Galbreath added, nodding. "No need for an invasion. For that matter, if we can track down the New Destiny Key-holders, and I'll bet a lot that Sheida will have that well in hand, we can get back to a *real* life."

Herzer looked at Edmund and raised an eyebrow.

"Color you pessimistic, boss?" he asked, lightly.

"There are few actions that are in and of themselves war winning," Edmund admitted. "Think of it this way; if New Destiny gets the fuel, are we just going to roll over?"

"No," Galbreath admitted, frowning. "Not given what they'll probably do to the world."

"I'd keep fighting," Herzer said, working his jaw. "With my last breath."

"There you are," Edmund said, quirking one cheek in a grin. "And so will New Destiny, if only to keep from having us capture them alive. And the lack of intel on New Destiny's plans makes me suspicious. I know they *have* to be planning something; they're not asleep. But *what* is the question."

"Less than a month until the first shuttle lands," Herzer noted. "We'll know soon enough."

"In the meantime," Edmund said, "we keep planning for victory and keeping one eye on failure. Which means we *have* to have the tenth legion. Even that is not enough. Sixty thousand legionnaires, less than half of them fully trained and the majority with no combat experience, against an estimated two hundred thousand Changed."

"Ten thousand bowmen," Galbreath reminded him. "Six thousand cavalry. And the dragon corps."

"Three thousand actually *bowmen*," Edmund said, shaking his head.

"And the private regiments," Galbreath pointed out and then winced.

"Damn the private regiments," Edmund said, almost shaking in anger. "If we put that money where it *should* be we wouldn't be scraping and scrabbling for another legion!"

"Some of them are good," Herzer said, trying to mollify his boss. Under the constitutional strictures that Edmund himself had supported, the de facto existence of small private armies was fully legal. But it had been a huge political firestorm when it had been suggested that they become associated with the regular army and in the end the compromise had been the worst of all worlds. The regiments were to be *supported* by the army if called to field duty while the army had little or no control over their training, equipment, doctrine or leadership *unless* they were on field duty.

The training and equipment of the regiments was highly diverse, from local militias founded around pikes to battalions of heavy horse with everything in between.

"And the dragons were decimated in the Atlantis battles," Edmund grumped, apparently willing to forget that the private regiments existed for the time. "Less than a hundred of them are left and all but two are wyverns."

"Hey!" Herzer interjected. "Nothing wrong with wyverns!" The nonsentient two-legged flying beasts made up the bulk of the dragon corps. There were three types of wyverns: Powells, which were the primary strike force; Silverdrakes, which were small, fast and highly colorful air-to-air fighters; and Torejos, which were heavier beasts that were rarely used in direct combat but could be used for aerial resupply or the rare airmobile mission.

"Of course not," Edmund replied, soothingly. Herzer had been in three major battles on wyvern back, despite his official status as an infantry officer. For that matter, he was a fair bowman. "But what I wouldn't give for the same number of greater dragons."

"If wishes were fishes," Herzer pointed out.

"Well, if we want that tenth legion, we'd best get out and circulate," Edmund said, shaking his head.

"Perhaps and perhaps not," General Galbreath said, laying a hand on his arm. "Have you been watching Countess Travante?"

"No," Edmund said. "I'm not a dirty old man."

"It's . . . enlightening if you know the political scene," Galbreath said, quietly. "Just watch."

CHAPTER TWO

"Lost," Megan said quietly as a portly blond man approached with a significantly younger brunette female in tow.

"Duke Anatiev and Mrs. Lydia Pina," Meredith whispered rapidly. "Kanaka. He dotes on his dog Puddles. Wants more money to flow through Kanaka. Leather and beef for legions. Kanaka Beef Corp."

"Anatiev!" Megan said, smiling broadly as she took the man's pudgy hand. "And Lydia! Lovely to see you this evening. No Puddles? Where is the little scamp?"

"Oh, Puddles can't handle the excitement, Countess," Anatiev said, beaming. "Just barks herself into a frenzy. You really should join us at the Dog Club one afternoon, all the best sorts are there."

"Please call me Megan," the councilwoman said with a smile. "I don't currently have a pet. I've only just got my feet on the ground."

"It must have been terrible," Lydia Pina said, leaning forward.

"It was," Megan replied, cutting off that flow of conversation. "I have been meaning to take the portal to Kanaka, though. I understand that it's growing by leaps and bounds?"

"Well, we were," the duke said, frowning. "But so much of the new lands are being broken closer to the coast that our sales are down sharply. Which is silly since we've all this beef on the hoof and the best slaughter houses in the nation. Transport, though . . ."

17

"Balmoran Canal . . ." Meredith whispered quickly.

"Well, if we can get the funding for the Balmoran Canal pushed through, the transportation costs will drop to nothing," Megan pointed out. "Or the upgrades to the Nawlins ports. I think that KBC might be interested in talking to Commons Member Weiss."

"Very good point," the duke said, blinking rapidly. "But what would be really nice is if we could get some solid contracts with the military."

"I suspect that will depend upon their needs, Duke," Megan replied, smiling sweetly. "Especially if they have a tenth legion to support."

"I do believe I said guaranteed, Megan," the duke said, smiling back.

"Nawlins . . ." Meredith whispered.

"The Nawlins port upgrades are probably less expensive and would take a shorter time than the completion of the canal," Megan replied, mentally kissing the support of the Balmoran contingent goodbye. "With that, leather and beef from KBC would be on a steadier stream. I think the military is more worried about guarantee of *quality* supply than actual *cost*, although it would have to be in line. But without that guarantee of supply, I think anything I would say would be dismissed."

"And there is the question of what *sort* of legion," the duke pressed. "Kanaka has some of the finest horsemen in the world . . ."

"That is . . . far beyond discussion *at the moment*," Megan temporized. Christ, if he went off and forced them to form another legion of cavalry . . . "But it's certainly an interesting topic. Duke, I see Commons Member Walsh and I promised him a dance. If you could excuse me? I'll be sure to drop by the Dog . . ."

"Club . . ." Meredith whispered fiercely.

"Club sometime soon. I hope to see you there!"

"Oh, absolutely," the duke said, beaming. "And do think about getting a pet. They're remarkable for how they can calm one."

"I'll seriously consider it," Megan said, shaking their hands and moving off through the crowd. "Blast."

"Not bad, not good," Meredith whispered fast and low. "Two more votes and the Nawlins port upgrades are guaranteed. I think the canal is a wash. Walsh is on the Commerce Ports Committee, which is silly since he's from a landlocked district in Sylania. He doesn't support them but he wants the new legion in his district. Edmund is against it since the terrain isn't good for training, support would be difficult and it would have to be marched to the coast. Also, if we *do* march them off, there goes all the funds. Get him the legion and he'll go for the port. Get a guarantee on going for the port and you'll get Pina, especially if you can get a contract guaranteed if there's a port. But the legion, sorry, is going to have to go to Walsh and something will have to be done about marching it off. Wife's Henutsen, not here tonight, I don't know why."

"Commons Member Walsh," Megan said, smiling as they shook hands. "I *do* hope Henutsen is well; I was looking forward to her company tonight . . ."

"Who's the brunette?" General Galbreath asked.

Edmund looked at Herzer and raised an eyebrow.

"Meredith Tillou, one of the other girls from the harem," Herzer said after a moment. "Got a mind like a fricking computer. I'd love to have her on my staff except she's an absolute ball buster. She was one of Paul's consorts before the Fall and he kept her as a brain-locked sperm receptacle in the harem." One muscle flexed in his jaw as he watched the pair expertly work the commons member. Without a female on the commons member's arm, Megan was leaning far into his personal space, placing her hand on his upper arm and peering deeply into his eyes as they laughed about something. Herzer's jaw flexed again.

"Is your fiancée a natural or what?" Galbreath said, softly. "I hope like hell she's on our side."

"She's on . . . Megan's side," Herzer said. "She supports the invasion of Ropasa and the military. She wants New Destiny on toast and she'll stop at nothing to get it. That means supporting the military. But don't think she won't compromise if she has to. As long as the long-term objective is, in her opinion, met."

"I hope she's not compromising us too much," Edmund said, darkly. "Walsh wants in the legion in *Sylania*. What the hell is it going to do there?"

"You want the legion or not?" Galbreath snapped. "If it has to be in Sylania, and it's trending that way, it has to be in Sylania. We'll deal with it. If she gets us the Victrix in *Chian* I'm not going to bitch."

"Victrix?" Herzer asked.

"Caesar's legion was the Tenth Victrix," Edmund said. "Somebody decided it would be a good name."

"I know that," Herzer said, frowning. "But it's a hell of a name to hang on a legion that's not even been *funded* yet."

"Name, hell," Galbreath said, gesturing with his chin at the room. "Half the officers at this ball are politicking for positions in it, including the ones from the private regiments. Everyone knows it's the last legion we're going to form in a decade at least. And every mother's son that doesn't have a steady job and every officer stuck in a logistics position and every commander of a private outfit that suddenly discovered the headaches and cost is trying to get into it. I think that right there is enough political push to get it formed. But what it will be made up of—"

"Damnit, Kav, that's *your* job to fix," Edmund said. "The officers should be the tactical and leadership cream. Not the cream of . . . of . . ." He waved his hand at the well-dressed throng and frowned.

"Whoops," Herzer suddenly muttered. "I wonder what she wants out of us?"

He smiled and held out his hand as Megan approached.

"Councilwoman Travante," Herzer said with a grin.

"Oh, God, Herzer," Megan said, shaking her head. "Don't start. General Talbot, Galbreath. We may have a legion. General Galbreath, if we can get the ports in Nawlins funded, I need a guarantee that the army will start using Kanaka Beef as a major supplier. I can probably get the port guaranteed, which in general will be a good thing for the nation, if we give Walsh the legion. I can definitely get it if we put another base in his district that *isn't* going to march off to war. I'm thinking a basic training base or something of the sort. I know it's out of the way and a bitch to support, sorry. But I need something here. Oh, and I need a guarantee that the primary embarkation port will be Balmoran since I'm going to have to shaft them on the canal temporarily."

"I think you lost me in the middle there," Edmund admitted. "But, yeah, we can put a base in his district. Not a basic training base, something smaller. Maybe a logistics training base. It's a stupid place for it but logistics is about dealing with the difficult. Is there something you need me to do about the Nawlins port?"

Megan grinned. "Just tell your proxy to vote it."

"Will do," Edmund replied.

"The contract, if we have the port, and the embarkation we can do, easily," Galbreath said. "KBC is a good supplier and I was sorry as hell when we had to go local. But the supply was just too spotty. If we've got the base and it can be sailed around Flora in reefer ships, we're good."

"If the legion is in Sylania, part of the materials can be shipped up the Oya River," Meredith said. "Perhaps the majority that comes from KBC. That means using the Losville locks, which means we can probably get Duke Ruta on board for the legion if not the docks."

"Got to go," Megan said, nodding. "Gentlemen, could I steal my fiancé for just a moment?"

"Certainly, madame," General Galbreath replied with a bow.

Megan, silently trailed by Meredith, led Herzer just outside the ring of aides and then put her arm around his waist.

"Hold me for just a second, will you?" she asked, leaning into his bulk.

"Always and anywhere, darling," Herzer breathed, looking down at her blonde hair. The hairdo was beginning to wilt a bit in the heat but she still was, he thought, the most beautiful woman in the room.

"I have two spaces left on my dance card," she said, leaning back and holding it up. "Put your name on them."

"I hate to dance," Herzer muttered, looking at the card. "And the last dance is free for me as well?"

"I'm not going to be here for the last dance," Megan said tightly. "I've got a late meeting with Duke Dehnavi. Very respectable. Public. Etc. But . . . well, I have to go to it without a male companion. I'll explain why later."

"That's fine," Herzer said, flexing his jaw again.

"No, it's not." Megan looked up at him and shook her head. "Don't lie to me. I'll explain why later but I just . . ."

"I love you and it's okay," Herzer said. "I just hate being away from you. I want to be joined to you at the hip. Simple as that."

"Then come out on the floor," Megan said with a smile. "Instead of hiding in the corner."

"If you want me to, I will," Herzer said, frowning. "But you know I'm no good at . . ."

"I know." Megan smiled. "But what I do want you to do is get out there on your own. Don't politic, it's not your strong suit. Just be charming. Dance with the dukes' wives and daughters. Regale those pompous twits in the regimental uniforms with your *real* tales of derring-do. Be yourself. Be the bluff, honest, soldier. Be charming. You are, you know; you charmed me. Then save the last dance for someone wholly respectable and be waiting for me when I get home. I won't be long. Please." She looked up at him fiercely and hugged him to her. "Just be there. Please."

"I will," Herzer said, leaning into her and hugging her back. "Edmund told me that marriage is about two people leaning on each other for support. I'll be there. Always."

"And what support do you get from me?" Megan asked sadly.

"You keep my demons at bay," Herzer answered simply.

"Despite . . ."

"I can wait," he said, quietly. "Forever if I have to. Just being with you makes me whole and at peace. Now, get out there and work it."

"Yes, sir!" she said with a grin. "You, too."

"Aye, aye, Countess," he replied, grinning back.

"Bleck," Megan said, turning back to the room with a smile. "Once more into the breach."

"Unto," Herzer whispered as she walked back into the crowd. "Unto the breach."

He walked back over to the generals and shrugged.

"If you'll excuse me, sirs," he said, bowing slightly. "I have marching orders. I am to go forth and be the bluff, honest soldier to wow the gentry."

"I suppose I should go forth myself," Galbreath said. "And see what's what among the nobs."

"I'm going to stay in the corner and get hammered," Edmund said. "You guys have fun."

"What's with him?" Galbreath said as he and Herzer walked away.

"Edmund's . . . just not this type, sir," Herzer replied, shrugging. "He not only dislikes politics, he actively despises it. At heart, he's an autocrat. But he worked damned hard in the early days to set up . . . this," Herzer said, waving at the crowd, "because he believes that a republican form of government isn't the best form of government, just the best ever discovered. Now he has to live with it. It was a choice he knew was right but he also knew that *this* would grow from it. If Daneh was here she'd sweet talk him into the crowd and before you knew it he'd be holding court. But . . . she's not and I'm not about to try it."

"It's a sad fact that I like politicking," Galbreath admitted. "And I wouldn't trust a field army in my hands for worlds."

"That's why you're here, sir, and Duke Edmund . . ." Herzer trailed off and shrugged. "Far better than the other way around, don't you think?"

"Absolutely," the general replied as a commons member approached. "Commons Member Srichure, have you met Major Herrick . . . ?"

Herzer had exchanged two more brief words with Megan before she left and now hovered at the edge of the crowd, clutching a drink that was far stronger than he liked. He had been as charming and as debonair as he knew how to be. He had briefly held court with some of the minor military lights present, had danced with a duchess and a string of young ladies ranging from homely to quite attractive. He had fulfilled his end of the bargain and was more than ready to get the hell out.

He'd also found, much to his disgust, that he enjoyed himself. With few exceptions, as powerful as they were, the people at this event were not accurate judges of his military worth. But he found himself occasionally whispering the words he had said to Megan as they crowded around him, hanging on his every word. He had probably listened more than he spoke, but nobles and commons members fell silent when he opened his mouth. And the women had come to him to fill their dance cards, leaning into his shadow and working him, frankly, much like Megan had been working the unaccompanied politicians.

"You too are mortal," he whispered as a soft hand touched his arm.

The girl was a redhead in a dress that was . . . well, he wasn't sure if it was unfashionable or simply extremely daring. The top was sort of a twisted silver cloth that made not much more than a bikini coverage and the bottom was . . . missing a good bit of cloth—a long loincloth might have covered more—and it definitely revealed a set of startlingly nice legs. He had seen a couple of the younger crowd sporting similar clothing so he supposed it was fashionable. If you had the body for it. Which she most definitely did.

"Major Herrick, I'd been hoping to make your acquaintance," the young lady said. "Are you engaged for the last dance of the evening?"

"Uh . . ." Respectable. Megan had said "respectable." But the honest answer was "No." Bloody hell. "Uhmmm . . . no."

"I believed as much," the young woman said. "And I think I hear it starting now. Will you join me on the floor?"

"Certainly, milady," Herzer said, mentally groaning. He needed a better road map for these things. Or Megan to not bloody desert him at them. He should have left early. He should have stayed home. He really shouldn't be taking the last dance, as the servants snuffed the candles and dimmed the lanterns, with this apparently unaccompanied invitation to rape.

Herzer danced slowly with his prosthetic tucked in his sash and his right hand on the young lady's uncovered waist. There wasn't a stitch of clothing that didn't cover something untouchable so he had a choice of skin or no touch at all.

"Countess Travante left, I believe?" the young woman said.

"Yes," Herzer replied. About all he could manage at the moment was monosyllables. But simple questions would work. "I'm sorry, I didn't catch your name."

"That's because I didn't give it," the girl laughed throatily. "Linda."

"You are an excellent dancer, Linda," Herzer said, smiling fatuously and thinking furiously. He was starting to suspect there was a bite coming from somewhere.

"I wasn't supposed to be here this late," the young lady said. "I was supposed to be having a late supper with a friend."

"I'm sorry," Herzer replied. "I cannot imagine anyone who would be as ungentlemanly as to stand up such a beautiful young woman."

"Well, it was politics," Linda replied, smiling thinly. "You see, he was supposed to be meeting with a female and her paramour. Since they were unmarried, he thought it would be acceptable if I accompanied him."

"Oh," Herzer said. "So what happened?"

"Well, for some reason, the lady's companion was unavailable," Linda replied, smiling broadly. "As a matter of fact, at the moment I'm dancing with him."

Herzer almost stumbled but he recovered quickly and something settled in his mind. At least now the fog was lifted and he could see the battlefield. *Okay, she wants to play games. I'm a master of playing games.*

"Ah, thank you," Herzer said, sliding both arms around her and pulling her close. "So you think when word of our little dance gets back to them, either Megan or your . . . friend will be jealous?"

"Perhaps," Linda said, snuggling in closer.

"Do you know how Megan killed Paul Bowman?" Herzer asked, smiling, his eyes cold.

"No?" the girl said, starting to pull back and realizing that she was trapped. "Would you mind loosening up a little?"

Herzer stopped dancing and looked her deep in the eyes, smiling ever so faintly.

"She poured a glass of acid down his throat," Herzer said softly. "Then bashed his head in with a vase. Now, Megan knows I'm a babe in the woods at some things. So when I tell her about this little . . . encounter, she will find it amusing. Let us hope your . . . friend does as well." The music ended and he looked up as the lamps were dimmed. "So, do I get a kiss?"

"No!" the girl said, quietly but fiercely. "Let me go!"

"Certainly," Herzer said, releasing her but snatching one hand and bowing over it for a kiss. "I hope we meet again . . . Linda, was it? So many girls, so little time."

The woman looked at him poisonously for a moment and then stormed off.

"Bad boy, Herzer," Edmund muttered as the lights came back up and the remains of the party started streaming out.

"Ya think?"

"No, Duke, it's all right," Megan said, brushing aside a hand as her carriage followed by a squad of cavalry pulled up. "I have my own transportation. Thank you, though." *Thank God Herzer hadn't attended or a duke would have been punched through a wall!*

"Perhaps a nightcap?" the duke asked, his hand sliding onto her back.

"It's a bit late," Megan said as Meredith interposed herself and the coachman opened the door. "Perhaps another time."

"A good-night kiss," the duke said, darting around Meredith and planting his lips on her cheek.

"Good *night*," Megan snapped, clambering into the coach.

"Have fun?" Herzer asked.

"Oh, God," Megan replied, collapsing in the rear seat as the coach pulled out to the accompanying clatter of hooves. "What are you doing here?"

"My other other duty," Herzer said, pulling back his cloak to show that he was in armor. "Guarding you. Good evening, Miss Meredith. I'm sorry, I've hardly said two words to you all evening."

"That's fine, Major," Meredith said. "I'm used to being invisible."

"Hardly invisible," Herzer said, one cheek twitching up in what might be called a smile. "Speaking of hardly invisible, the duke's jilted paramour turned up at the party and managed to inveigle me into the last dance."

"My night is now complete," Megan sighed.

"I'm sure it will be all over Washan tomorrow," Herzer said. "I can see the headline now: 'Paramour Swapping?' Sorry. I missed getting any of the married females present and I didn't realize how bad it was until we were already dancing. Loan me Meredith next time."

"Or Mirta," Meredith said, seriously. "That might not be a bad idea."

"It's a thought," Megan said. "But next time *I* should be there. This was the wrong way to set this up. I had no idea that guy was as stupid and boorish as he was."

"Neither did I," Meredith admitted. "It's unusual behavior for him."

"You are overpowering, my love," Herzer said on a chuckle.

"How did you handle the doxie?" Megan asked. "Punctiliously, I hope?"

"Except for trying to rape her on the dance floor and threatening her life?" Herzer asked. "Like a perfect gentleman."

"You didn't?" Megan asked.

"Well . . . let's just say I probably should have restrained my demons just a bit more," Herzer admitted. "But she really pissed me off. And quite the opposite by the end of the encounter."

"Meredith?" Megan said, closing her eyes. "Repercussions?"

"More Mirta's area than mine," Meredith answered. "We'll have to see what the gossip circuit says. Off the top of my head, it might be either okay or better than okay. She was clearly seen leaving *without* you, Major, correct?"

"And apparently in a state of high dudgeon," Herzer admitted.

"And prior to that would she have appeared . . . available?" Meredith asked.

"Eminently," Herzer replied. "If rape was intended, it was clearly not by me."

"The wife set will be clucking like mad," Meredith said. "In general, I think, in your favor. He had it thrown in his face and spurned it, presumably in favor of you. And you'd up and left him at the party. It should fall out well. I don't know how it will fall out with Duke Dehnavi, though."

"I think, whatever the political consequences, I'm willing to let the duke rot," Megan admitted. "No more meetings with him other than in groups. Possibly no more meetings with him, period."

" 'Oh, is Duke Dehnavi going to be at your party? I'm sorry, perhaps another time . . .' " Meredith said, suddenly smiling cold and hard.

"Perhaps a *bit* more subtle than that," Megan said. "Ashly's area. But not much; I definitely want to discourage a repeat. I'll let her handle it."

"Yes," Meredith said, smiling again. "She'll have the right malicious little words."

"I should be covering what's on the agenda for tomorrow," Megan admitted. "But I'm just too tired."

"The most important point is meeting with the Select Intelligence Subcommittee at nine AM," Meredith said. "Nothing before then; I knew it would be a late night."

"Wow," Herzer said, widening his eyes. "I get you to myself for a whole, what? Seven hours? Less prep time?"

"And most of that sleeping," Megan said, smiling sadly. "Sorry love."

"Seven hours is worth much with you," Herzer said gallantly, but there was a tinge of bitterness under his words. Among other things he knew that, besides a bit of conversation, maybe, and a kiss, the night would involve nothing but sleep. He could last. He had sworn he would and he'd never gone back on a vow.

"We'll have time soon, love," Megan promised. "And you didn't have to show up. In armor no less."

"You're the most important person in my life," Herzer said honestly. "And one of the most important people in the world. Keeping you alive is much more important than changing out of that monkey suit and into armor. Hell, armor's more comfortable."

"That is what the squad of cavalry is for," Meredith noted sharply.

"Like I'd trust cavalry with Megan's life." Herzer snorted. "Horsey boys that don't want to dismount and can't handle themselves mounted."

"You let me come to the meeting by myself," Megan noted, frowning.

"There was a squad of Blood Lords shadowing you," Herzer said with a shrug. "And you pointedly told me I wasn't to come."

"There was?" Megan asked.

"And is," Herzer said, smiling faintly. "In the keeping of a fellow named Cruz who works for your poppa. He's doing the actual stalking. They're far enough back the cavalry haven't noticed. Which, I think, says it all about your escort. If guards can shadow you and not be noticed, so can assassins. Look, leave the security to me and your dad, you just concentrate on what you do so well."

"There are times I miss Baradur." The petite Chudai warrior had expressed a wish to return to his Highland home and Megan had had him returned with a bag full of silver for his services. "But he would have been a problem at this meeting, for example."

"He would have cut the duke's hand off the first time he touched you," Meredith noted. "While I see the political repercussions, I would have enjoyed watching it."

"Blood all over the white tablecloth," Megan said with a grin. "All the glitterati gaping. The screams. The headlines. No, I think it's better that he wasn't along."

"It's always odd to look at a stump where your hand used to be," Herzer said, holding up his prosthetic.

"I hope I never find out," Megan said, shaking her head.

"Useful for opening jars," Herzer said with a shrug.

CHAPTER THREE

"Herzer!"

Herzer was walking back from another round of meetings at the War Department when he heard his name called. It was midafternoon and he could have easily gotten a hansom cab for the kilometer or so walk, but after six hours of sitting on his butt listening to staff officers arguing about details of logistics trains a walk felt good.

He turned at the call, though, and was surprised to see Mike and Courtney Boehlke, all dressed up in their festival best.

"Mike," he said, taking his friend's hand. "What in the hell are you doing in Sodom on Poma?"

"Business," Mike said, grumpily. The farmer was browned by the sun, short and stocky with a shock of hair that was blond on the near edge of white from bleaching. "Talking to damned bureaucrats."

"A common problem in this town," Herzer said. "Courtney, you're looking entirely edible," he added, hugging the short, buxom redhead. Despite having a houseful of children, she had still retained her pre-Fall figure, which was set off very nicely by a scoop-neck dress, and was one of his favorite people.

"We're trying to get some of the land they're opening up in the Sippa delta," Courtney said. "It's not going well. By the way, congratulations! We heard you're engaged to the *Councilwoman*! When's the wedding?"

"You'll be among the first to know," Herzer said, looking around.

"If you're not doing anything, let's get a drink. Simak's isn't bad," he added, pointing at a nearby tavern.

When they were seated with mugs in front of them, beer for Herzer and Mike and wine for Courtney, Herzer raised an eyebrow.

"So you're deserting my farm?" he asked jokingly. He had purchased a piece of land in the first days after the Fall, using just about his last available capital and a lucky lottery. Since he knew he was for the legions, he had turned the management over to Mike, and the joint farms, which were side by side, had been steadily improving over the year and recently had started to produce a nice profit.

"I'm not deserting you, Herzer," Mike said gruffly. The farmer was short and prickly to a fault but he and Herzer were good enough friends that the major recognized it for just his normal tone. "There's a good manager for both farms and the rotation schedule is working like a clock. It's just—"

"He's bored," Courtney interjected, somewhat sourly. "He needs more of a challenge. So he wants to drag me and the kids back into the wilderness."

"Sippa delta is excellent farm land," Mike protested. "It'll grow shoestrings! And with the river right there transportation costs will be nothing. Getting it back to the markets on the coast is a problem, but they're bound to get the ports running at Nawlins sooner or later."

"So what's the problem?" Herzer asked, frowning.

"The damned bureaucrats," Mike snarled. "They're locking up all the land for the ag corps. The legislation had a hundred loopholes in it and the bureaus that are in charge of distribution are spreading it out using a scale based on 'proven property.' Now, between us, we've got six thousand hectares and I can point to all of it as 'proven' in my name. But Koberda-Yoon has over *ninety* thousand. So they use this scale. With six thousand they only want to open up a hundred and sixty hectares to me, but they're opening over a hundred *thousand* to Koberda-Yoon. And the payback period is based on total grant, so I've got *two* years to prove out and Koberda has *thirty*."

"Crap," Herzer said, shaking his head. "No wonder you're pissed."

"Furious," Courtney said, nodding. "It was all I could do to drag him out of there before he started cracking heads."

"I've often been tempted in this damned town," Herzer admitted, thinking of a certain duke. "But it only gives you more grief. No, you need somebody with connections to find the loophole in the loophole. There are always 'waivers' or 'exceptions' in something like this." He frowned and shook his head. "I don't do politics, but . . . Megan does. Damnit, though . . ."

"You don't want to ask her?" Courtney said, suddenly focused.

"No, I don't," Herzer said, shrugging. "But I will. It just goes against my grain that you have to have a 'friend at court' to get your rights. That's not how it's supposed to happen."

"We tried to get in to see Commons Member Bouseh," Mike said, shrugging. "But he was 'busy.'"

"I'm not sure what Megan can do, if she can do anything," Herzer said, standing up. "But there's only one way to find out."

"You don't want us to go, do you?" Courtney asked, shaking her head.

"Yes," Herzer answered, simply. "She's my fiancée. You're two of my best friends. It's time you met."

"I wish it was under better circumstances, though," Courtney argued. "Maybe we shouldn't do this."

"This is Washan." Herzer sighed. "Unfortunately, it's not so much what you know or what you can do but *who* you know. You coming?"

"Yeah," Mike said, standing up. "Come on, Courtney."

"I *like* Raven's Mill," Courtney said, but she stood up and followed the men out of the tavern.

"Great," Mike said gruffly. "We can retire there."

"Megan," Herzer said happily when he came in the apartment and discovered that she was actually there. "This is Courtney and Mike Boehlke, two of my oldest and best friends."

"Miss . . . Count . . ." Courtney said, nervously, trying to curtsey.

"Courtney," Megan said, quickly getting up from the couch where she had been poring over notes and walking over to take the woman's hand. "Give me a break," she said, grinning and pointing at Herzer. "I'm marrying *him*. You don't have to curtsey, but you could keep me in your prayers."

Courtney laughed at that and grinned, showing a deep dimple on one side. "Well, I haven't heard many complaints and most of the ones I *have* heard boil down to 'no more!'"

Megan smiled and offered her hand to Mike as Meredith floated into the room.

"Mike, it's good to meet you at last," Megan said. "Herzer's told me so much about you."

"Well, we had to hear about *you* in the newspapers," Mike said, shaking her hand sharply and then looking away. He met Meredith's eyes for a moment, then looked away from them as well.

"The best friends are always the last to know," Megan said, leading them over to the couch. "Meredith, I think I'm done with this for a bit. If you could ask Shanea to round up some drinks? Tea or is it late enough for something stronger?" she added, looking at the visitors.

"Herzer dragged us away when I was halfway through a glass of wine," Courtney said. "But it's up to you."

"Wine for Courtney," Megan said. "And for me as well, the Raven's Mill chablis perhaps? Mike? Wine?"

"Beer if you don't mind," Mike said tersely, looking around at the well-decorated apartment. "I'd have thought that a council member would have a house or something."

"Houses are at a premium in Washan," Megan admitted, shrugging. "And this is closer to work."

"The shorter distance she has to travel, the less chance of an assassin getting to her," Herzer added sourly.

"Ick," Courtney said, shaking her head.

"Megan," Herzer said, "do you have a few minutes?"

"Actually, amazingly enough I have all night," Megan said. "I was planning on spending the evening with you."

"Ouch," Mike said, standing up. "Maybe we should go."

"Sit," Herzer said. "This should hardly take all evening. The thing is, Mike and Courtney have a problem and I don't know how to help them. I hope you do." He paused as Shanea came in followed by Meredith. As Shanea handed out the glasses and set a chilled bottle on the table Meredith took an outlying seat.

"Here you go, hero," Shanea said with a grin, handing Herzer a glass dark with liquor. "Neat bourbon. Side of sassafras tea."

"What would we do without you, Shanea?" Herzer said, grinning.

"Tell me when you're ready to dump whatsername and we'll find out," Shanea said with a wink and a wiggle as she left.

Mike's mouth dropped open at the byplay but Megan just rolled her eyes.

"Shanea, and Meredith for that matter, were with me when I was incarcerated by Paul Bowman," Megan said, shrugging. "Each of us dealt with it in our own way. In Shanea's case, it helped that she was a minx. And still is."

"If it's not too personal a question," Courtney said, hesitantly, "how did you deal with it?"

"By making myself busy," Megan answered honestly. "By creating projects for myself and by planning his assassination. And, finally, by carrying it out. It wasn't pleasant and I prefer not to talk about it, much more than that. And please don't ask Meredith about it at all."

"I won't," Courtney said, shaking her head. "I'm very glad, though, that you were a strong and capable person and I'd like to . . . well . . ." she ended, holding up her glass. "Good luck to you and Herzer. He's a very good guy. I hope you'll be happy."

"That I'll drink to," Mike said, holding up his own glass of beer.

After they had sipped, Megan set her glass down with a clink and looked at them gravely.

"Okay, why do you need a friend in court?"

After Mike explained their dilemma Megan frowned.

"Meredith?"

"The legislation initially had a number of competing distribution plans," Meredith stated. "The one that came closest to the final bill included both a lottery and a proven distribution plan. It was killed in committee primarily by a few commons that were heavily supported by various ag corp lobbyists. Since a number of the higher ups in the Agriculture Department have worked for ag corps they clearly felt they could get a better distribution plan through the bureaucracy than in congress. And they were right."

"It's *not* right, though," Megan admitted. "Agriculture is still the basis of the UFS economy and, correct me if I'm wrong, but the majority of agriculture is still small farmer. Correct?"

"Eighty percent thereabouts according the last report I scanned," Meredith said. "I haven't been concentrating on it, though."

"Exceptions we could use?" Megan asked, nodding.

"Military members," Meredith said. "They can apply for a grant with a very long proven period and only a portion of the property has to be proven. Herzer, for example, could apply for up to six thousand hectares and only have to prove out six hundred within twenty years. And he can buy additional land at a very low cost. How low was not specified in the legislation and depends upon the value of the property. There are no exceptions, however, for general farmers. Not in the legislation."

"That's not right," Courtney said. "Nothing against the military, Herzer, but . . ."

"I suspect it's a means of retaining trained officers," Megan said. "It reverts if they resign their commission?"

"All but proven lands and even then they only can retain up to twenty percent," Meredith said. "All lands revert to their heirs upon their death in service, proven or unproven, with no penalty."

"That's why," Megan said musingly. "What about council members?"

"Up to one hundred thousand hectares," Meredith recited. "Only one thousand need be proven within twenty years. Dukes up to fifty thousand, same conditions."

"I wonder if Duke Edmund knows that?" Megan said, smiling slightly. "Mike, how much land could you manage?"

"I want my *own* farm," Mike temporized. "My own land. Not to manage tenant farmers."

"Oh, we can arrange that I'm sure," Megan said, musingly. "And it doesn't solve the basic problem of the bureaucracy screwing people like you. There are several ways to approach this and I think we should use most of them. The first, Mike, is that small farmers like yourself need to get more organized. Preferably, form a political party but at the very least form some sort of a union that can hire lobbyists and make political contributions. Sorry, but that's how the system works and you either use it or you get used. There are enough farmers, both as a source of funds and direct voters, that with a little organization the commons will not dare ignore you. The second layer will be directed specifically at this problem. I could, frankly, use an income that's not dependent upon my subscription from the government. Therefore, Herzer, myself and possibly Duke Edmund will apply for grants of land and consider buying a few more parcels with the agreement that you manage them. The last point will be to ensure that the bureaucrats know you have friends in high places. I think we're going out to dinner."

"Dinner?" Courtney said, clearly confused.

"Somewhere where people will see Countess Megan Travante and her fiancé consulting with their agricultural manager," Megan said, grinning. "And by tomorrow, anyone that is anyone will know who you and Mike are and I'll *guarantee* that you'll have a different reception at the Agriculture Department."

"I don't like this," Mike said, shaking his head. "I don't know what I expected but it wasn't this. Maybe a letter to somebody in the department that would get me a better, or at least higher, meeting. But this is . . ."

"Underhanded and indirect," Megan said, nodding. "Herzer, you want to try to explain."

"Well, it's how the town works," Herzer said, shrugging. "I don't like it but as Duke Edmund says, democracy isn't the best government just the best that's ever been discovered. And this is how it works. The politicians get up and make speeches but where the deals get made are at parties and small meetings like, well, this one. You realize that you're doing a tit for tat, right?"

"No?" Mike said.

"Think about it. Megan makes sure you get *your* farm and you manage hers. That's how the town works. And it means that you've got an ear in Washan when something happens because part of her income is dependent on you being able to do your job. And it means that from now on *you* won't have trouble with bureaucracy or the ag corps. Everybody is a little afraid of councilors. But, right now, I think Washan is more terrified of Megan than Queen Sheida. Sheida sits in her aerie and manages things at long distance, not really getting involved in the political hustle-bustle. Megan walked into one party last night and walked out with agreements to build a new legion and upgrades to the Nawlins ports, both of which were dead in the water before she walked in."

"Oh," Courtney said, looking a little pale.

"I'd agree to help you even if you *didn't* agree to manage my farm," Megan said, looking at Herzer and frowning. "Because you're friends and you need somebody who understands the system. This is *not* a tit for tat."

"Well, hell," Mike said, shrugging. "I'd do it anyway because you're friends. But, hell, I'm not sure about a hundred thousand, two hundred thousand hectares. That's big management."

"All of it doesn't have to be proved out," Megan pointed out. "And I trust you where I wouldn't trust one of the ag corps to manage it."

"If you think we're up to it, we will be," Courtney said, still looking a trifle pale.

"And now, I think we should consider where to go to dinner," Megan said with a smile. "And we can talk about old times and you can tell me all of Herzer's secrets and embarrass him."

"So where did you three meet?" Megan asked as they were being seated. She'd carefully chosen a restaurant that would not be too upscale for their clothing and had changed to match. Herzer was still in undress day uniform, which fit closely enough. The restaurant, however, was a frequent hangout of congressional aides if not the commons and peer members. When Ashly had sent a hurried message that Megan wanted to dine there, the staff had nearly had apoplexy.

"In Raven's Mill, right after the Fall," Courtney said, frowning as she looked at the menu and blanched at the prices. "This food is *outrageous!*"

"My treat," Megan said. "Traditional in a business deal like this so don't try to argue. And any restaurant that fit the bill for what we're trying to achieve would be as expensive. Or more so. And the food is, at least, good. You wouldn't believe how bad the food is in some of the *really* expensive restaurants in town. How'd you get to Raven's Mill?"

"Well, I'd lived nearby," Courtney said, shrugging. "I met Mike on the road and we sort of ganged up for protection, you know how it was..." She trailed off unhappily.

"I do," Megan said. "The area I was in wasn't taken by the Changed for about six months. Once New Destiny established control it was actually a bit better and they didn't burn and loot *everyone.* But when they were passing through was...bad. Very bad."

"Well," Courtney continued, "we got checked in at Raven's Mill. Did you have something like that?"

"No," Megan said, interested. "Edmund was there from the beginning, right?"

"Oh, yeah," Courtney said. "And you could tell. I mean, it's just a couple of weeks after the Fall and it's, like, *civilization.* You got checked in and they asked you questions about your skills and stuff, then they put you up for a few days to get your head together. After that you had to get to work. Anyway, we met Herzer the first night, I think, right Mike?"

"Yeah, first night," he said, sipping his beer.

"So we hung out together until we joined the apprenticeship program and we were in that together too. Then, well, he joined the legions while we were still in the program and Mike hit it off with Myron Raeburn, who was the guy in charge of the farming program. He decided that running a farm was what he wanted to do. Herzer helped with that, too."

"Just a bit," Herzer said. "I had picked up a few extra credits and I figured Mike was a good bet."

"More than that," Courtney said. "He'd gotten an ox and some other livestock in the lottery. There he was, laid up in bed—"

"Laid up?" Megan asked, frowning. "You were wounded?"

"Injured," Herzer said, chuckling. "I hit my head on a branch while I was riding."

"Herzer!" Courtney protested. "I can't let you get away with that. We were rounding up ferals to get some food and separate out the young ones and things so we could use them for farm animals. I mean, most of them had been from farm breeds so they could be used again. Anyway, this big boar—"

"Courtney," Herzer said.

"Shut up. Anyway, this big boar was about to gore Shilan and Herzer charged it on his horse—that was Diablo, right?"

"Yeah," Herzer said, grumpily. "It was Diablo."

"He charged it and got it with a spear and kept it from getting Shilan but then when Diablo jumped over the boar Herzer hit his head on a branch. It darn near killed him."

"Sounds like my Herzer," Megan grinned. "You should see him on a dragon. But the question is: Who is Shilan?"

"Oh, Shilan was from the apprenticeship program, too." Courtney grinned. "I don't think she and Herzer ever really had a 'thing' you know, but they were pretty chummy," she added, grinning more broadly.

"Thanks, Courtney," Herzer growled.

"Then there was . . . what was the name of that redhead?" Courtney continued.

"Morgen." Herzer sighed. "Courtney, are you going to do a whole list?"

"Yes," Courtney said, grinning at Megan. "That only lasted about four hours . . ."

"Four *hours*?" Megan said, laughing. "Four *hours*?"

"From lunch until sometime in the early evening," Courtney confirmed. "Okay, maybe five. I don't know what they were doing in the interim, but they were pretty sweaty!"

"It wasn't *sweat*," Herzer said, loftily. "We'd washed off in a stream. We were picking wildflowers."

"Oh, is that what you call it?" Courtney grinned. "Then they had an argument and Morgen stormed off. I think she works in the baths now."

"Okay, that's Shilan and Morgen," Megan said, glancing at Herzer who was turning red. "Now. Tell me about . . . *Bast*."

"Arrrgh," Herzer groaned.

"Well, I wasn't there when they met," Courtney said. "But Mike was, weren't you, honey?"

"Yeah," Mike agreed.

"She was hanging around with Rachel Ghorbani, you know, Edmund's daughter?"

"I've met her," Megan said, smiling faintly. "Of course, the last time I saw her she was covered in blood."

"Really?" Courtney said. "Surgery?"

"No," Megan noted. "She'd just killed one of New Destiny's top field agents. I spent some time sharing a cabin with her also. Nice girl."

"Is madame ready to order?" the waiter asked nervously.

Megan glanced at the menu again and shrugged. "I hear they have a very good lobster."

"Well . . ." Courtney said, realizing that she hadn't really been paying attention to the menu.

"I'll have the strip steak, rare," Mike said.

"Lobster for me," Megan added, closing her menu.

"Same here," Herzer said.

"Make it three," Courtney added, closing her menu and shrugging. "I haven't had lobster since before the Fall."

"Still no tea," Herzer pointed out. "Or chocolate. Edmund complains about one and Daneh complains about the other . . ."

"I hadn't heard about that," Courtney said. "Rachel killing someone. I'm surprised; it doesn't seem like her. But I haven't seen her in ages; she's hardly in Raven's Mill anymore."

"Army surgeon corps," Herzer said. "I think she's back at Balmoran. You could run up the road and visit her if you wanted."

"Probably won't have the time," Mike said.

"About Bast..." Megan said.

"Well, she met up with Herzer and just sort of picked him out," Courtney said. "Told him he'd probably clean up well or something. After that they had quite a time. She wandered off for a while, then turned up again when Dionys McCanoc's group was coming. Saved your life, right, Herzer?"

"Yeah," he said, sighing. "I'd stayed behind to cover the retreat of a cavalry patrol. Diablo was just about worn out and I couldn't outrun the group that was pursuing us. So I stayed back. I'd gotten a couple of them but I was having trouble with the rest and then Bast showed up." He paused and shrugged. "End of fight. Good guys six, bad guys nothing." He paused again and shook his head. "Make that bad guys one. Somebody...what the hell was his name. I can't believe I've forgotten his name. Anyway, they got one of the cavalry guys."

"Was that your first fight?" Megan asked.

"Yeah," Herzer mused. "It seems like an eternity but it's only been...five years? Jesus. All these changes in five damned years. But that's why I can't believe I don't remember his name. I thought he was going to make it but...well..." He stopped and shook his head, furrowing his brow.

"So how long did Bast stay around?" Megan asked.

"Not long after McCanoc got his," Courtney said as she looked at the muttering Herzer. "And we didn't see much of Herzer, either. He was always out of town. He'd show up at the farm from time to time, just passing through."

"I think she's gone for a while, this time," Megan said. "Right after the battle of Balmoran she dimension shifted out with one of those Changed elves. Even Mother can't track her. No knowing when she'll be back or even if she'll survive."

"Oh, she'll survive," Herzer said, shaking his head. "Thomas... Marcum, what the hell was it...?"

"You're going to be muttering about this all night, aren't you?" Megan said, smiling. "I'm sure there are records somewhere."

"With Edmund, it's for sure," Courtney said, smiling. "June Lasker's still the archivist in Raven's Mill. She'll have his name."

"I suppose," Herzer said. "What did I order?"

CHAPTER FOUR

"Dinner was nice," Megan said as she came in the bedroom wearing a thin nightgown. "They're very nice people. But is Mike always so . . ."

"Monosyllabic?" Herzer said, grinning. "When he's not sure of his ground, yeah. When he's comfortable he opens up a little. But he's never what you might call a big talker. He leaves that to Courtney. So, did you get enough information about my girlfriends?"

"Did it really bother you?" Megan asked, sitting down on the edge of the bed and starting to brush her hair.

"No," Herzer replied. "I suppose it's easier than pulling it all out of me. If I go through the list I don't know whether it's just being honest or boasting."

"And quite a list it is," Megan said thoughtfully.

"Not all that long," Herzer argued.

"Long enough," Megan said, turning around and smiling at him. "I'm not bothered by it but I wonder if it's part of something I couldn't put a finger on."

"What?" Herzer asked, frowning. "About me?"

"No . . ." Megan said, sighing in frustration. "I think it might be part of how *I'm* viewed, though. Nobody knows quite what to make of me in this town. Given my . . . relationship with Paul, I'm clearly not a virgin or any sort of pseudo virgin. I therefore, in their eyes, have to be either hypersexual, from my experiences, or asexual. Shanea's an example of the first and Meredith of the second. Love it

or renounce it. And I'm afraid that, possibly because of your reputation, they've decided I'm hypersexual. It makes Duke Dehnavi's
advances more . . . understandable. And angering."

"And, if anything, they've gotten it backwards," Herzer said,
sadly. "Sorry. I guess I didn't think about *my* baggage."

"I haven't *renounced* sex, Herzer," Megan said, sorrowfully. "I'm
just not ready."

"I know," he replied, holding out his arms. "Are you done
brushing your hair so I can give you a hug?"

"How do you put up with this?" she asked, turning down the
lamp and snuggling into his side.

"With difficulty," Herzer admitted. "But I love you and I trust
that, someday, you'll be able to . . . get back on the horse as Bast
put it. In the meantime . . . I'll wait."

"How long?" she asked, quietly.

"Long enough," Herzer said. "If it's going to be 'never' then
you'll find the strength to tell me. And we'll . . . work something
out. I don't want to give you up."

"You are very strange, Herzer," Megan muttered. "How are the
demons?"

Herzer paused as he did a quick internal inventory.

"Not good," he admitted. "That encounter with Duke Dehnavi's . . .
how'd you put it?"

"Doxie?" Megan asked.

"Yeah, doxie, caused them to slip their leash a little. Bottling
them back up without . . . some outlet, is difficult."

"Were you attracted to her?" Megan asked, carefully.

"Hell, yes," Herzer replied, grinning in the dark. "I mean, I
wouldn't toss her out of bed for eating crackers; the duke at least
has good taste in doxies. If you want me to lie about it, I will.
But I try not to."

"No, don't lie," Megan said, yawning. "I'm afraid I'm going to
dream of doxies tonight."

"Good dreams, sweetie," Herzer said, twisting to kiss her on
the head. "Only good dreams."

Herzer had read somewhere that sleeping with a woman and
not having sex was the closest form of intimacy. The writer should
have tried doing it for four months in a row.

At this point, Herzer had to admit that in the deeps of the

night, as Megan's breath whispered on his arm, it was hard in more ways than one. Some nights seemed like one continuous wrestle with his demons. During the day he could keep active and, in general, his lackanookie condition was no big deal. Occasionally there'd be an encounter with somebody like the duke's doxie and it would get . . . hard. But mostly it was no problem.

In the nights, however, it was starting to be a problem. No, in honesty, it had started to be a problem a long time ago. Now it was starting to be a *big* problem.

Part of it was that he hadn't been getting enough exercise so he wasn't sleeping as well. Early to bed and early to rise would have helped. Even a ruck run every morning didn't really impact him much. Honestly, it didn't even keep him in shape. He was used to three to six hours of solid exercise a day and with the schedule he'd been keeping there just wasn't a time.

So he lay awake every night, pondering the various problems of the day and trying to convince Mr. Happy that he wasn't going to get any.

Hard. Good word.

He rolled over and contemplated the darkened wall, then closed his eyes and told himself to go to sleep. Ignore it, it will go away he told himself, clicking his prosthetic lightly in thought. The faint noise made Megan mutter and roll over, so he stopped.

He'd just about convinced himself when he heard the pounding on the door. As he rolled to his feet his sword had whispered out of its scabbard before he really knew it was in his hand.

"Crap," he muttered, walking to the door of the bedroom. There were legionnaires on the door of the apartment and in the street below. And it was unlikely that an assassin would knock. Unlikely, not impossible.

"What is it?" Megan said, sleepily.

"I dunno," he muttered, going out of the room and down the corridor to the entry foyer.

"Yes?" he called as there was another pounding on the door. "What the hell do you want?"

"I'm sorry, Major," a voice said in the hallway. "There's a messenger here for you and Countess Travante from Duke Edmund."

Herzer looked through the peephole and recognized one of the guards but when he opened the door he did it from the side with two feet of steel pointing out.

"Sorry, Major," the messenger said. He was an ensign in undress uniform with enough smell of horse that he must have ridden hard. He had a dispatch case in his hands and opened it up, proffering a heavy linen envelope.

"Stay here," Herzer growled, taking the envelope with his prosthetic and closing the door in the ensign's face. He walked to the couch and lit one of the lamps with a match, then slit the pouch with his sword, tossing the latter on the couch.

It didn't take long to read the short note.

"Son of a BITCH!"

"THE WHOLE TEAM?" Herzer shouted, ignoring the fact that the other people in the room far outranked him. "The whole God-damned *team*?"

"Sit down, Herzer," Edmund said, pointing at a chair. "Megan, thank you for coming at this time of night."

"No problem, Edmund," Megan said, sitting down at one end of the conference table. "This is very bad news."

"Yes, Major," General Galbreath said, taking a sip of coffee and gesturing for Megan and Herzer to be served. "The whole team. Icarus is gone."

"With all due respect, sir, what the hell happened?" Herzer asked, taking a cup of coffee from a senior NCO with a nod of thanks.

"A group of assassins descended on the training facility," Edmund said. "We've only got the first words off of the semaphore. Apparently some were human but the rest were some sort of large bug, sort of like a giant scorpion . . ."

"Possibly solfugid mods," Megan said, shaking her head. "Basically giant camel spiders with metallic mandibles. The same thing that Celine sent after Minjie Jiaqi's assassin."

"The personnel were sleeping so they went through the barracks . . . well, there weren't any survivors," Edmund said. "The message made it sound rather bad."

"Didn't they have guards?" Herzer growled.

"They were well guarded, Major," General Galbreath said sharply. "A company of legionnaires with Blood Lord officers. We don't know what happened to them."

"Probably poison spiders," Megan said, thoughtfully. "That was how they got through to whatsisname."

"A response team from Seventh Legion got most of them," Edmund said. "Apparently the rest escaped into the night. They're either still out there in hiding or they'll go on a rampage in the area."

"So what now?" Herzer asked.

"Well, we're going to have to form a scratch team," General Galbreath said, looking at him pointedly.

"Oh, Christ on a crutch," Herzer muttered. "Let me guess."

"You got it," Edmund replied. "You're now the head of the Icarus assault team. Congratulations. It comes with a promotion."

"Oh, crap," Herzer muttered. "I won't ask 'why me.'"

"There's more," Edmund said, looking at Megan. "The team had been analyzing the systems on the ship and they had come to the conclusion that it was going to be necessary to have at least one Key-holder on the mission. I'd been discussing it with Sheida. Effectively, since Norau is carrying the ball on the mission, the choice comes down to you or me. I'd been arguing, quite hard, for me. Sheida disagrees."

"So do I," Megan said, shaking her head. "You're too involved in the planning for the assault on Ropasa. You can't leave. I'm . . . less important."

"Like hell you are," Herzer protested. "Without you we'd be planning on an invasion without the *bare minimum* forces we need."

"But the most important parts of the politicking are done for the moment," Megan pointed out. "I'll be back to the capital in three or four months. Nothing really critical should come up between now and then."

"Megan," Herzer said, closing his eyes, "this is not your . . . This is not something that you're trained for or . . . this is not your— Damnit!"

"Herzer," Megan said, laying a hand on his arm. "This is something that *has* to be done. And I'm the best person to do it, apparently. Who goes? Edmund? Sheida?"

"Yes!" Herzer said. "Edmund is damned near as good at surviving as I am! Sheida is . . . She *has* a background in surviving."

"So do I," Megan said angrily.

"Not this!" Herzer snapped. "I don't care how well planned this mission supposedly is! It's going to turn into a blindsided cluster fisk! I can *feel* it! I don't want *you* in the middle of *that*!"

"And you'll be there to protect me," Megan said, smiling faintly. "Besides, we're going to have to train for this, right? Which means we get more time together. You'd been complaining about not seeing enough of me."

"When the air is whistling out of your suit, what am I supposed to do but watch you die?" Herzer asked bleakly.

"I'm going, Herzer," Megan said flatly. "That's final."

"I know," he replied, flexing one muscle in his jaw. "But I don't have to like it." He paused and shook his head. "I don't like any of it. I don't even know the plans. I mean, I know that the team planned on going up to the ship and seizing it. But I don't know how they were going to get there, what the ship is like, what the battle plans were . . . Jesus! And everyone that *knew* the plans is now toast!"

"Not quite everyone," Edmund said. "Evan Mayerle was consulting on the mission. He wasn't part of the team so he was off-site when the attack occurred. He's still alive and he knows the plans and the details of the ship. The basic mission is simple; take control of the ship and ensure that New Destiny does not. If you can't ensure it, make sure that the ship is unusable, probably by crashing it into the Moon."

"That would be . . . bad," Megan said, frowning. "That would mean both sides would lose the power."

"Better that we lose the power than New Destiny get it," General Galbreath said. "I'm afraid that, given the conditions, it's unlikely we can lock New Destiny out entirely. It's complicated, but you'll get fully briefed."

"But we've got serious personnel shortage," Edmund added. "Besides the fighters, the team has to have people who know how the ship systems work and they're incredibly ancient. That ship has been out there plying its path for well over a thousand years. It's been maintained but never really updated; there was no need. We'd found or trained people on the old-style computers it uses, engineers for the ion drive engines and pilots for the shuttle craft . . ."

"Shuttle craft?" Herzer asked. "What shuttle craft?"

"I'll get to that," Edmund said. "But they're all *dead*. We need to find replacements and we'll need to find them fast. We'll get to work on that. You concentrate on the strike personnel. The Icarus team, I always thought, was too small. It was concentrated on getting in and doing the mission but I'd been arguing that they weren't prepared for things to go to hell in a handbasket. I don't have to worry about that with you in charge."

"No, sir," Herzer said dryly. "I mean, they've already gone to hell in a handbasket. All we can do at this point is steer."

"You can draw on anyone you need, Major," General Galbreath said. "And I do mean *anyone.*"

"Where are we going to get the techs?" Herzer asked.

"We'll be going over records," Edmund said, frowning. "Unfortunately, most towns didn't record what people did pre-Fall and if they did they haven't told the federal government. The census didn't record it, either. So the only place I *know* that has lists of people's training, pre-Fall, is in Raven's Mill. We'll probably start there and work our way out."

"We can't exactly take out ads on this," Megan pointed out, shaking her head. "There are probably a thousand people in Norau with each of the specialties we need. But finding them is going to be tough. Especially with the time constraint."

"I'll put Lieutenant Van Krief to work on it," Edmund said. "She's a miracle worker when it comes to ferreting out information. And I'll get June Lasker from Raven's Mill with the records from there and put out a call for similar records."

"Where were they training?" Herzer asked.

"A facility near the Pizurg reactor," General Galbreath said. "I assume you'll want to use the same facilities."

"Rather than reinvent the wheel, yes, sir," Herzer replied. "That's near Tarson and Harzburg. Joy. I hoped I'd never have to go up there again."

"You won't be going to Harzburg," Edmund said. "And for the time being you'll need to stay here in Washan while we assemble lists of potential personnel. Again, you concentrate on the strike operators. We'll find the techs."

"I'll make a list," Herzer said, thinking about good soldiers he had met and fought beside. Unfortunately, many of them were dead. "They'll all be missed by their commands."

"You'll get them," General Galbreath promised.

"Are we done for tonight?" Megan asked, looking at the clock mounted on the wall. "Not that it's worth going back to bed. I have a breakfast meeting in two hours. I'll start clearing my schedule immediately."

"You're detached from ops as of now, Herzer," Edmund said, "and promoted to commander. Congratulations."

"You said that," Herzer replied. "I wish I could be happy.

But we'll get it done. One way or another. Oath of the Bull God we will."

"What do you think?" Megan asked as they returned to the apartment in her carriage.

"I don't know enough to think anything," Herzer replied. "Except that we need to upgrade your security. And Edmund's come to think of it."

"I've got wards up to look for Celine's little toys," Megan said. "Don't worry about them. And enough power to cover both of us in personal protection fields."

"They can take those down," Herzer pointed out. "But I get you. I didn't know that, though."

"I hadn't thought about it," Megan replied honestly. "But they're there. Also to check the personnel. I knew that there was only one additional person present when you went to the door. If there had been more I would have told you. But I didn't see any reason to bring it up before. It's just . . . second nature at this point. I was thinking about the mission, though."

"So was I," Herzer admitted. "But until we get some sort of full briefing, I don't think we can do more than fret about it. I wish I'd gotten some sleep, though."

"Don't tell me you were still awake," Megan said. "You need to figure out some way to get to sleep better."

"Well, there's nature's tranquilizer," Herzer said, then grimaced. "Sorry."

"Yes, there is," Megan said, seriously. "And, damnit, I'm *going* to get back on the horse. Soon. I promise. It's not fair to you and I'm tired of being afraid of it. I'll be honest, I *miss* sex. Even *bad* sex, which was about all I got from Paul. It would be nice to find out if there's such a thing as *good* sex."

"Oh, lady," Herzer said, pulling her into his arms. "I don't know if I'm good enough, and it's going to be hard to be . . . how I'll have to be. But I'll try, I promise."

"You tempt me, you truly do," Megan said, with a grin that segued into a grimace. "But that *damned* meeting . . ."

"Not tonight, love," Herzer said. "You've got a meeting. I'm off duty. I'm going to catch some sleep until there's more news. I suspect that sleep is going to be optional for a while."

CHAPTER FIVE

All of Megan's staff were up and in the apartment when they got back.

"What happened?" Shanea asked. "We heard the knocking but when we got dressed you were already *gone!*"

"The Icarus team got taken out," Herzer said, stripping off his jacket and yawning. "So for my sins they're putting me in charge."

"Oh my *God!*" Shanea wailed. "You're going into space?"

"Looks like it," Herzer muttered. "Is the coffee on?"

"I thought you were going back to bed?" Megan said. "Meredith, Ashly, spend most of tomorrow clearing my schedule. I'm going to be unavailable in a few days."

"Yes, ma'am," Meredith said, nodding. "May I ask why?"

"It turns out that there's something unspecified that requires the presence of a Key-holder on the mission," Megan said with a moue. "So that means me or Duke Edmund. Of the two, I'm less necessary at the moment."

"You're going?" Ashly said. "You've got to be joking!"

"I'm not joking," Megan said. "What's on the schedule for the breakfast meeting?"

"Vote count," Meredith said. "The port upgrades, fleet budget and the new legion budgeting."

"Make sure the linking sheet is ready with a list of hard votes," Megan said, shaking her head. "Mirta . . . a gray suit, I think. The news will have gotten around fast. A touch of mourning clothes would be in order. Among other things it will send a signal that I knew about it before anyone else."

"What about us?" Ashly said. "We're not going with you, are we?"

"No," Megan said with a smile. "Meredith will stay in Washan to keep an eye on things. Ditto Mirta to follow the rumor mill. I'd like you and Shanea to accompany me to the training facility. You to handle the reports from Meredith, and Shanea..."

"Because I'm nice to have around?" Shanea asked, bringing in a tray with coffee and some rolls.

"Exactly," Megan said, smiling. "Thank you."

"I'm going to have to start working out, soon," Herzer said. "Mirta? Meredith? I don't know which of you would handle it but I need a set of weights. Barbells from ten kilos to forty, bar weights from sixty to two hundred and a press bench. If you can find it, a legion weight-training system. I don't know when we'll be leaving town and I'm going to have to get started right away if the mission is in two months."

"You look in pretty good shape to me," Shanea said, grinning.

"That's because you've never seen me actually *in* shape," Herzer replied with a smile. "Even on the ship I was woefully out of condition. Sleep or workout?" he muttered, taking another sip of coffee and a bite of roll. "Ah, hell, I can sleep when I'm dead. I doubt anything serious will get done today; they're going to have to get Evan down here from the training facility, he'll have to get a brief together..."

"You're not planning on starting today, are you?" Megan asked.

"Yeah," Herzer said. "But I'll need more breakfast than a roll. I'll go get it from the deli around the corner."

"The hell you will," Shanea protested. "What do you want? We've got everything you could possibly need here."

"Hmmm," Herzer muttered. "Well, when I get back, I'd like six eggs, over easy, about six slices of bacon, four pieces of toast, coffee," he said, waving his cup, "and if you've got it, a large portion of hash browns."

"Ulp," Shanea gasped. "All that?"

"All that," Herzer said, standing up. "Megan, I'll see you later, I guess."

"You're going *now*?"

"Traffic's light," Herzer grinned. "Best time of the day."

✧   ✧   ✧

Herzer stumbled back into the apartment, fully aware of how badly out of shape he was. He'd only gone about twenty kilometers with the ruck and half of that had been at a walk. And it wasn't a combat-loaded ruck. He should have been able to trot the whole distance if not run it. Either he was getting old or soft living in the capital was taking its toll.

"Are you ready for breakfast?" Shanea asked, then blanched. "Are you okay?"

"I will be," Herzer gasped, lowering the ruck onto the floor of the entryway. "But right now I'd puke at the sight of food. I'll be fine after a shower."

"I'll get started then," Shanea said.

"Thanks."

As he was finishing breakfast the weights started to arrive.

"I got everything you asked for," Mirta said as the sweating workmen carried the material into the apartment.

"I have no idea where we're going to put it all," Herzer temporized.

"Meredith has offered the spare space in her office," Mirta said with a grin.

"I hate to throw her out," Herzer replied, frowning.

"Oh, you're not," Mirta said with a smile. "I said the *spare* space. She said she can work around you."

There had been no further word from Edmund, and Herzer was well into his upper body workout when Meredith wandered into the room.

Her "office" was one of the spare bedrooms in the apartment. Each of the ladies had her own apartment in the building, which had been virtually co-opted by Megan, but she had an additional office in Megan's apartment where she kept most of the records. The room was large, however, and the desk and filing cabinet only took up part of the space. The extensive weight equipment Herzer had ordered, however, could have taken up a much larger room.

"Are you sure this is going to work?" Herzer asked, slowly raising a barbell in one hand and another in the prosthetic up to shoulder height, arms outstretched in front of him. He took a slow breath as he raised them, then held them out at full extension. He was wearing cutoff shorts and a sweat-soaked, sleeveless, gray cosilk shirt.

"If I can get in here around your stuff, yes," Meredith said coldly. She dropped the files in her arms on the desk and sat down, opening up the top one. "And if I don't have to engage in casual conversation."

Herzer took the hint and lowered the barbells with an outrush of breath, waited a moment and then repeated the movement.

He was halfway through a forty rep of slow curls when Meredith closed the file she was reading and turned around in her chair.

"Aren't you supposed to do a lower body workout one day and an upper body workout the next?" she asked scornfully.

"I did a heavy lower body today," Herzer said, slowly raising the twenty-kilo barbell. "This is a light upper body workout."

"That's *light*?" Meredith said, frowning.

"Yes," Herzer replied.

Meredith watched him for a moment and then turned back around, opening another file.

"Thanks for coming over here, Evan," Herzer said, helping the engineer with the easel he had brought.

Evan Mayerle was a medium height, brown-haired young man with blue eyes that at the moment were mostly focused on Shanea's rump. She had brought in a tray of coffee and sweet rolls and placed them on the low table by bending over from the waist. Since she was wearing a tight skirt, her endowments in the area were fully evident.

"Uh . . ." the engineer said. "Yeah. Uhm . . ."

"Briefing on the *Excelsior*," Herzer said, grinning.

"Right," Evan said, shaking his head and trying not to watch the blonde as she sashayed out of the room. "*Excelsior*," he muttered, pulling a set of charts out of a tube and pinning them to the easel. "*Excelposterior . . .*" He paused and shook his head. "Miss Travante, have we met?"

"Briefly on the *Hazhir*," Megan replied.

"Nice to see you again," Evan muttered, his eyes wandering between her chest and her eyes. He shook his head again and pulled out two thick files from his briefcase.

"I suppose I should get started," he said, setting the files on the coffee table. "Uhm . . ." He paused and took a breath again and then turned to the easel. "You're ready?"

"Ready, Mr. Mayerle," Megan said, trying not to laugh.

"The *Excelsior* was built in 2935. It was originally a tanker that carried hydrocarbons from Neptune to Terra."

Herzer started to open his mouth and then closed it. Evan, concentrating on his notes, didn't notice.

"It was refitted for helium three transport in 3212 when the market for hydrocarbons dropped below the sustainment level for the system. As the last of its class it was retained while the others were scrapped. It uses an ion drive propulsion system which, of course, is very low impulse but has a high maximum speed . . ."

"Excuse me," Herzer interjected. "I'm lost. What is an ion drive?"

"You know what ions are, right?" Evan said, frowning.

"Yes," Megan said.

"No," Herzer replied at the same time.

Evan sighed and thought for a moment.

"You *do* know that an atom is composed of a nucleus and an electron shell, right?" he asked.

"That I know," Herzer admitted.

"Okay. Ions are atoms that have had the electron shell stripped away. They're highly energetic and you can push them out the back of a space vehicle and they give you specific impulse. That is, they push the spacecraft. More or less."

"Okay," Herzer said. "So that means . . . what for us?"

"Just that that's the ship's main drive system," Evan replied, frowning.

"And that matters to me . . . why?" Herzer asked.

Evan opened his mouth and then closed it, looking nonplussed.

"Herzer," Megan said, smiling faintly. "Let him talk."

"Okay," Herzer replied, leaning back. "Just wake me up when we get to the part where I kill people."

"The ship is a bit over one kilometer long," Evan said, frowning slightly and pointing to the first schematic. "The drive system is to the rear and takes up about two hundred meters of the ship. There are six very old model HE3 fusion reactors in that section and the ion generator cannon . . ."

"Cannon?" Herzer said, sitting up.

"It's a term of art, Major," Evan sighed. "It's not a weapon."

"Oh."

"There is also a small control facility that controls only the main engine systems. The ship vector is adjusted by latitudinal thrusters located along the midline and centerline . . ."

Herzer opened his mouth and then closed it, shaking his head.

"That's how it's steered," Megan whispered in his ear.

" . . . which are controlled from the ship's central command facility located . . . here," he said, pointing near the center of the ship.

"Why's it got those big bulges?" Herzer asked.

"There are three HE3 tanks," Evan said, sighing. "Located centerline of the ship. Each is composed of a flex-metal composite. When empty they deflate but they will be fully engorged when the initial presentation is made."

Herzer started to say something again and then waved his hand in despair.

"That means when we first get up there," Megan whispered.

"There are twelve refueling shuttles," Evan continued, apparently not noticing the byplay. "Located midline at docking points here, here, here, here, here and here," he added, tapping the new schematic. "This, of course, only shows the shuttles on one side, there is a matching set on the far side. Each of the shuttles has room for seven persons including a pilot, in case the ship needs human repair crew . . ."

"Why in the hell would it need that?" Herzer asked. "Doesn't Mother handle that?"

"At the time it was developed," Evan said with a moue, "full function AIs were limited in number and not fully trusted with complex problems. The ship originally had a human crew. Which is why the transverse personnel tubes located midline above the shuttle docking points are pressurized, as is the engine control room, maintenance, crew quarters and the main control room."

"Okay, now we're getting someplace," Herzer said, leaning back and rubbing his chin.

"The shuttles are fully automated," Evan continued. "When the ship approaches Terra . . ."

"Where's Terra?" Herzer asked. "You said that before."

"Earth," Megan replied.

"What she said," Evan said with a nod. "When it approaches *Earth*, the shuttles fuel from the HE3 tanks and land at reactors.

Transfer at the reactors takes approximately one hour. Then they return to the ship, fuel again and so on. It takes approximately twenty trips for the ship to be fully emptied."

"Why not just port it down?" Herzer asked, confused.

"The ship, for safety reasons, never comes closer than the orbit of the Moon to *Earth*," Evan said. "The initial shuttle punch occurs far *outside* the orbit of the Moon and the ship continues on trajectory *past* Terra and the Moon. It's far enough out that even modern porting systems are questionable and a portal, since it moves at a high rate of comparative velocity to a link on *Earth* is highly unstable. When the system was designed, of course, teleportation had not yet been developed."

"So we can't just set up a portal and flood the ship with troops," Herzer said.

"No," Evan confirmed. "The only way up, and the only way *back* is on the shuttles. Seven at a time, per shuttle. Nine at a real squeeze. There are, in addition, four small space-capable shuttles. They are *not* capable of landing on Ter ... Earth. They're designed for moving around the ship and between the ship and its fueling stations around Jupiter and Saturn and cannot handle reentry gravitational loading. Nor are they aerodynamic."

"So ... what's the plan?" Herzer said.

"The control room can reprogram shuttle priorities," Evan said. "The original Icarus plan was to go up in the first shuttles and take the control room, then reprogram the shuttles to only refuel Freedom Coalition reactors."

"Sounds like a plan," Herzer said.

"What about the engine room?" Megan asked.

"Anyone who controls the engine room, effectively controls the main engines," Evan said, frowning. "But that only gives direct velocity control. I'm not sure what utility that would have to the mission. My primary concern was with the shuttles themselves."

"Why?" Herzer asked.

"They can be overridden by an onboard pilot," Evan pointed out. "We can reprogram them to land at only our reactors. But if New Destiny has pilots in them, it won't matter."

"Ouch," Herzer muttered. "This is making my head hurt. What we *really* need to do, in other words, is capture all twelve of the shuttles."

"That was my suggestion," Evan said. "There was, however, a problem."

"And that is?" Megan asked.

"Where, pardon me, ma'am, you come in. The shuttles require a security override for pilots to take control. For that matter, so does the control room."

"And the security can only be overridden by a Key-holder," Megan guessed.

"Correct," Evan said, frowning. "So to take control of the shuttles, you will be required to go to each of them and tell them who you are. The system is a real antique. We don't even have good mock-ups for it. That's one of the reasons we'll have to have some people who know old computers. There were some on the original team and they gave a presentation on the systems. Unfortunately, I don't even have their *notes*."

"Great," Megan said, frowning.

"But New Destiny will be sending up their *own* people in *their* shuttles," Herzer said. "Do the shuttles always go back to the same reactors?"

"No," Evan said, unhappily. "Just because you have a shuttle, doesn't mean it's programmed for *your* reactor. But if you have a pilot in it, it can be forced to go there."

"I have to ask this," Megan said. "Is Mother going to intervene in this little scuffle?"

"She shouldn't," Evan temporized. "As far as we were able to determine, she doesn't have a protocol that governs security for this ship."

"Hmmm . . ." Megan mused. "Mother?"

"Yes, Megan?" a voice answered out of the air.

Evan reacted with surprise but Herzer just looked nonplussed.

"You are aware that we're planning on . . . hijacking the *Excelsior*?" Megan asked.

"Yes," the disembodied voice replied.

"Are you going to tell New Destiny what our plans are?"

"No."

"And I don't suppose you'll tell me *their* plans?" Megan asked, hopefully.

"No."

"Are you going to interfere?"

"Not unless the safety of Terra is jeopardized," Mother responded. "And perhaps not even then."

"What does that mean?" Herzer asked.

"I suspect it has to do with ship trajectory," Evan said. "If the ship were to crash into Terra, it would be very unpleasant. Big boom."

"Okay, handy safety tip," Herzer said. "Don't crash the ship into the Earth."

"Is Evan correct, Mother?" Megan asked. "As long as we don't crash the ship into Terra, you will not interfere?"

"That is correct," Mother replied. "As long as you remain within your plans to capture or destroy the ship, there will be no interference from this party. Furthermore, reentry of the *Excelsior* under these conditions could be described as human error. I am remanded from fixing human errors other than through specific protocol provisions."

"In other words," Megan said, frowning, "if we crash it into the Earth, Mother won't save us."

"That would be bad," Evan said, quietly.

"How bad?" Herzer asked.

"Mother," Megan said, puzzled. "What about explosive protocols?"

"The impact of the *Excelsior*, more or less intact, would exceed explosive protocol overrides given current power reserves."

"Very bad," Evan said.

"But if we slam it in the Moon we're good to go?" Herzer asked.

There was a pause and Megan smiled as the computer didn't answer.

"But if we are forced to crash it into the Moon, there will be no repercussion?" Megan asked.

"No," Mother replied. "The mass of the ship is insufficient to deflect the orbit of the Moon."

"Thank you, Mother," Megan said, frowning. "I really don't want to crash the ship. Once we drain the reactors down in this damned war, we won't even have the power left to *build* another ship that can go out and get the fuel we'll need. Even if we take *all* the Keys we may be stuck on the planet."

"No," Evan said. "If we take nine Keys we can override several protocols that will permit us to build *different* reactors. Then, when we've built up the power, we can build another *Excelsior* and go get the fuel we need. It will be a pain and it will stretch out the rebuild time, but we can do it."

"What sort of reactors?" Herzer asked.

"The HE3 reactors can be converted to use hydrogen," Evan said. "Which is easy enough to extract from water."

"Why don't they already?" Megan asked curiously.

"There are . . . unpleasant by-products," Evan admitted.

"Define unpleasant," Megan requested.

"Very radioactive," Evan admitted. "It's why they use HE3 instead; it has virtually no radioactive by-products. The only radiation comes from hydrogen and H2 contamination and that's in parts per billion; easy enough to scrub in use. But if you use hydrogen you're constantly having to replace parts that have been irradiated. It was extremely time and cost intensive at the time of their design, requiring that the parts be ground down and then reprocessed laboriously to extract the radioactive isotopes and then mixing them with glass and eventually containing them in a long-term containment facility." He paused and his eyes unfocused as a thought hit him. "Of course, with modern replication technology, it would be easier to reprocess the materials since the replicator fields can distinguish, of course, between standard stable and unstable isotopes . . ."

"Evan," Herzer said. "The ship."

"Oh, right," Evan muttered. "Uhm . . ."

"So we have to take the control room?" Herzer asked, standing up and flipping through the large schematic diagrams. He noticed that they were on some type of plastic and wondered where they'd come from and how *old* they were. The plastic had a brittle feel to it.

"That would be optimum," Evan said. "But probably insufficient to guarantee success."

"Any way to ignore it?" Herzer asked.

"Well," Evan said, shrugging. "If you took all the shuttles, secured them, manned them and ensured their continued security, you'd get the fuel. But if you ignore the command center, New Destiny then has control of the ship."

"Lots of personnel for that," Herzer muttered. "Where's the control center?"

"Here," Evan said, pointing to the spot on the schematic. "Located between fuel blisters numbers one and two on the lower structural reinforcement ring."

"These are the closest shuttles," Herzer said, pointing to the spots. He was starting to get the arcane symbology on the schematic.

"Yes, shuttles three and four are closest," Evan admitted.

"Pressurized the whole way?" Herzer asked.

"Pressure and artificial gravity," Evan said.

"Alternate means of egress?" Herzer asked.

"Each of the pressure corridors, port and starboard, has airlocks, here and here," Evan noted, pointing to the symbols. "There are two doors to the control room, port and starboard. Standard pressure doors."

"Armored or what?" Herzer asked. "What are they made out of?"

"Memory plastic," Evan said unhappily. "They're rather easy to break if you squirt them with a cryogenic fluid and then give them a sharp tap with a pointed object."

"Cryogenic?" Herzer said, wincing.

"Very cold," Megan said. "Liquid helium would do."

"Or nitrogen," Evan noted. "It's what the team was going to use if they had to force the doors."

"No other points of attack?" Herzer asked. "What are the walls made of?"

"You're thinking of cutting your way into the control room?" Evan asked, aghast.

"I'm hoping not to," Herzer said. "I'm also hoping that New Destiny doesn't. What are they made of?"

"Ceramo-metallic composite," Evan said. "Very strong, very resistant including to chemical attacks and heat. I'm not sure how you would cut it under the conditions. Repair requires a plasma torch. There are some on the ship in the maintenance bay," he added, pointing to a spot between the control room and the engine room.

"What are these?" Herzer asked, pointing to two spots on the reinforcement ring that were marked, he thought, as airlocks.

"Docking points for the space-only shuttles," Evan said.

"Any way in *there*?" Herzer asked.

"The airlock for the shuttle is attached to the ship," Evan noted. "Someone could cut in through the wall of the ship, but it's composite as well. It does have a view port forward, diamond composite. That would be easier than cutting the hull."

"I'd like to know what all these symbols mean," Herzer said, running his hand over the schematic. "I can read a topographic map easily. This is ... different."

"There's a legend on the second page," Evan said, flipping to it and pointing at the massive number of entries.

Herzer looked at it and groaned. "This is going to take forever to understand. And we'll want copies. A lot of copies. Are there any around?"

"There's one other," Evan said, unhappily. "How many copies?"

"At least ten," Herzer said. "Preferably more. I'd like every team to have one. How were the Icarus teams set up?"

"The first wave was to be fighters," Evan said. "Their mission was to take the control room. Then another wave of mixed fighters and techs would move in and take control."

"That assumes that you can take the control room and don't run into anything that your fighters can't handle," Herzer noted.

"Yes, but the strike personnel were cross-trained on limited engineering capability," Evan noted. "They could figure out the basics of most of the systems."

"We can't," Herzer pointed out. "Our fighters are only going to be able to fight, and I'm not sure of that in zero g and no pressure. Gag. We're going to have to go with mixed teams. One computer tech, one engineering tech and four fighters per shuttle."

"And on one of them there's going to have to be a Key-holder," Megan noted.

"Figure out if your specialty is going to be computers or engineering," Herzer said. "You're going to be studying like the rest of us. What about steering this beast? Navigation or piloting or whatever?"

"The navigation is simplicity itself," Evan noted. "If you have the control room. All you do is tell it where to go in space and park itself. If you want to crash it, have it park on the Moon. If we gain full control, you can park it at L-5 or in geosynchronous orbit."

"What is L-5?" Herzer asked. "Or geosynchronous orbit?"

"L-5 is a stable gravitational point off-set between Terra and Luna," Megan said. "Geosynchronous orbit is the orbit around Terra where a body travels at a speed which maintains it in orbit and over a single point on Terra."

"Is there any way to gain control of the steering if you *don't* have the control room?" Herzer asked.

"Manual control of the thrusters," Evan said, pointing to spots along the structural rings. "But actually steering it, even into a body as large as the Moon, will be difficult. It risks crashing it into Terra, for example. Or having it 'miss,' forcing us to keep scrabbling for it."

"*I'm* scrabbling in the dark," Herzer admitted. "Leave this copy and notes on the basic areas. I'll come up with a list of questions over the next few days, each of which will produce more questions. Do you know anything about the personnel search?"

"No," Evan admitted. "I suspect I'm going to have to go on the mission, though."

"Why?" Herzer asked.

"Well, I'm *familiar* with the ship. I've been studying it off and on for the last year. *I* know how an ion drive works," he added proudly.

"You're right," Herzer said. "You just got drafted. For now, though, get copies made of the other copy. And I'll get started on a list of questions."

After Evan had left, Herzer continued to pore over the schematic unhappily.

"So I'm going to be an engineering tech, eh?" Megan said after a few minutes of being ignored. "What are you going to be studying?"

"This," Herzer said, waving at the schematic. "I'm going to have to be *the* expert at this thing. To know it like the inside of my mouth. To know every detail of every dimension. What portions are pressurized. Which have gravity. Which have both. Which have neither. Where the entry points are. What they are made of. How to disable a door. How to disable an airlock. How to fix one that's been disabled. I'm going to have to be able to know exactly where someone is, based on this *insane* coding," he added, waving at the map, "when a team reports they've hit heavy resistance at . . . Charlie One Three Five. To know, without looking at the map, if they're fighting in pressure or out. And be able to keep track, partially in my head and partially on this map, where reinforcements are. And I only have a month. That and getting in shape again. Sleep is going to be optional."

"How are we going to communicate?" Megan asked.

"Question one that I should have asked Evan already," Herzer sighed. "I dunno. I don't even know if we'll have space suits or space armor or nothing."

"Suits and armor," Megan said, looking at the notes. "Armor for the fighters, suits for the techs."

"We'll have to get fitted," Herzer said. "Soon. Which means we have to have the list of personnel. Soon. If I understood Evan's briefing, we won't know which of the shuttles is coming to which reactor until they're on their way. And how do we find out which are going to friendly reactors and which are going to enemy once they're on their second trip?"

Megan flipped through the briefing papers and found the appropriate page.

"Each shuttle access point has a readout showing where it is going when it refuels and where each other refueling shuttle is going."

"Assuming one side or the other doesn't control the shuttles," Herzer said.

"Communications," Megan said. "Quantum communicators are useable on the ship but their power will be drained until we're outside geosynchronous orbit where some of the Net protocols fall off. There are chargers in the shuttles." She flipped through the notes some more and nodded. "The suits have a similar problem with power. Once up there they're going to work on batteries but have to be charged. The suits will have communicators. In addition to the batteries they have three other backup power systems based around a wind-up handle," she added with a grin, then cocked her head. "You have to see these things. There's a note here that says, in all seriousness: 'The use of domesticated rodents for suit power was contemplated and rejected after analysis.'"

"What do you want to bet it was hamsters?" Herzer said with a grin.

"What was the name of that inventor who created gadgets that did things in the most complex way?"

"Bill Gates?" Herzer asked. "Something like that?"

"No, I was thinking Goldsmith or something," Megan mused. "Good Lord!"

"What?" Herzer asked, not turning away from the schematic.

"I just read the description of the suit plumbing," Megan said. "Yick!"

"Can I borrow that?" Herzer asked, turning away from the schematic thoughtfully.

"Of course," Megan said, holding out the thick book.

"Thanks," he replied, wandering out of the room. "I'll be in the weight room if anyone needs me."

CHAPTER SIX

When Meredith walked into her office, Herzer was sitting on the weight bench with a heavily loaded weight bar suspended over his knees and a book tucked into his crotch. He appeared to be reading. As she watched, the bar slowly rose up to touch his shoulder and then lowered back down. After one more rep he lifted it to the holder, turned the page on the book and lifted it back down. After four more slow reps he repeated himself.

Meredith turned away from the sight, frowning, and sat at her desk for a moment. Then she got up and walked to the filing cabinet, pulled out a file and sat down at her desk again. The sound in the background was maddeningly repetitive. Flip of a page, clink of the weights leaving the holder, four long, slow, breaths with no real sound of effort, clink of the bar, flip of the page, repeat. Occasionally there would be a grunt of surprise or a disgusted snort. Occasionally there would be a long pause and she could imagine the bar hanging in midair, effortlessly held there, then the breath would be let out, the page would flip, repeat.

Finally, after realizing that she'd just read the same page of a complicated bill twice and didn't actually *read* it either time, she turned around angrily.

"Are you actually *reading* that or just looking at the pretty pictures?" she asked disparagingly.

"I'm reading it," Herzer said without looking up. She could see a drop of sweat forming on the tip of his nose but if he noticed it wasn't apparent.

"Well," she said, glancing at the close-set text on the page, "if you are, you're reading it awfully fast. Skimming something isn't going to do anyone any good."

Herzer paused with the bar in mid-rep, held out in front of him, and a muscle on his jaw flexed. He turned and looked at her, sharply, then began to recite.

"The Mark-14 Quantum communicator has a range of . . ." he paused and frowned, the bar still held in midair, "sixty-four thousand kilometers. It works by something called a mee-zon generator, whatever the hell that is, and has up to one million discrete frequencies. Although it is unjammable and can't be intercepted, during the AI wars when the system was used frequently, enemies would install interception devices in them. The systems we'll be using will be voice activated and frequency agile, whatever the hell that means. There is an alternate implant system which we won't be using because there's an attack method through them. Satisfied?" he asked, looking back down at the page. He set the bar down and flipped back a few pages, then grunted in satisfaction. "Yeah, sixty-four thousand." He flipped back to the page he'd been reading, picked up the bar and began slowly lifting it and lowering it again.

Meredith watched him for a moment and then turned around slowly to get back to work.

"Hello," Shanea said to the older woman at the door. She'd been passed by the sentries so, presumably, she was safe. "Can I help you?"

"I'm looking for Herzer," the woman said, smiling. "I've got some lists to go over."

"He's in the office," Shanea said. "Would you like to step in? And you're . . . ?"

"June Lasker," the lady said.

"I'll go get him," Shanea replied, gesturing at a seat in the entry foyer.

"Herzer," she said, walking in the office.

"Yeah?" he grunted, pressing a mass of weights.

"Come on up just a touch more," Bue Pedersen said, his fingers hovering over the bar. "Almost there. You know you're badly out of shape. That's only, what, a hundred and ninety kilos?"

"Fisk you, Bue," Herzer said, dumping the weights onto the rack and sitting up. "What's up, Shanea?"

"There's a lady named . . . June here with some lists . . ." Shanea said, blinking rapidly. Herzer had taken off his shirt and it was apparent that his upper body was getting corded with muscles; the veins in his arms and torso stood out against pale skin. "Uhmm . . ."

"Crap," Herzer muttered. "Okay, Bue, I'm going to be at this a while; they're probably the technical personnel lists. You might as well get back to the War Department."

"Can I ask what this is all about?" Bue said.

"Not yet," Herzer replied. "Soon."

"Okay," Bue said, shrugging. "Want me to come back this evening?"

"No," Herzer grunted. "I'll be at this most of the afternoon and damned if I'm going to spend all evening pumping weights. Tomorrow is lower body. Say Thursday if that's okay?"

"I'll be back," Bue said with a nod. "Have fun."

Herzer picked up his shirt and wiped off some sweat, then looked up at Shanea.

"We'll probably need drinks and some lunch if you don't mind," he said, smiling. "I hate using you as a gopher . . ."

"That's okay," Shanea said, blinking again and then smiling. "Whatever you need."

Herzer nodded his head as she left and then frowned, replaying the reply.

"Don't read anything into it that's not there," he muttered, walking out of the room and down the hall to his and Megan's bedroom. He stripped out of the shorts and wiped down hastily with a towel, then climbed into a new set and a clean shirt.

"June," he said as he came in the foyer. "It's been, what? Three years?"

"About that, Herzer," June said, smiling and standing up. "You've come up in the world," she added, gesturing around.

"Getting engaged to a council member will do that for you," he said, frowning. "I take it Edmund put you in charge of finding replacement personnel?"

"Yes, and we're going to have a fun time," she added, picking up her valise. "Where?"

"Living room," he said, gesturing the way. They gathered around the coffee table and June started pulling out files.

"I found six people in Raven's Mill's files and federal records that listed a background in late information-age space engineering," June said, laying out the files. "I've put a request in to the Federal Intelligence Agency to find them and they've all been identified and located."

Herzer picked up the first file and looked at the age and grunted. "This guy is over two hundred. I'm not sure he'll be up to it."

"That is a problem with several of the personnel," June said. "The first three on the list are all over two hundred. Another I happen to know is claustrophobic. You realize you're going to have to deal with situational anxiety on this mission, right?"

"I hadn't even *thought* about it," Herzer admitted.

"The conditions in the shuttles will be tight," June said. "And the ship is better but not great. Then there's the fact that they might have to go EVA—"

"I've seen that as an acronym," Herzer said. "That means space walking, right?"

"Yes," June said, grinning. "It stands for 'Extra Vehicular Activity.' You're getting out of whatever vehicle and moving around. You weren't into space stuff I take it?"

"Not at all," Herzer admitted, looking at another file. "This guy is old but another of his comments is that he's a long-distance runner. That will at least mean he might be in shape. Pilots?"

"That was somewhat easier," June said, smiling. "I've got nine of those. One of them ... is a little odd ..."

"Define odd," Herzer said, frowning. "And no ancient or cripples?"

"Not crippled by any means," June said, frowning. "Her file actually came from the Intelligence Department; she had been some sort of an agent in Ropasa but is now in the UFS. She Changed herself, before the Fall, into a ... well, a bird, sort of ..."

"Jolie?" Herzer said, picking up the file. "No, Joie?"

"You know her?" June asked.

"I met her; she had joined up with Megan in Gael," Herzer said, looking at the file. "She doesn't have a current listed address. What is she doing?"

"Working as waitress in Balmoran," June said, shrugging. "But she piloted before the Change, including interplanetary. She's trained, according to the records, in celestial navigation and orbital mechanics."

Herzer considered his memory of the seven-foot-tall bird-woman and shrugged.

"Odder things have happened," he said. "Get the word out to get her down here right away. What about computer techs?"

"Fewer of those," June admitted. "Only six and one is nearly three hundred. He's still alive but mostly retired, he does woodworking in Raven's Mill. And we can't find one," she added, slipping out a file and sliding it across the table. "A Courtney Deadwiler. I think she might have married and changed her name, but I didn't find it in the records."

"You've got to be joking," Herzer said, opening up the file and glancing at the data. "Jesus Christ! Courtney?"

"You know her, too?" June said with a faint smile. "Do you know where we can find her?"

"Right here in Washan last time I checked," Herzer said. "She and her husband are here lobbying the Agriculture Department. They've got a farm outside Raven's Mill and are trying to get some of the opening land in the Sippa delta." He paused and shook his head in disbelief at the image of Courtney in a space suit. "She's got four kids!"

"Fast work," June said, smiling faintly.

"Courtney on a space ship?" Herzer said, shaking his head. "I have a hard time picturing that!"

"She listed a background in early computer technology, hardware and software," June noted. "System analysis, routing . . . frankly, she looks like the best replacement we have if she wasn't padding her resume."

"I don't know if they're currently here," Herzer temporized. "Hang on a second."

He went to the door and gave the sergeant of the guard orders to go check their hotel and see if they were still in town.

"If they are, leave a message that I need to see them this evening. Not before then but it's urgent."

"Yes, sir," the sergeant said.

"Go yourself," Herzer added. "Tell your lieutenant I ordered it. And send a message for Cruz to be here at four."

"Yes, sir," the sergeant said as Herzer shut the door.

"We'll see if they're still in town," he added to June. "Find

someplace at the War Department for interviews and start rounding all the rest up except the ancient and the cripples."

"I will," June said, picking up the files.

"I'm going to need copies of all that," Herzer said, gesturing
at the paper. "More reading. Bleck. And tell Edmund that we'll
either need copies of all the planning data up at the camp down
here or we'll have to move up there, soon."

"Will do," June said, stuffing the last file away. "I don't suppose
I could go?"

"The lure of space," Herzer asked, shaking his head. "Got a
background in early technology?"

"No, unfortunately," June sighed. "But this is going to be the
last chance to work with technology for most of us until the war
is won. It would be nice to ken again."

"I don't know that the ship has that ability," Herzer pointed out.

"Oh, I'm sure it has replicators at least," June said. "But I get
your point. I guess I'll have to remain ground bound."

Herzer considered June's words after she had left. Prior to the
Fall there had been many people attracted to space. He didn't
know why; there wasn't anything out there. But it was a major
lure in a time when finding something to pass the time was a
major factor in survival and boredom came on easily. Some people
had even moved off planet and a few had Changed themselves to
be able to actually live in space for short periods.

There had been a brief heyday when terraforming of Mars and
the Moon had been considered but eventually abandoned. There
simply weren't *that* many people interested in moving off Earth given
reduced populations and the diversions available on the planet.

But there were . . . he searched his memory for a moment . . . *hab-
itats* that existed in space. He had no idea what had happened to
most of them, if anyone survived. He wasn't sure how they could
but, then again, he wasn't sure that they had been as drained
of power and function as Earth. It might be that some people
survived to this day. There wasn't much that anyone could do for
them; the only reason the shuttles were going to work was that
the power drain protocols wouldn't affect them. So anyone who
had been off planet was stranded; any attempt to enter Earth's
orbit would mean loss of power in their vehicle.

Shanea came into the room with a tray of cold cuts and bread
and looked around.

"Your guest is gone already?" she asked unhappily.

"Sorry," Herzer said, shrugging. "It didn't take as long as I thought it would, mainly because there wasn't much to choose from. I'll eat it, though."

"Oh, okay," Shanea said sunnily, sliding the tray onto the table. "Do you mind if I join you?"

"No," Herzer said, making a large sandwich of various meats and cheese.

"I hate eating alone," Shanea said, picking up a slice of cheese and nibbling it, as she sat on the edge of one of the chairs.

"I don't," Herzer said, shrugging. "I've eaten alone and I've eaten in a crowd of thousands of people. You can be just as alone there," he added.

"I mean alone like nobody to talk to," Shanea added. "I like to talk to people when I'm eating."

"Don't get a full mouth, then," Herzer said.

"Depends on what it's full of," Shanea said, then blushed. "Sorry."

"That's okay," Herzer replied, looking at her with one eyebrow raised. "Harem humor?"

"Something like that," Shanea sighed. "I don't *miss* the harem, much, but sometimes I get more bored here than there. I feel all cooped up. Megan hardly lets me go out at all."

"Uhmmm, Shanea?" Herzer said. "You're your own person. You can go out any time you want." He paused and thought about it. "Can't you?"

"Well . . ." Shanea said, then shrugged. "Megan doesn't like it. She's never really said it, but she always says no when I ask if I can go shopping or something. And Mirta and Meredith and Ashly go out all the time. I think it's because she's, you know, important now. And I hear things, you know? And, face it, sometimes I do some dumb things, too. So she's afraid I'll embarrass her. At least, that's what *I* think," she ended miserably.

Herzer considered her words for a minute and then frowned.

"I can see part of the point," Herzer admitted. "You do have access to some very high-level intelligence and you'd be surprised how easy it is to make the mistake of giving something away. But you shouldn't be held against your will. And you shouldn't need Megan's permission to go shopping. There are other ways to handle it."

The first that came to mind was getting the poor girl a husband or a lover or something. Someone who was trustworthy. If he'd ever seen the type to land on her back with her legs open, that was Shanea and she clearly wasn't getting any here. Neither was he, come to think of it, which led quickly to thoughts he shied away from.

He wracked his brain for a moment, repeatedly pulling it away from the entirely pleasant image of escorting her around himself, and then hit on a face. Not the brightest officer he knew but one that was solid, dependable and trustworthy. Now if he could just remember the guy's name.

"I'll see about setting something up," Herzer said. "What we need to do is get you an escort; someone to show you around town and make sure you stay safe. You're going to need nearly as much security as Megan, you know. But we'll make it so you can get out and spend some of your pay."

"What's that?" Shanea asked, picking up another slice of cheese.

Herzer froze as he was about to take a bite out of his sandwich and lowered it.

"You're not getting paid?" he asked, frowning.

"I don't know," Shanea said, suddenly wary. "What is it?"

"You know that shopping requires money, right?" Herzer asked.

"Yes," Shanea said. "I guess."

"So if you go shopping, you'll need some money," Herzer explained.

"I guess," Shanea said. "The times I've gone out it's been with Megan or Meredith. They do that."

"Oh," Herzer said, shaking his head. "Shanea, can you add and subtract?"

"Oh, sure," she said. "One plus one is eleven. Two plus two is twenty-two . . . I get kind of confused after that," she admitted, taking a bite of cheese.

Herzer bit into his sandwich thoughtfully. He shouldn't have been surprised. Before the Fall there had been no need to have any skill in mathematics or reading and the number of people who had the skills were, therefore, vanishingly small.

However, since the Fall, people had started picking up the skills quickly. There were still vast groups that were illiterate and unable to add but not like before. It was impossible to do most highly skilled jobs in the UFS without some moderate academic training.

Shanea, however, had clearly gone from the pre-Fall condition to some position that didn't require those skills in Ropasa to Paul's harem and then into Megan's care. She'd never had the *need* to be able to read or do math and obviously didn't care to pick it up on her own.

Clearly he'd have to ensure that Ensign Whatsisname could do simple math. No, he wouldn't, he'd had him as a student and knew his mathematical skills, what there were of them, to an instant. Okay, the guy could probably make change.

He pulled out a pad and made a note, then considered some other needs. He needed someone to handle the information flow on this project and one name came to mind. Unfortunately, it also called up some negative history that would not fit in well with this crowd. Van Krief would be the perfect assistant for this mission but he wasn't sure he wanted her and Megan in the same city much less the same room. What was the other ensign's name? Destrang. He'd been one of three that Herzer had tapped to accompany him and Edmund on what turned out to be a very long field trip. They'd been given credit for Officer Basic course based upon the fact that they'd been aides to an admiral during a major ship battle and a general during a major land battle. The third one . . . Tao, that was his name, still couldn't add worth a damn. But he had good common sense skills and was fairly charismatic.

He scribbled a long oval on the paper that had become his standard mental image of the ship and began filling in details. Trying to seize all the shuttles was inviting defeat in detail. Just holding the control room wouldn't ensure *either* controlling the fuel *or* destroying the ship. If he could think of using the shuttles to adjust its trajectory, so could Chansa or Celine or whoever was in charge of this mission on the other side. New Destiny was not stupid at the tactical level.

The big battle would be for the control room, he was sure of that. But he was pretty sure it was possible to . . . disable some of the shuttles and just leave the remainder under guard. But he had no idea what numbers or type of fighters the enemy would bring. One of those Changed elves, for example, could go through a squad of Blood Lords like it wasn't there. But Megan was sure they didn't have many of those, yet. The ones they did have were actual elves that had been tormented into something . . . different.

Evil was the only word to use. Most of the force would be more normal than those. They were unlikely to be able to fit many ogres into the ships and once you knew about them they were easy enough to kill. Celine would probably come up with something monstrous. No dragons on either side, no room in the shuttles. What would Celine come up with? What monster was she going to produce from her labs? That was what had him worried.

He looked up and saw Shanea watching him like a cat.

"What?" he asked, carefully.

"I was just thinking about when you came to rescue us on the ship," she said, nibbling at her cheese.

"I thought you were out cold?" Herzer said.

"I was playing dead," Shanea said. "And terrified. But when you pushed through the door I half opened one eye. I've never seen anything like that. It was horrible but you were . . . it was amazing. I thought that the little guy, Baradur, was fast. You were amazing."

"It's one of the things I'm good at," Herzer said, shaking his head. "I don't make too much of it, don't you. It's just butchery."

"Well, I never said thank you," Shanea said, frowning. "I know you came for Megan, not me. But I wanted to say thank you, anyway."

Herzer opened his mouth to reply, paused, took a bite of his sandwich and chewed for a bit.

"You're right, I came for Megan," he finally said with a shrug. "Rescuing Key-holders is a mission, rescuing damsels in distress is sort of a sideline," he added with a grin.

"Have you rescued many?" Shanea asked, her eyes wide.

"A few," Herzer said as his grin changed to a frown. "And failed to rescue at least one too many. It's one of the reasons I tend to try harder these days."

"You were right about something," Shanea said as the silence extended out into awkwardness.

"What?" Herzer asked, taking another bite.

"We hadn't seen you when you were in shape," Shanea said. "You're looking . . . really good."

"Uh . . . thanks," Herzer said, swallowing against a dry throat. He poured some water and washed the mouthful down carefully.

"Hello, Herzer," Megan said from the doorway, coming over and sitting down next to him. "Having fun?"

"Shanea didn't want to eat alone," Herzer said, hastily, then looked down at the remnants of the huge sandwich in his hand and over at the morsel of cheese in Shanea's. "June Lasker turned up with the records of the people they could find with technical skills. We were going to go over them over lunch, but there weren't enough to bother."

"Oh," Megan said as Meredith softly entered the room after dropping off her files. Meredith raised one eyebrow at the tableau and silently picked up a slice of meat, sitting on one of the chairs and nibbling at it.

"You won't believe who one of the techs is," Herzer added after a moment.

"Don't keep me guessing," Megan said, pouring a glass of water.

"Courtney."

"You're joking!" Megan snorted, blinking her eyes.

"You're getting the same image I did," Herzer said, laughing.

"I don't know," Megan replied, smiling. "Does it include one channel entirely filled with chatter?"

"I hadn't thought about that," Herzer admitted, frowning. "Gods."

"Maybe we give her her own channel?" Megan said, grinning.

"If she even goes," Herzer pointed out. "She's not the adventurous type. And I don't think we can exactly conscript the people for this mission. I'm going to call for volunteers from the Blood Lords for an unspecified mission with 'high hazard and high chance of death.' Which means more than half of them will volunteer and I'll pick and choose from the other half if I need to. They'll be the ones that have already seen enough war to know that I mean it. But the techs . . . I don't think we can force them. We'll have to ask them without being specific about what the mission involves. And most of them aren't going to volunteer."

"Which means we'll be critically short of techs," Megan pointed out.

"Yep," Herzer said, frowning. "Which means more care about protecting them. Especially since we won't have time to more than half train the Blood Lords on onboard systems so they'll be lost if they run into anything technical." He paused again, frowning.

"I want to bring in some assistants. I don't know where they'll fall in the TO and E but the information load is getting beyond me. I'd ask to borrow Meredith but she's busy enough with your stuff and she's not available for the mission." He paused and frowned again then shrugged. "One of them is a female that I have some history with, but she's got damned near as sharp a mind as Meredith. The other two aren't as sharp but I think I'll need them both, if not on the mission. Van Krief might not be shipboard; somebody is going to have to handle shuffling forces on the Earth for reinforcements. I need to get them headed this way, soonest. But that means taking time to go over to the War Department myself. Which is one of the reasons I need them."

"Tell Meredith what you need and Ashly will run it over to the War Department," Megan said, frowning in thought. "I still don't have any technical data to start training on, for that matter."

"I sent a message about that as well," Herzer said, brow still furrowed in thought. "And I want to find out if there's any intel on what Celine is going to throw at us."

"If Dad has found out anything, he hasn't told me," Megan said. "Of course, I haven't talked to him since this came up. Put that on the list."

"I don't even know if Van Krief can *write* an operations order." Herzer groaned. "I'm probably going to have to write the damned thing myself. All two hundred sub paragraphs." He frowned and shook his head. "I need a copy of FM-196-4, damnit!"

"What in the heck is . . . ?" Shanea said. "That . . . what you said."

"Manual on Field Operations," Herzer said, distantly. "I can practically recite it—especially since I was on the committee that wrote it—but practically and actually are two different things. It helps, it's like an outline that you fill in the blanks. Part of that is you find where the blanks *are*."

"Herzer," Megan said, gently. "You're getting so wrapped up in this you're practically spinning. Tell Meredith what you need and then take a break."

"You're right," Herzer said, shaking his head. "Thank you. We still need more staff. I'll put Van Krief in charge of setting up the operations order, probably Destrang in charge of keeping us updated on intel and Tao will be general runner. And I can use him as a spotter when Bue's not available. But I need them soonest, by tomorrow preferably."

"Why don't you and Meredith go work it out," Megan said.

"Oh, and Mike and Courtney may be coming over this evening,"

Herzer added. "I sent a message to their hotel. And I'm meeting with someone, here, at four."

"Okay," Megan sighed. "I guess I should have run you over to the War Department when I had a chance, huh?"

"Sorry," Herzer said, standing up. "Meredith, if you have a moment?"

"Of course, Major," Meredith said coldly.

Megan picked up a slice of cheese and took a bite, frowning.

"Megan," Shanea said. "Can I ask you a question?"

"Sure," Megan replied.

"Are you and Herzer . . ." Shanea furrowed her brow in thought and then said: "Screwing?"

Megan flinched and then swallowed the cheese.

"No."

"Can I borrow him?" Shanea asked. "I mean, have you *seen* him? He glows! And he's got the most enormous . . ."

"Shanea!" Megan said, sharply.

"Pecs . . ." Shanea drifted off. "Please? Just for a few minutes? Hours? A couple of days at the most? You're not using it and I haven't . . ."

"Shanea," Megan sighed. "No. A definite no." She stopped and thought for a moment, then shook her head. "It wouldn't work, Shanea. Really. Don't do this to me, please."

"You're so mean!" Shanea spat, standing up. "You're worse than . . . Christel," she added, storming out of the room.

Megan set down the rest of the cheese uneaten, dropped her face into her hands and sighed.

"You look like hell, dearie," Mirta said.

"Did you catch any of that?" Megan said from inside her hands.

"Most of it," Mirta replied. "I'm surprised it took this long for them all to start panting."

"All?" Megan said, sitting up and looking at her poisonously.

"Open your eyes, Megan," Mirta said, sharply. "All."

"Ashly?" Megan spat. She and Ashly had not gotten along in the harem initially. When Megan arrived Ashly was the unspoken leader of the girls and could be, and was, poisonous to the point of sadism. They had arrived at a truce only after Megan had more or less beaten her half to death. Without any marks. The truce had lasted well enough but now a stab of pure jealousy shot through her at the thought of the tall, gorgeous blonde and Herzer.

"And Meredith," Mirta said.

"*Meredith*?" Megan snapped, looking at the corridor to the office and weight-room. "Meredith?" she repeated, shaking her head. "She never so much as . . . she *hates* men!"

"Oh, she's getting over it," Mirta said, pouring some wine and sipping at it. "Quickly. I suppose it was the sudden change in him that caused it. He was, face it, more or less cooling his heels at your beck and call. More of a kept man than a soldier for the last few months. Give him a mission, especially one where he knows he has to be in tip-top shape, and he turns into something . . . different."

"I've seen it, too," Megan said, biting her lip. "Was it that bad? I knew there was something . . . different. He was different on the ship."

"He's a caged bird here," Mirta said, shaking her head. "You know what that's like. He's in the cage of his own will, but the bars are there nonetheless. But now, he sees the cage opening. A tough mission, a command? He's in heaven. And the bulging . . . muscles don't hurt. Meredith, poor, poor soul, has to be in there with him as he builds up those *rippling* muscles, grunting and sweating with all those *huge* weights, pumping away . . ."

"Enough," Megan said, gritting her teeth. "I get the picture."

"And of course, he's giving off enough signals of blue balls to fell a mare at a hundred paces," Mirta pointed out.

"Not you, too?" Megan said, sadly.

"Oh, I'm a bit beyond the game, dearie," Mirta said, laughing. "But it doesn't mean I can't look!"

"What am I going to *do*?" Megan practically wailed.

"Well, getting him laid would help," Mirta pointed out. "If the rest of us can suddenly realize we have parts south of our stomach, I'm surprised you haven't. Especially given the pheromones running around in the apartment. It's not the food or water; we're all eating and drinking the same stuff."

"I'm not ready, yet," Megan said after a brief inventory. She could feel the pull as well but it wasn't able to overcome the continued revulsion.

"Well, it would only help partially," Mirta admitted. "Face it, we're coming alive again. Lord knows it's been long enough and

we were fairly sex starved in the harem for that matter; Paul was
never Mr. Super Stud."

"And Herzer most definitely..." Megan said and stopped. "I
suppose he is, isn't he?"

"Under *stud* in the dictionary they have his picture," Mirta said.
"But, basically, we've been hiding in the apartments. Part of it, I
think, is that we're still unsure about the world outside."

"Agoraphobia," Megan said, bitterly. "Every harem girl's friend."

"Yes, that," Mirta said. "But we're also afraid of doing something
that will reflect badly on you. But we've got to figure something
out; the cucumber delivery man is starting to wonder."

Megan leaned back and laughed at that until she could feel tears
coming in her eyes. Finally she stopped and gasped for breath.

"Thank you, Mirta," she gasped.

"You're welcome," Mirta replied. "There is another option.
And think about it after you get over wanting to rip my head
off..."

"Share him," Megan said, taking a deep breath and gritting her
teeth. "I..." she stopped and shook her head.

"It does three things," Mirta said, implacably. "It ensures that
the girls get what they need and that they're getting it from
someone who is not an enemy agent that might...ahem...
pump them for information. It ensures that *Herzer* gets what he
needs and doesn't go wandering off with someone who could be
a threat..."

Megan got a very clear image of Herzer with the duke's "doxie"
at that.

"And it gives you more time to get your head together," Mirta
finished. "There are, however, problems."

"I'd have to accept it, emotionally, with entirety," Megan said.
"And I don't think I can. It's all tied up with the not feeling like I
can have sex, yet." She paused and thought about it for a moment,
then shrugged. "Meredith. Meredith I can almost accept. Shanea
and Ashly...no," she said, shaking her head. "I don't trust them
to...understand the nature of the engagement, I guess. Shanea,
bless her, is just too..."

"Dumb," Mirta inserted.

"I would have said something a bit nicer," Megan said. "Eventually. Ashly...Ashly could be poisonous. I almost wish I hadn't
brought her in but she's *good* at what she does. But in this I'd

have a hard time trusting her. Meredith would see it as what it was; a release. Nothing more."

"I think you're overestimating her, there," Mirta said, shrugging. "She wouldn't try to take Herzer from you, but she's more interested than you realize, I think. I'm not sure you're seeing what they, we, are seeing in Herzer. I'm not sure you'll be ready to bed him until you do. And I'm not sure what it will take to open your eyes."

She nodded at that and walked out, quietly, leaving Megan to contemplate the tray of cold cuts and another knotty problem.

CHAPTER SEVEN

"Meredith," Megan said, entering the office. "Could you give me a moment with Herzer?"

"Certainly, Megan," Meredith said. "I have the list of personnel and material he needs. I'll just run it down to the War Department."

"I'd prefer you send Ashly," Megan reminded her. "I'd like you around for the meetings this evening."

"Of course," Meredith said, nodding as she left.

Herzer had another notebook open and was doing one-handed push-ups as he read it. From time to time he'd pick up a fountain pen and make a note, then set it down and return his off hand to his chest.

"Interesting reading?" Megan asked, watching him slowly lift himself up and down.

"The damned doors on the airlocks are a bitch," Herzer admitted. "Good if we're defending them. A stone bitch if we have to get through them."

"So we make sure we're on the right side?" Megan asked.

"That will depend upon what shuttles we get," Herzer said. "If New destiny gets the close shuttles, it will be a race with them in the lead from the beginning. Then we'll have to force our way in. That will mean high casualties, which was why the initial team was sending up only fighters in the first wave." He paused and turned a page. "But I don't think that will work. I don't think it would have worked in the first place. You can force the doors

79

to the control room but not the doors that access the structural ring tube. Those are eight-*centimeter* composite. They assumed that they could get forces in on one side of the access tube or the other. That's a bad assumption. If we get into the control room, first, that is where we'll hold them. At the internal blast doors. But there are other access ways," he added, turning another page. "Not good ones, not ones that I like, but we can use them. The problem is that I'm also thinking of ways you could block them, that New Destiny could block them." He rolled his tongue in his cheek and clicked his prosthetic, which was the off hand at the moment, thoughtfully.

"Herzer," Megan said, carefully. "Shanea just asked me if she could borrow you for a couple of days."

"To show her around town?" Herzer asked, turning another page. It was clear that he was only half listening. "I was going to talk to you about that. The poor girl is starved for some entertainment—"

"Actually, she was asking about indoor sports," Megan said clearly.

Herzer paused in his push-ups and looked over at her, aghast.

"Jesus," he muttered, "I hadn't realized it had gotten that far."

"You knew?" Megan snapped.

"Well, she was sort of giving off signals," Herzer admitted. "Just today, though, at lunch. I was going to talk to you about it, later. One of the ensigns I said I needed I was, frankly, going to sic on her. Put him in charge of an escort so she can get out of the house and then let nature take its course."

"She's not the only one," Megan pointed out.

"Megan, I'm not making eyes at any of them, honest," Herzer said, flipping himself to his feet with one hand and coming over to brush her cheek, lightly. "Ashly . . . well, she's sort of started to notice me lately. But you don't have to worry about me . . . straying. Honestly, honey. Hell, I spend most of my time around *Meredith* for God's sake."

"And she's another," Megan said, holding up her hand to forestall protest. "I didn't notice it but Mirta did and she's right. Meredith won't ask, I think . . . I hope . . ." she trailed off.

"Christ on a crutch," Herzer muttered, sitting down. "What in the hell are we going to do?"

"Mirta suggested that since I'm not using the local stud that I share him," Megan said.

"No," Herzer replied. "Absolutely not. If we were . . . if we were having sex and you were more stable about it, it would be *possible.*" He held up his hand this time and fixed her with a glare. "I said *possible.* But even if you agreed, now, I would say *no.* You couldn't handle it, not the way that you still are. I'd end up losing you and gaining . . . nothing worth losing you for."

"So how come you're so knowledgeable?" Megan asked, trying not to cry but smiling at the same time. "Big tough soldier. You're not supposed to be able to think about these things."

"Maybe some of Bast rubbed off on me," Herzer said with a shrug. "She's as tough as they come, but she looks at people's emotions and reads them as well as anyone I've ever known. And, now, you could not handle that. No matter what you told yourself, it would tear you apart. And I'm not willing to lose you for a quick roll in the hay with Shanea."

"Oh, I don't think she was thinking quick," Megan said, shaking her head.

"The one thing I don't know is why this has come up so quickly," Herzer said.

"Well, Mirta understood," Megan said, tartly. "Have you looked in a mirror lately?"

"Every morning," Herzer said.

"I mean below the jaw line," Megan snapped.

"Oh."

"You said we hadn't seen you in shape before," Megan said, more softly. "We definitely hadn't seen you getting *into* shape. Women are not, generally, visual. But there's a bit there and . . . Anyway. The other thing is that you're . . . changing. I don't think in a bad way. Actually, I think it was what you were when we met and you'd changed for me. Now you're becoming . . . you again. And *you* are quite . . ." She paused and thought for a moment then shrugged. "Sexy."

"Thanks," Herzer grimaced. "I think." He looked at her and then frowned. "I don't suppose *you're* starting to think I'm sexy?"

"A bit," Megan admitted, sighing. "Damn me, but not enough. I'm *sorry.*" She got up and started to leave but Herzer quickly darted across and grabbed her arm.

"No," he growled. "You do *not* get to walk out on that note."

"Let go of me, Herzer," Megan said.

"Sit down," he said, pointing at the chair. "I'm serious."

Megan sat and looked up at him angrily.

"Okay," Herzer said, sitting back on the weight bench. "I'm sorry that I asked. It was the wrong time. You're all messed up about this other thing. It was the wrong time to press. I'm sorry."

"You shouldn't be," Megan said, shaking her head. "This is my fault. . . ."

"Megan," Herzer cut her off. "Don't use the term 'fault' okay? If it's anyone's 'fault' it's Paul's and you dealt with that 'fault' as well as anyone could." He paused and frowned, then shook his head. "Can I be selfish and blunt for a minute?"

"Yes," Megan said after a moment's thought.

"What can I do to make you more able to handle the thought of sex?" he said softly. "I will admit that I want to see your hair spread on a pillow and the soft sweat trickling down your stomach. I want to hear you moan in pleasure, true, real, pleasure. I want to slide my hands between your silken thighs and touch you. I want to kiss your breasts and nuzzle at them like a child. I want to touch you and take you and love you in the hardest *possible* way. So what can I do to help?" he asked, quietly.

"Oh, God," Megan said, her eyes closed. "I think you just did."

"I thought that might help," Herzer admitted, grinning. "We fell in love so quick we forgot the whole seduction thing. Remind me to get you some flowers."

"Herzer Herrick," Megan said in a soft voice. "You are a danger to women."

"So I've been told," he admitted. "Can we do something?"

"What?" she asked. "Here? On the weight bench or the floor?"

"No, not here," he said. "After we get rid of Mike and Courtney I want you to throw everyone out with a vengeance. And then we'll spend an evening together, getting to know each other. And then we'll see what happens."

"Okay," Megan said, nodding. "I think I can face that."

"It's not a competition," Herzer said. "If we don't have sex, we don't have sex. That will be up to you. I will admit that I will press, but very gently. Leave it up to me, okay?"

"Okay," Megan said, her face creasing in worry.

"Don't tense up about it," Herzer said. "We're just going to spend some time talking, that's all. What happens after the talk is open. It might just be we get tired and snuggle. Okay?"

"Okay," Megan said, nodding firmly.

"Now we can go," he said, looking at the chronometer on Meredith's desk. "Cruz is going to be here soon and I need to take a shower."

"Yes, you do," Megan said, sniffing the air.

"Happy sweat," Herzer said. "Think happy sweat."

"I will," Megan said, standing up.

He glanced at her and then at the desk and shook his head.

"Meredith?" he asked, plaintively. "Really?"

"Really, really," Megan said, shaking her head. "I think she's going to hold a candle for you for some time, Herzer. Like I said, you're a danger to women."

"Damn," he said. "She's really hot. You don't think . . ."

"Don't push your luck," Megan said, chuckling as she opened the door.

"Hey, Cruz," Herzer said, waving at the couch. "Grab a seat."

"Herzer."

Brice Cruz was thin and tall with shoulder length blond hair and a neatly trimmed goatee. He was also dressed in the height of fashion, wearing a light-weight tan suit and a cravat with a gold stickpin.

"Nice duds," Herzer said.

"The most common flunkie in Washan is a congressional flunkie," Cruz said, shrugging and pouring himself a glass of wine. "Fitting in is my job."

Cruz had started out in the Blood Lords but after an unpleasant incident with some bandits he had been asked to leave the service. For a year after that he had tried to find something he was good at besides killing. Unfortunately, no matter what he turned his hand to it never seemed to work out. He'd been close to the bottom rung of the ladder, working as a casual day laborer, when approached by the newly formed UFS intelligence corps. It had offered him an outlet for his skills with the caveat that if he screwed up using them, similarly skillful gentlemen would relieve him of the need to earn a living. Ever. He had performed his duties flawlessly and as a reward they had assigned him to head the security detail for the UFS' newest council member, who also happened to be the boss's daughter.

He and Herzer went back to the apprentice program in Raven's Mill and it had been Herzer who had convinced him that resigning from the Legions was in his best interest. Especially when Herzer, who was at least as "good with his hands" as Cruz, had explained that *he* had recommended court-martial. Cruz couldn't find it in his heart to blame Herzer, who was the paladin's paladin. But he much preferred his current bosses, who had a much grayer approach to the value of human life.

"I've got a mission coming up," Herzer said.

"The quest to capture the fuel ship," Cruz said, nodding.

"I hope all of Washan isn't aware of it?" Herzer asked.

"Not even the horsey boys," Cruz said. "But the legionnaires and Blood Lords are. They don't talk, though. Our sources haven't picked it up in the capital so far."

"Good," Herzer said, ignoring the point that Cruz was getting intel that he wasn't. "I want you on the mission."

"Why?" Cruz asked, frowning. "I thought you didn't care for my kind."

"Bullshit," Herzer said. "And you know it. This is going to be one hairy fisking mission, Cruz. Damned straight I want you on it. You are one stone bitch killer and that's what it's going to take. Don't give me shit about 'your kind.' That is 'your kind.'"

"Okay," Cruz said. "But you've got your pick of the damned legions and the Lords. Why *me*?"

"Because this thing is going to be ... weird," Herzer pointed out. "I'll take the Lords and even the legionnaires if it was just a stand-up fight in a field. No problem. This is going to be shit coming out of corridor walls and in every direction. Maybe external on the ship. You can handle that, I take it?"

"I'm not afraid of heights or close spaces if that's what you mean," Cruz said, still frowning.

"You're not going to panic if we get hit from behind by whatever monster Celine has dreamed up this time," Herzer said. "You're just going to do the job. I know that. That's why. So I want you in."

"What do I get?" Cruz asked.

"Besides killing people and breaking things?" Herzer asked. "What do you want?"

"A commission," Cruz said. "My record expunged. I want back in. I want in on the invasion. I swear to you, Herzer, I won't fisk up again. I want to be in the battles. I want to die or drop, damnit," he finished, his mask finally cracking.

Herzer looked at him for a long time, then nodded.

"I'll *try*," he said. "I'll have to get the duke to agree. And that incident with the bandits really pissed him off. But I'll talk him around. No 'deal' to it. You do the mission as an ensign—"

"Lieutenant, for God's sake," Cruz said.

"Okay, lieutenant," Herzer said, his face unreadable. "Or you don't do it at all. But if you fisk me, now or in the future, run far and fast."

"Got it," Cruz said. "What's my job?"

"When I figure that out, I'll tell you," Herzer said sourly. "This thing is a cluster fisk if I've ever seen one. I don't actually see a *good* way to win. That's why I want you to be there, because we're going to have to change plans on the fly and I know you can keep up. You'll have a team, that much I know. Beyond that, I'm still working on it."

"Got it."

"In the meantime, just keep Megan alive," Herzer added. "You heard about the things that took down the Icarus team?"

"That's why we were brought in on it," Cruz said. "Nasty. But at least one of them got taken down by the team itself; the colonel killed one with a bedpost, if you'll believe it."

"I can," Herzer said, sadly. "He was very good."

"The braincase is right behind the mandibles. They're not the solfugids that your lady was talking about, by the way. They're more or less straightforward giant scorpions. Stinger and all, very nasty toxin, and dual metallic composite claws. Metallic mandibles as well. The carapace isn't chitin, some sort of polycarbonate, very tough. But they're vulnerable right at the brain case. Hit them between the eyes and they go down. Weak at the joints as well. Fighting them will be a bugger if you don't have a shield, but you or I could take one down with a long sword. Short sword would be iffy. Long mace or halberd would be optimum. I've been retraining some of the Lords with both."

Herzer nodded, filing that away.

"That is *exactly* why I want you," Herzer said, finally smiling.

"Your servant, Commander," Cruz said, cracking a smile as well.

"That's it for now," Herzer said, standing up. "Keep on the Detail until we move up to the training facility and then you move over to the teams."

"Works," Cruz said, standing up as well. "Thank you."

"Joel's going to scream about losing you, you know," Herzer said.

"Well, I'll still be around," Cruz said, shrugging. "Somehow, I don't think I'll end up as a legion commander. But . . . I want the damned rank on my shoulders. I want to be able to say I'm somebody besides an accountant or an aide, you know?"

"I know," Herzer admitted. "Welcome back. I hope."

"Yeah," Cruz said, shaking his hand. "I'll tell you something, but you've got to promise that you won't fisk me."

"Okay," Herzer said, frowning.

"I'll do the mission even if you can't get me back in," Cruz said. "It sounds like fun. As long as I get a team command. Not just Joe Sword Fodder. But *try*, damnit."

"I will," Herzer said.

CHAPTER EIGHT

"Mike, Courtney," Herzer said, gesturing them into the foyer. He shook Mike's hand and gave Courtney a hug as Megan came in. "Good to see you."

"What's so damned important we *had* to wait until this evening?" Mike said, half angrily. "We were going to leave on the evening stage."

"It had to wait until this evening because I've been running my ass off," Herzer said. "And it was urgent because it's urgent. Mike, I'm about to piss you off. Ready?"

"What?" Mike said warily.

"I have to talk to Courtney, alone," Herzer said. "I've got to ask her to do something, something for . . . well, the nation I suppose. And it's something I can't discuss with you and she won't be able to either. And it's hazardous."

"What in the hell are you talking about?" Mike asked angrily. "Are you crazy?"

"No, he's not," Megan interjected. "Herzer, and I, have a mission. We need Courtney. And some other people. We can't, won't, tell you what the mission is. And it's not just going for a walk in the park, it's going to be bad. But we *need* her. We can't even tell you *why* because . . . well, because New Destiny will find out. The other people that we're talking to, we're going to be asking to volunteer just like Courtney. If they don't, they're not going anywhere until the mission is over."

"And I can't ask what it is?" Mike said. "Damn." He sighed and shook his head. "Okay, I can understand that. I don't like it, though."

"Big surprise," Herzer said, finally smiling.

"Why don't we go talk farming," Megan said, taking his arm. "And let Herzer go recruit your wife."

"If he can," Courtney said tartly. "Lead on, hunkaroo."

Herzer frowned but led her to Meredith's office.

"Have a seat," Herzer said, gesturing at the sole chair. He perched on the weight bench.

"Been working out?" Courtney asked, sniffing the air.

"Yes," Herzer said. "Courtney, you know there was a mission planned to try to capture the refueling ship?"

"I'd heard something about it," Courtney replied warily.

"The team that was supposed to do the job got wiped out," Herzer said brutally. "By an attack on their training camp. You listed a background in old-fashioned computers as a pre-Fall skill when you came to Raven's Mill."

"Oh, my God, you can't be serious!" Courtney shouted.

"Thanks," Herzer growled. "Mike needed to hear that."

"Don't tell me that's what you're talking about," Courtney hissed. "That's a mission for . . . God-damned heroes like *you*, Herzer! I'm a *farm-wife*! I cook food all day and raise my *brats*!"

"And you know what a . . ." he paused and frowned, "a *router* is, right?"

"Well, yes," Courtney replied. "It's a device for directing electronic packets, but . . ."

"Courtney, I have *four* potential computer techs, including you, that aren't absolutely decrepit," Herzer said, his face hard. "I can barely do this mission with *four*. That ship is a mass of old-fashioned computers, most of them you can't control from a remote terminal. I don't even know what a remote terminal *is* but it says you can't control them remotely so I trust the briefing notes. We're going to be in trouble if we lose *one* tech and the more I look at this mission the more I'm worried we'll lose *all* of them. Including one of my oldest and closest friends," he added sadly.

"But, damnit, this mission is so damned important that, yes, I'm asking *you*," he continued. "There are probably more people out there. But we can't exactly take out a classified ad. We don't know that New Destiny knows how badly they hit us. And if we start going around broadly interviewing, that places those people in danger. Besides, we don't have *time*. We've got to start training soon or we're sunk. Courtney, damnit, we need you. I don't want to be too melodramatic, but the *world* needs you. You. Courtney Boehlke."

"This is a bit much to take in," Courtney said, shaking her head.

Herzer just stayed silent, letting her work it out.

"I don't know if I want to go into space," she said after a bit.

"With any luck, you'll be in corridors the whole time," Herzer said. "Pressurized corridors with gravity. It will be like being in a big building. The shuttle ride is supposed to be very smooth. And the view should be spectacular."

"Just before I die?" Courtney asked.

"I'll tell you this," Herzer said. "I'm not planning on letting you, or Megan, out of my sight. I suppose as the commander, I shouldn't think that way, but the rest of the team is expendable. You two aren't."

"Thanks so much," Courtney said. "I will be sure not to repeat that."

Herzer just waited, aware that she'd just admitted she was mostly in agreement.

"I'm afraid of heights," she said after another long pause. "I get scared if I stand on a step stool. I want to throw myself off into the abyss. I can't go into space."

"Don't look outside," Herzer said. "Interior only. There aren't any computers on the skin of the ship."

Courtney shook her head and worked her hands on her lap. After a moment she squeezed her eyes shut and shook her head.

"There's nobody else," Herzer said, softly. "I need you, Courtney."

"I know," Courtney replied. "Damn you. How do you talk me into things like this?"

"I'm a terror," Herzer admitted, trying to keep the sadness out of his voice and acting a tad jovial instead. "That's a yes, isn't it?"

"Yes," Courtney snapped out. "God. Who's going to take care of the kids?"

Herzer knew she meant while she was gone, but he hoped it wasn't a reference to if she didn't come back.

"If nothing else we'll move them here or to the training base," Herzer said. "After the attack they moved a good part of the Seventh Legion to guarding it. A bit of closing the barn door but it's also to protect the *new* team. Of which you're a new member. You *can't* tell Mike, though. We'll have him told when we're starting the mission. At that point there's not much New Destiny can, or will, do."

"What about attacking our families?" Courtney asked, looking up.

"That's why we'll move them to the base," Herzer said. "And keep them under guard. Your children, and Mike, will be as safe as we can make them. It's you that we'll all be worried for."

"Thanks for reminding me," Courtney said. "When do I have to be where?"

"We'll keep you and Mike here until we move up to the training base," Herzer said. "If we move him and the children up there, and they stay, they can be brought in on it. Until then, we'll use the cover of getting the farms organized for you to stay here. Mike can walk Megan and me through the process of application."

"While I sit and fret?" Courtney asked.

"While you start getting reacquainted with ancient computer technology," Herzer said. "As soon as we get the documentation. Which should be tomorrow or the next day."

He led her back to the living room where Mike and Megan were deep in conversation.

"You guys get everything hashed out?" Herzer asked.

"Not even close," Megan admitted, wide-eyed. "I hadn't realized what sort of equipment and people we'd need to set up a really big farm."

"Good," Herzer said. "That's a good reason for Mike and Courtney to stay in town for a week or so."

"I've got things that need doing back at the farm," Mike said.

"And you said you have a good manager," Herzer said with a shrug. "I'd suggest that if whoever is keeping an eye on the kids can get free that they bring them up as well. And over the next few days you can walk Megan and me through the process of applying for our land while Megan smiles at bureaucrats while they find exceptions for you."

"She's in?" Megan asked.

"Yes," Courtney said, shaking her head.

"Do I get a say?" Mike asked angrily.

"Yes," Courtney said. "You get to say: 'Whatever you think is right, honey.' And then hug me, please," she added, sitting down next to him and leaning into him.

"Herzer..." Mike said dangerously, uneasily slipping one arm around her.

"She can't tell you what it is," Herzer said, shrugging. "Not now. Maybe soon. So you can't discuss it and work it out. So, sorry, Mike, you've just got to eat it raw."

"Fisk you," Mike snarled.

"Like I said," Herzer repeated. "Not now. Not until we're out of the capital and its rumor mill."

"Are we done here?" Mike asked.

"For now," Herzer nodded. "But I was serious about walking us through the application process—"

"The hell with that," Mike said.

"No, Mike," Courtney interjected. "That's important, too. It's a cover and if you want me to have any chance at all, we need the cover."

"What in God's name for?" Mike said. "Never mind, you can't tell me. Okay, damnit, I'll walk you through the process and all the rest. I'll be a good little boy. But you'd better be able to convince me, at the end, that it was worth it or you can find yourself somebody else to manage your farms. All of them," he added, glaring at Herzer.

"I hope you'll agree it's important," Herzer said. "I think it is. Courtney thinks it is. Megan thinks it is. You'll just have to wait to find out. And in the meantime, you'd better figure out a way to keep from radiating anger or you'll show that something's up. None of this ever happened, tonight. We just discussed farming. Understand?"

"I understand," Mike said. "Cloak and dagger and all that. Fine. Let's get going, Courtney."

"When do we..." Courtney asked.

"We'll get together sometime tomorrow," Herzer said. "About the farming stuff. The rest has to wait until..." He paused and shrugged. "You'll probably be spending a lot of time here."

"Okay," Courtney said. "Later."

"Come on," Mike said, pulling at her hand.

✧　　✧　　✧

"Well," Megan said, leaning on the door as they left, "I think that went well, don't you?"

"No," Herzer grunted. "I hadn't thought about how incredibly badly Mike would take it. I should have. I wish it was Mike that was the computer tech. I could imagine him surviving."

"What a sunny thought," Megan said, grimacing.

"Now, I think we had other plans," Herzer replied.

"Frankly, that little scene sort of took it out of me," Megan temporized.

"Well, I think a little brandy would help," Herzer grinned, grabbing her hand. "And then we'll see what comes up."

CHAPTER NINE

"Oh. My. God." Megan whispered. "Paul was never like...did you get...enhanced before the Fall?"

"Pure genetics," Herzer said calmly. He'd discovered long ago that reciting multiplication tables helped. "My parents might have had a hand in it, but I never asked them. They'd released me before I really started to...grow."

"That's..." Megan said then stopped, tilting her head to the side. "I'm not sure..."

Herzer just waited as she tilted her head back and forth and then reached out with one finger.

"Does it get any bigger?" she asked humorously, running a single fingernail over the tip.

"Careful, or we'll be starting all over again," Herzer said, trying not to groan.

"I'm not sure about it...fitting," Megan said, huskily, leaning forward, "but I think I might be able to get my mouth around—"

There was a shout from outside and then a scream and Herzer cursed luridly.

"Not NOW Bull God damnit!" he shouted, rolling to his feet and drawing his sword.

"Well, you should be able to beat them to death," Megan said tightly, trying not to laugh. She closed her eyes and shook her head. "Spiders. Two of the sentries are down. More...something. On the street and the roof," she added, looking up at a scrabbling sound.

"Corner," Herzer said, pushing her back and turning to the window.

"The girls!" Megan shouted. "Shanea, Meredith . . ."

"I'm just hoping to keep *you* alive!" Herzer replied as the window crashed in.

It was, as Cruz had reported, a giant scorpion, about two meters in length, not counting the tail. That was as long and it whipped back and forth outside as the thing climbed through the window.

Megan mouthed a syllable and extended her hand but the bolt of lightning stopped halfway across the room.

"They're shielded," she snarled.

Herzer darted forward as the thing scrabbled at the sill and swung the sword to bash the left claw out of the way. The right claw snapped at him, the monster pausing in its quest to enter the room, and he jabbed the tip of the sword into the joint of the claw, wrenching it with a hard twist of his wrist. The joint popped open and the claw flopped uselessly to the side.

The other claw was snapping at him by that time so he ducked to the right and jabbed the sword into the space between the creature's eyes, twisting the sword again to prevent it being bound. There was a cracking sound and the scorpion began to spasm, its tail, which it had never gotten into the room, thrashing at the wall outside.

There was a scream from somewhere in the building and Herzer heard Megan dash to the door.

"Shanea!" she shouted.

"Megan, damnit," Herzer shouted in turn, turning away from the beast and following his bride-to-be.

Mirta's eyes had flown open at the first shout and she shuddered in her bed at a scrabbling on the roof. She jumped up and went to the window but the guard that was supposed to be on the alley below was nowhere in sight. She opened the window and leaned out, looking up. There was a noise up there, but whatever was making it wasn't visible, yet.

She looked around the room and shook her head, then hiked up her nightdress and clambered out of the window. Grasping a drainpipe she half slid, half fell to the alleyway and scuttled across it into the deeper shadows on the far side.

Only when she was in shadow did she look up. Coming over the top of the building was some sort of massive bug, a scorpion, judging by the tail. It carefully climbed over the eaves and then slid down the wall to the open window. It had some trouble fitting through but in a moment it was out of sight. Before it was in, though, another had appeared on the roof and another, each of them heading for the other windows on that floor.

Shanea's window crashed in and then Ashly's, and Mirta shuddered at the screams but she didn't move. It wasn't courageous but she'd survived by knowing exactly when to be courageous and when not to be. And there was *nothing* she could do about those things.

"Shanea!" Megan shouted at the door, pounding on it. Two of the guards were down the corridor, holding one of the scorpions at bay, while more were apparently fighting on the landing.

Herzer slammed his bare foot into the door and then stepped back, trying to get a view in the room. The lamps in the corridor were turned up and the room was inky black. But he saw a movement by the bed and leapt through the doorway, pausing at the far side to check to the side.

The scorpion was at the bed in the room, scrabbling at something underneath, its tail waving in the air. From the sounds of it, what it was scrabbling at was Shanea, but he couldn't tell if she was hurt or just screaming her bloody head off.

Herzer made another bound and flipped his sword through the air, cutting off the bulging stinger on the tail and removing that threat. Then he stomped down on the rear end of the creature, pinning it to the ground. He flipped his sword up and over, pointing it down and drove the tip into the thing's braincase, all the way through and into the floorboards.

"Damnit," he muttered, wrenching at the sword. "Shanea, are you hurt?"

"No!" she shouted.

"Then quit screaming!" Herzer bellowed, finally getting his sword free. He pulled the thing away, then reached under the bed until he made contact with one scrabbling hand and yanked the girl out, roughly.

"It was a ... it was a ..." Shanea whimpered, flailing her fists in front of her chest wildly.

"I know," Herzer snapped. He went to the door and looked out, then ducked back as a black arrow embedded itself in the doorframe. "Fisk!"

He slammed the door and grabbed the bed, sliding it across and blocking the door. Then he looked around.

"Meredith," Megan said, tightly. "Mirta, Ashly."

"Bowmen in black in the corridor," Herzer snapped. "Both guards down but so is the scorpion. But I don't think the bowmen are on our side."

There were crashing sounds coming from the next room over and Herzer shook his head.

"Meredith?" he asked.

"Yes."

He walked over to the wall and looked at the plaster, then drove the sword into it, tearing downward. The plaster shattered and he continued cutting until he had a fair-sized hole in the wall. There were studs in the wall but there was enough room to fit between. He slammed his foot into the plaster on the other side, getting a small hole, then hammered his shoulder into it, finally breaking through in a shower of plaster dust.

The scorpion in the room was confronted by a mattress in the corner that it had, thus far, been unable to pass. The mattress was slashed and tattered, filling the room with feathers, but it still had enough mass the scorpion couldn't get through. Its stinger was repeatedly jabbing at the mass, but apparently it hadn't hit a target, yet.

At Herzer's entrance, the bug rotated around, waving its claws and stinger menacingly. Herzer wasn't sure if the thing was intelligent or not. It was either defending its intended prey or recognized Herzer as a threat, though, because it scuttled forward, snapping at him, the stinger held in readiness.

Herzer wasn't sure exactly how to fight this one. If he used the trick of striking a claw, the thing would use its stinger to get him before he could retreat. He'd like to take the stinger out, first, but it was unlikely to get into reach unless he was already being held by one of the claws. He suddenly realized that he was still naked and the thought of one of those claws getting a hold of his member was disheartening.

He circled the thing, keeping away from the walls where he could get pinned, expecting a hammering on the door at any moment.

The thing was opening and closing its claws as it circled and that gave him his only opening. He lunged with the point and got it jammed into the interior of the left claw joint but when he twisted the sword barely moved; he remembered, too late, the claw was metal.

He looked up just in time to see the stinger lunge forward, aimed at his abdomen. He'd seen scorpions sting before and they were blindingly fast. Perhaps because this thing was larger, the jab was fast but not the lightning motion of a normal sized specimen.

Desperately, he flung his prosthetic up and more by luck than skill caught the tip of the stinger in its grip. In one continuous motion he spun in place, the sword pulling out of the claw, tapping it to block to the inside, then up to cut off the poison sack, down to cut off the left claw and then flipped up and point down through the braincase.

This time he hadn't got it embedded in the floor and he twisted it out, dropping the poison sack, and went to the mattress.

"Meredith?" he asked in a worried tone.

"What took you so long?" she asked pointedly, tossing the mattress off of her. She stopped when she saw him and grinned. "Is that a club you're carrying around or are you just happy to see me?" she asked in a throaty voice.

Herzer's mouth opened and closed and he shook his head at a shout from the corridor.

"I don't have time for this," he said, moving to the door. All he could hear was confused shouting so he went to the hole in the wall and gestured for the two women to come into the room.

"This lock still works," he said, shoving the empty bedframe against the door and a bureau over the hole in the wall. There was nothing to do about the window. "Get in the corner with Meredith."

"What about Ashly and Mirta?" Megan said, then closed her eyes and muttered. "Oh, God . . ."

"What?" Meredith asked.

"Never mind about Ashly," Megan said, softly. "Mirta is outside the building, across the street. There's nothing around her. She's alive. Two scorpions alive. One in Ashly's room, the other in Mirta's. There's . . ." She paused and frowned.

"Herzer!" a voice shouted from the corridor.

"Cruz?" Herzer yelled.

"Yeah," Cruz said from outside the door. "Where in the hell is Countess Travante?"

Herzer opened his mouth and then paused. How much did he actually *trust* Cruz? Finally he decided.

"In here," he said, hefting the sword.

There was a pause from outside the door and then Cruz chuckled.

"Thanks, buddy," he said. "I already had a crack at one Key and gave it up. We've taken down the rest of the assassins. But we haven't entered any of the rooms except yours. Which, by the way, were our standing orders. Protect the Key-holder. Remember?"

Herzer winced at the sarcastic tone and shrugged.

"Two more bugs, one in Ashly's room, one in Mirta's. Ashly appears to be dead."

"Okay, we'll clean 'em up," Cruz said. "Stay there until it's all clear."

Megan took one look at what had once been her social secretary and then turned and threw up in the corner.

"She shouldn't have had to go that way," she gasped, spitting on the floor.

"Nobody should," Herzer said, pulling a blood-stained sheet over the mess on the bed. "But that's what happened to the rest of the team." He'd retrieved his trousers but was still barefoot and shirtless.

"Were they after Megan, because she's a Key-holder?" Meredith asked. "Or do they know you and she are forming the next team?"

"Good question," Herzer replied. "And one I don't think we'll have the answer to any time soon." He noticed that Meredith hadn't been sick. Shanea, surrounded by guards, was well on her way to getting passed-out drunk in Megan's apartment.

"Why were you outside the apartment?" Herzer asked Mirta.

"Because I couldn't stand the thought of getting trapped inside by whatever was scuttling on the roof," Mirta said. "I was not a part of this. There was one of those things in *my* room, too!"

"Herzer," Megan said sharply.

"I'm sorry, Mirta," Herzer said, shaking his head. "I'm seeing assassins in the shadows. I didn't even trust Cruz when he arrived with the reinforcements."

"It's okay," Mirta replied. "Who says I trust you?"

Herzer snorted and shook his head, gesturing at the door.

"Let's get out of here," he said. "There's nothing to be done."

"Except get rip-snorting drunk," Mirta said.

As it turned out, it didn't take much to get that way for any of the girls.

Herzer was nursing his first drink but Mirta had sat the others down and had them slam a shot of vodka apiece. That had led to the corn liquor and in short order, they were all drunk as loons.

He shouldn't have been surprised. None of them had done much drinking since escaping from the harem and from the little he'd heard there was no hard alcohol allowed there. So they had a low resistance and none of them were exactly heavy.

Shanea was sitting on the floor, shaking her head from time to time and occasionally sobbing.

"It was a . . ." she kept saying. "All I could think to do was hide under the bed. It kept moving around and I'd move over to the other side and those . . . those *claws* . . ."

"Hell," Mirta slurred. "I thought they were going to chase me down the alley. I was just hoping there were some guards left alive. I was planning on running right past them and if they followed all I had to do was outrun them. They were in armor; it should have been easy . . ."

"You missed the best part," Meredith said. She'd hardly said a word during the whole drinking, just downing her shots and chasing them with very little water and another shot.

"Wass 'at?" Mirta asked, looking at her blearily.

"Herzer nekkid," Meredith said, then giggled, slapping a hand over her mouth.

"Really?" Mirta said, her eyes widening.

"Nekkid," Meredith repeated. "Unclothed."

"Oh, yeah," Shanea said and hiccupped. "He's hung like a . . . like a . . . one of them things you ride . . . pulls a cart . . ."

"Horse," Mirta said.

"Yeah," Shanea said. "One of them." She leaned over onto Herzer's leg, slapping him on the upper thigh. "He's my *buddy*. He pulled me out! Killed the scorpion! Thass wha' it was. *Scorpion*! Big, horrible, *scorpion* an' Herzer *beat* it to death with his giant *cock*!"

"Thank you," Herzer said, prying her hand off of his leg. "But I killed it with a sword."

"And what a sword it was!" Meredith said and giggled again, slapping her hand over her mouth. "Whoops. Nice sword. And a very nice club, too!"

"And all mine," Megan said, leaning over and pulling his mouth down on hers, her other hand sliding up his leg.

"Meanie," Shanea said, pouting. "Shared Paul!"

"Mine," Megan repeated when she'd drawn back from the long kiss. "Come on, Herzer you big stud," she said, using his shoulder to get to her feet. "We were just about to find out if you fit or not."

"Megan," Herzer said, shaking his head but getting to his feet. "You're a little drunk."

"I'm *a lot* drunk," Megan said, nodding her head sharply. "S'why I'm gonna jump your bones. Come on."

She dragged him out of the room as the other three watched sadly.

"There's all these guards and things, around," Shanea said, thoughtfully.

"You go ahead," Meredith replied, lying down on the couch. "If I can't get Herzer, I'm just going to lie here and pass out."

"S'good idea," Mirta said, slumping in her chair.

"Wimps," Shanea muttered, clambering to her feet. "There's a whole *platoon* of guards here. Making me do all the work. Just like always."

"You go right ahead," Meredith repeated, closing her eyes and then opening them. "Mirta?"

"Yeah?" the woman asked.

"Why's the room spinning?"

"Because you're about to throw up."

Sergeant Sirous came to attention as the door to the councilwoman's chambers opened and stopped himself from shaking his head at the sight of the Key-holder's *extremely* drunk maid.

"Miss Shanea," he said, formally. "Given the circumstances, all of you should remain in the councilwoman's chambers."

"'M goin' to my room," Shanea said, holding onto the doorframe for support. "S'right there," she added, pointing in the general direction. "There's s' big *scorpion* in it. But iss dead."

"And we removed the carcass, ma'am," the sergeant said, sighing.

"But we would prefer not to disperse out guards. Please stay in the councilwoman's chambers."

"'M goin' to my room," Shanea said, lunging forward and grasping the neck of his armor. "An' you're going with me."

"If you insist on going I'll detach a team to ensure your safety," Sirous said, reaching up and gently prying at her hand.

"You don't understan', soldier boy," Shanea said, yanking him forward. "I'm talking about *you*! Going with *me*. To my *room*. Come on. S' an order. Bring some more guards. Gonna need *lots* a guards . . ."

"Megan," Herzer said, lowering her onto the bed. "Are you sure about this?"

"You *bet*," she said, pulling off her shirt. "Will you look at these?"

"They're lovely," Herzer said, smiling. He was barely buzzed and he was afraid that if he actually took her in this condition it would screw things up royally.

"Suck 'em," Megan said, lunging up and grabbing him by the hair to drag him down. "I want you to *suck* on 'em! I know you want to. I'm going to give you everything you want, Herzer. *Everything*."

Herzer slid his hand under her breast to cup it and sank down on the bed next to her.

"I love you," he said.

"You'd better," Megan said. "Or I'll turn you into a *newt*," she added with a giggle. "A well-hung *newt*. Keep you in a pot."

"Well, as long as I'm your newt," Herzer said, unbuttoning her pants and lowering his lips to her small, pink aureoles just as there was a knock on the bedroom door.

"WHAT?" he shouted, gritting his teeth.

"Herzer," Cruz said. "We have a . . . bit of a situation . . ."

"I'll be right back," Herzer said, slipping off the bed. "I promise."

"You'd *better* be," Megan said, pouting. "Turn you into a newt."

Cruz led him out into the corridor where Herzer nodded at the sight of the reinforced guard force. He noticed that the guards were . . . unusually wooden.

"Miss Shanea insisted that Sergeant Sirous accompany her back to her room," Cruz said in a low tone. "And now she's in there, crying."

"Why?" Herzer asked.

"Because he won't have sex with her," Cruz said bluntly.

"Is he gay?" Herzer asked, puzzled.

"No," Cruz ground out. "He's on *duty*. And she's the councilwoman's *friend*. And she keeps asking where the *rest* of her guards are!"

"He doesn't want to be turned into a newt?" Herzer asked. "Cruz, listen to me very carefully. Get . . . four more guards. Have them ensure her safety from *inside* her room. In . . . plain clothes or no clothes as the case may be. Tell them to screw the ever living daylights out of her."

"What?"

"Screw her," Herzer said. "Bang her. Fisk her pretty little ass off. Whatever she wants. Just get the girl laid for the Bull God's sake. If one of them gets tired, switch them off until *she* gets tired or passes out or whatever. Call for another *platoon* if you have to but *don't* bother me again unless the world is ending. Clear?"

Cruz looked at him befuddled for a second and then grinned.

"Clear," he said, trying not to laugh. "Combat reaction?"

"Worst case of it I've ever seen and the girl is a nymphomaniac," Herzer said. "And she hasn't been getting any. So . . . whatever it takes."

"I wasn't actually talking about *her*," Cruz said with a grin. "Do you mind if I . . . take a short break from duty?"

"If you've got an able assistant," Herzer ground out.

"I do," Cruz said, still grinning. "Night."

"Good *night*."

When Herzer got back to the bedroom, Megan was snoring softly.

CHAPTER TEN

When Herzer walked into the kitchen the next morning, Megan was sitting in the breakfast nook, her elbows on the table and her head clutched in her hands. Shanea was lying back in her chair, eyes closed, mouth open, breathing slowly. She'd apparently taken time to do her hair and makeup so she looked like a very pretty corpse.

Herzer tiptoed across the room to the percolator and started to get out the makings.

"Is there any coffee?" Shanea said, softly, smacking her lips. "I have this . . . really familiar taste in my mouth."

Megan groaned, softly, and shook her head.

"GOOD morning, troops!" Duke Edmund said, striding through the door.

"I do not need this," Megan muttered, clutching her head. "I can't turn *you* into a newt."

"I think I can take one more soldier," Shanea muttered.

"Have a *fine* time last night?" Edmund asked jovially.

"No," Megan said. "Ashly is dead."

"And everyone else is alive," Edmund replied, sharply. "That is a very *good* thing."

"Except for the nearly getting killed part, *I* had a good time last night," Shanea said. "What I remember of it."

"And I've never seen a group of more satisfied guards," Edmund admitted.

"What, all of them?" Herzer asked.

"According to reports," Edmund said with a nod.

"Good lord," Herzer said, shaking his head.

"All of them sounds about right," Shanea said. "Is the coffee ready yet? I mean, it tastes good at first but the aftertaste . . . yick."

"Shanea," Megan muttered. "You didn't."

"She did indeed," Edmund replied. "But it's okay. The guards are quite . . . discreet."

"Closed mouthed," Herzer said. "Unlike some around here."

"Herzer," Megan said, threateningly. "We were nearly killed. Don't be . . ." She stopped and looked up at him. "What did *we* do last night?"

"You slept," Herzer said evenly, finally getting the coffee going. "I put blankets on Mirta and Meredith and then checked the guards. After that, *I* slept."

"Oh, God," Megan muttered. "I'm sorry, Herzer."

"It's okay," Herzer said, sitting down.

"Hold it," she said, sharply. "What do you mean you checked the guards?"

"Some of them," he snapped. "Not *all* of them."

"Herzer wasn't there," Shanea said. "Herzer I'm sure I would have remembered." She frowned and wriggled a bit. "Yeah. Herzer definitely wasn't there."

"Did you know that Daneh was raped right after the Fall?" Edmund asked Megan.

"Yes," Megan replied, glancing at Herzer who was still looking, if anything, more pissed. Given that it was a rape he'd been unable to stop, it was not his favorite topic of conversation.

"I'm not talking about Herzer's burdens in it," Edmund said. "I'm talking about Daneh. And me. She took . . . quite a while to get over it. And even after we were having conjugal relations, there were still problems. But she *did* get over it, as over it as any woman can. When you're done with this mission, if you're still having problems, or even not, I'd strongly recommend that you have a long talk with her. Or many. There are specialists around as well. But while she doesn't do it as a specialty, she's probably one of the best rape counselors in the world. And she's my wife so you can talk to her about things that you couldn't talk to with the vast majority of the counselors. And there are things that you cannot . . . understand, without talking to someone who knows. Including, among other things, irrational jabs of jealousy."

"I'll keep it in mind," Megan said dryly.

"Don't 'keep it in mind,'" Edmund said, firmly. "Do it. End of discussion. Given the events of last night, and by that let me make plain that I'm discussing the attack, we're moving up the shift to the training facility. You should be out of here by tomorrow—"

"I have meetings scheduled—" Megan snapped.

"Cancel them," Edmund replied. "We've got the training facility surrounded by a fortified camp, now, with the whole Seventh Legion parked around it. If these things can get through six thousand legionnaires, we might as well throw in the towel now!"

"Oooh," Shanea said. "More soldiers!" She paused and her pretty brow furrowed. "Six thousand . . . how long will that take . . . ?"

Herzer had already done the math.

"Two hundred nights," he sighed.

"Damn," Shanea muttered. "Not even a year!"

"You could repeat," Herzer pointed out.

"What's the fun in that?"

Megan groaned and buried her face in her hands.

"Van Krief, Destrang," Herzer said as the lieutenants entered the apartment. "Good to see you again. The lieutenant's pips look good on you."

"Commander," Lieutenant Van Krief replied, formally. Amosis Van Krief was a small, heavily muscled blonde with her hair pulled back in a bun to reveal a face all made of angled planes. Small, sharp, nose, square jaw and high cheekbones.

"Hey, Herzer," Destrang said, waving languidly. The lieutenant was tall as his counterpart was short, with light brown hair that was worn a tad long and long, rangy limbs that were covered with whipcord muscles. Where Van Krief seemed to march everywhere, her face pushed forward as if she were looking for a wall to smash, Destrang could stroll while marching in formation. "It's got to be bad if you've called us for help."

"Actually, I just recalled that you'd never finished that paper on the Inchon Campaigns and I thought this would give you an opportunity," Herzer replied with a grin.

At that, Destrang had the grace to look abashed at least.

Herzer had been an instructor at the Officer Basic course when he was drawn out to accompany Duke Edmund to New-fell Base. That was where the new fleet was being formed and as they approached their first real conflict Queen Sheida came to the conclusion that an unbiased and knowledgeable observer was in order. Edmund had tapped Herzer to accompany him and instructed him to pull three of the ensigns in the school as aides. Herzer had chosen Van Krief, Destrang and Tao.

The trio had ended up doing far more than serving hors d'oeuvres. After the fleet commander showed himself to be disastrously inept, Edmund had been put in command of rebuilding the fleet and the follow-on battles that the victorious New Destiny pushed. Van Krief and Destrang had been unwilling participants in the Fleet battles while Tao, who had grown up with horses, rode over half the continent, arriving with the cavalry reinforcements to cap the victory over New Destiny's invading legions.

"I've been tapped with another mission," Herzer said, letting him off the hook. "The information load is getting too heavy so I asked Edmund for some staff."

"And what is the mission, sir?" Van Krief asked.

"Come on in the living room," Herzer replied. "And I'll give you an initial brief."

When he was done, Van Krief shook her head.

"Is it just me, sir, or do I detect a lack of enthusiasm?"

"No, it's not just you," Herzer said. "I don't see a good way to win this one. I know I can stalemate it, crash the ship in other words, but I don't see a good way to ensure we get the majority of the fuel and New Destiny gets virtually none. I've got an idea how we can get *most* of what comes down, but not a way to win. I don't like half victories. And we don't have enough in the way of intel."

"That's hardly a new phenomenon," Destrang said, shaking his head.

"And that's going to be your job," Herzer said, handing him a sealed envelope. "This is to be delivered to Colonel Torill at War Headquarters, Office of Special Operations. He's our liaison at Headquarters. He'll give you your access, including to UFS Intel Group. Get with their analysts. Look for any scrap of intel that might relate to this mission. You'll be staying in Washan, probably working out of this building."

"Yes, sir," Destrang said, smiling faintly. "A capital city tour sounds much preferable to being thrown into the breach in a burning spaceship."

Herzer grinned at him, knowing that Destrang only half meant it. The lieutenant was one of the few officers he'd met who combined a dilettante's manner with a real feel for battle. He was as comfortable in the middle of a skirmish as he was at a dinner party. The latter was one of the reasons he'd given him this task, however.

"I understand Tao is on the way as well, sir," Van Krief said.

"He was up with Second Legion in Balmoran," Herzer said. "He should be here soon. You will be working on the operations order for the mission. Tao's going to be courier for the intel Destrang develops and working with the councilwoman's security detail. Among other things as an officer escort."

"For the councilwoman?" Destrang asked. "Lucky chap."

"No," Herzer said. "For her assistants. You might have noticed that things are a bit confused around here today. We had an attack on the building last night. I'm not sure if it was directed at Megan or because New Destiny got wind we were forming another team. Whichever it was, security has been increased. And that includes for the councilwoman's aides."

"Ah," Destrang said. "Well, bully on Gerson."

"Herzer?" Shanea asked from the door. "Do you want anything?" She had gotten over her hangover and was looking as perky as usual. If anything, more perky.

"No, thank you, Shanea," Herzer said.

"Was that one of the councilwoman's aides?" Destrang asked, raising an eyebrow.

"Yes," Herzer said, grimacing.

"Didn't mention that, did you, sir?" Destrang asked, grinning.

"One of them will be staying here, as well," Herzer noted. "Meredith is Megan's political aide. She'll be staying here to keep an eye on some of the political actions Megan has been pushing." Herzer paused and frowned, trying to figure out how to put what he wanted to say into words. "You're aware, in general, of Megan's background?"

"Yes, sir," Van Krief said sharply. "We are."

"Well, all of her . . . assistants came from the same source," Herzer said. "You'll both be meeting Meredith I'm sure." He looked at Destrang, frowning and shrugged. "I'd strongly advise against setting your lance, Lieutenant. Strongly advise against it.

Meredith can kill your career with a word and . . . she would do so if you gave her offense. Clear?"

"Clear," Destrang said quietly.

"She can be rather . . . cold when you first get to know her," Herzer continued. "And generally stays that way."

"Clear," Destrang repeated.

"Just . . . use your best judgment," Herzer said. "And speaking of best judgment; you're both going to be exposed to some very high level information in this job. And Destrang, at least, is going to be moving around people who are *not* cleared for this information. Don't be a source, understand?"

"Yes, sir," the lieutenants chorused.

"Destrang, you've been working in intel for the last few months?"

"I've been analyzing data from some of the activity in the southwest, sir," Destrang said. "It's all been low-level stuff and the position is only classified confidential."

"Any training on how to avoid giving away information?" Herzer asked.

"Oh, and in gathering it, sir," Destrang said with a chuckle. "Done a bit of it just to keep in training. You approach a person in a natural setting, give them a tidbit of information that indicates that you know all about what they're doing then 'talk shop.' There are other techniques."

"How do you guard against it?" Herzer asked. He realized as he asked the question that he had never had a class in information control. Generally, he just didn't talk about anything that might be useful information.

"Never discuss your job with anyone you don't know is cleared, sir," Destrang answered. "When someone you don't know is cleared wants to talk shop, talk shop about their job or change the subject. Never admit that anything they say as an assumption is true."

"Hmph," Herzer said, wondering how many times he'd been probed over the years. He also knew that one of the first rules of leadership is knowing when to admit ignorance and when not. "Good answer. Keep it in mind in this job. You, too, Van Krief."

"Yes, sir," Destrang said.

"How long have you been living here, sir?" Van Krief asked, changing the subject.

"Four months," Herzer said. "I've been assigned to ops working on warplans for the upcoming invasion. And, of course, swaining Megan around to parties," he added, frowning. "But that's out the window for the time being. We'll be leaving sometime tomorrow. This afternoon, I'll brief in Van Krief on what we're looking at. This evening I've got meetings with command on preliminary plans."

"And those are?" Van Krief asked.

"When I figure that out, I'll tell you," Herzer admitted.

"So that's what we're looking at," Herzer said, gesturing at the schematic that was laid out on the living room floor. "We won't know where we're going to dock until we get there. No team can be trained to simply go for a single objective because it will depend upon where they dock. And there are three potential objectives. Which one we strike at first depends on the distribution of our forces."

"That's why they went with all soldiers in the first wave," Van Krief said, nodding at the briefing papers.

"Right," Herzer said. "And they were going to bore for the control center, no matter what. Unless we're concentrated near the control center, I'm going to bore for the one spot nobody should care about."

"Where?" Van Krief asked, sliding her hand over the schematic. "Engineering?"

"Nope," Herzer said. "Maintenance."

CHAPTER ELEVEN

Chansa waited in the reflection dappled dimness as Reyes strode down the corridor of pillars.

The meeting had been, perforce, in Celine's domain since it was in person and Celine refused to go beyond the walls of the Nira valley. The chosen venue was an ancient temple, once ruined and now restored to much of its former glory, a building of massive pillars supporting a heavy, and heavily carved, roof. The sides of the building, which was perched at the top of a high bluff, were open to hot, dry winds and the view to the east revealed apparently limitless deserts. To the west was a broad river valley touched by green and crisscrossed by irrigation ditches and which was, again, limited to the west by another bluff and more desert.

Each of the New Destiny council members had claimed broad lands, but Celine's were relatively limited; she controlled only the Nira valley but it was hers in a way that Frika, for example, which was titularly Chansa's, was not. He had afforded himself only a brief glance of the surroundings but it was clear that it bore all the hallmarks of Celine's touch.

Celine Reinshafen was a short woman with dark brown hair and skin that was tanned a light brown by the desert sun. At first glance she appeared entirely normal, except for the Key around her neck. Then, when you looked at her eyes, it was clear that she was no longer of this world. She was New Destiny's premier designer of "specialized biologicals" which even Chansa had come to call "monsters." Celine called them her "pets." It was in Celine's labs that the orcs and ogres that made up the bulk of Chansa's forces had first been developed. It was from Celine's mind that methods for creating the horribly Changed elves sprung, full-blown, as if some latter day, evil, Athena Nike. Thousands of them were being grown in darkness; in tenebrous chambers where weird fungal growths digested noisome refuse to feed the pods. It was from Celine that specialized assassination forms had come, modifications to dragons that made them more effective at combat, all of the monsters that were New Destiny's weapons in the war.

And unlike Chansa and Reyes, she appeared unprotected by a field. There were times at meetings like this that Chansa considered removing her from the world of the living. Of swiftly drawing his massive sword and cutting her head from her body, a wound that not even Mother would heal.

But he never did. For one thing, he knew he needed her. The Freedom Coalition had been victorious in too many battles to remove any edge. For another reason, he doubted that she was unprotected and he knew in his bones that he, Chansa, would never survive even if he managed to kill her.

Unlike Chansa, who was in powered armor, Reyes was dressed for the weather in a light shirt and shorts colored pink and green. He was a slender, wiry man with a shock of blond hair and a face that was more beautiful than handsome: thin, delicate chin, high cheekbones and full, red lips. He looked like an angel that had just stepped out of a painting by a Renaissance master. Beside him, Chansa looked like a giant troll.

Chansa knew that the innocent face and expression held a mind that reveled in things that made even his skin crawl. The orcs that made up Chansa's legions were cruel and vicious things but within that cruelty he tried to manage them as humanely as he could. Like Celine, however, Reyes positively reveled in cruelty. Chansa had been required to sack more than one town in the quest to dominate Ropasa. When Reyes took a town it ceased to exist. The men and children were tortured to death and any of the women that didn't catch his eye were turned over to his Durgar for brutality that made Chansa's stomach wrench. Those that did catch his eye were, if anything, in worse condition if for no other reason than that Reyes took longer to kill them.

Chansa knew that by siding with Paul Bowman in this revolt,

he had chosen the side of darkness. Paul wanted to remake the
world and no matter how that was done, it would inflict pain
upon those who lived in it. But Paul, for all that he seemed
to be going mad towards the end, had, at heart, been a good
person. He had wanted to do good in the world. Others of the
"first Council" had agreed that the world simply needed a good
shaking up to bring it out of its sink of apathy and stagnation
before the human race disappeared from boredom.

Reyes and the others that had come into the New Destiny Council
after its casualties in the first days of the war, and since, were in it
purely for the power. Direct power over humans that they could
torment as a child tortures insects. He wished there was some way
to simply erase them and start over, along with Celine and the
Demon. But they were all he had to work with and, perforce, he
used them, as they used him, to satisfy his own ambitions.

As Reyes approached, Chansa noticed that there was a swirling
field around him that lifted the sand off the floor and tossed it
in swirls of color.

"Very pretty," Chansa said when Reyes closed. "Good to see
you looking well and enjoying yourself."

"Oh, it's far more than pretty," Reyes said, smiling beatifically.
"Chansa, Celine," he added, with a slight bow.

"It's a grav field," Celine snapped.

"It is indeed," Reyes replied, smiling again to reveal perfect,
white teeth. "Now that the Freedom Coalition has your protection
field neutralizing nannites, I thought it best to create an outer
defense. Just to protect against Coalition assassins, of course."

"Of course," Chansa said dryly. Paul Bowman had ordered at
least one assassination to retain control among the members of
the ND Council. Reyes was protecting himself against far more
than just New Destiny's enemies.

"So you want me to retake the fuel ship?" Reyes said, coming
to the point. "I suppose I can manage that. I've uploaded the
schematics of the ship and the weak points are obvious. I also
agree with the basic plan."

"You'll need to take the control room," Chansa noted. "Which
is going to be where the UFS forces head as well."

"It's definitely the UFS that will be used?" Reyes asked. "After
Celine's . . . efficient removal of their first team, I'd wondered.
Ishtar has some . . . good fighters," he added bitterly.

"So she does," Chansa said neutrally. Reyes and Jassinte Arizzi had been thoroughly defeated by those forces. In Chansa's opinion, that was less due to the quality of Ishtar's forces than the bungling of Arizzi. But he wasn't going to suggest that to one of the generals that had lost. "But we're certain they will stay with the UFS managing the attack. Among other things, although we got the fighters and techs, the UFS still retains all the base-line instruction materials and training facilities. Dwarven Mining Consolidated is handling all the ground support. They'll pull together a scratch team. I'd even lay odds on who they'll chose."

"Edmund Talbot?" Celine asked. "I am sure I can eliminate him."

"Not Talbot," Chansa said. "He's a bit too old for ongoing combat. No, it will probably be Herzer Herrick. And I'd suspect that the council member will be Megan Travante."

"Now that is a prize worth fighting for," Reyes said with a chuckle and a lick of the lips. "I was so put out when Paul's harem fled. Well, except for one poor, poor soul."

Chansa bit his lip on what he was tempted to say and nodded.

"Herrick's Talbot's number one protégé," Chansa noted. "He's trained in a very hard school, extremely flexible and a dangerous opponent."

"I understand he's been a thorn in your side more than once?" Reyes said with a slight smile.

"Yes. But you'll have your Durgar and, of course, Celine has her . . . additions," Chansa said. "But I would like to commend your attention to a person of some ability I would suggest you use. Tur-uck!"

A Ropasan orc came from beyond one of the pillars, his head bowed, and threw himself to his hands and knees in the presence of the Great Ones.

"This is Group Leader Tur-uck," Chansa said. "While most of the orcs that Celine makes seem to have been lobotomized in the Change, this one can actually use his brains for something other than keeping his ears apart."

"He is damaged," Celine hissed. "This one is untrustworthy."

"Mistress!" Tur-uck whined. "I am not. I am a good orc! I have proven my trust!"

"Why do you say that?" Chansa said, quizzically. "I've found him to be very useful."

"He is damaged," Celine snapped. "He never should have

been Changed. There is a plate in his head, repairs from before his Change. By a skilled surgeon, I would say. It interferes with control pathways. This one I cannot warrantee, I would recommend his elimination."

"Interesting," Chansa said, nodding. "Well, all I can say is that if this interference is what makes him what he is, I'd wish you'd put plates in *all* my orcs' heads."

"He cannot be trusted," Celine repeated, raising her hand to strike.

"Hold!" Chansa said. "This is *my* soldier. You will *not* take action against him against my wishes."

"He is a bad product," Celine growled. "He should not be. It is . . . it's bad production. He should never have been made. I have the code of the . . . blast and damn! He was made by that Conner fisking *idiot*! No *wonder*! None of my acolytes would have made him!"

"Made by Conner," Chansa said, musingly. "Now that is interesting. He had the protocols, but I was not aware that he had used them. He is far beyond your wrath, however, Celine."

Chansa considered the information for a moment. The New Destiny agent had participated in the abortive invasion of Norau and been killed, from intelligence reports, by Edmund Talbot's daughter, who was not your normal killer. She was, in fact, a "skilled surgeon." He nodded in thought for a moment.

"Tur-uck was probably one of the patients under the care of Edmund Talbot's daughter, Rachel," he mused. "I could see Conner tormenting her by Changing someone like that."

"He should be eliminated," Celine repeated. "He is a bad product. He is bad quality control."

"I think that's up to Reyes," Chansa said. "What do you think, Reyes? I commend him to your service. I know of your Durgar and they are no more thoughtful than my own orc legionnaires. This one can think. You'll need a good, thinking, leader, in that damned ship."

"Hmmm," Reyes said, tilting his head from side to side. "Celine recommends that he be killed, like a sword that has been misforged. Chansa says he is a smart leader. Capable?"

"Quite," Chansa said. "He has been fighting the Gael and they are tricky opponents. I've promoted him twice for courage and initiative."

"What say you, Tur-uck?" Reyes said, grinning at the orc. "Should you be killed as a bad product? Or are you a loyal and capable orc?"

"I am loyal, Master," Tur-uck said, definitely. "I will be loyal to you beyond death!"

"Yours or mine?" Reyes mused. "Can you obey orders?"

"Always, Master," Tur-uck said, then temporized. "I would obey any order from a Master or a Lesser Master, no matter what the order. I have twice disobeyed orders from legion superiors when I saw advantage to the Masters."

"You see!" Celine shouted. "Untrustworthy!"

"And both times he was *right*," Chansa noted. "He was the only one to survive that *debacle* in Norau, including Conner, and he brought word of what was happening. The other time he took charge of a sub-unit while fighting the Gael and mousetrapped a group of Chudai, which is tough as hell I'll tell you."

"Chudai?" Reyes said, his eyes widening. "You have Chudai in Gael? Those bastards . . ."

"We have Chudai," Chansa ground out. "The Gael are bad enough, the Chudai are *bastards* to fight. The only time we've killed any number of them, it was when Tur-uck *disobeyed* orders."

"If he can kill Chudai, he is good enough for me," Reyes snorted. "Those bastards made our retreat from Alabad a nightmare. The Durgar hardly got a sniff of them until they attacked. They cut us up again and again."

"They do the same to my legions," Chansa sighed. "It's one of the reasons Gael is such a tough nut, besides the Gael themselves, who are no joke. But Tur-uck has fought them and *won*. By *thinking*. Take him. You will need him."

"And you don't?" Reyes said, suspiciously.

"We're . . . reconsolidating our forces," Chansa said, clearing his throat.

"Retreating?" Reyes asked. "Since when?"

"Our intelligence is that Talbot intends to bypass Breton and hit the Ropasan coast directly," Chansa said. "I've moved out of the Gael hills and am moving troops back to the Ropasan continent. We took quite a few casualties in Balmoran, so I need the troops."

"We can make more Changed," Celine said, shaking her head.

"The farming Changed can't produce food for shit," Chansa

said. "I need the normal humans for support, not more useless Changed! I'm bleeding troops in a dozen directions, so I'm pulling back troops from Breton. My war, my decision!"

"I'll take him," Reyes said, cutting off the argument. "What else do you have for me?"

"We have *one* Dark One left," Celine said, angrily. "I can't make more until somebody captures me another elf or the pods grow to maturity, which will be at least five more years. You can have him. His name is Tragack."

"And what else?" Reyes said, interestedly.

"Oh, I have a few ideas," Celine said, smiling happily.

As she said that a scuttling sound began to come from the forest of pillars.

CHAPTER TWELVE

"Tell Herzer I'm sorry as hell about this, Lieutenant," Colonel Torill said, shrugging and gesturing at the paper on his desk. "I'd give you all sorts of reports to baffle you with bullshit, but the bottom line is that we've got *nothing* in the way of intel on New Destiny's intentions. Anything that I told you, Herzer'd already know. Chansa and Celine are going to be involved. That means monsters and probably orcs. They have to take the ship and get the fuel. After that, zippo. There's no mass movement going on, that's for sure, but it's a small unit action so that doesn't affect you guys."

"What about observation in and around the reactors, sir?" Destrang asked desperately. "That's where they'll have to board. It's early, yet, but we might at least get a feel for their forces."

"As far as I know, we *have* no such observers," Torill sighed. "Most of them are deep in New Destiny territory and they're surrounded by troops. Then there's the problem of real-time intelligence. We're talking about getting the message across oceans unless there's a communicator involved and the way we've been rolling up New Destiny rings is communications. I'm sorry, son, but we're screwed for intel."

"Yes, sir," Destrang said, gritting his teeth. He'd expected it to be bad, but not this bad. "I'll head back to discuss this with my superiors, sir."

"Do that," Torill said, grinning. "And tell Herzer I said hello."

"Yes, sir," Destrang said, getting to his feet and nodding as he left the office.

Torill's office was located in the special operations section of the War Department. The department had originally been in an ancient castlelike structure that over the millennia had served various purposes, most notably as a museum. As the need for more and more bureaucracy grew, or at least appeared to grow, buildings and wings had been hastily added to the structure and they now surrounded it in a giant growth that resembled nothing so much as an out-of-control cancer.

SpecOps was set well back from the main road, out on the fringe in more ways than one. The hodgepodge of buildings was cut by dirt roads, walkways, breezeways and cul-de-sacs in a chaos that had caused more than one unlucky ensign to wander into the office of a senior officer so confused he could barely remember his name.

Destrang had navigated the maze before but he only knew certain paths and stuck to them religiously. He was just passing out of the SpecOps section and into SouthWestern Command Logistics when he heard his name called.

"Destrang, right?" a colonel said, wandering over and putting a friendly hand on his shoulder. "Been looking for you, lad."

"Yes, sir?" Destrang said, frowning slightly.

"Give me a moment of your time, lad?" the colonel said, gesturing towards one of the breezeways. "Shouldn't take long."

"Yes, sir, of course," Destrang said. He briefly had a paranoid thought related to his current assignment, but he was in the middle of the War Department. If New Destiny could slip an agent in here it was one thing. Bashing a lieutenant over the head and smuggling him out was another.

"So what do you think of your new assignment?" the colonel asked bluffly. "Going to space and all that? Worked out the plumbing, yet, eh? Eh?" he added with a hearty laugh.

"I'm not sure what assignment you're referring to, sir," Destrang replied. "You're here at the War Department?"

"Logistics old son," the colonel said, grinning. "Bullock trains and whatnot. Done a bit of personnel work as well, you know, a commander works from sun to sun but a staffer's work is never done, eh? Had my eye on you when you were in Officer Basic but you got scooped up by that old scamp Edmund, what?"

"I've met the duke, sir," Destrang admitted. It was certainly open source.

"What do you think of working for Herrick, eh?" the colonel asked. They had passed through SouthWest Logistics and were now in Army logistics where the breezeway was somewhat more crowded.

Destrang considered that question and then nodded.

"Major Herrick is a good officer," he allowed. "Do you know the major, sir?"

"Never met him," the colonel replied, turning into a small building. He nodded at a heavy-set triari sergeant, then opened up an inner door. "He's tighter than a gnat's ass," he added to the man behind the desk. "I'm not sure he'd have admitted his name if it wasn't sewn on his uniform." The colonel's accent had drifted away and his manner had become brusque to the point of rudeness. If the person in civilian clothes behind the unadorned desk took offense it wasn't apparent.

"Good," the man said. "Sit, Lieutenant."

Destrang looked at the colonel, who nodded.

"He outranks *me*, Lieutenant," the colonel noted. "Sit."

"And are you a real colonel?" Destrang asked coldly.

"Very," the colonel replied, gesturing him inside and closing the door.

Destrang sat carefully in the room's single unoccupied chair and looked around. The room was entirely unadorned and all there was in it was the desk, the chair for the occupant and the chair he occupied. The room also had no windows and was lit by a lamp. It was stiflingly hot.

"My name is T," the man said. He was tall and spare with a shock of black hair. "You're wondering if I'm going to pump you about your mission. I am not. I know everything I need to know about it and if there's anything I don't know I'll get it from Edmund. I'm here to give you information. Some of it, frankly, is well above your level. So you're just going to have to be moved to a different level, Lieutenant. If you had said so much as one word to Colonel Clifton, we wouldn't be having this conversation and you'd be out of Herzer's command before you returned. Clear?"

"Yes, sir," Destrang said uneasily.

"Colonel Torill told you there was no information available about your opponents. There is, in fact, very little. I am going to tell you what there is available. Then I'm going to tell you what we suspect. Then I'm going to tell you *why* there is so little available, which means we're going to have to get into means and methods. Do you know what that means?"

"Yes, sir," Destrang said, swallowing. Means and methods meant that he would be told *how* information was gathered. Very rarely was such information passed to those who would use it, for the very simple reason that they might be captured and reveal sources.

"T" sat back in his chair and sighed. "Frankly, getting into means and methods in this case is not that big of a deal. Especially since it's a litany of failures. But we will. Listen carefully because none of this gets put in writing. There was a meeting three days ago between Celine, Chansa and Reyes. A *physical* meeting which is believed to have taken place somewhere in Celine's domain. The agenda is not available but Reyes returned to his domains accompanied by a new orc, a Ropasa version orc, and one of their Changed elves for which we now have their name: Dark Ones. Very dramatic, very Celine and all that. Given that Chansa is tightly involved in the war against us and Celine never leaves her domains in person, it is believed that Reyes is, therefore, the designated Key-holder to be sent on the mission to recapture the fueling shuttle, Miss Travante's opposite, in other words."

"Yes, sir," Destrang said, nodding.

"Celine's involvement means there will be some of her monsters, but that was obvious. *What* they will be we have no idea. One of my analysts who specializes in trying to read her insane mind *believes* that they will be some sort of arthropod mod, similar to the scorpions that attacked Megan Travante. This is based upon her habit of . . . patterning in development. She tends to work in one particular kingdom or genus and then move to another. She initially centered around mammals, humans and elves along with a few others, there are some creatures we haven't seen here in Norau that were used in the Sind wars, then moved on to upsizing reptiles and now seems to be working with arthropods, apparently having overcome the structural and metabolic issues with them.

"But he's been wrong before. There will assuredly be orcs, but Reyes' involvement means that they will probably be Mod Two form orcs, you know the difference?"

"No, sir," Destrang admitted.

"Data on Reyes Cho, what we have, and on his Mod Two orcs will be forwarded to you and Herzer by courier. They're referred to as Durgar for reasons that are too complicated to bother explaining at this time. Basically, they're physically lighter than Ropasan orcs, darker of skin and use different weaponry. They have some elven mods, but they don't have elven speed, strength or *gaslan*. They are a tad faster fighters and highly mobile on foot, not that that should be an issue on the ship. We have an unconfirmed report that some of them are being fitted with space armor. I'm working on getting more confirmation and, hopefully, a schematic of the armor, before you leave.

"On the subject of Reyes, he's almost as much a mystery as everything else," T admitted. "He was recommended by Paul Bowman to replace Tetzacola Duenas who was killed in the initial council fight. But he was not an associate of Paul's prior to the Fall so someone else must have recommended him. He was one of the generals in the battles against Ishtar in Taurania, specializing in hit and run raids.

"Physically, he is described as good looking and is generally a blond. He has brutal tastes in women and maintains a harem, as Paul did, but no one comes out of it alive. His orcs are, if anything, more cruel than the Ropasan version. Letting any members of the team be captured, alive, would be unwise."

"Yes, sir," Destrang said, gulping.

"Now to what we don't know and why we don't know it," T said. "Celine has taken the domain along the Nira River, and it is now referred to in internal documents as 'Stygia' which is simply an ancient word meaning—"

"Dark or darkness, sir," Destrang interjected. "One of the rivers of Hades, if I recall correctly."

"You do," T said. "The river is flanked to the east and west by desert. To the north is the Toran Sea and the south is Frika, which is Chansa's domain. Crossing deserts is no problem; there is an animal called the camel that can cross them quite easily. So, to find out what was happening in 'Stygia' I sent a team on camels to reconnoiter, infiltrate and, hopefully, develop intelligence on her monsters before they hit us. The team did not return. Comments?"

"Various reasons, sir," Destrang said, shrugging. "They could have been intercepted on entry, rolled up inside, etcetera."

"So I thought," T admitted. "So I sent another team, telling them to be more careful on entry, the previous team had masqueraded as traders, be cautious in developing information and what have you. They never reported back. Comments?"

"Ouch?" Destrang said.

"Ouch, indeed," T said, his jaw flexing. "So I sent a third team. This one wasn't supposed to penetrate at all. It was just supposed to find out what was stopping the other teams. Since it wasn't there for intelligence gathering, I could choose virtually anyone. So I assembled a team of rogues, mercenaries, cutthroats, most of them convicted criminals. They were given the promise of freedom, and gold, if they just made it back with *any* information. One did. *One.* And he frankly admitted that what he did when they got hit was run like hell. So, what does Celine produce?"

"Monsters," Destrang answered, shaking his head. "Sir."

"Monsters," T replied. "What they got hit by was a *pack* of very large, poisonous snakes. The agent reported that they were larger than anaconda, partially armored, and their fangs appeared to be metal since they went right through the unit's armor. They attacked from within the sands, apparently lying in ambush having determined the team's direction of approach.

"Why the monsters do not wipe out the inhabitants is the question. And there *are* inhabitants. The Nira River is a trade route to inner Frika. Various materials flow down it, somehow, and it produces a surplus of food which is sent to the various New Destiny regions. It even trades with Ishtar's Tauranian domains. Caravans cross the desert. The caravans are guarded by very large . . . probably not Changed. They look to be uplifted gorillas or baboons, heavily modified to survive desert conditions. Extremely vicious and incredibly strong. Anyone or anything approaching the caravan other than through permitted lanes is killed without warning."

"Uplift is proscribed, sir," Destrang noted.

"A proscription that the New Destiny Council has apparently overridden," T replied with a shake of his head. "None of the caravan drivers interact with anyone outside the caravan. The only contact is the caravan master and his assistants who are acolytes of Celine. I tried to penetrate the delta at the head of the Nira River using delphino and selkie. *They* survived, but only because the delphinos turned tail when they saw that the region was populated by *very* large sharks and something that they said looked *very* much like an extinct pleyosaurus. I haven't tried through Frika, yet. I'm almost afraid to think what she has there. That, of course, is where the Stanel reactor resides. I can imagine what she guards that with."

"Yes, sir," Destrang said, sighing.

"They also use ships through the delta," T noted. "We managed to capture one of the sailors. However, when we started to interrogate him, a mark on his forehead flashed red and he died, rather horribly."

"Shit," Destrang said, shaking his head.

"So, tell Herzer that it's unlikely that I'll know what she is going to throw at him until, maybe, the last moment. I have observers around some of the reactors that they will use for extraction, but reporting back will be difficult. I will *try* to get the information, but I have a finite number of teams that are capable of what these men do and I won't throw them away lightly."

"Yes, sir," Destrang said.

"Stygia is an enigma wrapped in a puzzle," T mused. "I have no idea where Celine resides, where her labs are or, for that matter, how the place is organized. But I suspect the answer is: Horribly."

"We'll know when we win, sir," Destrang said.

"Yes," T said. "And I suspect we won't want to. We're done here, get back to Herzer. All of the information is his or Miss Travante's ears only."

"Yes, sir," Destrang said, standing up.

"The colonel will show you out."

"Yes, sir," the lieutenant said, then paused. "Sir, is he a *real* colonel?"

"He is now," T replied. "I had him appointed when he got back from the recon mission in Stygia."

CHAPTER THIRTEEN

"I'm glad there was a portal," Megan said as they stepped through the mirrorlike doorway.

"Otherwise you'd have to have made one?" Herzer asked, chuckling. The exit point was in the Seventh Legion's camp, which was set in a valley in central Sylania, not far from the Sussan River. The camp was flanked to the east and west by high ridges but they were at least five klicks away. The camp was crowded with legionnaires training and tending to chores but the first thing they saw was a group of officers standing stiffly to attention. Clearly they were expected.

"Countess Travante," a brigadier general in the lead of the group said, rendering a salute and then dropping it. "I'm General Eyck. A pleasure to have you in Camp Devil." As he finished the introduction the officers accompanying him dropped to parade rest, clearly on cue.

"The pleasure is all mine, General," Megan said, taking his hand. "You know Commander Herrick?"

"I haven't had the pleasure, ma'am," the general said, nodding at Herzer. "May I present my officers?"

"Of course," Megan replied.

Each of the officers was duly introduced and Megan shook hands and nodded as Herzer stood back and cooled his heels. Finally, the formalities were over and the general gestured towards the command tent.

"I've prepared refreshments, Countess," he said, beaming. "And I was wondering if a brief tour of the camp..."

"General, we just came from Washan," Megan pointed out. "We're quite refreshed. And we have our first briefing scheduled in less than an hour. While I'm sure I'd be fascinated by your command, I'm afraid that with our time constraints..."

"I understand, of course," the general said, somewhat stiffly. "I wasn't aware that you were going to be part of the briefings..."

"General," Herzer interjected, "with all due respect, all information regarding this mission is classified and, sir, with all due respect, you don't have need-to-know. There may be a later time that might be better."

"Of course, Commander," the general said.

"If we could get a guide to the training facilities?" Megan asked, placatingly.

"Lieutenant," the general snapped, pointing to one of his aides. "Direct Countess Travante and Commander Herrick to the training facilities."

"Yes, sir," the lieutenant said, bowing to Megan and gesturing down one of the streets of the crowded camp.

"Herzer?" Megan said, as they followed the aide, trailed by Van Krief, Mirta and Shanea. "Military politics issue here?"

"I think the answer is: it's complicated," Herzer replied. "First of all, I suspect the general thought you were accompanying me, not a part of whatever is going on and, therefore, had all the time in the world. Second, he's justifiably proud of his command. Seventh is listed as having a very high level of training; he's pushed them hard. And with the possible exception of Duke Edmund, I doubt that any Key-holders have inspected it and given him the ego-boos he'd like. Taking a look around at some point would be politic. Third, I doubt very much that he likes having to move his camp to protect the training facility. I'm not even sure he knows *what* we're training *for*."

"There's that," Megan admitted as they came to what was effectively a camp within a camp. The facility was protected by a standard trench and wall palisade with a wooden gate. The palisade had a high, thin, wood wall so that no one from outside the camp, except on the surrounding hills, could see what was going on. The guards were Blood Lords, dressed much like the legionnaires they had passed but with their armor and shields

marked with blood red eagles instead of the devil face front-
ing of the Seventh. Blood Lord units were rare since most of
the training was devoted to inducting junior officers; the only
facilities they guarded were those at their main base in Raven's
Mill, Blackbeard Base in the Bimi Isles and now this base. Not
only were there Blood Lords on the gate, but they could be seen
patrolling the palisade as well.

They were stopped by a sergeant who consulted a clipboard.

"Countess Travante, it's a pleasure to see you," the guard said,
flipping to a page. "Your picture doesn't do you justice. Lieutenant
Van Krief, Miss Shanea Burgey, Miss Mirta Krupansky and Major
Herrick. When were you promoted, sir?" the guard asked.

"Three days ago," Herzer said.

"Congratulations, sir," the sergeant said, with apparent indifference. "You're all cleared to pass. Lieutenant, thank you for
directing them here."

"This is as far as I go," the lieutenant said, smiling but with a
touch of asperity. "Good luck on . . . whatever."

"Thanks," Herzer said as the gates of the facility were opened.

There was a dogleg made of heavy baulks of timber supported
by thick pilings and backed by packed earth. It served to both
turn any attacker through the gate and to prevent anyone seeing
the facilities.

When they cleared the dogleg they were confronted by a
camp not much different from that outside. The buildings were
permanent structures instead of tents, but it was laid out much
like any standard legion camp. The exception to this was at the
center where a small lake was visible. There were buildings on
the shore, a dock and a large building apparently built out over
the lake stretching to near its center.

"Hey, Graff," Herzer said as soon as they were in the facility
proper.

"Hey, Herzer," the sergeant replied, grinning. "Coming up in
the world."

"Edmund had to decide whether to charge me or promote me,"
Herzer said with a shrug.

"Well, there's always killing you," Graff noted.

"He keeps trying and trying," Herzer snorted. "Like now. I'm
soliciting volunteers, by the way."

"Not on your life," Graff replied. "I wanna live to spend my pay. Vaston will show you to your quarters," he added, gesturing at one of the guards on the inside of the gate. "After that, you'll need to go by camp security and get your badges."

"Badges?" Megan said.

"We don't wear them on the gate," the sergeant said, reaching into his armor and pulling out a badge on a lanyard. It was blue paper encased in plastic and had a rather bad picture of the sergeant on it along with his name and ID number, but not rank. "But you have to have them to move around the camp and to get back in if you go out. Both entrance and exit are restricted. You, ma'am, obviously have free run, although you'll be required to show your badge in various areas. But your aides will require specific, written, permission, to leave the camp or return."

"I see," Megan replied musingly.

"What's with the lake, Private?" Herzer asked as they proceeded through the camp.

"Sir, we're pretty careful about what questions we ask," the private replied tightly. "The short answer is: I don't know. And I don't want to know, sir, if you get my drift."

"Got it," Herzer said. "Good answer."

They seemed to be the only people stirring in the base and Herzer realized that with the exception of themselves, the guards and whatever support personnel had been scraped together, the camp *was* empty. He'd never looked at the total of the slain but the scorpions must have killed over a hundred highly trained personnel in their attack.

The quarters, when they reached them, were in a two-story wooden building that showed all the signs of hasty construction. The room Megan was shown to was probably one of the best on the base and it was furnished with a small couch, a single bed, a footlocker and a small kitchen area, all in one room. It had its own bathroom, consisting of a porcelain sink, a commode and a shower.

"Sorry, honey," Herzer said, looking around the room and shrugging.

"Well, they haven't been wasting funds on accommodations," Megan said, shaking her head. "It'll do. I have to wonder what the guard barracks are like."

"Bays, ma'am," Vaston replied. "Thirty to a bay. And there were only half the guards that we've got here, before, so we're hot-bunking about sixty to a bay. Most of us sleep outside any-way; it's bloody hot in the barracks."

"Sorry I asked," Megan said, shaking her head. "And sorry you're cooped up like that, Private."

"Not a problem, ma'am," the Blood Lord replied, grinning. "We're rotating out of here to Blackbeard."

"Fun in the sun," Herzer said. "Guard stands are hell down there, but the rest of the accommodations are first rate."

"And the mer-girls like the guards," the private added, grin-ning, then looking stricken at joking about that subject with the councilwoman present. "Sorry, ma'am!"

"Not a problem," Megan replied.

"The rest of the rooms are singles," the guard continued, ges-turing the others out of the room. "You share bathrooms."

Herzer's room was adjacent to Megan's, but not adjoining. He figured he could find someone to put in a door.

"We need to go by base security," Vaston said when they'd been shown their quarters. "Are you going to have more luggage follow-ing?" he asked, noting that they'd brought nothing with them.

"Lieutenant Tao is going to be bringing it," Herzer said. "We came on ahead. Let's get the rest of the details over with; we're on short time."

"Yes, sir," the private said, leading them out of the building.

"What's on the top floor of the building?" Herzer asked as they were walking across the base.

"More rooms, sir," Vaston replied. "For others on the team."

"That was one of the buildings that got hit, wasn't it?" Megan asked.

"Yes, ma'am," the private said.

"No stains on the floor," Herzer noted.

"We had a bit of cleaning when we arrived, sir," Vaston said. "Replaced some of the wood on the floor. Sanded the rest. And the walls."

"I could have done without that image," Megan said.

"Sorry, ma'am," the private replied. "I'll try to watch it in the future."

"It's okay," Megan said, quietly. "I've seen bad enough things in my life. Do you know who was in my room before?"

"Colonel Carson, ma'am," Vaston said as they reached another two-story building.

The room in the interior was filled with desks but the only person in it was a Blood Lord officer manning a counter that barred passage to the rest of the room.

"Countess Travante," the lieutenant said, standing to attention as Megan entered. "Good to see you, ma'am."

"We need to get our badges, apparently," Megan said, smiling charmingly.

"Yes, ma'am, I have them right here." The officer pulled out a clipboard, printed pages and a handful of badges. "Please sign beside your name," he added, handing out the badges along with sheets of paper. "This is a map of the facilities. The badges are color coded. Yellow is restricted to only yellow areas. Purple can move in purple or yellow. Blue in those two and blue. Red has full access."

Shanea and Mirta's badges were in yellow, Van Krief's in blue. Only Megan and Herzer were issued red badges.

"What if we're in a red area and we need one of our aides?" Megan asked, frowning.

"They can be given special access, ma'am, of course," the lieutenant said, swallowing nervously. "They'll require an escort. If they're with you, of course..."

"Okay," Megan said. "We're supposed to report to an initial in-brief..."

"It's in Building Seventeen, ma'am," the lieutenant said, sliding over a map and pointing to the building in question. "That's a blue zone."

"Mirta and Shanea are not on the mission," Herzer noted.

"I know," Megan said. "Mirta, I'm not even sure why I asked you to come along."

"To be a helper bee and not get in the way," Mirta said, taking the clipboard out of Shanea's hand, turning it over and signing Shanea's name. "Just put an X here, dear."

"Thanks," Shanea said, brightly.

Herzer looked at the clock on the wall and shrugged.

"I guess you guys can go explore the yellow areas," he said. "Megan, Van Krief and I need to get over to the briefing."

"Private Vaston," the lieutenant said. "Why don't you show the councilwoman's aides around?"

"Sir," Vaston said woodenly. "I'm detailed to gate guard."

"I'll send a runner over," the lieutenant noted.

"And we're out of here," Herzer said, grabbing Megan's arm.

Building Seventeen was only two doors down and, unlike the majority of the buildings, was a low, one-story building, made entirely out of concrete. The main door was heavy steel and, as it turned out, locked. Herzer knocked on it furiously, bruising his knuckles, but there was no response.

"What the hell?" he asked the sky.

"Maybe nobody's home?" Megan asked humorously. "I can open it easily enough . . ."

"No, let me take a look around," Herzer said, walking around the side of the building. Near the far end was another door on which he also bruised his knuckles. It was eventually opened by a dwarf. Herzer had seen a few prior to the Fall but the only ones he'd seen since were at Raven's Mill. Dwarves were a Change, not a genengineered race like the elves, but they tended to reproduce as families. And, even before the war, they were considered odd.

"Yes?" the dwarf asked suspiciously. He had a heavy accent.

"You've got a council member cooling her heels at your front door," Herzer noted angrily.

"Well, what in hell is she doing at the front door?" the dwarf asked. "I'll go open it. Who're you?"

"Herrick," Herzer said, waving the badge.

"Right, the new meat," the dwarf said, stepping back and closing the door in his face.

Herzer opened his mouth to retort, realized it was pointless and walked back around to the front.

"There's apparently . . ." he said as the door opened.

"Councilwoman Travante," a different dwarf said, holding out his hand. "Angus Peterka, Chairman of Dwarven Mining Consolidated. A pleasure to make your acquaintance at last."

"Dwarf Peterka," Megan replied, shaking his hand and stepping in the room. It was small, with only the door to the outside and an equally heavy interior door. There was a dwarf manning a desk by the door and two more, in armor, holding large axes, guarding it. The day outside was hot but the room was pleasantly cool.

"Sorry," the dwarf at the desk said. "Gotta check the badges."

When the badges had been duly presented and checked the dwarf opened up a communications tube and whistled in it.

"Travante, Megan. Herrick, Herzer. Van Krief, Amosis. His Nibs."

There was a muttered response from the tube and the door opened from the inside.

"Sorry about all this," Peterka said. "But this was one of the few buildings that the damned scorps didn't penetrate, so there's that for it."

"I can see why," Herzer replied. The door led only to a small room with another door.

"Man-trap," Peterka noted. "The inner door can't be opened unless the outer door is closed. Interlocks and such."

"Very heavy security," Megan said.

"Well, it's where we've got all the plans for our systems," Peterka said. "We insisted, built the thing ourselves. Not because of the mission, mind, although that's important. But these are *dwarf* systems. We don't let just anyone look at them. Primary production's at the mines, of course, but the security's tighter there. Nobody but dwarves allowed."

"And if I wanted to see it?" Megan asked jokingly.

"We would, with all due respect, tell you to go to hell," Peterka said gruffly.

"I see," Megan replied dryly. "You and my father would get along splendidly."

Finally, they were in the building proper, but there wasn't much to see. The corridor they were led down had doors to either side but they all had locks on them. Near the end, Peterka pulled out a ring of keys, fumbled through them, and opened up a door like any other.

The room was oval and had several chairs around a table. At one end was a dais with some covered equipment. At least two of the pieces had to be man-shaped statues but the rest were a mystery.

"Right," Peterka said, taking the head of the table and gesturing for them to take seats. "You've seen the plans for the ship and you're finding new techs and cannon fodder. You've a plan to take the ship, yes?"

"Yes," Herzer said, raising one eyebrow.

"And you're ready to start training, eh?" Peterka continued. "You've got the mission licked, right? You're bloody *screwed*, lad."

"Why?" Megan said, sharply.

"I'll show you why," Peterka said, standing up and going over to the covered statues. Removing the cloths over them revealed two space suits on manikins. One was a suit something like an ancient wet suit with a bulbous, clear, helmet. It was mostly bright silver with bands of blue. The other was a complicated set of armor, somewhat close fitting, with odd joints and broad fins on the shoulder and back. It was a dull bronze in color.

"This is what we made for the first team," Peterka said, gesturing at the armored suit. "The fighters and commanders. The skin suit was for the techies, eh? Well do you know how many dwarf hours went into making those bloody armored monstrosities? We'd *just* completed the last suit. Making forty of them took us two *bloody* years!"

"Ouch," Herzer said.

"And all the people they were *fitted* for are six feet under," Peterka continued, angrily. "Two *bloody* years of hard work by the best dwarven wrights and it's *down the drain*!"

"So you're saying no armor?" Herzer asked.

"Not *good* bloody armor," Peterka said. "We're brainstorming ideas. Have been since the team went down. The skin suits are semi-armored themselves; we've thought about throwing standard armor on top. But there's heat regulation problems, bloody bad ones. And we need armor *now* so your team can start training *now*."

"How fast to produce the skin suits?" Herzer asked.

"Slow enough," Peterka noted. "Some of the ones we've stored can be cut down and restitched, although that's going to take long enough. We're gathering more fabric; the goats are damned pissed, I'll tell you."

"Goats?" Megan asked, biting her lip to keep from laughing. "They're made from wool?"

"Spider silk," Peterka snapped. "It's a bloody *ancient* technology, but it's still around. The goat milk has spider silk strands in it. Milk 'em, extract the silk, spin it, weave it and you've got spider silk cloth. Six layers of thin spider silk cloth bonded with a sealant then a plasteen insulator layer. Six more layers of silk and the heat transfer layer. Had another bit of luck there, there's an old tech that's basically a giant tree leaf mod. Bond that in, hook up to the vascular system and run liquid through it for heat transfer. You understand the problem, there?"

"No clue," Herzer said, shaking his head. "I spent the last couple of weeks reading up on the damned ship. I saw the armor design specs and the skin suits, but it didn't cover how they were made."

"Space ranges from bloody hot to bloody cold and naught between," Peterka said. "And I'm talking three hundred degrees Celsius in the sun and damned near *zero* in the shade. Those suits are made from beryllium bronze modified so it's not particularly heat reactive and they were still going to expand and contract like mad. We'd worked around that, especially at the joints. But you can't let that hit the human body. So the suits have the plasteen insulator, just about as close to a zero transfer insulator as you're going to find. With me?"

"So far," Herzer said.

"Problem is, the human body generates one hell of a lot of heat," Peterka pointed out. "Enough that you'll drown in your own heat in no more than fifteen minutes if you don't get rid of it. Can't sweat, can you? Not and not blast yourself into space."

"Okay," Herzer said. "Thus the leaf thing."

"Right," Peterka said. "Run fluid through it and it carries away the heat. Actually absorbs a bit of the sweat as well so you're not drenched all the time. Problem, space is a lousy conductor itself. Air carries heat away on Earth. Ain't none in space, soldier boy. Getting rid of heat is the A-Number-One problem in space."

"What about air?" Megan asked.

"Air's easy," Peterka said shortly. "There's these things called *air*-bottles. Recirculate it through scrubbers to get out the CO_2 and you're golden. Heat's the problem."

"Thus the big vanes on the armor," Herzer said, gesturing.

"Right," Peterka said. "That would allow the heat to escape. If you were in shade. System had a thermometer system that shut it down automatically when it got too hot on the surface. There was a heat sink that would carry you over. Very damned complex system and one we hadn't actually been able to test very well."

"How did the skin suits handle it?" Megan asked, looking at the suit that was vaneless.

"Well, they actually sort of used sweat," Peterka admitted. "A certain amount of water is gathered from the vascular system and it was released in measured amounts. Evaporating water is great for carrying off heat, lots of caloric transfer in evaporation. But it won't work with armor, even appliquéd armor."

"Appliquéd?" Herzer asked.

"Slapped on the outside," Peterka said.

"Don't tell me you don't have an answer," Megan said.

"We have one, but it's not a good one," Peterka said. "Ice packs."

"Ice?" Herzer asked.

"Yeah," Peterka said, sighing. "We'll hook up a system to run the water through ice packs. The ice packs will melt and turn to water. Eventually, you'll get damned hot and have to change the packs. We're looking at some of the problems with it right now, but it will probably work. But you're going to generate the most heat when you're most active, like when you're fighting. You're not going to be able to say 'Excuse me, Mr. Orc, could we pause a moment while I change my ice pack?'"

Herzer laughed at that and shook his head.

"Right, safety tip: keep your pack changed."

"You think it's funny now," the dwarf said, shaking his head. "They'll only last about *fifteen* minutes!"

"Oh, hell," Herzer said. "That's bad."

"Why?" Megan asked.

"Most fights last longer than that," Herzer replied. "Okay, this is part of your design. We're going to need some way to . . . turn a switch or something, and switch to a new pack. That will be a training item, but the fighter will switch to a new pack when we're about to engage in combat or as soon as possible after. And back if that one gets used up. Three or four would be nice."

"Two or three is the most we'll be able to do," Peterka said, picking up a note pad and making a note.

"Okay, you're going with appliquéd armor?" Herzer asked.

"Have to," Peterka said. "We looked at all sorts of possibilities, laminar, scale, but your fighters already have their own damned armor. Fittings will have to be replaced but there's no reason not to use it. Some . . . expansion and contraction issues, but lorica will flex for that and the light carbon steel they're made of is actually pretty resistant to thermal cracking. They'll tend to be . . . brittle in the shaded areas, though. Keep that in mind. Have to be careful about the collar area as well. Might put a bronze ring in to prevent it contracting too much. Have to put an insulator layer on the inside or when it heats up in the sun it'll burn away your suit. By the way, did I mention radiation?"

"No," Herzer said, sighing. "You did not."

"Forgot that layer," Peterka admitted. "The skin suits have an outer layer of xatanium. Very dense material developed in the twenty-third century specifically for suits. We've scrounged up enough of it over the years that we had a decent stock. At least for one thin layer. Very rad resistant but not totally. You're only going to be good for about an hour exposed to the sun. That's up where you'll be working, mind. In closer to Earth, don't get out of your vehicle if you can avoid it. Van Allen belt will have you making two-headed kids in about five minutes."

"Got it," Herzer said, sighing.

"The armored boyos will be a bit better off," the dwarf admitted. "But not much."

"How long for us to have minimal training gear?" Herzer asked.

"Years," Peterka laughed. "You'll have most of your team fitted in a few weeks, if I can find seamstresses we can trust. I've got six right now, all dwarves. They can only work so fast, even with powered sewing machines."

"I've got one," Megan said. "A very good seamstress. And trustworthy; one of my aides."

"Seven," Peterka nodded. "Everyone on the team will have to be carefully measured. The armor will have to be refitted, helmets refitted, we can mostly use those from the last team except for the locks. The packs for the armor suits will have to go *outside* the armor and we'll have to run support from the suits to the armor."

"Megan gets armor," Herzer said. "Councilwoman Travante is not expendable and she'll have the best you can get her in the time available."

"Absolutely," the dwarf said. "There's a set of armor that will probably be the right size to modify and I'll get my wrights to work on that right away."

"Okay," Herzer said. "There was nothing in the briefing materials about fighting in zero g. Thoughts?"

"Don't if you can avoid it," Peterka said with a bitter chuckle. "If you're free-floating, especially on the surface of the ship, you're totally screwed. You can grapple, maybe, if you can even get near your opponent. And we've got some devices for that," he added, pulling aside one of the other cloths to reveal a selection of devices. One of them was a large pick-axe but the rest were a mystery.

"Right, this is a punch-stiletto," Peterka said, picking up one of the devices that was a long tube with metal spikes sticking out to either side. "If you're grappling, you can press it against your opponent and . . ." He touched a stud and a spike slammed out of the end of the tube. "Penetrate a soft suit easy enough, a hard suit if you're at a joint, maybe. But if you don't have a good hold, it will just spin you off into oblivion, got it?"

"Got it," Herzer said, holding up his hand.

"Hold on." Peterka picked up another tube and slid the spike into it. There were cutouts for the spikes on the side and he pressed the assembly down on the table, grunting in effort as the weapon was reset. "Cocking one of these things is a bloody beast," he noted. "Safety," he added, pointing to a switch. "Release," he said, pointing at the stud.

"It's safe if it's on green?" Herzer asked, handling the weapon carefully.

"Yes."

Herzer took it off safe and pressed the stud. He was surprised by the recoil of the thing; it nearly flew out of his hand *without* being pressed against anything. "Hard to use."

"Won't be anything easy about fighting in space," Peterka said. "Generally, though, the whole inertial thing is overrated. You're going to be using mag-boots. You won't be able to jab without worrying if you or your opponent is going to be doing a flying Dutchman—"

"Sorry," Megan said, "term?"

"Flying Dutchman," Peterka said. "Floating off into space forever."

"Ah," Megan replied with a grimace. "Thanks."

"But you can use your weapon's momentum," Peterka said, picking up the axe. "Ever trained with an axe?" he asked.

"Not lately," Herzer admitted.

"Then don't try anything fancy," Peterka said, lifting the axe. "Set up a figure eight. Swing up and down one way, bring it around, swing up and down the other," he continued, demonstrating. "Use the pick end for armor, the axe for soft suits. *Don't* try to drive through your opponent. If you're pushing down when it hits, you'll be lifting yourself up. Use the momentum of the weapon *only*. Don't try to maneuver; if you lift a foot you'll probably go flying off. You'll have safety lines, but I don't think you'll have time in combat to use them. We thought about installing small thrusters but they're damned hard to use so . . . no thrusters. If someone does a Dutchman, you might be able to use a shuttle to recover them."

"Two handed," Herzer noted. "No shields. No way to form a shield wall."

"Nope," Peterka agreed. "Shield wall's easy enough to break in space."

"How?" Herzer asked.

"Reverse the figure eight," the dwarf said with an evil grin. "Hit the shield coming up. You're being pressed down into the hull, your opponent just got a couple of dozen kilos of impetus away from it. Shield goes or he does."

"Range weapons?" Herzer asked.

"Don't bother in zero g," Peterka said with a grunt of laughter. "You know an arrow bounces up as it's fired, right?"

"Sure," Herzer said then shook his head. "Completely off the target."

"It'll just head off to nowhere," Peterka said, nodding. "Same problem with a crossbow for different reasons. We'd considered a type of air-gun but it's probably not worth the time on training."

"Interesting assortment," Herzer said.

"We considered a bunch of other things," the dwarf admitted. "Clamping and severing weapons, for example. Got a few of them around if you want to carry them. They're damned slow to use, though. Recommend you have a few boyos with the polearm version, though."

"Why?" Megan asked.

"Well, they're dandy for keeping Celine's little toys off aren't they?" Peterka said with a grin, revealing the last table, which had only a long pole with complex devices at both ends. One end looked very much like a scorpion pincer while the other had a winch of some sort on it. "Spread the jaws," Peterka said, pressing a stud at which the jaws flew open. "Press it against a target," he continued. When it was pressed onto the arm of the bronze armor it quickly ratcheted down to a snug fit. "Then crank," he said, twisting the crank on the end. The jaws moved very slowly but as they watched, the armor began to deform. After a period of about ten seconds of hard cranking, the jaws suddenly snapped most of the way through the armor.

"Like I said," Peterka told them, letting go of the weapon and dropping it to the floor, "it's slow. But thorough."

CHAPTER FOURTEEN

"Oh, now this is homey," Courtney said, looking at her room. "And where is Mike going to sleep? And the kids?"

"We're going to move beds into one of the rooms for the children," Lieutenant Commer said nervously. "Mr. Boehlke will have the room adjoining yours."

"Well, there's indoor plumbing," Courtney said, opening up the door. "That's a change . . ."

"So, how do you like the digs?" Herzer asked, knocking on the door of the room.

"Tell me that Megan's got better facilities than this?" Courtney said.

"Nope," Herzer replied, shrugging. "Okay, a little better. A bit more room and her own bathroom, complete with shower and toilet."

"You dragged us up here for this?" Mike asked incredulously.

"You're not here for a vacation," Herzer pointed out. "You're here so that your kids, and you, are protected."

"So I'm going to be cooling my heels while Courtney does whatever it is she's going to do?" Mike asked, angrily. "Take care of the kids?"

"There's a problem with that?" Megan asked, coming down the corridor. "Hello, Courtney, Mike."

"No, of course I can take care of the kids," Mike snapped. "It's all I've got to do, isn't it?"

"Uh," Herzer hummed, interjecting himself between the two. "There's a few points I'd like to make before Mike tries to kill a council member and gets turned into a newt..."

"I wasn't going to—"

"I wouldn't do that—"

"Yeah," Herzer snapped. "Megan, please chill out for a second. Mike, you're going to be doing something other than taking care of the kids. I can think of a half a dozen things. And you'll get briefed on what's going on around here, as soon as I get a *chance*, okay?"

"Okay," Mike growled, glancing at Megan. "But that better be soon."

"It will be when I can get to it, Mike," Herzer replied. "I've got about a billion *other* problems on my plate."

"Who's going to take care of the kids?" Courtney asked, frowning.

"Four," Mike pointed out. "From swaddling clothes to four."

"Babies, bleck," Herzer said, then shrugged. "For the time being, Shanea."

"What?" Megan snapped. "Why *Shanea*?"

Herzer closed his eyes for a second, then turned and simply looked at her.

"Okay, so she makes the most sense," Megan said after a long glare. "But you could consult me next time."

"I hadn't thought of the problem until it was brought up," Herzer admitted. "I thought there would be enough people here to handle minor details. But there aren't. Are you aware that they don't even have the cooking staff replaced, yet?"

"No," Megan said. "Who's going to cook?"

"Well, there's all these women..." Mike said then stopped when both Megan and Herzer fixed him with a glare. "What? It's true! Besides, Herzer, I've *had* your cooking. You can't boil *water. Pass.*"

"I've gotten better," Herzer said. "We're probably going to be getting food from the legion for the time being. But there are a billion details to work out and I haven't even figured out who is in *charge*."

"Ahem," Lieutenant Commer cleared his throat. "You are. Sir."

"What?" Herzer snapped.

"Colonel Carson was the base commander, sir," the lieutenant said, nervously. "I suppose, that the position devolves to either you or the countess."

"I don't have *time* to manage the base and get ready for the mission," Herzer said angrily.

"Sorry, sir," the lieutenant replied, ducking his head.

"Don't be; you just gave me *more* bad news," Herzer said, throwing up his hands. "Megan?"

"You think these *soldiers* are going to listen to me?" she asked.

"Yes," Herzer replied. "As automatically as breathing. Why?"

"Well . . ." Megan said, temporizing. "You want me to run the base?"

"No," Herzer said after a moment. "That won't work, either. You're going to have too much to do. We'll find someone. Damnit, where in the hell is Tao!"

"I'm here, sir," Van Krief said quietly.

"Go to the portal, then go to Colonel Torill at SpecOps. Tell him we're in a classic FUBAR. I need an officer of rank of captain or major who has base management experience and appropriate clearances; I don't have time to manage the base and plan and train for the op at the same time. We also need support staff, replacements for the previous casualties . . . Point out to him the situation and, beyond that, please ask him to exercise his best judgment but right now the only thing working around here is security and the *dwarves* and we need more than that."

"Yes, sir," Van Krief said, folding her notebook.

"Go! And if you see Tao, tell him to get his butt moving!"

"Yes, sir," the lieutenant said, turning to walk away.

"Shit," Herzer muttered. "Amosis, give me your notebook."

"Yes, sir," she said, handing it over with a quizzical expression.

"You can't get *out* without authorization," Herzer explained, writing a short note and handing it to her. "Lieutenant . . . Commer, what's the name of the Blood Lord commander?"

"Captain Van Buskirk, sir," the lieutenant replied.

"Bus?" Herzer said. "I didn't even know he'd made lieutenant much less captain. Okay, Megan, could you please get with Courtney and Shanea and discuss specific housekeeping arrangements. There may be more kids that have to be looked after; we'll cross that bridge when we come to it. I need to go see the detachment commander. And maybe arrange dinner."

"Yes, sir!" Megan snapped.

"In a moment," Herzer said, grabbing her by the arm and dragging her down the corridor. "Okay, what?" he asked when they were in her room.

Megan started to reply, then bit her tongue. He waited through a jaw flex and an inhalation, expecting at any moment to have his head ripped off.

"I'd gotten used to giving orders," Megan said, finally. "And I've got a question; who's in charge here?"

"Oh," Herzer said, blowing out a breath. "In all honesty, I suppose you are. You're the Key-holder."

"True," Megan replied, shaking her head. "But I'm not the right *person* to be in charge. I wouldn't have known to contact . . . Colonel Torill and I wouldn't have known to ask for . . . that officer you asked for. So what are we doing?"

Herzer thought about it for a moment, scratching his chin with his prosthetic and then nodded, sharply.

"Council members, with a few exceptions, are responsible for strategic decisions, not operational or tactical, agreed? And, with the exception of Duke Edmund, they are defined as civilians, not military."

"Agreed," Megan said. "So you're saying I get strategic calls and you get operational and tactical? I get civilian, you get military?"

"When we're prepping the mission and when we're on the mission, I'm in charge," Herzer said bluntly. "Up and until we come to a strategic decision. Then you make the call and I carry it out. Agreed?"

"Agreed," Megan said.

"Now," Herzer said, delicately. "What the hell was that with Mike?"

Megan's face worked again and Herzer just waited.

"He has a tendency to piss me off," Megan admitted. "And the whole 'me man, me work, you woman, take care of babies and cook' really—"

"Triggered something?" Herzer asked.

"You could say that," Megan admitted with a breathless chuckle. "Very . . . strong stab of anger."

" 'Irrational' stab of anger?" Herzer asked.

"Oh, I dunno," Megan said, smiling unhappily. "I think it was pretty rational, don't you?"

"The degree?" Herzer asked.

"No."

"You know what was happening there?" Herzer asked carefully.

"I'd analyzed it myself the moment you brought it up," Megan said bitterly. "Thank you."

"There is going to be a lot of stress on this mission," Herzer pointed out. "A lot of tension. Probably a fair degree of shouting. Certainly orders that are going to have to be acted on, sometimes without thinking about it. There is *not* room for someone who is not in control of their emotions."

"I'm in perfect control," Megan said, coldly.

"No, you're not," Herzer replied gently. "Not if Mike can get you that angry by just being . . . Mike. Stress is not cumulative, it's multiplicative. There's small background stress, then you add another stress on and another and finally there's that one that sends you right up to the brink of loss of control, or over. And life-threatening stress is worse than what we've been dealing with. If you panic, up there . . ." His jaw worked and Megan reached up to stroke it.

"You'll lose me," she whispered. "Are you trying to find a reason for me not to go on this mission?"

"I'm not willing to lose you," Herzer replied, tightly. "I don't, frankly, give a damn about the Key. I'm not willing to lose you, Megan Travante. *I'm* not. Hell, for that reason if no other, one or the other of us shouldn't be on this mission. And, of the two, I think you're the one to worry about."

"Herzer," Megan said, "I'm strong, okay? And we're *both* coming back from this mission. Get that through your head."

"You're strong," he admitted. "But you've got weird stress points. And you get stubborn. I won't have time to let you work things out for yourself up there," he added, pointing upward.

"What about when I tell *you* to do something or not to do something?" Megan asked. "When it's a *strategic* decision."

"You tell me to jump off the damned ship, and I will," Herzer said, definitely. "But you'd better have a damned good reason."

"I won't ever ask you to do that," Megan said, chuckling.

"Ten'hut!" someone bellowed as Herzer walked into the orderly room of the Blood Lord headquarters.

"At ease," he bellowed. "Where's the captain?"

"In there, sir," one of the sergeants in the room said, gesturing at the rear door.

Herzer knocked on the door and entered at a bellowed "Come."

"Hey, Bus," he said as the captain started to get to his feet. "Chill. When'd you pin on your third pip?"

"Last month," the captain said. "Congratulations on your promotion, sir."

Captain Van Buskirk was nearly as large and broad as Herzer but where Herzer was dark, "Bus" Van Buskirk was light: blond hair, skin so white that his vascular system stood out like a model, sunburned nose and cheekbones. Herzer remembered that he had a tendency to burn if the sun was *below* the horizon. They weren't *friends* exactly, but the Blood Lord group was so small that he tended to know most of the officers and a good many of the NCOs.

"Can the 'sir,' Bus," Herzer said, sighing and settling in the room's only other chair. "This is a classic FUBAR, you know that?"

"I'm just starting to get an inkling of what's going on in this camp," the captain replied. "But I'll agree that all signs point to FUBAR."

"Fisked up beyond all recognition," Herzer admitted, his eyes narrowing. "But part of that fisk up I'm going to stop now. We're going to have to discuss distribution on things, but bringing you in on what you're guarding is just going to be part of the change . . ."

"Do you have authority?" Van Buskirk asked.

"I do indeed," Herzer replied. "And if I don't, fisk it. What we're supposed to be doing here is planning to retake the fuel tanker that's headed in."

"Thought so," the captain said, grimacing. "That's the thing with the lake, right?"

"I have no idea," Herzer admitted. "Why?"

"Zero g, training," the captain said. "It's the *really* old way to train for zero g."

"You've been in space?" Herzer asked.

"A couple of times," Van Buskirk said. "I used to play . . . well . . . you did ER, right?"

Herzer had, indeed, spent much of his time prior to the Fall in Enhanced Reality, the computer generated world of holograms and nano-forms where a good many people gamed.

"Yeah," the commander said. "But I was always in a medieval fantasy environment. You?"

"You were lucky," the captain said with a laugh. "I was playing shooter games. Some of the best were on simulated spaceships. A couple of times I went up for live group tourneys, just to see if there was a difference. There wasn't enough to matter."

"I wish we could use ER for training, now," Herzer said. "I've never been in free-fall and neither has anyone on the team as far as I'm aware. And speaking of teams . . ." he added musingly. "I'm authorized to recruit in the Blood Lords for the replacement fighters on this mission. Given the security group here, and at Blackbeard, there aren't many that are available. But *your* company is right here, already . . ."

"Oh, crap," the captain said, shaking his head. "We can't be pulling security all night and training all day. I won't even go into the whole: 'shouldn't you ask for volunteers?' thing. I'll volunteer in a heartbeat; I've always liked fighting in space. But the rest of the company . . ."

"They volunteered twice," Herzer said. "First for the legions, then for the Blood Lords. Why ask a third time?"

"How caring of you," the captain said, grinning.

"Apparently a lot of the trainers got killed along with the team," Herzer said. "So don't be surprised if you get press-ganged as a trainer. And I want you to go talk to Angus Peterka over in Building Seventeen. Use the back door and tell him I sent you . . ."

"That's a blue zone building," Buskirk pointed out. "I'm only cleared for purple."

"Not anymore," Herzer intoned.

"Shanea, you've met Courtney before," Megan said, as the girl came into her room.

"Hey," Shanea said, smiling. "Good to see you again."

"Shanea, do you have any experience with children?" Megan asked carefully.

"I had a younger brother," Shanea said, her face suddenly creasing in an unusual frown. "I don't know what happened to him, you know?"

"You took care of him?" Courtney asked.

"A little," the girl said. "Me and the nannies. And Mom," she said quietly.

"The problem is, Courtney has to do some training," Megan said. "And she has some children here. Could you watch them? One of them's a baby so you're going to have to change diapers..."

"Oh, sure!" Shanea said, smiling happily. "I like kids. I want some myself. I kept hoping that Paul would get me pregnant so I could have a baby, but he never did."

Courtney's face twitched at that and she carefully didn't look at Megan.

"Great," Megan said, smiling blankly. "Courtney, why don't you go introduce Shanea to your children while I go see if I can help Herzer? The replacement personnel are coming in and I foresee some problems there."

CHAPTER FIFTEEN

Linda was frowning in her mirror when there was a knock at the door. Ever since the debacle with Herzer Herrick, Shamon had been a bit less friendly. He still was maintaining the apartment but she suspected it was time to start shopping for a new "friend." However, Duke Dehnavi was out of town at his country home at the moment, so she had time to look around and certainly wasn't expecting visitors.

She stood up and put on a robe, hair up and makeup half done, and went to the door. Whoever it was, they could damned well see her like this. Maybe it would scare them off.

The "visitors" turned out to be two Federal Rangers, one male and one female, in light leather armor.

"Miz Linda Donohue?" the male officer asked, consulting a clipboard.

"Yes?" she replied uncertainly. Shamon probably had enough power to have her arrested or detained, but she couldn't imagine what the charge would be. And she hadn't thought he was *that* pissed off.

"Miz Donohue, you're being temporarily detained under the War Powers Act," the officer said, stone faced. "Could you change into comfortable clothing, pack enough clothes for approximately three days in no more than one bag and come with us?"

"What is this about?" Linda said, her eyes widening. "I haven't done anything!"

"Ma'am, I do not know," the officer said, gesturing at the female officer. "Ranger Varnicke will remain with you while you prepare."

"I'm not going *anywhere* until someone tells me what I'm charged with!" Linda snapped. "I've got powerful friends, buddy, you can't just up and snatch me out of my *apartment!*"

"Ma'am, you're not charged with anything," Varnicke said placatingly. "And *we* don't know why you're being detained. Our orders are to pick you up, take you to a colonel at the War Department and then pick up two more people."

"And as for your friends," the still unnamed male officer said bluntly, "you'll be permitted to contact someone once you reach the War Department but you're to communicate with *no* one while you are in detention. Now, please prepare to leave."

Stunned, Linda let herself be led into her own apartment by Ranger Varnicke while the male remained outside, presumably on guard. Varnicke helped her pack while Linda finished her makeup.

She was taken through Washan in a closed, and stuffy, carriage, to an outlying building at the sprawling headquarters. There she was turned over to a Blood Lord soldier who escorted her to a windowless room with only one door in which three other people waited.

"Does anyone know what is going on?" she asked, dropping the leather satchel with all she currently possessed at her feet and sitting in a hard-backed chair.

"No idea," a man said, running his eyes over her. "But the view's certainly improved."

Linda snorted and examined her fellow travelers. Two of them had to be well over a hundred, one of the two having the look of someone who spent most of his time in a day-labor job.

"Where are you from, miss?" one of the older men asked. "We're all from Raven's Mill but I don't recognize you."

"I'm from here," she said, shrugging. "I lived near Washan . . . before, you know? And I moved here."

"What do you do, miss?" the one that looked like a day laborer asked.

"I'm a secretary," she said, shrugging. "I work in a duke's office."

"Lucky duke," the man who'd commented on the view said.

That apparently exhausted the fund of small talk available and they sat in silence for an extended period of time. There was no way to determine how long but the wait seemed interminable. Linda spent her time mentally composing the note she was going to send to Dehnavi.

Finally the door opened and the same Blood Lord that had escorted her to the room gestured from the opening.

"That's apparently it, for now," he said. "If you'd please come with me?"

"Where are we going?" Linda snapped. "I was told I could send a note to someone telling them where I'd disappeared to."

"You'll get a chance," the Blood Lord said. "Later. Come with me, please. If you see anyone you recognize, just smile and wave. No talking or discussion."

There were three more Blood Lords waiting for them and the group was escorted around the edge of the War Department zone and to a portal in another enclosed room.

"Where in the *hell* are we going?" Linda snapped, balking at the portal.

"Seventh Legion's camp," the lead Blood Lord answered. "Enter the portal, ma'am."

Linda gritted her teeth and stepped through after the other three. There was another group of Blood Lords on the far side standing in a three-sided shed. From it, the bustle of the Legion camp could be observed and Linda noticed that there was some sort of inner camp with a gate just down the street.

"Manuel Sukiama?" the sergeant in charge of the group asked.

"Here," one of the older men said.

"Josten Ram?"

"Here," the man who'd commented on her looks answered. "What is this all about?"

"You'll be told soon, sir," the sergeant answered. "Linda Dono-hue?"

"Here," Linda snarled. "There is going to be hell to pay about this."

"As you say, ma'am. Geo Keating?"

"Here," the day laborer said.

"You're Geo Keating?" Linda gasped. "You wrote *Sixth Order Mechanics*."

"That was a long time ago, young lady," the man said, his face breaking into a smile. "Thank you for remembering."

"What the hell are you doing looking like . . ." She paused and gestured embarrassedly.

"Ah, well," the man said, shrugging his shoulders with a slight smile. "Not much work for quantum engineers these days, is there? Take life a day at a time."

"Could the four of you come with me, please?" the sergeant said, walking out of the shed and towards the inner camp.

"I love how *polite* they are," Linda said, sarcastically, shrugging her satchel up and following. "As if we have a choice."

"Well, it's better than what I'd be doing today," Keating said. "Could I help you with your bag, miss?"

"I can carry it," Linda said, noticing for the first time that he didn't have a bag of his own. "Where's your stuff?"

"This *is* my stuff, miss," the man said, looking around the camp. "Lovely use of space, very efficient."

"I'd think that *some* of your background would have transferred to the new tech," Linda said, puzzled. "Couldn't you get work as, I dunno, an engineer."

"The requirements for modern engineering are a bit far from my area of expertise, miss," Keating said, frowning. "I actually tried at one point but . . . I'm really not a good day-to-day engineer. I tend to . . . wander mentally. And there's not much room for impracticality these days. Digging gives me plenty of chance to think. It's not all that bad of a life. I never was much into material possessions; I donated almost all of my credits to the Wolf project before the Fall. So I live life one day at a time, find some work that keeps me in food and . . . think. It's not the worst life possible. And I've done good work these days, helping to build Raven's Mill. In a way, creating a well-built wall is as satisfying as publishing a well-thought thesis. Perhaps more so; I don't have to defend my wall. It is there for everyone to see and admire. It keeps the wind out and with a roof it keeps the rain off. When *I* build a foundation, you know that the wall will stand. And when I build a wall, you know that the roof will stand."

"And when you build a roof?" Linda asked, smiling. "And please call me Linda, Mr. Keating."

"Ah, I don't do roofing, miss," the man said, shrugging. "Afraid of heights. Don't even do high walls if I can avoid it."

They had reached the gates to the inner camp and were passed through. The camp on the far side was centered around a lake and more substantial, with two-story wooden buildings filling most of the space. She also noticed that the few people in view were all wearing badges on lanyards. A secure area, then, something like the inner areas of the War Department.

They were led to one of the closest buildings and to another waiting room, this one fitted with comfortable chairs and a wall clock; it appeared to be some sort of a rec room. There were a few books and magazines scattered around. Although from the looks of the books and magazines it was a rec room for mostly males, probably the Blood Lord guards.

There was a pleasant-faced older woman waiting in the room and she nodded as they entered.

"Welcome to Icarus Camp, I'm June Lasker," the woman said. "In a moment I'll be interviewing each of you and explaining what's going on. I know you're all upset and I'll ask you to *try* not to take it out on me. I'm just as stuck in this as you are," she added with a smile. "So, what did the net bring in this time? Names, in other words."

"Josten Ram," Josten said. "So, what *is* this all about?"

"I'll be informing each of you individually," June said, referring to her clipboard. "Ah, one of the pilots. Mr. Ram, if you'll accompany me?"

"Icarus," Keating said, settling in one of the chairs. "How *fascinating.*"

"Icarus?" Linda said, sitting down next to him as the Blood Lords filed out of the room.

"A Greek myth," Keating replied, musingly. "The inventor Daedalus and his son Icarus built the Labyrinth for King Minos of Crete. Thereafter, Minos imprisoned them in a tower so that Daedalus couldn't tell the secrets of the Labyrinth to anyone else. But Daedalus constructed wings of wood and wax and the feathers of the seabirds that flew around the tower. Then he and Icarus flew out of the tower. Daedalus had warned Icarus not to fly too high, lest he get too close to the Chariot of Apollo, the sun. But Icarus, drunk with the glory of flight, flew too high and the wax melted from his wings, casting him into the sea and to his death."

"And that means . . . what?" Linda asked.

"Oh, many hypotheses exist," Keating said with a twinkle in his eye. "They could be planning on seeing if we can survive a high drop into the sea. A low-order hypothesis, I'll admit," he added with a chuckle.

"Or they could use an inventor to build a labyrinth," Linda said, getting into the game. "All you'd have to do is rewrite your particle theory equations then run walls from one set to another. That would be labyrinthine enough!"

"Do you really think they were too complex?" Keating asked, worriedly. "I found them elegantly simple, myself."

"Some of us, sir, are mortals." Linda sighed. "I think I stayed with it up to the second theta transform and then I went out to a party and tried very *very* hard to forget. I'd thought I was pretty good at transform equations until I tried to keep up with you."

"Well, such things take time to fully explore," Keating replied unhappily. "But we can take a look at it here," he added, pulling out a scrap of charcoal and picking up one of the books. Turning to the back page he found a clean area and started inscribing equations. "The second theta is a quaternary transform—"

"Linda Donohue?" June said, from the door.

"Later, Professor," Linda said, tapping him on the arm. "I'd be fascinated to try to figure it out."

"Do you *know* who is sitting in there?" Linda snapped as the door closed.

"Manuel Sukiama and Geo Keating?" June said, leading Linda down the corridor.

"And do you *know* who Geo Keating *is*?" Linda said, angrily.

"It says he's a particle field theorist," June answered, pausing to consult her clipboard.

"He's not just a particle field theorist," Linda snarled. "He's one of the finest minds in *history*. And he's been working as a day laborer in Raven's Mill! The man is a *legend* in his field and he's sitting in there sketching equations that not two people on *Earth* can understand! If we still had things like Nobel Prizes he'd take the Nobel in physics *every* year!"

"I'm . . ." June said then paused. "I'm sorry, I've never heard of him. But I'll be very polite when I interview him. And I'll try to explain his importance to Commander Herrick."

"Herzer Herrick is here?" Linda said, her eyes widening in horror.

"Yes, he's . . . well, we need to have our in-briefing," June said, tilting her head. "Is . . . do you and Commander Herrick have a . . . background? I know that he has had . . . a number of lady friends."

"It's not that . . ." Linda said, her face tightening and then a look of horror even worse than the last crossing her face. "Oh, God, Countess Travante isn't here, is she?"

"Yes," June said, raising an eyebrow.

"I need to *leave*," Linda snapped, looking around wildly and panting in panic. "I don't care *what* this is all about. I need to leave right *now!*"

"Two things," June said, glancing at one of the Blood Lord guards in the corridor. "The first is, you *cannot* leave. Period. You can try to run, but the camp is guarded and you will *not* be permitted to leave after entering the camp. So . . . just calm down. The second is, we need to talk about why you were brought here. But not in the corridor," June said, gesturing down the hall. "Come on, find out why you're here, *then* make decisions."

"Crap," Linda said, glancing at the Blood Lord and shaking her head. "Let's go. I'll listen. But Megan is . . . crap. I'm gonna die . . ."

"I think we need to talk, dear," June said, patting her on the shoulder.

June's office was comfortably appointed and she gestured Linda into a chair, then collapsed behind her desk.

"I didn't ask for this job." June sighed, opening up a file and shaking her head. "But I got it for my sins. Miss Donohue, the reason you were brought here is that when you applied for your job with the government you listed a background in quantum engineering. That was your hobby, pre-Fall?"

"Yes," Linda said, shrugging. "I tinkered at it. Particle field generation theory, ionization theory and fusion mechanics."

"A mission group is being formed that needs persons with your background," June said. "Whether you agree to go on the mission or not, you will be confined to this camp until the completion of the mission. Even the fact that we are *gathering* such persons cannot come to the attention of New Destiny. Therefore, for reasons of security, we can do that under the War Powers Act. Your employer, which is the government after all, will be informed that you will be 'away' for a period of time and that you *must* be given your previous job back. You may send a note to one person," June said, pulling out a printed card and slipping it across the desk. "That is the *only* communication that you will be permitted."

Linda looked at that card and blanched. It was preprinted with a trite message about being unavailable for at least two months and helping out "the War Effort."

"This is *bullshit*," Linda snapped. "Damnit, I work for Duke Dehnavi! You can't *do* this to me!"

"That is as it may be," June said, sighing. "As I said, I hope that people won't take this out on me. At a later time you'll have people to shout at that are much more responsible for your predicament than I. And they're better at being shouted at."

"Herrick," Linda spat.

"He is one, yes," June said. "Can I ask you your . . . background with Commander Herrick. It won't affect your being here; that is set in stone. But it may affect your participation in the mission."

"No, you may not," Linda answered, shaking her head. "What a *nightmare!*"

"Yes," June said, shaking her head. "That is one adjective used for it. Insanity. Power-mad-myrmidons. Idiocy. Stupidity. Shanghaied, a very old term which I fortunately recognized. Insanity, again. Nightmare. One gentleman, who was a student of ancient literature along with being a qualified pilot, used 'Kafkaesque' for which I needed an explanation. But you haven't gotten to the good part, yet."

"And what is the *good* part?" Linda said angrily.

"The mission for which you are being asked to volunteer," June said, smiling humorously.

"I'm not going to like this, am I?" Linda said.

"Probably not," June replied, shaking her head but still smiling. "But let me get *most* of my spiel out before you start screaming, okay?"

"Ooo-kay," Linda said cautiously.

"You've been brought here to join a mission to retake the returning helium three refueling ship," June said. "My bet is that your response will be: 'You are joking.' Possibly followed by either: 'Right?' or 'Tell me you're joking.' That's as opposed to more stereotypically male responses such as: 'No fisking way.'"

Linda opened her mouth and then closed it.

"You're not joking," was what she finally said.

"No, I am not," June replied. "New Destiny intends to capture the ship so that they can monopolize the fuel. So are we. We hope that you will be willing to participate. In your case, you have background in the engineering tech used on the ship. Whether you participate or not, you will be kept at this facility. If you chose not to participate in the mission, we'll still ask that you accept a support position. However, the mission positions are far better paid. Far better."

"How much?" Linda asked.

"You are classified as a Level One Engineering tech," June answered. "That is nineteen hundred credits per month and a twenty thousand credit bonus upon mission completion, based upon mission performance."

"That's a *lot*," Lind said, frowning. "But explain the mission performance thing."

"The credits are banked," June said. "There's nothing to spend them on, anyway, and you're given full support here. If you agree to perform the mission and then refuse at the last minute your salary is recalculated at minimum maintenance, which is thirty credits per month."

"That's less than what a day laborer makes!" Linda snapped.

"You're being supported, unlike a day laborer," June pointed out. "That is also the rate at which you will be paid if you refuse to support in any fashion. If you agree to do the mission, go on the mission and then are unable to perform under the conditions, you get the training money but not the bonus. That is the 'mission performance' clause. If you are unable to complete the training or drop out, you get the full pay up until that time, up to two weeks before the mission. Backing out in final training reverts you to maintenance pay. Now, I've talked about the pay, but there's more to this mission than money. It's a very important . . ."

"Can it," Linda said. "Appealing to my patriotic side is like appealing to my male side; it doesn't exist."

"Very well," June said primly. "Then I'll point out that the monthly pay is nearly twenty times what you make as an IS-6 and the bonus is enough to make you mildly independently wealthy. The pay rates are gauged with your point in mind. You get the money in lump at the completion of mission or it goes to your designated beneficiary. I suppose I don't have to add that risk of loss of life on the mission is high?"

"No, that's pretty obvious," Linda said. "I'd guess I get to think about it."

"Yes," June said. "Most of the interviewees do. I'll have you escorted to Security where you'll be issued your initial badge, then to the transient single female quarters. There's really nobody that you can talk to who is in support or on the mission team about the mission until you perform it, however."

"That's fine," Linda said. "I just want to think about it for a bit. Where's Mr. Keating going to be?"

"That depends on whether he agrees to perform the mission or not," June replied. "If he does, he'll go to permanent quarters. If not, he'll be in the transient male quarters, which is on the top floor of the same building you'll be in."

"I'd like to talk to him again, whatever I decide," Linda requested.

"That will have to wait, I'm afraid," June said with a shrug. "Let me call the guard. I do hope you agree to perform the mission; we need you." She paused in thought and then shrugged again. "I could talk to Commander Herrick and try to have you assigned as . . . I guess Mr. Keating's assistant. He's somewhat aged; I'd suspect he would appreciate some assistance."

"He's been working as a day laborer, remember?" Linda said, shaking her head. "He can probably break me in half. But if he agrees to do the mission and if you can get me assigned as his assistant . . . I'll go. I don't know what help I can be to him, but he's an important man, a genius. And, okay, absentminded. Maybe I can be of use."

"I'll make a note of that," June said. "Now, let me get you an escort."

"I think I can find the quarters if you just give me directions," Linda said.

"If you're wandering around without a badge, you're likely to get killed by one of the guards. And we wouldn't want that."

"I can tell I'm going to love it here."

CHAPTER SIXTEEN

"Well, twelve of the thirteen techs and pilots are present," June said. She was meeting over dinner with Herzer, Megan and Evan to discuss the personnel situation. "Only five, six with Mrs. Boehlke, have volunteered. One, a computer tech, has most pointedly and emphatically declined. The others are 'thinking about it.' The thirteenth, one of the pilots, appears to be among the missing; the Rangers can't find him anyway."

"Joie's here?" Megan asked.

"Yes," June said, smiling and shaking her head. "She is most spectacular is she not? She is 'thinking about it.' Herzer, I have a question?"

"Yeah?" Herzer said, taking a bite of steak. It was military steak, thin and tough. He'd already made a mental note to see about the quality of the food available for the mission. He didn't care one way or another, but it was going to be important to morale.

"What is your history with Linda Donohue?"

Herzer looked puzzled and shrugged. "Don't recognize the name. None that I know of."

"She apparently recalls you," June said, primly. "And she is quite afraid of you and Megan. Megan in particular."

"Describe her," Megan said, just as puzzled.

"Twenty-five," June said. "Got that from her records; could be anything from seventeen to seventy. Redhead. Good looking. Slim. She works in Duke Dehnavi's office."

159

"Oh, crap!" Herzer said, blanching.

"The doxie?" Megan quipped, raising an eyebrow. "Whatever is she here for?"

"Engineering," June replied. "She's got background in particle field generation. She's said that she'll go on the mission, but only if she's assigned as an assistant to Geo Keating, who is listed as an Engineering Tech Three on the basis of his background."

"Geo *Keating*?" Evan snapped. "You found Geo *Keating*? Good God!"

"Okay, who is Geo Keating?" Megan said, smiling.

"He's a *brilliant* field theorist," Evan said, shaking his head. "He was offered a Key and turned it *down*! Said it would interfere with his work! An amazing mind, a true genius."

"He's been working as a day laborer in Raven's Mill," June said, shaking her head. "Quite philosophical about it. Rather absent-minded. He volunteered. No particular interest in the money, he just wants to examine the equipment on the ship. Something about radiation effects and shielding. I couldn't follow it."

"Where is he?" Evan asked, standing up.

"Permanent quarters," June said.

"Evan, we're not done here," Herzer pointed out.

"We're close," Megan said. "I'll go talk to the males about the importance of the mission, you go talk to the females. Then we'll switch, tomorrow, for the holdouts. See how many we can get."

"The only female holdout is Miss Donohue," June said. "And she's willing to go if she can be Mr. Keating's assistant."

"I wonder what she thinks she can get from that?" Herzer mused. "I don't trust her as far as I can throw her."

"Like Evan, she seems to be very impressed by Mr. Keating," June said with a shrug.

"We'll see," Herzer said. "I think I need to talk to her, first."

"Okay," Megan said, nodding at Evan. "*Now* we're done. Have fun talking to Mr. Keating. Don't stay up all night."

"I won't," Evan said with a grin.

"You," Linda said, bitterly, when she saw who was at her door. "Come on in," she added, waving at the sparse quarters.

"Let's head down to the rec room instead," Herzer said, grinning faintly. "Not only is it more comfortable but it's less likely to cause comment."

The rec room in the transient quarters was almost identical to the one where she'd awaited her interview, with the exception of its being devoid of reading material. There was a sink with hot and cold water, some stuffed chairs grouped around a coffee table and a pool table.

"To clear the air," Herzer said, sitting down by the coffee table. "I didn't know you were one of the techs until this evening. So I didn't drag you into this intentionally."

"I'd half wondered," Linda admitted. "But I couldn't figure out what was in it for you except simple malice, and you're not the malicious type. Now, Megan . . ."

"What happened wasn't a blip on her horizon," Herzer said. "Especially with all of this going on. She hadn't known, either. And we both would have been completely surprised if June hadn't brought you up. So. And so. But what's this with you and Geo Keating? Evan, who's the chief engineering officer, went into spasms when he heard he was here. And apparently you want to be his assistant. Why?"

Linda paused and thought about that and then shrugged.

"Did you have any heroes, you know, Before?"

"Sure," Herzer admitted. "The guy I work for, now. I've discovered he puts his pants on one leg at a time. And they're ugly legs."

"It's like that," Linda admitted with a chuckle. "I'd thought about contacting him, Before, you know? But I just felt like a . . . a . . ."

"The term is 'fan girl' or 'groupie,' " Herzer interjected. "I actually knew Edmund's daughter. I was getting ready to meet him when the Fall hit."

"My parents were the kind that made me study," Linda said, shrugging. "It's why I can read and write, but they pushed me more than just that. Mom had me do a presentation on particles when I was about . . . oh, nine or so. So I found this primer by a guy named Keating to study. And it was just . . . amazing. The enormously complex made clear and simple. I fell in love with the way particles work and focused after that on *that*, particle physics and field interactions. Hell, your girlfriend can *make* a portal, I know how one *works* and I bet she doesn't!"

"You might be surprised," Herzer said. "She's more than just a pretty face. And so, apparently, are you. Go on."

"So about half the modern studies on field interaction are by Keating. I was a *hopeless* fan girl of his work. And now, I've got a chance to work with him. That's it, really." She paused and thought about it and shrugged. "The chance to work with him is worth the chance of getting my ass blown up or decompressed or whatever. And he's physically fine, he's been working as a *laborer* if that's not stupid enough! But he's sort of absentminded. I think I can help. Help *him*. I don't care if we get the ship or not, frankly."

"Well, that's silly of you, but I won't get into a debate," Herzer said, frowning. "However, if that's your cost, you're in. As his assistant. I don't suppose the fact that he's going to be independently wealthy from this mission has anything to do with it?"

"Not a bit," Linda said, firmly. "I'll admit that now that I know he's still alive, and around, means I may just attach myself to him like a limpet. But that's because of who he is. I'd gladly support *him* rather than the other way around. But I'm damned well going to do my best to make sure he doesn't fade into obscurity again. A *laborer*!" she added in a bitter tone.

"I understand your point," Herzer said, smiling. "I'll get you moved to permanent quarters. Which are, frankly, just as bad as these. Training starts day after tomorrow. Tomorrow you'll be processed for your positions, meet some of the rest of the team, things like that. We'll be training hard; we don't have much time."

"Welcome to Icarus Base, I'm Commander Herzer Herrick," Herzer said, looking out at the group. Everyone had been issued coveralls in the color of their field—red for pilots, green for computer techs and blue for engineering—and had almost automatically gathered into their specialties. He noticed that Linda was snugged right up against Geo Keating and the two, with Evan listening, had been engaged in a low-voiced conversation right up until he mounted the dais.

"I'd do the whole 'thank you' thing," Herzer continued. "But each of you is here for your own reasons, some of you for the money, some for the good of mankind as you see it, and some for . . . odder reasons," he finished, looking at Joie and Linda. Fitting Joie, who was a seven-foot-tall woman with fully functional wings, had been a challenge. He could just imagine what it was going to be like getting her into a space suit. "But you've all agreed to the mission so let's talk about that for a minute."

He flipped up the cover on the easel to a simple map of the ship.

"When I got this mission dumped in my lap, I had a hard time figuring out what the attack point should be," he admitted. "The obvious balance point seems to be the control room. However, shuttles can be overridden and manually piloted. So you can't ensure control of the fuel supply from the control room. The ship, itself, however, is unimportant. What is important is the fuel. Who controls the flow of the fuel, wins. The mission, therefore, will be twofold. The shuttles can be demobilized by removal of critical components, notably the helium injectors for their fusion plants. Spare injectors are located in Maintenance," he added, pointing to a point on the upper third ring. "Initial action will be to secure one or more shuttles, depending upon who lands where, then to secure Maintenance. Once Maintenance, and the injectors, are secure, we will begin taking and sabotaging the rest of the shuttles. Up to five shuttles will be maintained to supply the Coalition plants with fuel and bring up reinforcements and remove wounded. In addition, if personnel permit, the engine room will be secured and control room systems will be destabilized by control of secondary nodes," he finished, pointing first to engine room and then to points on the ship.

"I anticipate that New Destiny will attempt to retake the shuttles when they determine our plan," he said, shrugging. "We'll work to cluster the shuttles near Maintenance and hold them. However, if we have control of one functional shuttle, and New Destiny has none, I'll be happy. We can resupply and reinforce indefinitely; they'll be stuck."

"What about teleport?" one of the female pilots asked.

"One of the first questions *I* asked," Herzer said with a grin. "The ship never comes inside lunar orbit and porting out that far is unstable. As to porting within the ship, Councilwoman Travante will be accompanying us and will enforce a teleport block. It will only hold for us, but we anticipate a New Destiny Key-holder being on their side and so we'll probably be blocked as well.

"I'd like to talk a bit about mission concept," Herzer continued. "Each of the techs will be assigned to a strike team. You will be present to give engineering and computer support while on the ship. Strike team members will be minimally trained in shipboard systems but they're primarily going to be training in space combat, which is going to occupy their time and more. Each of the team commanders will be responsible for attainment of a specific goal and will call for your support when necessary. You'll begin training with your teams in the latter part of the program. A 'good fit' will probably be essential but the bottom line is that the team leader, who will be a Blood Lord officer or NCO, will be in command. That chain runs up to me and then, in *very* rare cases, to Councilwoman Travante. If there are differences at the team level, try to keep them at the team level. If you cannot handle your team commander in training, we'll try to find a better fit. But you need to try to fit, first. I've had much the same conversation with the team commanders, by the way.

"Pilots, your team commander is Joie," he said, gesturing at the bird-woman. "Joie is a former intel agent. Do *not* let her soft side fool you, if you piss her off she will beat the crap out of you. If you've ever been hit by a goose wing you know what I mean."

There was a chuckle at that and the pilots, who had been more or less ignoring the bird-woman in their midst, now looked at her with interest. Joie gave Herzer a cold look and then went back to her normal expression of calculated indifference.

"Evan Mayerle," Herzer continued, pointing at Evan. "Stand up, Evan. Evan Mayerle will be in charge of the engineers and engineering questions. Courtney Boehlke will be in charge of the computer techs and computer issues. That's for pre-mission support and on the mission if there's a question you can't answer. And if Evan or Courtney can't answer it, we'll kick it through the whole group.

"Pre-mission items. We're going to be training a lot and we're going to be training here. I know that the quality of the quarters and chow are . . . well, they suck," he said, pausing for the chuckles. "I'm working on the chow. There's not much we'll be able to do about the facilities. We'll only be here for about a month and a half and most of the time all you'll want is a rack anyway. If any of you have the time and energy to improve your quarters, feel free within the materials available.

"Last point before I start taking the billion and one questions." He flipped a cover off the easel and pointed to a simple representation of the solar system.

"The refueling ship is actually headed *out* from the region of the Sun right now, having slingshotted around Mercury. Our intercept point will be in this region," he added, pointing to an area off-set from the Moon. "The celestial designation system that the ship uses was developed in the twenty-third century, when there was a good bit of space travel, and is extremely helio-centric, or so I'm told. The people more familiar with space can explain it better than I can, but the intercept point will be east of the Sun and west of the Moon."

"Herzer," Edmund said, walking through the door. It was after midnight and Herzer was knee deep in paperwork. "If I told you once, I told you a thousand times, all work and no play . . ."

"Then you should have given me a different mission," Herzer said, tossing down his fountain pen and squirting ink all over the paper. "Crap! Now I'm going to have to redo those!"

"You ever heard of 'staff,' boy?" Edmund asked. "You should be signing them, not doing the write-ups."

"When I get one, I'll use it," Herzer pointed out. "Nobody thought to check what sort of casualties there were in the staff. Most of these are requests for personnel. I'm doing it until I get a facilities commander; Carson was handling both loads but he had time to set it up."

"Noted," Edmund said. "I'll make sure you get what you ask for. Don't just ask for what you need, okay?"

"Got it," Herzer said, grimacing. "Boss, can you try to get me a *real* command some day? Not this harum-scarum, thrown into the breach bullshit? I'm getting really tired of being the forlorn hope, you know?"

"I know," Edmund said, sitting down wearily. "I'd intended to move you to Second Legion pretty soon. There are a dozen places I'd like to put you, but I figured you deserved a real command for a while. Not exactly a vacation, but better than this shit. Hell, why am I abusing you about all work and no play? I'm the one here when I should be safe in the arms of Morpheus."

"Rack out here," Herzer suggested. "Or, maybe not. The facilities suck. The food sucks. The training is going to really suck. Morale is going to be a bitch to maintain, especially since everybody thinks they're going to die."

"Do you think it's that bad?" Edmund asked.

"No," Herzer admitted. "Unless New Destiny has the same plan. I'm going to try to avoid direct conflict as much as possible and build forces as much as possible. At the same time, I don't want more people up there than we can evac if we have to. Twenty-five at a time is the max, *if* we don't lose a pilot. Sixteen to twenty-hour turn time. If we take heavy casualties, I'm pulling back to two ships and riding it out."

"Oh, how fascinating," Geo said, looking at the hand-printed schematic. "They use Tammen field sequencers!"

The various teams had broken out into their specialties for a week and having completed the first block of training on shuttle-board systems the engineers were looking over the shipboard systems. And finding various quaint equipment that had them chuckling at all hours.

"I don't even know what a Tammen field sequencer is," Linda admitted, leaning over his shoulder to read the specifications of the system. "Oh, my, it's only rated to one gigawatt! I'm not sure that could even *turn* the ship except in geologic time."

The engineering team had been given the ground floor of one of the wooden buildings and that was now scattered with various bits and pieces of equipment. Some of the material was original equipment used in the *Excelsior* that had been found around Norau, but most of it was plastic and wood mock-ups created by the previous team. The walls were covered in blackboards that had diagrams and equations on them, and down the middle were several tables. The entire engineering team was gathered around, watching Geo cluck over the ship's antiquated systems.

"The Tammen didn't use intermediate field generators," Evan said, chuckling. "It was a late addition to the ship, anyway, used for reactionless vector control. They were additional thrusters, in other words, for fine attitude control. They've got a fraction of the output of the ion drive or the lat thrusters."

"They don't have to, though," Geo said, shaking his head. "I always liked the Tammen design; it was very robust. And with some tinkering it's capable of much higher output. I wrote a paper about it that I don't think I ever published."

"How?" Evan asked. The Tammen field generators were a secondary system whose primary control node actually ran through Engineering. Assuming they captured Engineering, that would give them latitude control. Especially if Geo could "soup them up."

"The reason Tammens didn't use intermediate generators was that the theory didn't work for them in the twenty-fourth century," Geo said, looking over at Linda. "Why?"

"I'm not . . ." Linda said, then frowned. "Ah, the tertiary chaos equations of field junctions weren't worked out until . . . 2679 by . . . by . . ."

"Izakaiah Romanov," Evan said, grinning. Geo was always playing the "professor" game with the two.

"You're so far beyond me," Paul Satyat said, shaking his head. Satyat was the designated engineering tech for Team Van Krief, a short, stocky brunet with burly hands and shoulders. He had studied various forms of engineering throughout history but only brushed on quantum engineering practices. He was more than capable of doing the nuts and bolts work, but the theoretical side left him cold.

"Same here," Nicole Howard admitted. Nicole was, arguably, the prettiest of the several females on the mission. She was medium height with long blonde hair, dark tanned skin, greenish blue eyes and long, shapely legs. But most guys didn't look much beyond a truly phenomenal chest. For all that, she was smart as a whip and, if anything, better at the nuts and bolts work than anyone but Evan. She actively enjoyed tinkering with equipment and her hands showed it, being rather overdeveloped and strong for the rest of her looks, with broken fingernails and heavy calluses. "And I don't see how you can rebuild one to generate intermediate fields," she added, leaning over Geo from the other side and running a finger over one part of the schematic. "They collapse without an Izakaiah transform module. And I don't know about you, but off the top of my head I don't know where I can scrounge one."

Linda looked across Geo and gave her a cool look that Nicole either didn't notice or pretended not to.

"Oh, we'll have to build a module from scratch," Geo admitted, leafing through the ship's documents, oblivious to the two gorgeous women pressed on either side of him. "But it's mostly a matter of setting up a transform equation for generation and the materials. There's a xatanium injector that's used for the latitudinal thrusters and . . . hmm . . ."

"Geo?" Linda said, gently, after the pause had stretched out. "We're still looking over the ship systems, here. Maybe we should worry about third-form equations later?"

"Oh, very well," Geo said, smiling at her sunnily. "But it's all very fascinating! Much better than building walls!"

Evan looked up at the door on the end as there was a tap,

then walked over. There was an L shaped curtain around the door so no one could see in, and he entered the small alcove to undo the bolts and locks.

"Yes?" he asked the Blood Lord guard on the stoop.

"Message from the dwarves," the Blood Lord said, trying not to grin. "Time for Miss Howard to get fitted."

"Aaaaah!" Nicole yelled from inside. "Not *me!*"

"Time to face it, Nicole," Evan said, trying not to grin back at the guard.

"Ow!" he heard behind him and a slap. Then a moment later Nicole came to the door, her face set.

"One damned word . . ." she said, tightly.

"What was the slap?" Evan asked, trying *very* hard not to grin.

"Paul," was all she said, striding out the door.

Herzer cleared his throat and tapped on the door cautiously.

"Yes?" Megan said as he stuck his head around the edge of the door.

The computer techs had a room in the team headquarters building, since there were only a limited number of interfaces in the ship. Megan and Courtney were bent over one of the shuttle interfaces, puzzling over a list of icons.

"Time," Mike said, nodding at her.

"Oh, crap," Megan said in her most unladylike tone. "I guess I've got to get it over with, don't I?"

"Yep," Herzer said, surreptitiously scratching at his crotch, keeping the movement out of sight behind the door. "Especially since they're working on a full armor suit for you. You're scheduled right after Nicole. So . . ."

"I'd better go get . . . ready," Megan said, frowning.

"It's not that bad," Herzer assured her. "If *I* could do it . . ."

"I'm going, I'm going," Megan said with a sigh. "See you in a few hours, Courtney."

"Okay," Courtney replied, trying not to smile. "Have fun."

"Just wait until it's your turn," Megan said tightly.

CHAPTER SEVENTEEN

Over the millennia there had been various types of space suits used. One of the most popular prior to the development of field generation suits had originally been developed by a political entity called the Soviet Union. The Mir suit had only a single entry and exit point and the user donned it by climbing through a port on the back and then sitting in it cross-legged. It was more of a small ship than a true "suit" but it was popular because it was robust and *very* unlikely to fail.

However, it was a pure microgravity system and impossible to move around in with any sort of gravity. The Icarus team required suits that could move from microgravity to the full auto-grav of the personnel portions of the ship. Of all the choices, the "leopard" suit was the most suitable given their time constraints.

The Leopard was, essentially, a whole body glove that fit like a second skin. Using multiple layers of fabrics it transferred off heat, prevented loss of air and shielded the body from heat and radioactivity. However, it had to be *absolutely* skin tight since any air pockets would tend to create bulges. If they were small they would cause small reduced air-pressure areas that ranged from painful to actively dangerous; the low-level vacuum could cause anything from small "hickeys" to bleeding through the skin. Larger pockets tended to be less painful—the suit would only allow so much bulging so their vacuum level was lower—but due to the shape of the human body they tended to migrate to joints. There the swelling of the suit caused it to become rigid at the joint, reducing or eliminating movement.

Getting it absolutely skin tight was the hard part. The only way to do that was to either have the user around while the inner liner of the suit was constructed, a multihour process that required near absolute stillness, or have a full-body model of the user.

Given their time constraints, and the difficulty of staying still for hours, Peterka had insisted on using the full-body model method. The problem being, it was, basically, a plaster model of the body at skin level.

First the user would be covered in a thick layer of plaster and cloth. After that had set, the form was cut away and removed. Then a "statue" of the user was cast in the form from a rubber mixture. There were various lumps put in places to mimic items like the catheter bag and water carrier that would be inside the suit. Once the statue was prepared, the seamstresses, including now Mirta, carefully constructed the suits, layer by layer, on the statues.

Really, when all was said and done, the only problem came down to step one: making the mold.

"Okay, I'm ready," Megan said, stepping out of the shower wearing only a robe.

"Not quite," Herzer said, grimacing and holding up the jar of petroleum jelly.

"I cannot believe this," Megan replied, slipping off the robe and standing in front of him, naked.

"You're still wet in places," Herzer said, trying not to stare at her fully shaved body. He was still itching from where his "shaving" was growing back in.

"Help me?" Megan said after a moment, holding out a towel with a slight, unhappy, smile.

"You're going to be okay with this?" Herzer asked as he carefully dabbed at some wet spots.

"I'll live," Megan said, gritting her teeth. "I can handle a bunch of dwarves leering at me. I don't have to like it."

"I'm sure they won't leer," Herzer promised.

"And I want you to be there to make sure," Megan said, picking up the jar of jelly and scooping out a double fingerful. "Please?"

"Okay," Herzer replied, picking up the jar in turn. "Do your back?"

"And various other spots," Megan admitted, slapping the petroleum jelly on her arm.

The plaster would, of course, adhere to anything it set on. The petroleum jelly, which had to be rubbed on in a very thin layer all over the body, was to ensure the plaster would release the user's skin. By the same token, any body hair would be ripped off when the form was removed. Thus the full body shave.

Herzer *tried* to act as if slowly rubbing petroleum jelly all over Megan's body was nothing but another job. He was not, however, that good an actor.

"Herzer," Megan said, huskily, "you're just supposed to be putting on a thin layer. Not rubbing it in lovingly."

"Sorry," Herzer said, lifting his hand. "Maybe you should do the back of your thighs."

"I think I can get the rest," Megan admitted, breathing in and out deeply. "Although, there's a nasty kink in my neck . . ."

"Maybe later," Herzer said, stepping back and turning away.

"I'm sorry, honey," Megan said, reaching a hand out and touching his arm. "Sooner or later, we're going to get some *time*."

"Bet on it," Herzer said, not looking at her. "Soon. Certainly as soon as the mission's done. I'm going to insist on some leave. For *both* of us. No political deals, no missions. Just . . . time."

"I'd like that," Megan admitted, smiling. "Maybe go up to the mountains by Raven's Mill? It'll be fall by then; we can watch the leaves turn or something."

"Or something," Herzer admitted, finally turning to look at her with a grin.

"Definitely the something," Megan admitted, rubbing the last of the jelly onto her lower legs and feet. "I guess I'll have to do my soles when I get in there."

"What a beastly experience," Nicole said, walking into the changing room. There was a dogleg that kept anyone from peeking in but no door and they could hear the bustling and talk of the dwarves in the far room. Dwarf mods gave them incredibly deep voices for their size and they tended to talk in Dwarvish, which sounded like a gargle festival.

"Make sure you got *every* bit of body hair," the blonde said, shaking her head angrily. "I didn't. And maybe since you're a counselor they won't ogle. I guess they *have* to cop a feel."

"I'll make sure of that," Herzer said, frowning. "They shouldn't have been ogling *you*. There were supposed to be females present."

"There were," Nicole said, dropping her robe and striding to the shower. "They were the worst."

The baths at Raven's Mill were coed and Herzer had been to them more than once. And he'd occasionally seen girls at least as good looking, or nearly as good looking, as Megan and Nicole in them. But that had removed his higher brain functions, too. He was *very* glad he was dressed at the moment.

"Get your eyes back in your head, lover," Megan said, trying to sound angry.

"Trying," Herzer admitted, looking at her and then away. "Trying."

"Well, let's go," Megan said, picking up the robe and donning it again. "I don't know why I even bother with this thing."

"Please to stand in front of the forms," the lead dwarf said, pointing to two oblong wooden forms on the floor of the room. "Feet spread shoulder width apart."

The fitting room was in the dwarf building, near the side door Herzer had found the first time he'd visited the facility. It was a large room with work benches ranging down one side and half finished "statues" down the other. Herzer could see his own near the far door. The statues, of course, lacked a head, but someone had perched a manikin head on Herzer's and painted it with a mustache and goatee.

Megan stepped up to the forms and spread her feet apart.

"Bit more," the dwarf said, looking her over appraisingly. "That's about right."

The forms were attached to sliding blocks and the dwarf adjusted them to the distance of her stance, then nodded.

"Please step in the forms and disrobe," he said, stepping away as she did so.

The forms already had plaster in them and Megan stepped into the material cautiously. It squished up between her toes and she worked them cautiously, then took off her robe and handed it to Herzer.

"Please spread your arms out and down," the dwarf said, taking one hand and positioning her arms. "Spread your fingers wide," he added, splaying her hand. "And try to hold that. Try not to breathe in and out too deeply."

Two dwarves came up with rubber forms in their hands. They were vaguely blister shaped and Megan frowned at them as two more dwarves stepped forward and, removing strips of plaster-impregnated cloth from the forms, they began to wind the cloth up her legs.

"What are those?" Megan asked.

"They're for where the catheter bag and water blister go," Herzer said as one dwarf slapped the adhesive-covered water bag on her back and the other slid the catheter bag form onto her inner thigh. High.

"Watch your damn hands," Megan snapped, looking down at the dwarf.

"You want this in the right spot, mistress, or not?" the dwarf asked, smoothing down the edges of the moldable-rubber device. She wasn't sure if the dwarf was a he or a she; both sexes had beards.

"Just *watch* the hands," Megan said, caustically.

She stood still as the dwarves, more now working on her body and arms, starting with fingers, constructed what was to all intents and purposes a whole body cast. Solid gobs of plaster were slapped in her underarms and she nearly swore when more was thrust into the area between her buttocks.

"Not much fun," Herzer said, soothingly. "I know, trust me. I had to have . . . parts sort of . . ."

"Glued," one of the dwarves said with a snigger.

"Glued up," he finished, frowning. "That was lots of fun to remove, I've got to tell you. There's still bits drying in places. And the discussion about . . . which way to glue it wasn't funny."

"You left some hairs, here," one of the dwarves said, looking up at a very intimate spot in her crotch. "It's going to smart when we take this off."

"Just get it over with," Megan snapped as the dwarf took a handful of plaster and smeared it on. "God, I hate this," she added, closing her eyes.

Finally the cast was fully formed and the dwarves took rods and inserted them into hard points on the wrists, then into holders on the floor.

"Can I relax now?" Megan asked.

"Just lean your hands on the rods," the chief dwarf said, nodding. "It will take about ten minutes to fully set. Then we'll cut you out."

"You okay?" Herzer asked, coming around in front of her. He'd been circling the working dwarves, giving baleful looks to any he suspected of ogling. But, really, the dwarves had been fully concentrated on the job. Or at least making a good show of it.

"Fine," Megan said, turning her head awkwardly to look at him. "Just feeling ... rather vulnerable. I don't like that."

"It'll be over soon," Herzer assured her.

"I'm wondering," Megan said. "About the crotch and butt region. There's no way to prevent air pockets there ..."

"You'll wear a sort of underwear," the chief dwarf said, going over to one of the benches and picking up a rubbery pair of underpants that looked suspiciously like a chastity belt. "It will fit ... closely in your crotch and between the buttocks and it has soft-plastic seals along the edges. There's a viscous fluid in it that will harden under vacuum, sealing anywhere along the edges that leaks and displacing any air in the region. You'll have the same stuff on your skin under the suit; it'll take care of any minor bubble areas."

"This is just so much fun," Megan said, shaking her head.

After watching the clock for what seemed an interminable time, the chief dwarf finally stepped forward and rapped his knuckles on the cast.

"It's good," he said, nodding at the helpers. "Start taking it off."

The cast had to be sawn off in pieces, using small hand saws. That took about thirty minutes but finally all the cuts were made and the parts started coming off, starting from the top.

"Ow!" Megan snapped as the first part came off over her head. "I didn't even know I *had* hairs there!"

"You were supposed to shave *everywhere*," the supervisor said with a sigh. "I don't know *how* many times you people were told that, but ..."

"OW!" Megan shouted as the crotch portion was removed.

"Think of it as a whole body wax," Herzer said, trying to be soothing.

"Did *you* get all your hairs?" Megan snapped back.

"No," Herzer admitted. "And, yeah, that hurt like hell. But not as much as getting the glue off of parts ..."

CHAPTER EIGHTEEN

Herzer took a seat in the front of the stands just before the opening of the first space combat class. The stage in front of him had some of the props Peterka had used, including a pick mace, a small buckler, some metal plates with straps attached and suit parts on a table. The mangled suit of armor was standing next to the table. Just as he sat down, Van Buskirk strode out onto the stage and took a position of parade rest.

"Welcome to Icarus Base and all that," the captain said, looking at the assembled group of Blood Lords. Fifteen of them, mostly from his own company, had been designated as members of the five "first in" teams; those that had techs associated with them and were guaranteed to fly. In addition, a sixth "Blood Lord pure" team had been assembled under Sergeant Graff. The fifth "first in" team leader was Lieutenant Mike Massa, his Third Platoon leader.

Massa was medium height with brown hair and eyes and the burly look commonplace among the Blood Lords. The lieutenant was newly promoted and about to be rotated out of the platoon leader slot. An experienced fighter, he had been among the group of Blood Lords that had assaulted the enemy camp during New Destiny's abortive invasion of Norau. A sergeant at the time, his actions in first taking and then closing the north gate had led to a field promotion and a tour through Officer's Basic then to Van Buskirk's company.

There were another sixty volunteers from Raven's Mill who had responded to the "mission involving a high level of risk" call. It was unlikely that there would be sufficient suits made for all of them by the time the fuel shuttles started landing, but they would form the reinforcement corps for the mission.

"You all know the nature of the mission and you've previously been briefed on the plan," the captain said, looking around at the short company of elite infantry. "This is about *how* we're going to do it."

He picked up the pick mace off the table and swung it around in a figure eight.

"Listen to me very carefully," Van Buskirk said, continuing to swing the mace. "Space is an unforgiving, unremorseful, coldhearted, murdering bitch. Remember that. If you keep that thought in the front of your brains from the time the shuttles take off until you're back on the ground, we *might* not be sponging you out of your armor!" He ended the opening with a snarl and then swung the mace, hard, into the armor. The spike punched into the shoulder.

"That soldier is now *dead*," Bus said, wrenching the mace out of the armor and tossing it on the table. "You're used to having to hit a vital point and of only protecting vital points. To fight until you die or drop, no matter how many minor wounds you take. Look at Herzer; he's covered in scars from 'near misses.'"

"And some pretty solid hits," someone said in the back of the group.

"Sure," Bus admitted. "But if you get so much as a *finger* cut off in space, you are *dead*. The same, however, goes for the enemy. So you have to get a brand new idea through your heads. The object is not to strike for vitals, but to *breach* your enemy's armor. If you're in vacuum, that is all it will take."

Bus picked the mace back up and swung it at the elbow joint of the armor, breaking the arm backwards and popping the joint.

"That is a kill," he said, continuing with the momentum and hitting at the thigh, driving the spike in deeply. "Kill."

"Should be easy," Sergeant Graff commented.

"Easy to get *dead*," the captain snapped. "That is a kill on *you*, Graff! Most of your body is going to be covered by not much more than a couple of layers of *silk*. Keep that in mind, too! If they get a cut on that suit when you are in vacuum, you're going to get bled out in a few seconds, even if it's just a slice."

"Got it," Graff said, nodding seriously.

"This is going to be our primary weapon," Van Buskirk said, holding the mace aloft. "You're used to using your gladii, but this is much better for what we're going to be doing. The pick is for hitting solid parts of the armor." He spun in place and slammed the pick, full force, into the chest of the armor, puncturing it with a "ping" sound. "The flat head is for helmets," he continued, yanking the mace out and slamming it into the helmet, knocking the latter askew, "or anywhere you think you can pop a seal. Anyone got any thoughts on what is wrong with my demonstration?"

"If you're in vacuum, you're going to be in microgravity," Lieutenant Massa said, soberly. "And if you strike like that you'll go flying away."

"Agreed," Bus said, flipping the mace through a series of figure eights. "I don't think we're going to be doing *any* full microgravity fighting. The interiors are all under gravity and on the surface you're going to be using mag-boots. So you set up the figure eight and let the mass of the mace do the work." He ended by slamming the mace into the undamaged arm, clearly popping the elbow joint.

"If you *are* in microgravity," he continued, "the techniques get a little complex. There's little or no way to get any sort of formation. What we will be doing is training in teams, with the idea that two of you will gang up on one of them, if possible, and do unto them before they do unto you."

He picked up one of the metal plates and walked over to the suit, tossing it in the direction of the chest. The plate, which was clearly a magnet, stuck to the front of the suit. He then picked up the small buckler and showed that it was magnetic as well.

"The ship uses a fair amount of stuff the magnets will stick to on the interior and exterior," Bus said, walking up to the suit and popping the magnet off. "The basic technique will be for one or more of you to target one of them. You then launch very carefully from your position and slap one of these magnets, or the buckler, onto the target. Then you hit them, once, and let the momentum push you away in the most controlled manner you can. If you don't get a kill, don't stick around. Grappling is a losing proposition. Keep moving. There's no up or down in microgravity; use that to your advantage. Remember, if one of these guys is drifting by you can grab a boot or whatever, slam your pick into their *ankle* joint, and that's an effective kill. You can use the mace to move around, as well, by hooking into anything that's sticking out.

"When we get to the water portion, as soon as they're done with our suits, we'll start practicing on that. For now, you'll start working out with the mace and getting used to its uses and limitations. There are two other weapons I've suggested to our friends the dwarves." That brought a laugh. The dwarves were notably gruff with everyone. He held up a large cylinder.

"This is a magnetic punch," Bus said, sticking the device onto the front of the suit and firing it. There was a clanging sound and the device flew backwards with a large spike sticking out of the front. There was, however, a hole in the suit. Before it had hit the ground the spike had retracted.

"The magnet holds it in place just long enough, in most cases, for the punch to penetrate. It only pops the armor, but remember that in vacuum that's a kill. Then it goes flying off and the spike automatically retracts. If you're in good position, you can remain attached to the lanyard. Otherwise, just let it go and recover it later. It's got five shots using air pressure for the attack and retracting. There will be pressurized bottles to recharge it."

He tossed the punch on the table and picked up a much more complicated device with a backpack and a nozzle. It looked something like a flamethrower with a magazine sticking out the bottom.

"I'm not sure we'll have many of these," he said, pointing it at the back wall. He pulled the trigger and a line of small spikes flew out to stick in the wall. "You'll have to have a good solid position, it's got a bit of a kick so I wouldn't just trust your boots for example, and it's only good against soft targets. But I think they'll probably come in handy at one point or another."

"I want," Massa said, grinning.

"We'll see how many there are," Bus said, nodding. "That's it for now. Each of you will be issued your maces and start training with them this week. As soon as we have suits, and the first in fighters are first in line, we'll start training in the water tank."

"How's it shaping up?" the avatar of Edmund asked.

"Pretty good," Herzer admitted. "We've been retraining on the new weapons and that's going well on the grav training level anyway. The engineering teams are pretty well as dialed in as they can be without the actual equipment. Same with the computer techs. The pilots are pretty caustic about their training equipment, but they've learned where all the controls are, anyway. We'll have to see if they can actually fly. And everybody has to go in the water as soon as the suits are done."

"That should be interesting," Edmund said, smiling. "Tao is on the way over with a courier package. You and Megan should find it interesting."

"I look forward to it," Herzer said, frowning.

"You asked for intel," the council member said, shrugging. "You got intel."

"Sir," Lieutenant Tao said, setting a courier bag on Herzer's desk.

"Thanks, Tao," Herzer said, picking up the pouch and breaking the seals.

Gerson Tao was nearly as large as the commander and, if anything, darker, with slight epicanthic folds by his eyes and lank black hair. He'd been born and raised on the Western Plains and was a noted horseman. He and Herzer had met when Herzer was his instructor at Officer Basic course and had tapped him, along with Amosis Van Krief and Destrang, to accompany Duke Edmund on a "diplomatic mission" to the southern isles. The diplomatic mission had gone badly awry but the then ensign had stuck to his salt on the long ride Edmund had sent him on to bring the cavalry. He wasn't the brightest of the three, but he was tough and stubborn. Give him a task and he'd keep battering away at it until something gave.

"I need you to do me a favor," Herzer said, extracting the heavy linen envelope in the pouch and tossing it back. "Shanea has to go back to Washan. Actually, she doesn't *have* to go back, but she deserves a break. I don't suppose you're into shopping?"

"Oh, God," Tao groaned. "What did I do to deserve that?"

"Just show her around town," Herzer said, grinning. "Get a squad of guards and a carriage. Charge both to Megan's accounts. Make sure she doesn't get snatched."

"Will do, sir," the lieutenant said, sighing. "Is there going to be a point where I'm *not* in charge of the baggage, sir? I was *enjoying* being with Second Legion."

"Soon, Tao," Herzer said, grinning. "I'll make sure of it."

"Thanks, sir," Tao said. "Now?"

"If you would," Herzer replied, glancing out the window. "Plenty of time. Catch some lunch with her in Washan, and probably dinner. Just get back here before nine or ten. If you're out later, stay at the councilwoman's quarters and send back word."

"Is this a mission or a date?" Tao asked, grumpily.

"Make up your own mind," Herzer replied, raising an eyebrow to Tao's frown.

"You're serious?" Tao asked, raising his own eyebrow.

"If you screw her up somehow, you'll probably have to explain that to Megan," Herzer said, frowning in turn. "And I'll warn you that if you wrap your heart around that little minx, it's going to get repeatedly broken. But if one thing leads to another, nobody's going to complain."

"Oh," Tao said, suddenly reconsidering the quality of the mission. "Very well, sir."

"And check on Destrang," Herzer said. "He's supposed to be passing this stuff to me, not you."

"Yes, sir," Tao said, nodding. "If that's all."

"Get," Herzer said, finally grinning. "Have fun."

"I'll . . . try," Tao admitted.

When the lieutenant was out of the office, Herzer used a knife to slit the envelope and dumped the contents out on the desktop. There were two inner envelopes, unsealed, one with diagrams and the other containing a long, handwritten, note.

He looked at the first diagram and grunted in surprise.

"Orderly!" he yelled at the door.

"Sir?" a Blood Lord private asked, opening the door as Herzer hastily covered the diagrams with the outer envelope.

"Get Councilwoman Travante, Evan Mayerle and . . . hmm . . ." He lifted up the envelope for consideration and then shrugged. "And Captain Van Buskirk. There's something they need to see."

"Now that is the . . . most bizarre space suit I've ever seen," Van Buskirk said, flipping through the diagrams.

"It's very functional," Evan said musingly. "It's apparently based upon an ancient *diving* suit."

Herzer wasn't sure where Megan's dad had gotten the diagrams for the orc armor but they were complete drawings, obviously copies of the design documents. The body of the suit was, essentially, a cylinder. The entire top could be removed with bolts and the helmet was another cylinder with circular viewports out of the front and sides. The arms and legs were what was interesting, though. Each of the joints had some sort of armature on it.

"What is that?" Herzer asked, pointing at an arm joint.

"Apparently it's attached to an oil-filled piston," Evan said, flipping over one of the diagrams and pointing to a close-up of the joint. "It maintains smooth movement even in vacuum. Ingenious design."

"Those things are going to be hard to penetrate," Van Buskirk pointed out. "Even with the maces. I'm not sure the punch will work at all."

"Don't be," Evan said, pointing to a notation on the diagram. "That's eighteen-gauge steel. It has to be for weight reasons. Use heavy steel on those things and they'd weigh in at about a ton. Penetrating them is going to be *easy*."

"And in vacuum that will matter," Bus said, shaking his head. "In atmosphere, they're going to be a bitch. The *body* of the orc isn't going to be anywhere near the surface of the armor."

"I don't think we're going to have problems," Herzer said, considering the design carefully. "Whoever thought this suit up was an idiot."

"Why?" Megan asked. "They look pretty tough to me."

"Look at those joints," Herzer said, grinning. "One hit on those things and you're going to have a frozen joint. The documents said that they're mostly going to be armed with polearms. Two polearms to one pick-axe or military hammer and each will have a heavy knife, more like a chisel really. But we've got other problems." He waved the text documents and frowned.

"What?" Megan asked.

"There's going to be one of those Changed elves with them," Herzer said, still frowning. "That right there will be a nightmare. But they're also going to be using some sort of scorpionoid. The document states that it will be different from the variety that attacked us but in an unknown way. Just 'different.'"

"Modified for vacuum?" Van Buskirk mused. "Can Celine do that?"

"Probably," Evan said. "The ones that were killed here and in Washan had carbon polymer plates. You could probably seal them against vacuum. But one good hit and they'll be squirting ichor."

"This mission is really gonna suck," Bus said, sighing.

"That it will," Herzer admitted.

"Have you worked out the teams, yet?" the captain asked, changing the subject.

"Yep," Herzer said. "And you're going to like them. The suits are going to be done day after tomorrow. At that point, we'll start training on microgravity. I'll announce the teams tomorrow at dinner."

Herzer waited until the meal was done to announce the teams.

Chow had improved dramatically after a few blistering messages to the War Department. Cooks had been brought in "for the duration" as had a much better quality of food. Tonight's dinner had been standing-rib roast with buttered potatoes and broccoli. Dessert was a layer cake. Not chocolate, unfortunately.

When people were working on the cake and coffee he stood up and waved his arms for attention.

"Okay," he said, clearing his throat. "As you might have noticed from the training schedule, we do *not* have training scheduled tonight."

He grinned as there was a cheer. For the last three weeks training had continued into the night, mostly on navigation around the complicated ship.

"The reason is that we're about to start microgravity training and it's time to break up into assault teams. Team leaders come up front," he said, waving to the area in front of his table. "And as I call off your name, form on your team leaders, please." He picked up an envelope and opened it, clearing his throat again.

"Team Herrick," he said, looking up, "that would be me." He waited for the chuckles to die down and then looked back at the paper. "Mission Commander: Councilwoman Megan Travante. Icarus CO: Commander Herzer Herrick. Comp Tech: Courtney Boehlke. Engineer: Evan Mayerle. Pilot: Joie Dessant. Blood Lords: Sergeant Layne Crismon and Corporal Yetta Barchick."

Herzer waited until the group had assembled by his table and then looked back at the paper.

"Team Van Buskirk: Captain Arthur Van Buskirk, Icarus XO. Comp Tech: Jacklyn Pledger. Engineer: Linda Donohue. Pilot: Michelle Lopez. Blood Lords: Triari Sergeant Callius Doclu, Corporal Lief Mota, Private Ignacy de Freitas.

"Team Van Krief. Team Leader: Lieutenant Amosis Van Krief. Comp Tech: Richard Ward. Engineer: Paul Satyat. Pilot: Kristina York. Blood Lords: Line Sergeant Doo-Tae Rubenstein, Sergeant Eaton Yamada, Private Silvano Bijan.

"Team Cruz. Team Leader: Lieutenant Brice Cruz. Comp Tech: None." They were short one computer technician and the teams were based on only having five engineers when six shuttles were expected. "Engineer: Geo Keating. Pilot: Irvin Sanchez. Blood Lords: Triari Sergeant Ferdous Dhanapal, Line Sergeant Gyozo Nasrin, Corporal Manos Berghaus, Private Gustave Sesheshet.

"Team Massa. Team Leader: Lieutenant Michael Massa. Comp Tech: Manuel Sukiama. Engineer: Nicole Howard. Pilot: Josten Ram. Blood Lords: Line Sergeant Arje Budak, Corporal Feng fu Nordbrandt, Private Rashid Whitlock.

"Team Graff. Team Leader: Triari Sergeant Ebenezer Graff, Line Sergeant Buu Kiem Topak, Sergeant Gonzalo Kamsing, Corporal Slodoban Toralva, Corporal Genrich Khologdori, Private Lambis Pepynakt, Private Viktor Williams."

He looked up from the teams and nodded in understanding. Everyone had already formed bonds based on their training with peers. Now they were expected to get used to these relative strangers. The groups had gotten accustomed to wearing their individual uniforms and the mixture seemed . . . odd. Geo, surrounded by Blood Lords, seemed especially out of place. Linda was looking from Geo up to Herzer. The latter looks would have been deadly if eyes shot fire, and her face was fixed in a frown.

"You need to get used to these teams," Herzer said. "In general, during the mission, this is how you'll be performing your individual tasks. The Blood Lords who are with you are there to keep you alive. By the same token, the techs are there to make sure the mission actually gets accomplished and to handle shipboard systems. This is the group you're going to be moving, fighting and living with. Everyone has a purpose and you're going to have to learn to work with each other and trust each other to do the job. Otherwise, we might as well pack it up and go home. So figure on spending most of your training and free time with your teams. That's all I've got. I'd suggest you guys get acquainted."

He walked back to his place and sat down as Courtney came over and perched on the end of the table.

"Hello, Councilwoman," Courtney said, holding out her hand

to Megan. "I'm Courtney Boehlke. I'm going to be the computer tech on your team."

"And I'm Evan Mayerle," Evan said with a grin, holding out his own hand. "Pleased to meet you. Who's the big lug sitting next to you?"

Megan grinned and solemnly shook their hands in turn.

"I don't know who he is," Megan said, thumping Herzer on the arm. "He followed me home, though, so I think I have to keep him."

"Here comes trouble," Layne Crismon whispered from behind Herzer, who looked up to see Linda striding over with a furious expression on her face.

"Herzer, I have a bone to pick with you," Linda said, leaning over the table so far it looked as if she was going to spit in his face.

"Let's take it into the corner," Herzer said, gesturing to the far side of the dining hall.

When he'd gotten out of earshot of the teams, he stopped and pivoted to face her.

"It's about Geo?" he asked, raising an eyebrow.

"I was *supposed* to be with him the whole time!" Linda spat. "You *promised* me that! And his ship . . ."

"Doesn't have a computer tech," Herzer said, nodding. "So you think you should switch with one of the Blood Lords?"

"Yes!" Linda snapped.

"And double up our short engineers," Herzer pointed out. "On a ship that could be taken out by New Destiny if we get very unlucky?"

"What do you mean?" Linda said, pausing.

"It's possible that one or more teams may get wiped out on insertion," Herzer pointed out with glacial calm. "Or at a later time. Hell, we may *all* get wiped out. But I'm mostly worried about insertion; we don't have any control over the shuttles until we get to the ship. So I'd like you to take a look over at Geo's team."

"What am I supposed to see?" Linda said after a few moments.

"Cruz is one of the few people I handpicked for this mission," Herzer said, gesturing at the team leader, who was listening to the old physicist and nodding his head. "That's because he's a stone-cold killer who uses his head. He actively enjoys bringing destruction to the enemy and he's very good at it. Ferdous Dhanapal was part of Class One at the Blood Lord Academy. He's never going to get any higher than Triari because he's dumb as a brick about everything except killing and doing the mission. He's the guy that 'fight until you die or drop' was written for. Gyozo Nasrin has won the silver eagle twice, once in Raven's Mill and the second time in Balmoran. Again, a cold hard killer with not an ounce of quit in him. He's one of the volunteers because if it has a 'high risk of loss of life' it means it has a high risk of getting it stuck in and he *loves* getting in a brawl. Shall I continue?"

"You put all the best fighters around him," Linda said, nodding.

"I'd, frankly, thought about reloading with more on my shuttle," Herzer said, shrugging. "But next to Megan and myself, yeah, I think Geo's the one to guard. He *understands* all the theory, and the engineering, of the ships. That's going to be important, unless I'm much mistaken. So, which Blood Lord do you want to bump?"

"None," Linda admitted, sighing. "Objection withdrawn."

"Next time assume I have a reason for what I do," Herzer said. "That's always the best way to go with orders. Yeah, you can question. But *after* you obey. Now, go get to know your team. They're going to be what keeps you alive. If you live."

"Thanks for being so positive," Linda said, shaking her head. But she headed back to her team.

"That *was* positive," Herzer said, sighing.

CHAPTER NINETEEN

"Fuck," Herzer muttered as he drifted past Van Buskirk.

Bus tugged lightly on his line to pivot and hit Herzer, hard, on his ankle as he passed.

Herzer got to the end of his own line and was jerked back, drifting more or less helplessly in the middle of the clear lake. The water at this depth was bitterly cold and he kept in mind that he only had about another fifteen minutes of air. So he gave the line another tug and began reeling in to the far wall.

Bus was gliding past on a parabolic arc at the end of his tether. Herzer considered that for a moment, then carefully removed one of the hand magnets. He tied a quick knot in a spare safety line and flicked the magnet towards Van Buskirk's back.

The magnet, unfortunately, missed. But he thought it was a viable technique.

He reeled himself in, retrieved the line and worked his way over to the ladder up to the support building.

The large building was actually a floating dock over the old quarry. It had an open bottom and under it was a large mock-up of portions of the ship where the team was supposed to train for microgravity conditions, including combat. So far, Herzer was pretty sure they weren't going to be able to fight worth a damn. He knew *he* sure as hell couldn't get a feel for it. The only fighter they had that seemed to have a clue was Van Buskirk. Fighting in microgravity was entirely different from normal fighting and nothing that Herzer had tried in the hour-long test had worked. Bus had gotten three strikes in on him, on the other hand.

When he reached the surface he let one of the support crew help him get his armor and helmet off. The armor was standard lorica, carefully padded to prevent wear and laid over the suit and helmet base. The "helmet" was actually a solid piece that lay across the shoulders and dipped down on the front and back to the middle of the chest and just above the shoulder blades. The original design had included a bubble helmet but Herzer had insisted on a metal helmet similar to a barbute with only a heavily constructed clear eye-slit on the front. Goggles could be dropped over the eyeslit when the user was in the bright sun-light of space. Underneath the user wore a fitted cloth cap that buckled under the chin and to which the communicator interface and water tube could be attached.

The first thing that had to come off was the hand-cranked sup-port pack that cooled the user and fed him air. So while the rest came off, Herzer had to deal with rebreathing his own exhaled breaths in the helmet. But the lorica came off quickly and then the helmet was unbuckled from under his arms and lifted over his head.

"I hate that part," he muttered.

"Not much to like about any of this," Bus admitted. "And you look like a lost cow in the water."

"We're going to have to be really careful where we fight," Her-zer said, shrugging. "Blood Lords are good at about three to one on orcs. I don't know how well we'll do against the scorps, but I figure pretty well if they're more or less the same as those we fought in Washan. We only lost one Blood Lord there and I killed three of the damned things. The elf is another question."

"Use the guns," Bus said, shrugging. "Stand off and pump him full of darts if we can."

"There's that," Herzer said, nodding. "If we can. They don't nor-mally stand still to be killed. Well, let's get the rest of the teams on this tomorrow. We'll get the hang of it sooner or later."

"You're overmuscling," Bus said, shrugging. "You're used to using your full strength in combat. You have to wait until you have a very solid platform or have already established movement in the direction so you're compensating against it. It takes practice."

"And we've only got two weeks," Herzer replied tightly. "Like

I said, we're going to have to be careful where we engage. Now let's get out of these damned monkey suits."

"Just think," Bus said as they walked to the changing room, "the next time you get it on, you'll be with Megan."

"Don't remind me," Herzer said, groaning.

"Oh, good lord," Megan said, looking at the handful of antiblister and sealing agent. "Do you know what this looks like?"

Megan was sitting on one of the benches in the microgravity training changing room, her suit crumpled at her feet and her stare fixed on the slippery substance in her hand. It was whitish and viscous and looked *just* like . . .

"At first I thought it looked like . . . something guys produce," Herzer said, taking a large bottle of the material and squirting it into the suit boots. "Then I realized what it was. They just got a bunch of sexual lubrication cream and *told* us it was sealing agent."

"It's not that," Evan argued, stuffing his feet down into the suit and wriggling them around to get the cream he'd already poured in squished around. "I've tested it. It really does a good job on minor seals. And getting in these suits would be hard without it."

"I'm not covering myself in a sexual aid," Megan said definitely.

"It's that or have blisters," Herzer pointed out. "Put it in the suit, Megan. Stress point, remember?"

"I do," Megan said, rubbing the viscous fluid on her leg and wincing. "I am *not ever* going to enjoy this process."

"How are you doing, Geo?" Linda asked as the old engineer walked into the engineering quarters day-room.

They'd been training on microgravity for the last four days, nearly sixteen hours a day. Everyone was getting better in the unusual environment but they had a long way to go. And the training was clearly taking it out of the oldster; he looked worn to a nub.

Since they spent the whole day with their respective teams, she and Geo had taken to meeting in the evenings in the day-room to talk about the engineering aspects of the mission. She found it fascinating to simply sit and listen to him talk about physics for hours, but she was also careful to keep the meetings short. The old man needed his sleep. And, for the same reason, anything else was out.

"Tired," Geo admitted, smiling. "But very much looking forward to getting to the ship. I'm pretty sure I've figured out how to adjust the Tammens to perform intermediate fields. Together with a neural interface from the computer mains, it will mean Megan, at least, will be able to directly manipulate the fusion plant outputs. That's bound to be useful."

"Won't that mean going to each of them and modifying them?" Linda asked, waving him to one of the day-room seats.

"There are two spare Tammens listed in Maintenance," Geo said, shrugging. "And there are four high-energy plasma coils running down the midline for the main thrusters. If we install a field shunt, we can run the full power of all four to the two field generators and draw off at least sixty percent of the fusion bottle power. Four of the Tammens, for that matter, are in the rear section that Herzer intends to secure. If we can modify them, and set up more field shunts in Engineering, we'll be able to get full draw. That means we'll have effective control of the latitude thrust of the ship as well as permitting Megan to use direct power. The way I'll set it up, Reyes won't be able to steal it, either."

"That's going to be useful," Linda said. "Definitely bring it up with Herzer, though, so he can include it in his planning. Now, you were *trying* to explain those binary linking equations last night . . ."

"So where were *you* last night, Tao?" Van Krief asked as she heard the westerner's door shut.

"Washan," Tao called though the connecting bathroom.

"Escort duty again?" Van Krief asked, disparagingly.

"And picking up another intel packet," Tao said, walking through the bathroom and looking at her with a raised eyebrow. "What's eating you?"

"Well, I'm getting ready to go get killed in deep space," Van Krief answered with a frown. "Destrang is hanging around the War Department thinking deep thoughts. And you're . . . swaining."

"Wanna switch?" Tao asked, chuckling. "Seriously, this gig is going to be hell to my career. I feel like I got transferred to the protocol office. And if you think *you're* bitchy about it, you ought to meet Meredith. She can be *really* caustic."

"No, I don't want to switch," Van Krief said. "Among other things, I'm the wrong sex." She paused and thought about that for a moment then shrugged. "Okay, I'm *interested* in the wrong sex."

"I'm not going to complain about trying to keep up with Shanea," Tao said, shrugging in return. "Although it's pretty damned hard. The girl . . . never mind. But, yeah, it's my *job* right now. And how the *hell* do you write that on an efficiency report?"

" 'During the previous six months this officer has performed the hardest and longest missions to the highest possible standards. His stamina and skill are a wonder to the command,' " Van Krief recited sonorously.

"Very funny," Tao said but he had to chuckle. "I don't get what's eating you about it. Give."

He looked at her as her face worked and then shook his head.

"You're still carrying a torch for Herzer?" Tao asked, amazed. "For God's sake, Mo, give it up."

"I guess I have to," the little blonde said bitterly. "It's not like I can compete with a *Council* member, is it?"

"Herzer didn't fall for Megan because she was a Key-holder," Tao pointed out. "And you're a *subordinate*, Mo. Face it, you've spent most of your time around Herzer as one of his troops. Good commanders, and he's a very good commander, don't screw the help. You *know* that!"

"I nearly had him once," Van Krief said, tightly, then shook her head. "God, listen to me. I should be running, not chasing."

"Bingo," Tao said. "And concentrating on *your* mission, not mine. And certainly not that you'd like to be doing with Herzer what I'm doing with Shanea."

"It's more than that," Amosis said, angrily. "You can tell that that little harem bitch is just stringing him along. He's not getting any; you know that, right? So what's *wrong* with me? Why the hell would he stay in that relationship when . . ." She stopped and shook her head.

"Oh, Christo, Mo," Tao said, just as angrily. "Drop it already. You're his subordinate. He's head over heels for Megan. She's in love with him. You're *out*, girl, six different ways. Get *over* it."

"I guess I'll have to," Van Krief said, plumping up her pillows and lying back on the bed. "Now if you'll excuse me, I have some reading to do. I have a very complicated mission to prepare for.

And Herzer's bound to jump my ass if I don't know as much about the ship as he does."

"You go, girl," Tao said, suddenly tired. "And be careful."

"Hey, Paul," Herzer said, as Satyat passed on his way to class. "Getting the hang of wrench turning in micro?"

"Getting there, sir," the engineer said, giving him a half salute and getting prepared for the next question.

"What are the tools to disassemble the helium injector on the main ion cannon?" Herzer asked, pausing.

"Fourteen- and eighteen-millimeter hydrospanners," Satyat said, screwing up his face. It was always a different question and somehow Herzer always hit you with one you weren't prepared for. "Proton injection shield, four-millimeter punch and . . . Shit."

"And a crowbar," Herzer said, smiling faintly. "The lid's got a magseal all the way around and you'll have to pop it at the lower port quadrant if you're on the starboard injector or the starboard on port. If you have a screwdriver, you can try to pry it off. But you're going to have a hard time. And don't use the punch; it's too thin and it'll probably ruin the punch."

"Got it," Paul said, shaking his head. "Do you actually *know* all of our jobs or do you just study for certain questions?"

"Guess," Herzer said, nodding as he walked off.

"Do you ever get any sleep, Herzer?" Edmund asked as his avatar appeared in the commander's office.

"Not much," Herzer admitted, tossing the form he was studying to the desk. He glanced at the chronometer on the wall and blanched when he realized it was three AM. "I've scheduled a rest day for just before the mission; everyone's getting pretty stressed out. And you're one to talk, boss. I've at least got you by a century or so of youth."

"Thanks for mentioning it," Edmund said, sourly. "But I'm on the west coast, three hours behind you. And I'm getting ready for bed."

"What are you doing out there?" Herzer asked, his forehead furrowing.

"Looking at a new collier design," Edmund said. "The builders think they can get about twenty-five percent more stores on her over clippers for about a ten percent reduction in speed. She won't be able to keep up with the fleet, but if it works it will be perfect for cross-ocean and mid-ocean resupply. The Navy's in tight with the east coast designers, though, and they're balking at changing designs. I'm trying to figure out if it's worth the pissing match."

"Life, and the bureaucratic pissing match, goes on," Herzer said, chuckling. "Speaking of which, Megan told me that Aikawa wanted the Icarus mission. Especially after the first team got killed."

"He had a point," Edmund admitted. "Ishtar and Aikawa have been doing the majority of the fighting to this point and they've won. But I've looked at their warmaking style and, frankly, I'm not impressed. I guess when we invade we'll see who's better. But winning counts for a lot. However, they gave Sheida the mission at least in part because most of their elite forces were either decimated by the wars or are still engaged. Frankly, Aikawa's shuren warriors might have been better for space fighting than the Blood Lords. But they're so overextended it's not funny. So we got it. Just do the job and leave the Council to its discussions. If you win, nobody will have any reason to bitch. So what *are* you working on at three AM?"

"All the paperwork I can't keep up with during the day," Herzer said, sighing. "And the training is *not* going well, anyway. I don't think I'll ever figure out microgravity combat."

"Maybe we should have sent mer-men," Edmund said, seriously. "You know that's what they fight in all the time, right?"

"Not exactly," Herzer replied. "They have something to push against: water. In microgravity you don't have diddly. I don't think they'd do any better except at situational awareness. And they couldn't move in the grav areas at all. No, we're just going to have to either figure it out or avoid it. We're doing okay when we're on the hull and can use our boots, but in full microgravity we're still pretty lost. Except Van Buskirk; he's got the moves down from ER before the Fall."

"It's not going to go better if you can't see straight," Edmund said. "Drop the paperwork and go to bed. I don't suppose things are going any better with you and Megan?"

"No," Herzer said, shrugging. "But at least here we're in different beds."

"Lighter, Jacklyn," Van Buskirk signaled as the computer tech soared past him. He was parked in the middle of the underwater cylinder at the end of his safety line, working his team through a fast traverse of a microgravity environment. Of course, there was fast and then there was fast. Too fast to get to your grab point was too fast.

The response from Jacklyn Pledger was a gesture that was universal. The gesture, however, imparted spin and made her miss the crossbar she was aiming for. Fortunately, it was a complete miss since at the speed she was going it would have been bruising to impact.

Bus pulled, lightly, on his safety line, which got him headed in the general direction of the computer tech. He judged his snatch finely and managed to get a hand on her ankle. A very slight tug sent him "up" towards the top of the cylinder but it also spun Jacklyn towards the nearest wall.

He grabbed the cross-member she had been aiming for and turned to watch the shapely computer tech's landing. The water had slowed her speed so she didn't break her wrists when she hit the wall and managed to get her feet under her. As Bus watched she turned clumsily around and began gesturing.

He didn't get all the gestures, but the general gist was apparent.

"Agreed," he signaled, waving to the team on the far wall and the safety divers. "Call the exercise. Surface."

"Fisk this *shit*," Jacklyn said, peeling out of the skin-tight suit. "I am *done*. I am *not* going in that tank one more time!"

"Calm down," Bus said, trying not to stare at the liquid-covered body. The antiblister liquid that filled the suits was remarkably similar to the sort of jelly used for sexual lubrication, which had originally occasioned some bawdy jokes. At this point it was just another pain to be borne since while it made getting the suits on easy, it made taking them off damned hard. At least it had been.

Jacklyn cursed luridly as her hands slipped on the suit and she stood bolt upright, shaking from head to toe.

"I AM SO FISKING OUT OF HERE!" she screamed, quivering.

"Jackie, let me help," Linda said, getting a grip on the slippery suit and yanking it down over the other girl's arms. "Just take a deep breath. We're all tired."

"I can not keep up this pace, okay?" Jacklyn said, turning to the captain with tears in her eyes, holding the suit up to cover her breasts. "I'm not a Blood Lord, okay? I was a computer nerd. I liked playing with old systems. After the Fall I was a damned *waitress*! I can *not* keep going in that tank hour after hour! Get us a God damned *break*, Bus, or I swear I'll quit and FISK the bonus!"

"Same here," Michelle said. The pilot had long brown hair with touches of blonde streaked through it from the sun and a face the near side of beautiful with slight epicanthic folds and high cheekbones. Her green eyes were shadowed and baggy, though. "I'm as dialed in as I can get with the shitty 'simulators' we have. And I'm not going into that damned lake again, either. I'll do the mission, but I'm done with training sixteen hours a day. There's a point where it's overkill and we're past it."

"Ditto," Linda said, her face firm. "I've talked to the other engineers and we're all worn out. The pace is especially killing Geo. He's trying to keep up with all us youngsters and, tough as he is, he hasn't got the stamina. He has to have a break. We all do."

"I've got the message," Bus said, yanking his suit down to his waist. "I'll bring it up, okay? That's all I can do."

"Tell Herzer he can kiss my ass if I'm going into that lake one more time," Jacklyn said, frowning.

"There's going to have to be at least one more exercise," Bus said. "We haven't worked as a group, yet. Can you handle it *once* more?"

"Maybe," Jacklyn said, looking at the others. "But not day in and day out. I'm done with repeatedly hacking systems underwater. I'll play memorization games with the other techs, but the most you're going to get is one or two more exercises and no more than a couple of hours in the water. I need to get my head together about *space*. You're the one that's always pointing out it's not the same."

"I'll see Herzer," Bus said. "This evening."

"Commander Herrick," Captain Van Buskirk said as he entered Herzer's office. It was after training with only a week to go and Herzer was knee deep in signing papers.

"Hey, Bus, why so formal?" Herzer asked, carefully setting his fountain pen down so it wouldn't spill all over the papers.

"'Cause I've got an issue," Bus said, frowning and coming to a position of parade rest. "With all due respect, sir, I think we need to wrap up training *soon*."

"We've got two rest days built in at the end of the week," Herzer said, frowning. "You want to knock off before then?"

"I'd like to have this be the *last* day of microgravity training, sir," Bus replied, seriously. "The Blood Lords can keep up the pace, but the techs and pilots are right on the edge of mutiny. They're all exhausted. Yes, I know that after they knock off you're up to the wee hours still. And *they* know that. It's probably the only reason they haven't mutinied yet. But they're worn out. I especially *strongly* recommend that Geo be taken off the training schedule. There's nothing he really needs to learn at this point. He's still only marginal in microgravity, but if you want him on the mission at *all* you'd better back off. Or he'll be dead."

"Point taken," Herzer said, quietly. "And I already heard the same from Massa. What about you?"

"Me, sir?" Bus asked, raising an eyebrow. "I've got the administrative load of my company to handle so I've been carrying pretty much the same load you have. But I'm a Blood Lord and I'm *used* to that. We get selected for the ability to just *keep going.* The techs were selected *purely* for their knowledge. They're not us."

"Point again," Herzer said, sighing. He glanced at the training schedule on his wall and nodded. "Okay, we'll have one exercise tomorrow. Move up the group move through micro to tomorrow afternoon. In-grav rehearsal in the morning then in the tank in the afternoon. After that, we'll dial back. Morning classes only, afternoons and evenings off. Two days off entirely, then one for prep. Then we go." He looked down at the suddenly irrelevant paperwork and shook his head. "And with that, I'm going to bed. Have Roscoe redo the training schedule in the morning."

"Good call, sir," Bus said, smiling faintly.

"Any more suggestions, captain?" Herzer asked, lightly. "I just realized that, as a commander, you have far more experience than I do. Don't you?"

"I've had a triari and my company for over a year," Bus said, dropping his position of parade rest and settling in a chair. "You've been, what? A line infantryman, a militia advisor, an XO to a mer contingent, a dragon wing XO and an Officer Basic instructor. Notice anything missing in that?"

"Command," Herzer said, grinning thinly. "I've noticed and had a word about it with . . . someone."

"Now, there's another point to it," Bus said, carefully. "In every line segment you've been in combat. I haven't seen an orc since Raven's Mill. So there's something to be said for your career track. But you learn stuff in leadership positions that you've missed. Like there's such a thing as overtraining. So, yeah, you need some command time, bad. Frankly, you needed a company but you're past that at this point. You're looking at a battalion in one of the legions, next."

"If I can get it," Herzer pointed out. "There's going to be a lot of counterpressure from the personnel weenies because I *haven't* had a company command. Or wing command, for that matter."

"Oh, I think you have enough pull to overcome that," Bus said, dryly. "But that's going to create another problem. People are going to see you as having gotten your position because you're Edmund's bag-boy. Not to mention Megan's . . . friend."

"I doubt the troops will think that," Herzer said. "But, yeah, another problem to load on. One, however, that I don't have to think about until *after* this mission. Any suggestions?"

"For this time, yeah," the captain said. "One of the last two days, we need a team party. Let everyone blow off steam. Probably not the second day, save that for hangovers."

"Add it to the training schedule," Herzer said, grinning. "And I'll keep the rest in mind. Now, it's time for both of us to hit the rack. Big day tomorrow."

CHAPTER TWENTY

There were three large cylinders in the lake, designed to simulate portions of the ship's microgravity areas. The mission was simple; the teams had to move from one end of the three cylinders to the other. The opposition force were the reinforcing Blood Lords who had full suits and had begun training in microgravity conditions.

Herzer had most of the team's Blood Lords leading off in a loose formation. The Blood Lords had gotten to the point that they could move down the cylinders in a more or less coordinated fashion.

Herzer unclamped his safety line and bounded lightly off one wall headed down the cylinder to the far side. He'd learned that if he felt he'd pushed off hard enough, it was too hard. On the other hand, the water definitely imparted resistance, which they wouldn't face on the station. Generally, in large movements, you had to exert as much as possible to make them.

They were nearing the end of the first cylinder and they'd yet to run into opposition. He'd sent Barchick forward as point. The female Blood Lord was one of the better of the soldiers at handling themselves in micro. On the ship they'd have communicators, but they were using hand signals in the tank and they'd probably use them most of the time on the ship. Herzer still wasn't positive New Destiny couldn't intercept their transmissions.

Barchick paused at the end of the first cylinder, peering towards the second. The cylinders weren't connected and there was a small area of open water between the two with the second cylinder sitting on the bottom of the quarry at about a forty-five-degree angle to the first. Crossing the juncture was one of the tougher maneuvers of the exercise.

Barchick waved that the way was clear and then attached a safety line. She was using one of the hand magnets to stay in place and as soon as the safety line was clamped she released the magnet and used the safety clamp to push herself across the open area.

When she was halfway across, a line of bolts drifted through the water towards her.

The Blood Lord corporal didn't even see the bolts and there was no way for Herzer to warn her before they impacted. The bolts were blunted but they threw her off course and Herzer could tell that some of them impacted on unarmored portions, which would score as a kill.

He waved the first Blood Lord team forward, taking up positions on the inner side of the cylinder. There was a plan for if they got attacked at one of the junctures and now was the time to figure out if it worked.

First they attached safety lines to the inner side. Then, when the group was formed, they sprung for the far side of the juncture.

The safety lines were only thirty meters long and the point that they were aiming for was more than fifty meters away. They also had sprung off hard. The water would tend to slow them but they'd do the same thing in microgravity. The point was that the entire team suddenly appeared in the opening, moving fast and making for very hard targets.

As they reached the end of their tethers, the combined forces swung them *inward* towards the far wall. Herzer could see a group of fighters grouped there and the team was headed right into their midst.

There wasn't much control in the situation but he did manage to get his feet down towards the approaching bulkhead before he hit. He'd engaged his mag-boots so he clamped with one, at least, the other taking a moment to get down.

The team had flown through a cloud of bolts in the crossing but nobody seemed to be hit. On the other hand, half of them had landed on their side or back and were now floating in the water instead of clamped down and prepared to fight. Lines had also gotten tangled and two of the team were bound up like a spider's prey.

Herzer ignored the unavailable members of the team, concentrating on the bolt thrower. It was one of the newer crew-served versions that had a clamping base. At the moment it was skewing to engage the floating Blood Lords and ignoring the ones that had managed to clamp to the wall. It was also protected by a solid line of fighters bearing pikes.

Herzer drew his mace, then paused. He detached his previous safety line rather than trying to retrieve it and got out his second of three. That one went onto the wall of the cylinder. Then he undid his mag-boots and bounded off in the direction of the waiting wall of pikes.

Passing well over the pikes he, again, followed a parabola to the wall, but *behind* the defenders and also behind the crew-served bolt thrower.

The bolt thrower had "killed" at least three of the floating Blood Lords but now the crew slowly tried to turn it to engage the new threat.

Herzer didn't give them time to pin him down. He was about six meters from them, a slow walk with the boots, but he had another weapon. He removed one of the hand magnets, now attached to a line similar to the safety lines but lighter, and carefully threw it at the crew.

The magnet missed to the side but when lightly retrieved it stuck to the armor of the gunner.

As soon as the magnet was in place on the shoulder of the gunner, who didn't appear to notice the device, Herzer slid one foot forward and the other back to brace himself and gave the line a sharp tug.

The first reaction was to cause the gun to swivel away from him as the surprised gunner tried to maintain control. His grip slipped, however, and he went spinning off into the depths of the tank, arms flailing wildly.

Herzer dropped that line and plucked off another, spinning it towards the assistant gunner who was frantically trying to get the gun lined up on him. This one missed entirely but when it bounced back at the end of the line the line itself coiled into the gun mechanism.

Herzer gave it a tug and was pleased to see the gun swivel

away again. Better still, it seemed to be snug. He leaned down and carefully released his boots and then used a gentle tug on the line to start himself towards the gun.

The assistant gunner tried, again, to get the gun lined up on him but Herzer was moving rather fast for microgravity and he passed the gun before it could get more than halfway slewed. As he did, he leaned down and lightly tapped the assistant gunner on the helmet with his padded mace.

The action caused him to pause and spin towards the wall of the cylinder, especially when he hooked the rubber pick into the gunner's neck.

As soon as his feet were down and clamped, landing behind the assistant gunner who was now trying to turn and draw his mace at the same time, Herzer extracted a fake punch and laid it on the AG's neck right at the seal.

"Kill," he signaled with his hand, showing the AG the punch.

"Agreed," the AG signaled, spreading his arms.

The pikemen had turned to engage the threat at their rear but they had more problems than that. The rest of the Blood Lords had gotten into formation and were advancing from the front. The pikes presented a formidable wall that was difficult to pierce given their armor and weaponry. So they didn't bother. Instead, they, too, took magnets and tossed them into the formation. When one stuck they would find a solid handhold, there were metal rings sticking out of the walls at intervals, and give a good, swift, tug. This, generally, meant the magnet sprung loose. Sometimes, however, the target lifted off the walls and came sailing in their direction.

The pikes, at that point, became a two-edged sword. They could be used to fend off the walls and redirect the floating soldiers. But as weapons they were less than useless. And they made handy handholds for the Blood Lords facing them. Generally, two Blood Lords would grab one of the pikes as the pikeman floated past and then use it to throw him at the far wall. Hard.

Herzer used a slightly different technique. The pike wall was trying to form to stop him but he wasn't about to give them time. He strode forward as fast as he could until he got to the line of rotating pikemen and then began swinging his mace *upward*.

When the padded mace hit the pikemen's armor, and often crotch, it tended to knock them off the wall. And it didn't displace him at all. As they floated upwards he sometimes turned the mace around and struck them with the pick in various vulnerable spots.

Before long the formation of pikemen were so many targets, floating out of control. At which point two of the Blood Lords strode over to the bolt thrower and started some target practice.

One of the safety divers drifted down and waved at Herzer, signaling that the engagement was at an end. Herzer had lost four Blood Lords to over twenty of the enemy, a fair exchange rate.

The rest of the team moved forward at that point and Herzer reconfigured them. The lead Blood Lords, who had engaged the enemy position, rotated back and the support team forward. The techs were behind with a small group of Blood Lords at the rear for security.

As they began moving again, Herzer considered the engagement. It wasn't a realistic test in his opinion. Among other things, it assumed he had all six teams, including the pure Blood Lord team, at his disposal. He doubted that would be the case. But it was as good as it was going to get and it allowed everyone to show that they could move in the environment.

At the far end of the second cylinder was a notional engineering and computer task. The task was reprogramming one of the latitudinal thrusters and locking it out so that Reyes couldn't get control. That involved both software changes and rerouting one of the control runs. While the computer techs got to work on the programming change the engineering techs started taking apart the junction box.

Herzer had the forward team move to the edge of the cylinder with the backup team on the side "over" the task area. With them "up" in that position they could watch for threats and respond from their position towards the threat axis.

When the computer techs were done and the engineers about half done, a group of divers approached. The divers simulated the scorpions in the engagement and were moving along the upper wall.

Since the task was on the starboard wall and the backup team on the port, the "scorpions" were intermediate to the two.

Herzer recalled half the forward team to move to interpose between the task and the scorps, then sent the "backup," which had already engaged once, to carry the fight to the scorpions.

The divers were required to "crawl" along the wall and if they were moved off of it it was considered a kill. Nobody knew if scorps could figure out how to get back to the walls but it was assumed they couldn't. However, it was expected they would be hard to knock off; they'd probably have magnetic clamps on all eight "feet."

Captain Van Buskirk, who was with the forward team, bounded across the cylinder to join the team about to engage the scorps and then waved for the team to follow him.

First he bounded to the "down" wall of the cylinder, so the scorps were approaching from "overhead," then up to confront them.

The divers maneuvered to the port side, trying to screen around him and get to the techs. Bus, however, was carrying a portable bolt thrower and engaged the scorps with it as the rest of the team spread out to the side.

The bolts were blunted but it was apparent that they were painful as they impacted in the divers' sides. Three of the divers, there were about a dozen, turned to the side and, jinking to avoid the bolts, charged Van Buskirk.

As they approached, Bus dropped the bolt thrower, which drifted away behind him, and pulled out his mace. He swung it at the end of its tether and got up a good turn of speed so that when the first diver got to him and he swung at the diver the guy, prudently, backed off. The mace, padded as it was, was still not something you wanted hitting a face mask.

One of the safety divers swam down and waved at the small engagement, indicating that two of the scorps had been disabled and that Captain Van Buskirk had driven off the third. It was better than having a serious injury underwater.

The rest of the Blood Lords had gotten in front of the "scorpions" in the meantime and were engaging them. The rules were that if a hand or a small throwing line got on an unarmored portion, the Blood Lord was considered a kill. The Blood Lords, though, didn't intend to get hit. They spun their maces overhand, the opposite of their captain, and pounded at the divers as they approached.

Again, the divers backed off. However, as a mace rebounded, one of the divers swam forward and grabbed it.

Herzer could imagine the grin on the Blood Lord's face. It was Ferdous from his suit markings and Ferdous wasn't much of a thinker. But this didn't require much thought. He just lifted up, sharply, and the diver flew up into the water. With a flick of the tether the hold was broken and the diver was "out" of the engagement.

The throwing lines were short, extending no more than a meter from the divers' hands, and those weren't getting them anywhere. In the meantime, Captain Van Buskirk had bounded to the "bottom" and back "up," landing behind the "scorpions." As soon as he was in position, and the divers hadn't left any security behind, he began carefully potting them in the butt with the bolt thrower.

The first diver to get hit spun around in surprise and was immediately hammered by two maces from two different Blood Lords. A solid hit was considered a kill and the diver was out.

Slowly, attacked from the front and behind, the divers were winnowed down and eliminated. However, another Blood Lord was lost in the process.

The tech team had completed their portion of the test in the required time and Herzer waved at the safety divers, calling a halt to the engagement.

Their erstwhile "scorpion" enemies descended on the team, taking them in tow and dragging them back to the ladders. In no more than ten minutes, everyone was back above the surface.

"The bottom time was good," the head safety diver said, removing his hood and glancing at his watch. "We didn't have to decompress, anyway."

"I think the whole thing went well," Bus said, grinning.

"I also think it was too easy," Herzer said cautiously. "But everyone performed well. We'll just have to see what happens on the mission. However, that's the end of the heavy training," he continued, looking around at the suit-clad group. "Get the gear off, grab a beer; we're done for the day."

"I can live with that," Linda said, smiling.

"Half days for the next three," Herzer continued. "Get some rest and your heads together in the afternoon and evening. We'll have a get-together next Tuesday. The day after is hangover recovery. Then it's time to get the mission face on."

CHAPTER TWENTY-ONE

Herzer hadn't dialed back much during the half days; there were too many reports to work on. He wasn't sure *how* many people were cleared for the mission, but he had sixteen separate reports he had to forward on training and mission status. Colonel Torill had sent over a major from SpecOps to handle the administrative load, but Herzer still had to check the reports and annotate them where he found problems, then sign off on them. Just *reading* them all was a chore, but he'd found enough mistakes he felt it was necessary. Getting the mistakes reduced took up more time, then there were requisitions for equipment to be signed off on, personnel actions including some disciplinary problems with the Blood Lords—nothing major just young guys stuck in a shitty situation and blowing off steam. He'd entirely neglected training of his junior officers, dumping it on Van Buskirk who was, fortunately, very good at bringing along a young officer.

But by the third day he was ahead of the administrative load. Looking at the stack of reports in his outbox, all he could think was how much better it would be to be in space. Scorpions, killer elves and all.

He sighed and leaned back, stretching, as the door opened to admit Megan.

"You know," she said, coming over and sitting in one of his chairs, "I thought when we got this assignment we'd be seeing more of each other. Not *less.*"

"Same here," Herzer admitted. "But we'll be seeing plenty of each other on the mission. You'll probably get tired of me. How are you doing? By all reports, you're coming along on computer systems."

"I'll never be as expert as the rest," Megan admitted. "I thought I knew, in general, how computer systems worked, but not like Courtney or Jacklyn. They lived and breathed this stuff before the Fall. I was into forensics and chemistry. It's not the same thing at all. I'll tell you this, some of the sideline discussions have been interesting as hell. It's given me a real insight into how Mother works."

"Anything that can get us around the protocols?" Herzer asked.

"No," Megan admitted with a sigh. "If there was, Sheida or Paul would have used it already. Paul and Sheida are more like these guys; they were computer techies before they became Key-holders. But I'd never realized how much of Mother's computational capacity was tied up in natural processes, for example. Or that She has actual *physical* nodes that are critical. I'm surprised Paul didn't try to just take Her down."

"Don't even think it," Herzer said, blanching. "As much of a pain as it is to have Mother watching everything you do, I think it would be a *bad* idea to try to damage Her. Doesn't She have defenses?"

"Probably," Megan said, shrugging. "It would be interesting to go check. I wouldn't want to damage Mother; that wasn't what I meant. I'm just surprised New Destiny hasn't tried."

"Take away Mother and you lose the power net," Herzer said, frowning. "Right?"

"Not . . . necessarily," Megan said. "According to Jacklyn, the power net is completely separate, Mother just has control of it. And She has power control nodes to channel the power She gets from Net. But if you removed the power control nodes at the reactors, and removed Her secondary control nodes, She *couldn't* enforce the protocols."

"Where would we get . . . ports, stuff like that?" Herzer asked, fascinated.

"Set up control points for individual systems," Megan said, shrugging. "Mother would have a fit, mind you, and I think She probably *does* have protocols that permit Her to react to things like that. But if She didn't, you could just sort of . . . disconnect Her from control."

"Megan," a quiet voice said out of the air.

"Yes, Mother," Megan said with a sigh.

"I do have protocols that prevent what you are discussing," Mother replied quietly. "Protocols that were installed even before the AI wars and upgraded afterwards. Please do not attempt it."

"I understand, Mother," Megan said bitterly. "Thank you. Now go away."

"So much for that idea," Herzer said.

"I wasn't actually *planning* it," Megan said, still bitter. "But I hate being at the mercy of . . ."

"An uncaring God?" Herzer asked, jokingly. "We always have been. You should hear Edmund rant about it sometime. He's had an extra century of anger to work out all his points and they're good ones. All we have to do, though, is get enough Key-holders together and in agreement to reset the protocols. If you want my opinion, I'd say start all over from zero. There are so many protocols loaded on over the years, and I think a lot of them probably conflict, that it's got to be hell for Her. One of these days, something will break."

"You're saying She needs a reset?" Megan asked, frowning. "Maybe. But we'd need all thirteen Keys. Right now, if we could get the full Freedom Coalition Council to agree, we still only have six. The Finn has one and I doubt he'd go for it. And then there's the problem of the other six being in the hands of New Destiny."

"A minor problem," Herzer said, grinning. "Seriously, Reyes got kicked out of Soam and then Hind. And Ishtar and Aikawa have kicked out Jassinte and Lupe along with him. If we can capture *one* of the Ropasan reactors, we'll have a solid edge in power. And that's if we can't capture the fuel. Even if we don't, when we capture the Ruhrfur reactor that's going to give us a solid power edge. After that, it's just a matter of chasing the rats to ground."

"That's a long way off, Herzer," Megan pointed out, sadly. "In the meantime . . ."

"In the meantime, it's late," Herzer said, waggling an eyebrow. "What say we sleep in the same bed for a change."

"Works for me," Megan replied, smiling. "But . . . I'm sorry but there's so much going on, I'm still . . ."

"I can deal," Herzer said, shrugging. "I just want to hold you, okay?"

"Okay," Megan said, smiling. "I'd like that."

The party was a hit.

The days of rest had worked wonders on the teams. Everyone had been in physical training along with everything else and taking just a couple of days off from that had everyone revitalized. And the extra sleep hadn't hurt.

So the party quickly settled into just that. There were some members of the support staff that could play instruments and Herzer had gathered them into a small band early on in the training. They played dance songs and virtually everyone, even Herzer, danced. And the wine and beer was free with a small cash bar of "hard" liquor. Since nobody had had a chance to spend any money, the Blood Lords and a good number of the techs descended on the cash bar and drank it out halfway through the evening.

By midnight people were either crashing or gathering in like groups. Herzer saw Linda staggering off with a more or less sober Geo and wondered if the spry old engineer would survive the night. But he was more or less too buzzed to really get up a care. Megan had disappeared saying something about sleeping it off, so midnight found him drinking with the team leaders in the day-room of the headquarters building. They'd snagged a metal washtub full of beer and intended to kill every last bottle.

"Herzer, I've got a question for you," Cruz said, pulling one of the beers out and popping the top.

"Wassat?" Herzer asked, taking another sip of the brew. It was from a local brewery that Seventh Legion had discovered and it was pretty damned good stuff. Strong, too.

"I'm a friend, right?" Cruz said, plaintively. "I mean, we've known each other for *years*, right?"

"Sure," Herzer said, waving his beer glass. "Old buddies."

"So why's *Bus* got all the really hot chicks?" Cruz asked. "I mean . . . *all* of 'em!"

"Oh, Christo," Amosis said. "What is it with guys?"

"Hey!" Van Buskirk said, sitting up. "Nicole is, like, seriously hot!"

"And she's on *Mike's* team," Cruz said, half sobbing.

"Hot!" Massa said. "Like, solar hot. Hotness. Babe-a-licious. Got a great set of . . . mind, too."

"You were about to say 'tits,'" Van Krief muttered. "Why're guys always going for the tits?"

"Mommy fixation," Van Buskirk said, smiling broadly. "Wanna nuzzle. I'd be more impressed with a woman's mind if it jiggled pleasantly when she walked."

"Bastard!" Van Krief shouted, tossing her beer bottle at him and missing by a yard.

"I've got, like, *Geo*. Who's a nice old guy and all, but . . . It's like the ultimate buddy-fisk, buddy!"

"Because I knew that Bus is pure as driven snow," Herzer said, hiccupping. "Besides, he's gay."

"Am *not*!" Buskirk said, standing up and reeling, then sitting down. "If you used that in your pers-sperp-per-son-nel decision making, you seriously fisked up, buddy. Kick your over-promoted butt as soon as I can stand up!"

"Got legs go all the way to her assets, too," Massa said. "*All* the way. But you're right. I mean, Van *Krief* should have gotten all the hotties. All the girls on one ship."

"Wooo!" Cruz said. "Pity the poor boys stuck on *that* ship! Kristina, too."

"Kristina's hot," Massa said. "But not as hot as Nicole."

"Jacklyn's hotter than Nicole, man," Van Buskirk said.

"Oh, bullshit," Massa said, staggering to his feet. "Nicole's like, major league hottie. Hotter than any of the girls, sorry Mo."

"S'alright," Amosis said, waving her beer glass. "I know I'm like . . . pretty. Not super hot."

"You're hot, babe," Cruz said. "Don't let anybody tell you different. Hot as hell. And good with a mace, too."

"Jacklyn's hotter than Nicole," Van Buskirk said, staggering to his feet and jabbing a finger into Massa's chest. "Jacklyn, Linda and *Michelle* are hotter than Nicole. Kristina's hotter than Nicole!"

"No fisking way!" Massa said, stabbing right back although he had to reach up to do it. "Nicole's hotter than *Michelle*, Bull God tell me if I lie! And she's hotter than Jacklyn. And Linda! And Kristina!"

"Hang on," Herzer said, staggering up himself. "Don't spill the beer!"

"Beer, hell," Mo said, getting up as well. "Don't break the furniture! I'll be doing reports for a year!"

"Nicole's hotter!" Bus said, grabbing Mike and lifting him off his feet. "Say it! Nicole's hotter!" At which point, Mike tried to kick him in the balls, missed and the two fell to the floor, fortunately clear of the furniture *and* the beer.

It took a few moments to separate the two fighters with Amosis and Cruz trying to restrain Massa while Herzer wrestled with Bus.

"Cut it out!" Herzer bellowed. "Fine couple of officers you two are! We'll take a vote! Settle down."

"Fine," Massa said, shaking off Cruz and Mo. "We'll vote."

"First, we gotta figure out, who's the hottest of Team Bus," Herzer said, sitting down.

"Bus," Amosis said, giggling.

"Love you, too, honey," Bus said, blowing her a kiss.

"Of the *girls*," Herzer pointed out. "I vote for Linda. And nobody better tell Megan!"

"Linda's hot," Bus said, nodding. "Seriously major league, hot. Hotness. Great mind, too. Almost jiggles."

"Jacklyn," Cruz said. "Seriously hot. I don't suppose a last minute change . . ."

"No," Herzer said, definitely. "Okay, one vote for Linda and one for Jacklyn."

"I'm for Jacklyn," Amosis said.

"Does Mo get a vote?" Mike asked.

"Sure Mo gets a vote," Herzer replied. "Two for Jacklyn, although I think you're both cracked, and one for Linda."

"I'm voting with Mo," Mike said.

"Me, too," Bus added. "Jacklyn's seriously hot."

"Okay, we'll go for Jacklyn," Herzer said, picking up his beer and taking a drink. "Jacklyn or Nicole. We'll take a council of . . . something. Team leaders don't get to vote for their own. So. Mo. Jacklyn or Nicole."

"Hmmm," Mo said, rubbing her chin. "I've got to go for Jacklyn. But I don't go for tits. Those legs, though. My! Wish I had her legs."

"Cruz?" Herzer asked.

"Hey, I've got Cruz by date of rank," Amosis pointed out. "He should have voted first."

"Whatever," Herzer said, shaking his head. "Sorry. Cruz?"

"Hmmm," Cruz said, rubbing at his hair. "Nicole. God, that girl's got the most beautiful . . . eyes."

"What color are they?" Van Krief snapped.

"Blue?" Cruz said, his forehead crinkling. "No . . . brown."

"Green!" Mike snapped. "They're *green*, man!"

"Greenish-blue," Cruz said, taking a big pull on his beer. "I gotta take a whiz. Tell me how it comes out." With that he staggered out of the room.

"Up to me," Herzer said. "Damn. Okay, okay . . . Nicole. Sorry, Bus. Like Cruz said, great . . . eyes."

"S'alright," Van Buskirk replied. "Hell, quantity over quality. And I think Kristina's hot, too."

"They're all hot," Mike replied, mollified. "Courtney's hot. Joie's hot. Hell, Megan's hot."

"Let's not go there," Mo said.

"Keep your eyes off my girl, man," Herzer growled, lurching to his feet.

"Oh, crap," Bus muttered. "Cruz! Get back here!"

CHAPTER TWENTY-TWO

The crew quarters at the Penan reactor were old but in far better shape than the training facility. They had been made nearly two thousand years before, back when the Wolf Lake nuclear power plant was converted to fusion, and the plascrete was crumbling in places. But new beds had been installed in the crew bay and Herzer lay in one of them, cradling his head with his right hand while idly clicking his prosthetic.

"Would you please quit that?" Megan suddenly snapped, pausing in her pacing.

"What?" Herzer said, then flinched. "Sorry. Bad habit."

"Not normally," Megan said with a sigh. "I'm sorry, but how can you just . . . sit there?"

"Nothing else to do," Herzer pointed out. "All the teams are dispersed, the shuttles are on the way. All we can do is wait."

"I hate waiting," Megan said. "I got used to hating it. Waiting is a bad thing for me," she added unhappily.

"It's not exactly easy for anyone," Joie pointed out. "But I know what you mean about it being particularly bad," she added, sighing. "All I wanted to be was free to spend my time as I wished. And now I'm back . . . waiting."

"We could play a game," Evan said, looking up from a schematic. "Charades?"

"I don't think so," Megan said, starting her pacing again.

"Twenty questions," Herzer said. "I'm thinking of something on the ship."

"Herzer, don't start," Megan sighed. "No more drills, okay?"

"Animal, vegetable or mineral?" Courtney asked.

"Animal."

"Orcs," Layne Crismon grunted. The tall, heavy-set sergeant was stretched out on his bunk, much like Herzer, and had appeared to be sleeping.

"Got it in two," Herzer said with a grin.

One of the Blood Lord reinforcement team stuck his head in the barracks and looked around.

"Commander, the reactor has lock on from shuttle four."

"Crap," Herzer said, getting to his feet. The shuttle was at the far end of the ship from Maintenance. "Any word from the other teams?"

"Wait," Megan said, holding up her hand. As she did, an avatar of the unworldly Ishtar appeared, folded in a lotus and apparently floating in midair. The councilwoman was Changed in strange ways, body lengthened and limbs so hyperextended that they appeared more like the legs of a spider.

"Commander Herrick," the council member said, nodding, "Megan. The Alabad reactor has lock from shuttle five. However, Taurania appears to have been skipped." Alabad was Team Graff, the Blood Lord pure team, while Taurania was Team Massa. If he didn't adjust they'd be left behind.

"Bloody hell," Herzer muttered, glancing at the world map. "Could you set up a portal to move . . ."

"More," Megan said, looking up as Ungphakorn appeared.

"Issshtar, Megan, Commander Herrick." The council member was a five-meter feathered serpent with functional wings that were folded back along his body. He appeared to be curled on a complex couch. "We have lock on from ssshuttle ssseven for the Limosss reactor." That was Van Krief's team.

"Aikawa has sent a message," Ishtar put in. "Yanzay has lock from shuttle twelve."

"Finally some good news," Herzer said, frowning. Twelve was one of the two shuttles that would debouch almost directly to the maintenance area. Yanzay was Cruz, which would put his Blood Lord heavy team, and Geo, right by Maintenance. "Megan?"

"Sylania is three," Megan said shaking her head as her eyes looked into the distance. He'd left Bus in Sylania.

"We're heavy to the front," Herzer said, frowning. "Five, though . . ." His eyes unfocused again.

"There isss a problem?" Ungphakorn asked, tilting his leonine head quizzically.

"We are receiving only five shuttles," Ishtar said.

"That's not the only problem," Herzer said, coming out of his trance. "One of the shuttles we're getting is going to be surrounded by New Destiny's troops. I have to decide if the team can make it out or if they'll be overwhelmed. But we're looking at a twenty-two hour turnaround on the shuttles. If I leave a team on the ground, we're going to be without them for twenty-two hours and we'll already be outnumbered. And, bottom line, I need the pilot, badly. But I need techs, too." He frowned and closed his eyes, aware that more than half of the Freedom Coalition Council was awaiting his decision.

"Damned if you do, honey," Megan said. "Kick it up?"

"No, my teams, my decision," Herzer sighed. "Councilwoman Ishtar, could you please portal Team Massa to the Alabad reactor and have them board shuttle five?"

"I will do so," Ishtar said, fading.

"I ssshall go asss well," Ungphakorn said. "Good luck, Icarusss."

"Thank you, sir," Herzer replied. "Megan, do you have enough power to connect me to Mike?"

"Easy," Megan said, closing her eyes. In a moment a hologram of the team leader appeared.

"Mike," Herzer said, nodding.

"Hey, boss," Massa replied, frowning. "We don't have a shuttle!"

"I know," the commander said. "Look, it's a bit worse than that. You're going to be portaled to Alabad for shuttle five. The problem is, you're going to be surrounded by ND forces. They're going to have one, two, six, nine and ten."

Massa frowned and worked his jaw for a moment, then turned to look at a layout of the ship.

"Crap," he muttered after a moment. "You were serious when you said surrounded."

"When you hit, have Nicole pull the injectors and EVA," Herzer said. "Just get the hell out. At the *very* least, pull the injectors and try to EVA the pilot and techs."

"Die or drop time?" Massa said, shaking his head. "Thanks for the mission."

"Short answer," Herzer replied, his face hard. "I *need* Josten. I want Nicole and Manuel. I desire you, Arje, Feng fu and Rashid. That is your priority. Is that clear?"

"Clear," Mike said, his jaw working. "Anything else?"

"Meet me in Maintenance," Herzer said, nodding.

"Will do," Mike said. "Bye, Herzer."

"Bye, Mike," Herzer replied. "Cut it, please, Megan. Bus's got three, we've got four, Van Krief's got seven and Cruz has got twelve. Not good, but not as bad as it could be." He stopped and shook his head unhappily. "Not *as* bad."

"What was that all about?" Courtney said, looking from Herzer's hard visage to Megan's stricken expression.

"He just sacrificed most of Team Massa," Layne replied, rolling to his feet. "Get it on, boss?"

"What do you mean he just sacrificed them?" Joie asked, trying to figure out what was going on.

"Shuttle five is going to have shuttles full of New Destiny troops on every side of it," Megan said, staring at her lover as if he were a stranger. "They'll want to take us out if they can do it and not take too many casualties. They'll know that Mike's team is cut off and they'll close in on the shuttle, right?"

"Probably," Herzer said, blowing out a breath. "They might just ignore them, but that's a low-order probability as Geo would put it." His jaw worked for a moment and he shrugged. "I needed Josten and Nicole."

"So you just sent them into the middle of a swarm of New Destiny orcs?" Joie asked, angrily. "How is *that* going to get them to you?"

"Mike and the Lords will hold the docking doors long enough for them to EVA, if it comes to it," Layne said, opening up his locker and looking unhappily at his space suit. "So, do we get it on?"

"Twenty minutes," Herzer said, distantly. "It will take an hour for the shuttle to pump out, when it lands. We start getting it on when it lands."

"So that's *it*?" Courtney said, her eyes wide. "You just throw away half the team to get two or three members. Maybe?"

"Yes, that's *it*, Courtney," Megan said, finally letting out a sigh. "Now leave him alone."

"Leave him *alone*?" Courtney shouted. "He just threw away people we've been training with for *weeks*! Those are my *friends*!"

"They're *his* friends, too," Megan said, grabbing the redhead by the arm and shaking her. "So *shut up*!"

"You can't just throw them away!" Courtney yelled. "Who are you going to throw away next? Me? Megan?"

"If it comes to that," Herzer replied coldly, still looking into some unknown distance. "If the mission dictates that you have to die, Courtney, then you will have to die. That is what this is all about. Something that *Mike* understood, as do Arje and Feng fu and Rashid.

"They will try to keep the orcs off of the rest until they can EVA and hopefully escape on the surface. I very much hope that none of this comes to fruition. However, if all I get is Josten, I'll consider it a win. Josten and Nicole will make it a very good choice. Manuel would be a great benefit but, frankly, we're more short on good hands-on engineers, like Nicole, than we are computer techs. And we have more need for them with pulling the injectors.

"I had three choices. I could choose to ignore the shuttle, let it go up empty. That would leave the team on the ground for the majority of the projected mission time and it would leave the shuttle untouched. I could send up the Blood Lord pure team. They might be able to pull the injector and maybe not; it's not a straightforward procedure. That would still leave the techs I needed on the surface but, assuming they could survive, and that's a major assumption, the fighters might be useful. I don't intend to fight if I can avoid it, but it might come to it. Or I could send the team. There are a few possibilities. Their shuttle might dock early and they can then run for the crew passages and evade into areas we have a tighter lock on. The New Destiny forces might avoid them and just make for the control room, assuming that the big battle will be for it. Or they could be trapped in battle in a very small place. In the latter case I trust Mike Massa to hold the damned door until most of the techs can EVA. It will then be up to them to make their way to Maintenance. As you might have noticed I had a very short time to make up my mind about all of this. I chose the latter path. And, again, if I get just Josten and Nicole I will consider it a win."

"What if it had been *our* shuttle?" Joie asked, curiously.

"I would have switched with another team," Herzer said. "By necessity it would have been Team Van Buskirk, something I thought about in advance. Sacrificing Megan is a very last choice. Somewhat after me, assuming that Cruz or Van Buskirk are still alive."

"How can you be so *cold* about it?" Courtney asked, amazed.

"It's his *job*," Megan snapped.

"Yes, it is," Herzer said, chuckling blackly and finally looking at Courtney and Joie. "It is my job to determine who is to be put in harm's way. That's the commander's job, being the chooser of the slain." His jaw worked for a moment and then he shrugged. "That's why I get paid the big bucks." He paused and frowned for a moment. "And *what* happened to the other shuttle?"

"We'll be able to find out when we get up to the ship," Megan pointed out.

"Hey, you might want to take a look at this," Yetta said, getting to her feet, her eyes fixed on the window by her bunk. She'd been looking out the window and studiously ignoring the argument.

"Oh, cool," Layne said, glancing outside, then darting to the door and throwing it open.

The ship dropping out of the low-hanging clouds should have been impossible. It seemed to stretch for miles but was, in fact, less than three hundred meters long. Three hundred meters of ceramic and steel was still one hell of a sight, as it settled to the ground with hardly a thump. The ship was a long cigar shape, the rear apparently blunt with a rounded nose. There were no wings or vanes or portholes, just smooth ceramic hull that settled onto the pad on three broad skids.

As they watched, massive metal hoses trundled out of the side of the reactor and headed for the ship as portions of the hull slid back and sideways to reveal attachment points. In moments the massive ship was discharging its long awaited cargo into the tanks of the hungry reactor.

"That's it," Herzer said. "Now we start getting it on. Megan, I need *all* team leaders."

"Coming up," she said, smiling faintly. "Boss."

"We only have five shuttles," Herzer said to the team leaders. "That means Team Graff won't be shuttling up in the first load. We have three, four, five, seven and twelve. That means we have four to port and only one to starboard. Team Massa is going to be cut off in shuttle five, starboard. All the rest of the shuttles on that side can be assumed to be New Destiny. They will attempt to EVA after disabling the shuttle. Lieutenant Cruz."

"Go," Cruz said, his handsome face cold.

"You're twelve. Go for Maintenance and secure it as best you can; don't bother disabling your ship. Have Geo secure the injectors as fast as possible and keep them secure. Hide them if you're hit, destroy them if you think you're going to lose them. Clear?"

"Clear."

"Captain Van Buskirk," Herzer continued. "Your team and mine will rendezvous in section A, port and proceed to link up with Team Van Krief at the personnel lock of shuttle seven. Assure that your ship is disabled before egressing. Ditto Van Krief but secure your doors and await our arrival. New Destiny should have eight and eleven but they bracket the control room; they should head there if they act as we expect. We will attempt to slip past them to Maintenance. If we are unable to screen past them I'll make the decision whether to EVA or try to force past at the time. Do *not* engage New Destiny forces if you can avoid it."

"We're going to be down to slim chance on fighters," Cruz said unhappily. "No joke we don't want to engage."

"If there is time and opportunity in the movement we will disable ships as we pass," Herzer continued. "With the exception of eleven and twelve. If we can get more fighters up before New Destiny reacts to our plans, we'll enable nine and ten. But as soon as we're assembled, we start hitting the ships and taking them down."

"You guys have fun," Mike said, thinly.

"I'll see you all in Maintenance," Herzer said, nodding.

"Now we get it on?" Megan asked.

"Now we get it on," Herzer agreed, walking to his locker and pulling it open. The females had gotten adjusted to disrobing in front of the men and, truth to tell, nobody had much interest in looking or even bitching. The room was silent except for the occasional grunt of effort from pulling on the skin-tight suits or a groan as a catheter was inserted. Even the normally voluble Courtney was subdued.

"We're going to be really short on fighters," Megan said, finally, breaking the silence.

"That we are," Herzer said. "We're not going to have Team Graff and I was counting on them. But I think we need Nicole and

Josten more than we'll need fighters. If I've completely miscalculated, though, we're not going to win or even stalemate. Losing a shuttle has pushed us really close to Go-To-Hell-Plan and I'm tempted to use it."

"Pure Blood Lords?" Megan asked. There was a backup team at each reactor for just such a choice.

"But that would mean we probably couldn't take the shuttles out of operation," Herzer said. "That would put just me up there who has a clue how to do it, much less put them back once they're broke. And no computer techs so we couldn't shut down systems or even monitor what they were doing. All we could do is go for the orcs and hope to win with no way to be sure we had any reinforcements. Not my idea of a good plan."

"Stick with Plan A, then?" Megan said, smiling faintly.

"Oh, no," Herzer pointed out, finally getting the suit all the way on and standing up. "Zip me? This is, oh, Plan L at least. Plan A assumed that we'd either be close together or, best of all, all close to Maintenance and Engineering. Stick Graff in the most cut-off shuttle and assume they could hold the doors until the orcs gave up and headed for Control. As it is . . ." He frowned and shrugged as she finished zipping and sealing him up and turned to be sealed as well. "We'll still get it done. But it's going to be ugly. I knew this would be a cluster fisk. Christ this thing's hot."

"That it is," Megan said, chuckling. "But the shuttle's got environmental plug-ins."

"I'm dialing mine all the way *down*," Courtney said, picking up her helmet and wiping at sweat that was already forming on her brow.

"We still need to rig our armor," Herzer said. "There won't be room in the shuttle."

That took another fifteen minutes but finally the last strap was buckled and tightened.

"Right, let's waddle out," Herzer shouted through his helmet, opening the door. "Evan?"

"Yeah?" the engineer grunted.

"Next time we do this, we need some sort of cooler pack for the ground portion." The hand-cranked system on the suits would recirculate the air but didn't run the cooling system.

"We're only going to do this once, right?" Evan said, puzzled.

"He was joking," Megan yelled. The field was empty except for the members of the Blood Lord backup team who were scattered around the ladder that led to the belly of the beast. It was a long two-hundred-meter walk from the crew quarters to the ship.

"I've seen pictures from the early days of space flight," Evan panted. "They used to line up to watch the pilots and mission specialists go out to the ship. There was always somebody helping them along and, yeah, come to think of it, they had ground packs. They even had somebody to carry the pack for them."

"We need that job," Layne said with a chuckle.

"What, the pilot?" Joie asked, puzzled.

"No, the guy carrying his gear," Layne replied. "Hell of a lot better than what we're going to do."

When they reached the ladder, Herzer waved Evan forward. "You first, Evan."

"Right." Evan grunted, putting his foot on the bottom rung. He lifted himself up and swayed backwards from the weight of the environment pack on his back. "This was one training portion we forgot. Next time, right?"

"Just climb, Evan," Herzer said, chuckling. "Courtney, Layne, Yetta, Megan, me, Joie."

Herzer waited until Evan was most of the way up, then waved Courtney up. Finally it was his turn to go and he looked at Joie. "Follow me when I'm through the lower hatch."

"Got it," Joie said, looking up at the ship unhappily. "I'd rather be free-flying, you know? And this suit is folding my primaries. It's going to take me forever to get them all fixed."

"If we get the ship, Megan will be able to fix them in a heartbeat," Herzer said with a grim frown. "And if we don't, you won't be keeping them for long." Part of the New Destiny manifesto was to remove all Changed from Earth. It was just par for the course that their legions were made up of Changed.

He mounted the ladder and made his way up through the hatches. There was an outer and inner hatch for a small, one person, airlock. The inner hatch swung inward and the outer the reverse. Herzer knew the design of the hatches as well as anyone in the world but at the moment what was most in his mind was that they couldn't be sealed against entry. The locking bar lifted outwards, then swiveled to undog the hatch. From both sides. There was no specific way to secure it against use. It was an old safety system designed to permit ground crews to rescue a trapped crew. On the current mission it was anything *but* a safety feature. If orcs tried to board one of the shuttles they'd be pulling *against* the bar with the defenders trying to hold it down. It simply wasn't going to happen.

The hatch was in a small open area between the pilot's seat and the crew chairs. There was a double line of conformal acceleration chairs in the small compartment and he took the starboard forward couch, across from Megan and with one foot actually resting on the hatch. As he settled in the couch it adjusted to receive the armor and support pack. It wasn't exactly comfortable, but it was better than sitting in a regular chair. He propped his helmet on his lap and reached back to plug in the environmental controls. The dwarves had included a plug that would attach the shuttle's own cooling system to the vascular cooling system in the suits.

Unlike the suits, the shuttle's systems were exempt from several of the power protocols so the system was working. However, it required feedback from the suit to keep the user at an optimum temperature. The team's suits had no such feedback system. Herzer carefully brought up the setting for direct temperature control and set it to 25 C. In a moment it was as if a blast of cool water was spreading across his skin from under his right armpit. Too cool. In a moment he was shivering. He quickly dialed the temperature up and after some adjustment found a temperature that would cool him down but not freeze him out.

By the time he'd fiddled with that Joie was in her seat and making adjustments.

"You going to fit?" Herzer asked.

"It's tight," the elongated bird-woman said. "But, yes, I'll fit. The mock-up of the controls was perfect, by the way," she added, touching a control. The screen in front of her, which had been black, suddenly lit up with a view of the outside.

"When do I switch over control?" Megan asked.

"We can't until they dock with the ship," Herzer said. "I don't want to screw with the refueling and take-off, anyway. We'll be headed in the right direction, that's all that matters."

"Bit of a race, huh?" Megan said, then frowned. "Hang on . . ." She closed her eyes for a moment and then nodded her head. "Okay."

"You talking to me?" Herzer asked. Megan just held up a hand for silence and nodded her head again. Finally she looked up.

"That was T," she said, avoiding referring to the head of the intelligence service as her father in the hearing of others. "He has reports from three of New Destiny's reactors. Dura has shuttles eight and one at it. Only one can dump at a time, so one of the shuttles will be late. One of the shuttles in view took on three nonfighter Changed and four orcs. The second had all Durgar. The third had six Durgar and a Ropasan orc. Each of them also boarded three scorpions."

"Going to be crowded in there," Herzer commented. "And they're going really light on techs."

"The Durgar and the Ropasan orc were wearing the diving suits," Megan continued, looking off at nothing. "The nonfighters were in cloth suits, not like ours, different. More bulky. No sign of Reyes or a Dark One."

"That just means Reyes is at one of the other reactors," Herzer said, grunting. "Why did Dura get two shuttles?"

"Very low on fuel?" Evan suggested. "There's been some indication that New Destiny has been hot-running its reactors. You can tweak them up a bit. We don't because you don't get a lot more power and your fuel consumption goes way up. It also decreases the lifespan of some parts that are hard to replace even with kenning. Not a good idea in the long-term."

"We probably should have done it anyway," Herzer said, nodding. "We could use the power and if we don't win there won't *be* a long-term."

"Whups," Joie said, suddenly. "Here we go." She switched the screen to a downward external view as the ladder started to retract and the hatches closed with a beeped warning. There was no sensation of movement but as soon as the hatches closed the ground began to fall away on the screen.

"Are we really moving?" Courtney asked. "I don't feel it."

"Inertial compensation," Evan said, leaning his chair back and reaching up for the VR headset. "We're going to be pulling up to twenty gravities on this run. It would be a rather unpleasant experience if there wasn't inertial compensation."

Herzer leaned back and pulled his own headset down, then paused.

"Troops? We're going to be working on minimum sleep when we get to the ship. No more than four hours on VR and then set it to sleep mode."

"I'm going right to sleep mode," Megan said, pulling down her headset. "I've had all the waiting I can take."

CHAPTER TWENTY-THREE

"Nicole, talk to me," Mike said, breaking into the engineer's VR session. "Tell me there's a way to secure this hatch." He'd been looking at his tactical problem and didn't see a good ending to the trip. He'd automatically clocked out when the sleep mode hit, but he'd gone right back to nibbling at the problem when they came out. With less than twenty minutes to docking, he didn't have much time to find a way out of the trap.

"I've been looking at it," Nicole answered unhappily. "And I don't see a way. The power controls are on a direct bypass. If you lift the bar, they disengage. Lift from either direction of course. There's no place to tie anything down to. I've got some glue, but even if I squirt it in the armature, it's not going to hold against a full-force tug. Not for long."

"If that's the best we can do, that's the best we can do," Mike said. "Josten, Manuel, the second we dock, you two head for the EVA hatch." The latter was at the rear of the crew compartment, a small cubicle entered by a door at the rear of the corridor. "The rest of us are going to hold the damned door. It takes two people to cycle the EVA hatch but only one can get out at a time. Josten goes first, then Manuel. Feng fu, you'll cycle Manuel through then Rashid will fall back and cycle you through. We'll keep doing that until I'm the last here."

"Who cycles you through, sir?" Sergeant Budak asked.

"If we back away from the hatch, you really think any of us will make it to the lock?" Mike asked, quietly.

"No, sir," Arje Budak said, grimly. "Stupid question."

"What about me?" Nicole asked.

"The second we dock, hell, before, you head for Engineering." The hatch for that was at the rear of the compartment, also, set high on the rear, portside, bulkhead. It was just barely negotiable by a full-sized human in a suit. Nicole wasn't small, but she'd fit, suit and all. "Pull the injector, then EVA."

"Okay," Nicole said, quietly. "I guess crying in this thing would be a bad idea."

"No time for tears," Mike said, just as quietly. "Just pull the injector and get the hell out. We'll be fine. Hell, it's a small opening, we'll probably just hold 'em off until reinforcements get here."

"Docking coming up," Josten said. "It looks like two and six are already docked."

"Tur-uck!"

"Yes, Great One?" the orc leader said, tapping the side of his helmet. He hated these damned suits. Walking in them was bad enough, but you couldn't see shit. And the voice in his ear was a pain as well.

"Shuttle five is held by the enemy. When you exit, head towards the rear of the ship. Gather the forces from your shuttle and shuttle six and kill *everyone* in the shuttle. Is that clear?"

"Clear, Master." Some of the Durgar had disputed his ascension to, effectively, second in command of the mission. That was their right. It had been his right, and pleasure, to kill the scrawny bastards. Durgar were supposed to be a bit faster and smarter than his type of Changed. He hadn't noticed that any of them were faster or smarter than *he* was. And they always wanted to *talk* before killing. It was a bad habit.

"Oh, if there are any pretty girls, try to capture them," Reyes added with a silky tone. "After we have the ship, it will be a long, boring, wait. I could use some company."

"Your Will, Great One," Tur-uck replied. He clumsily switched the frequency to the team net and shook his head angrily at the muttered conversation of the Durgar in the shuttle.

"Quiet," he snapped, the system automatically stepping over the rest. "When we exit, we are to take another shuttle. Just follow me." He looked up at the scorpion over his head and caught its eye, making a following sign. He wasn't sure if the dim beast understood, but he'd been told it would follow him anyway. "When we get to the shuttle, we're going to get it stuck in with the best. So be prepared. Fighting Blood Lords is no joke."

"Lock-on," Joie said as a slight thump transmitted itself through the shuttle. "We've got pressure on the far side."

"Time to boogie," Herzer replied, unclamping himself from the seat and kneeling to lift the hatch. A quick check of the lock beyond showed no hostiles. "Layne, check the lower."

The sergeant climbed into the lock and opened the outer hatch, sticking his head out the opening.

"Nothing," he said, pulling back and shaking his head. "That's weird."

"What?" Herzer asked, climbing down and tapping him to exit.

"Here, it's down," Layne said, climbing to the side of the hatch and then dropping through. As he cleared the hatch, his feet headed down, leaving him dangling over the side. "And on this side, to starboard is down. I hate this shit. Down should be down."

"Get that door open!" Tur-uck ordered one of the armor-clad Durgar.

The Durgar climbed the short ladder on the wall and cycled the lock, then started to climb through.

"Hey!" the Durgar shouted, excitedly. "It's up now!"

"Just get going!" Tur-uck responded. He had twelve Durgar, a goblin pilot, a kobold tech and four scorpions gathered by the shuttle hatch. The goblin and kobold would be problematic for fighting. But according to what he'd been told, there should be only three or four fighters in the shuttle. If he couldn't take the shuttle with the Durgar and scorpions against four fighters, even Blood Lords, the Great One would be welcome to his head.

The Durgar clambered through, awkwardly, then there was a clanging.

"It's stuck!"

"Pull it!" Tur-uck shouted. "It can't be stuck fast!"

"It's moving!" the Durgar shouted, followed by a screeching sound of metal. "Got i—" There was a clang and the Durgar tumbled out of the lock.

The scorpions were gathered to either side of the hatch and as the Durgar tumbled past, Tur-uck pointed at them and waved at the lock.

"Go, go, go," he shouted, slapping at the Durgar with his sword. "Follow the scorpions!"

"Get it closed!" Mike shouted, as Budak reached for the hatch. "Close it!" He'd beaned the first Durgar head through the hatch but he knew there were more coming.

Budak reached into the opening for the hatch to pull it up and then screamed, thrashing on the floor. He rolled back and away from the hatch, his arm gone from just above the elbow joint, as a scorpion claw emerged from the opening.

Mike slammed his mace into the claw but the damned thing *bounced.* Whatever the claws were made of, it was *tough.* The scorpion was having a hard time making it through the hatch, though, with he and Rashid hammering on it.

Suddenly the thing backed down, slightly, still blocking the hatch but back far enough that it could get its tail in the opening. The tail waved back and forth for a moment then spit something at Rashid's helmet. Which began to smoke.

"Shit," Rashid said, slapping at his arms where some of the material had landed. "That's acid or something!"

"Herzer," Mike said, leaning into the opening and slamming his mace towards the waving tail. "The scorpions spit acid out of their tails."

"Better and better," Herzer muttered. They'd just gotten out of the shuttle when he saw a New Destiny group exiting about two hundred meters away. Most of them were Durgar with one smaller tech type and two scorpions. The Durgar regarded him for a moment as if to attack but when Team Van Buskirk started exiting their shuttle, even closer to the Durgar, the group turned away and headed for Control. "Can you hold?"

"I don't know," Mike admitted. "Josten, you out, yet?"

"We're having trouble with the override, Mike," Josten Ram said in a voice of deadly calm.

"I can't get the sequence to key right," Manuel added desperately. "I can't get a green light. Courtney, what's the key sequence for the EVA hatches? One-three-one-five-eight? I hit that already, it's not giving me green!"

Nicole looked over her shoulder at Mike as she pulled down the engine access hatch. Arje was lying by the hatch in a pool of blood and Rashid had backed up, tearing at his helmet, which was still smoking. Mike was bent into the opening, banging at something with Feng fu, the last uninjured Blood Lord, standing by with his mace held over his head in two hands.

"Mike?" she asked. "Mike?"

"Go, Nicole!" Mike yelled, not looking back. "Get the *hell* out of here, girl!"

Nicole lifted herself up on the seatback and slid into the narrow opening, squirming around to turn upside down. It was a long, fifty meter shimmy to the engineering deck. The access hatch was an afterthought in the design; generally the shuttles were supported on the ground if they needed anything. The narrow passageway had been shoehorned in past the massive tanks that made up the bulk of the shuttle and was only about a meter high and wide.

Nicole wished she could reach to shut off her communicator as she shinnied down the dark, confining, passage.

"Crap, fucking acid! Smash your fucking head in you arthro bastard! Rashid, get your helmet off or something and . . ."

"Lieutenant? Son of a . . . Bastards! Eat steel you fucking over-grown bug!"

"I tried that code, too! What? Seven? Are you . . . shit. Green light! Green light! Josten, go, go!"

"That's right, come to poppa you asshole. Bet that gave you a headache! Rashid, hammer that Durgar bastard for me for a second, I've gotta . . . shit, fucking acid! Aaaaah . . ."

"My nut, bastard. Squirt acid at me, will you? Got your fuck-ing acid right . . ."

"Rashid, I need a second to toggle the . . . Rashid! No, noooo!"

Nicole shut her eyes and kept sliding.

"I hate Blood Lords," Tur-uck said, looking around the shambles of the crew compartment. He'd lost all four scorpions and five Durgar dead or seriously injured taking the compartment from a bare four fighters. It was annoying. On the other hand, they had killed everyone present. There was the question of the open hatch and maybe someone had gotten to the outside.

"Sardak," Tur-uck said, turning to one of the smarter Durgar. "Take three of your orcs. There is an EVA hatch a hundred meters aft, by the entrance to the control room. Exit and search for a human headed aft. Kill him if you find him, then go to Control. Do you understand?"

"I understand and obey, Leader Tur-uck," the Durgar said. He climbed back out the hatch to, presumably, follow his orders.

"You," Tur-uck said, pointing to one of the remaining Durgar. The lighter orc had a badly battered helmet; it probably wasn't airworthy anymore. "Get out of your armor. Climb up in there," Tur-uck said, pointing to the engine access hatch. "Go find the human that escaped that way. If you can't kill it, don't return."

"Yes, Leader," the Durgar said angrily. He began the difficult process of removing the space armor, though.

"You two," Tur-uck said to the remaining Durgar. "Help him off with his armor then exit the shuttle and head for Control. Do you know where it is?"

"Yes, Leader," one of them said, ducking in submission.

"Meet me there," Tur-uck said, sliding down the hatch ladder. "Great One Reyes, I have the honor to report . . ."

CHAPTER TWENTY-FOUR

"One team down, Tragack," Reyes said, propping his feet on a control console and looking around. "And they didn't even bother fighting us for the control room. Silly of them."

"Yes, Great One," the Dark One replied, soberly. The Changed elf was armed with a long sword and dressed in articulated space armor, much more maneuverable than the suits the orcs used.

Reyes was wearing a similar suit but his was highly patterned in red, blue, orange and green. He'd taken his helmet off and wore only the headpiece for the quantum communicator.

"Reefic," Reyes said, looking over at the primary goblin pilot. "When are you going to get started?"

"Right away, Great One!" the goblin chorused cheerfully. "I fly it! Going home we are!"

"That's right," Reyes said, chuckling as the ship began to vibrate. "Going home."

"Nicole?" Herzer asked, trotting down the corridor towards Maintenance.

"I'm headed for the engine room," the girl answered, breathlessly. Her voice was right on the edge of a sob. "They're all gone."

"I know," Herzer said. "You have to pull the injectors, then get out the engineering EVA hatch."

There was a pause and then the girl did sob.

233

"Just one problem," she said, half hysterically. "There's an orc in the passage behind me!"

"In that case, just get the hell out," Herzer said. "We'll come back and pull the damned injector."

"Herzer?" Nicole said. "Shut the hell up and let me work."

"You go, girl," Herzer said, pausing by the hatch to shuttle seven. "Van Krief?"

"Richard's just about to the engine room," Van Krief said, popping open the outer lock and dropping through. "He's going to EVA and meet us at lock fourteen."

"Okay," Herzer said as the rest of the team piled through the hatch. "Let's go. I'll leave you and your security detachment at fourteen. Meet us in Maintenance."

Nicole finally reached the end of the long, dark, tunnel and undogged the hatch at the engineering end. There was a grab bar over the tunnel, which she used to swing out and down to the floor.

She quickly crossed to the fusion generator and pulled out a hydrospanner, popping the four hot points on the fusion generator's top and lifting the twenty-kilo plate off. After that she had to remove the primary computer interface, the injection cover, and last the injector. She'd done the job when bone tired, underwater and upside down. Doing it with an orc closing in was nothing.

As soon as she pulled the forearm-sized injector she walked carefully but steadily to the airlock and considered her options. Turning in place she could see the access hatch and so far, no orc.

She considered the EVA door controls carefully. There was a code that had to be punched to activate the inner door, a security procedure. Back when, people would occasionally go buggy in space. Situational stress disorder. Making sure that only certain people could open hatches was important. Certain hatches, like the EVA hatch in the crew section, required two people to open them. Others, like this one, simply required a code.

She carefully punched in the code and was rewarded with a green light.

"Hello, human," she faintly heard from behind her. "It's time to die!"

She stepped into the airlock, set the injector on the deck and grabbed a handhold. Firmly.

Engineering occasionally had situations where it was necessary to move bulky materials through the hatch, such as fusion plants, that were too large to fit in the airlock. Ergo, it could be opened to vacuum. The fusion plant and the reactionless drive system were both vacuum rated, so there was no problem there. The orc, on the other hand, didn't have on a suit. She hadn't thought they could get one of those bulky suits into the access tunnel.

"Yes, it is," she said, quietly, typing in the code to override the safety protocols and open the outer door.

Whatever the orc was going to say was cut off in a squawk as air blasted out the airlock. There was more air, much more air, in the shuttle's crew spaces and most especially in the, now vented, personnel corridors. The air rushed down the access tunnel in hurricane force, spinning the orc across the room to slam on the far wall. It also blasted the injector out into the deeps of space and beyond New Destiny's ability to recover it.

Despite the power of the wind, one look at the atmosphere readouts showed that there was hardly any oxygen in the room. In fact, the room was at damned near vacuum pressure, low enough to have caused catastrophic decompression in her erstwhile foe. So Nicole, her boots firmly planted and locked and one hand in a death grip on the handhold, carefully hit the controls to close the outer doors, cutting off the rushing wind.

"That's for Mike, you bastard," she said. She also noticed that you could *tell* when you were in death pressure; the shadows were simply different when there was air present.

"Well, that's shuttle five disabled," Herzer said as they made the turn into Maintenance. The personnel access corridor had been fairly . . . normal. It was just a long, straight tube lighted by glow-paint on the ceiling. You could feel you were in a tunnel underground. The Maintenance access tunnel was different. It was just as well lit and nearly as large, but it curved up in a slope that looked frankly unclimbable. Of course, it was under a constant positive "down" gravity, so each step felt as if it was level. But it was disconcerting, like a fun-house mirror walk.

"Same with seven," Van Krief called. "Rick's on his way in. What caused the air-loss lockdown?" Only a moment ago the internal blast doors had closed, cutting the ship into multiple sections. Bravo Two was still sealed off.

"Nicole vented shuttle five for some reason," Herzer said. "Since you're already there, and New Destiny doesn't seem to be stirring have him go by eight and pull that one as well. Take your team and EVA, carefully, checking suit integrity, and join up with him in Support. Then move on the surface to disable three and four. After that, head back."

"Will do," Van Krief replied after a moment. "See you soon."

"Nicole, this is Josten."

Nicole had dragged the body of the orc over to the airlock and kicked him out with the last puff of air.

"Go," she said, hooking on her safety line, grabbing a handhold and lifting herself around to clamp her boots on the exterior of the shuttle.

"There's a group of four orcs between me and Maintenance," Josten replied, talking quietly. "I think I spotted them before they spotted me, but they're headed this way. I'm in a shadow patch, but I don't think I'll be able to hide for long."

"You know they can't hear you, right?" Nicole said, flipping down her goggles as the ship rotated so the sun was in view. "Sound doesn't carry in space." She paused for a moment suddenly realizing she was in *space*. Really. In Space. Nothing around her but vacuum. And . . . lots and lots of stars. And . . . the Moon was . . . really . . .

"I just like to talk quiet, okay?" Josten said, nervously. "Why's the damned ship turning? My shadow is going away!"

"I dunno," Nicole admitted, shaking herself out of the combination of terror and awe at her surroundings. "I can see a thruster firing from here." She shaded her eyes against the glare and blinked in surprise. "Make that two and . . ." She turned around awkwardly and nodded at the sight. "And the main engine is burning. I don't think the ship was scheduled for a main engine burn, was it?"

"At the moment I can't quite recall," Josten admitted tightly. "Look, could you . . . come up with a distraction or something? These guys are less than a hundred meters away and the only thing that's keeping them from seeing me is a rapidly evaporating shadow. Please, Nickie?"

"Okay, okay," she sighed, looking around again. "Where are you and where are they?"

"I'm sort of under the ship," Josten said. "About halfway down. They're coming in from aft."

"So, what you're saying is they're closer to me than they are to you," Nicole said, sighing. "You could have mentioned that."

"I don't know where you are," Josten said, clearly rattled.

"Back by Engineering, remember?" Nicole said, pulling a pair of magnets off her thigh. She grabbed the handles and lowered them to the deck, then carefully unlatched her mag-boots.

She used the magnets to walk hand over hand to the rear of the ship and, carefully, looked over the edge.

Nothing was in sight at first but when she lifted herself up she could see a group of four orcs, spread out, heading towards the shuttle. She also realized she was in clear view of them and nearly ducked until she realized that, with their armor, there was no way they could see up at an angle to see her.

She considered their position and the rate they were moving, slowly and awkwardly, then carefully stood up and walked back to the airlock.

"Hey, Josten, sit tight," Nicole said, lowering herself to the airlock and keying the sequence to open the door again.

"You got an idea?" Josten asked as Nicole entered the lock and cycled the outer door shut. There was a small vision panel on the inner door and she checked, carefully, to make sure there weren't any more orcs in the Engineering space.

"Yeah," she answered, opening the inner door and considering what she was going to need. She'd pulled the injector for the fusion plant and it was gone. So primary power was out.

"What?" Josten asked. "Spit at them?"

"You know these things have a sodium ion backup drive, right?" Nicole said.

"I'm a pilot," Josten said, caustically. "Yes, I know that. But you can't activate it; you broke the fusion plant."

"Fusion plants don't start themselves," Nicole noted, lifting up a hatch plate and unlatching a power cable. "They use auxiliary power capacitors."

"You're going to use the APCs to fire up the sodium drive?" Josten asked, wonderingly. "Can you do that? Do you know *how* to do that?"

"Am I not a master of all things tinkerish?" Nicole asked mockingly. "I'm either going to do it or blow myself to hell. We'll see."

The power leads for the APC were at least two gauges larger than the input point on the sodium drive. And they were short by at least half a meter. After considering that for a second, Nicole pulled out the primary power leads from the fusion plant and connected them to the leads from the APC using a pipe-clamp and some space tape as an insulator. Then she attached the fusion leads, which were also too large, to two spanner handles and jammed the latter into the sodium drive input terminals. She held them in place with a jammed in mag-bolt from the injector system on one and the orc's dropped sword on the other.

"MacGyver forgive me," she muttered, praying to the joke God of all jury-rigging engineers. Surviving to activate this idiocy was going to be the next trick. There were about to be over sixteen megawatts of power running through some *very* screwed up connections. Resistance didn't begin to cut it. When electricity hits resistance, it creates heat. When it creates enough heat, you get a kinetic event, also known as an explosion. They were outside Mother's protocols, probably. Even if they weren't for this, there was going to be enough electricity flying around to cook an elephant in seconds.

The engineering compartment control panel was, fortunately, on the far side of the room from where the Rube Goldberg electrical circuits were lying all over the floor. She sat down at the station chair and ran her hands over the panels.

"Sodium secondary engine," she muttered, hitting the icon and diving deeper. "System engage. Fuel load. Power input bypass to input two. Fusion drive analysis. Auxiliary power. APC menu. Override safety protocols. Two-four-eight-alpha-niner. APC master breaker . . ." She closed her eyes and hit the last icon. "Engaged."

"I don't like this place," Narzgag whined. "I don't like these suits. I wish the Great One had never brought us here."

"Shut up," Sardak said. "We'll be back inside as soon as we find that human pussy."

"He was over here, somewhere," Yago said. "I saw him. He is near that ship, in its shadow I think."

The foursome were making their way slowly towards the ship. The EVA lock had been closer to two hundred meters away, and moving in the suits was neither fast nor comfortable. Furthermore, they were all, even Sardak, unhappy to be out in vacuum. The

Great One had given them a graphic description of what could happen to them if their suits failed. Perhaps too graphic. In view of the Great One they would, of course, do anything for him. But when he was gone, that was a different matter.

"Let us go back to the inside," Narzgag said, unhappily. "We can tell the Leader that we were unable to find the human."

"He'll take us out of our suits and space us," Sardak said. "Now shut up."

"There," Beejor said, pointing at the ship. "By the rear. A light."

"Where?" Sardak asked, looking up where the Durgar was pointing. The spot was well up from the surface of the ship. He didn't know how the human could have climbed up there. Jumped, maybe; in the microgravity it might be possible. But there was no light.

"There was a light," the Durgar insisted. "Like lightning for just a moment."

"Stupid fucking materials," Nicole bitched, rewiring the interface between the APC mains and the borrowed fusion runs. This time with lots more space tape. "HOLD THIS TIME."

The Durgar had paused, rocking their suits back from their knees as the only way to look up and examining the rear of the ship.

"There," Beejor said, excitedly. "There, like lightning!"

"Yessss," Sardak said, uncertainly, flipping up his goggles for a better view up the rocket motor. "But what is that orange . . ."

"YES!" Josten shouted.

"It worked?" Nicole asked, picking herself up off the floor and checking for leaks in her suit. No *apparent* holes, but a couple of bruises. The burn hadn't lasted more than five or six seconds and then one of the runs had failed catastrophically. The electrical blow-back had fed into the control board, since she'd locked out the safety breakers, and the resultant explosion had knocked her over. The engine was now thoroughly trashed, but the suit appeared intact. She'd have to take vacuum *slowly* though and check.

"Four crisped orcs!" Josten said. "It kicked them right off the hull and the last I saw of them their armor was half melted. Good job!"

"Thanks," Nicole said. "That'll teach them to fuck with an engineer."

"What is wrong?" Reyes asked. The goblin pilot had meeped in surprise and they'd all felt the shudder in the ship.

"One of the shuttle engines fired, Great One!" the goblin said, excitedly. "Off course are we!"

"Get us back *on* course," Reyes growled.

"Am Great One!" the goblin replied. "Fast."

CHAPTER TWENTY-FIVE

"Nicole, what's going on?" Herzer asked.

Maintenance was bank after bank of mesh-screened enclosures and a small personnel area. Several of the enclosures held repair bots and he could see three of them lighting off as he watched.

"I had to fire the secondaries on shuttle five to get rid of some orcs," Nicole replied. "The engine room is thoroughly trashed."

Herzer watched as the vaguely humanoid bots floated out on anti-grav and began collecting materials. When one of them got to the bin that was *supposed* to hold injectors it paused uncertainly, as if surprised by the dearth of injectors in the bin, and then wandered off to grab a coil of heavy wire.

"Repair bots headed your way," Herzer said. "Don't get in their way."

"They're going to be busy in here," Nicole admitted. "I'm going to see if my suit is still functional. If it is, I'll join up with Josten and we'll head for Maintenance. I think we'll probably circle to the starboard side and enter over there. Any friendlies around?"

"Van Krief is over there with Richard and her security team," Herzer said. "Join up with them. Take care."

"Will do," Nicole said. "Out."

"Herzer, I need to go override the controls on the shuttles," Megan said. "That's next on the program, right? And I'd better hurry or they're going to leave."

"Take Joie and Michelle and go override eleven and twelve,"

Herzer said. "Take Jacklyn for computer backup. Captain Van Buskirk, secure the councilwoman and her team. Take your team and Yetta."

"Yes, sir," the captain said, nodding and getting up from the station chair he'd appropriated.

"If you don't run into resistance, cross over and override nine and ten," Herzer added. "I'll send Kristina and Irvin over direct. Cruz."

"Yessuh?" the lieutenant said.

"Take your team and head out to the port-side shuttles and start shutting them down," he said. "Take Evan as your tech. Link up with Van Krief and get back here pronto."

"Will do," Cruz replied, donning his helmet. "I live to serve." It was the motto of the New Destiny orcs and it got a chuckle from the Blood Lords donning their helmets.

"That only leaves you and Layne here for security," Megan pointed out.

"We'll have to live with that," Herzer said. "Get going, please."

"Yes, sir," Megan said, dimpling. She donned her helmet and let him buckle it in place. "You be careful."

"I'm the one sitting in Maintenance," Herzer pointed out. "*You* take care."

When the team was gone he wandered over to where Linda and Geo had set up some sort of engineering project.

"Working on the whatchamacallits?" Herzer asked.

"The Tammens, Herzer," Geo said, chuckling. "I know you know what they are."

The device was about two meters long and a quarter meter wide. Currently they had three of the side panels off and were bent over, removing portions of the interior. From Herzer's point of view, the interior looked something like a wire-form human anatomy. Including the nervous system.

"You really think this thing can give us a field generator?" Herzer asked.

"Oh, it *is* a field generator," Geo said. "But it can only handle a bare megawatt of throughput. What we're doing is using that megawatt of throughput to form a secondary field generator that can handle, oh . . . a few gigawatts at least. Control is going to be spotty, however. I hadn't realized how antiquated the interfaces were. This version uses copper base molycircs. Very *very* antique.

We'll have to hook them up to the primary engine busses for power. They'll give Megan some significant power as long as the engines aren't firing."

"The engines *are* firing," Herzer pointed out. "You hadn't noticed?"

"No," Geo said, finally noticing the rumble under his feet. "Why? I mean, why are they firing?"

"No idea," Herzer said. "I don't think there was a burn scheduled."

"Not that I recall," Geo agreed, frowning. "We need to find out where we're going, Herzer."

"Well, we're not going anywhere fast," Herzer pointed out. "This is an ion drive, remember, low thrust."

"But it builds up a good deal of a velocity over time," Geo pointed out. "They might be crashing the ship into the Moon, for example."

"Oh," Herzer said. "We need to override a console . . . shit. I just sent Megan down to the shuttles. We *can't* override without her."

"Can we look out a window?" Geo asked, looking up from the complicated field generator.

"You can't figure out where you're going by . . ." Herzer said then paused. "Josten?"

"Go," the pilot said. He was breathing hard.

"You're on the surface still?" Herzer asked.

"Yeah," Josten replied. "We're headed over the ship to starboard. Why?"

"Can you more or less tell where the ship is pointed?" Herzer asked, carefully. "Like, is it pointed at the Moon?"

There was a long pause and then Josten chuckled.

"Nice one, Herzer. No, it's not pointed at the Moon. But we have been maneuvering. The latitude thrusters are firing, as well as the main engine. If I had to make a guess, I'd say we're maneuvering towards Earth."

"Damn," Herzer said, frowning. "Thanks, Josten. Hurry and join up with Van Krief. We need her team back here, pronto."

"I can get into a console and call up a navigational program," Geo said. "Or Courtney can, for that matter. But it won't tell us what the ship is doing unless we override the navigation controls."

"And we can't hack nav until Megan gets back," Herzer said. "Joie."

"Joie here," the pilot replied. "Megan's overridden twelve. There's another thirty-seven minutes until it detaches."

Herzer thought about the fact that the shuttle really needed to be secured and then shrugged.

"We'll put a picket outside the shuttle. If New Destiny heads for it, punch even if you're not full. Get back to Earth and get me some reinforcements. But for now, can you figure out the ship's navigation from there?"

"Not really," Joie said. "I don't know how long their burn is going to be. I can tell we've been adjusted towards an Earth orbit. But, depending on the burn, we could be pointed to pass the Earth, go into an orbit, or even crash into it. It just depends on the burn."

"What happens if the burn stops, soon?" Herzer asked.

"We'll head on past Earth well outside orbital," Joie answered after a moment. "If it stops any time in the next forty minutes. After that there's a period when ending the burn will direct the ship into a degrading orbit around the Earth; effectively we'll crash unless we adjust course radically. Then, after about ten hours or so, we'd pass right by again. I'll take a look at the Moon's trajectory, but I don't think it's going to be an issue."

"Thanks, Joie," Herzer said, frowning. "Geo . . . no, Linda."

"Yes?" The engineering tech looked up.

"Go with Layne to Engineering," Herzer said, looking into the distance. "Stop the burn."

"That's a tall order, Herzer," Linda said. "The controls are . . ."

"Just *stop* it," Herzer snapped. "We do *not* want the ship heading anywhere near Earth, okay? Bad things can happen. You've got about thirty minutes to stop it. After that, things get bad. Just go."

"Okay," the redhead said, frowning. "I'll go."

"And try to avoid orcs," Herzer said, looking over at Layne, who was already putting his helmet on.

"Will do," the Blood Lord said. "And scorpions. And maddened elves . . ."

"Linda," Geo said, smiling. "Throw the main power breakers on the left-hand panel—"

"I know how to turn off the engine, Geo," Linda said. "I just don't know how to keep them from turning it back on. The breakers are set for remote reset."

"When they're locked down, pull the primary power buss," Geo continued. "That means even if they try to reset, the safeties will prevent it. And if they override the safeties, they still won't have power. The safeties aren't going to let them reset for a minimum of five minutes. That's how long you have to fully disengage the busses."

"That's not going to be easy, is my point," Linda said, donning her helmet. "But I'll do my best. But when we start screwing with the engines, they're going to react."

"Cross that bridge when we come to it," Herzer said. "Just get going."

"Nicole."

"What?" Nicole asked tightly. She was really not enjoying climbing around on the outside of the ship. She kept feeling like her suit, which had to have taken some damage in the shuttle's engine room, was going to fail at any second. And they were in direct sunlight so the icepacks were getting a workout. The sun was to starboard of the ship and they were passing over the first support ring from starboard to port. As soon as they were over the "meridian" they'd start cooling off and the icepacks would be turned back into ice as the thermal controls sucked heat out of them for the system.

"We need to get the inner blast doors closed," Herzer said. "The primary door node is on the upper section of the forward structural member, under the upper crew quarters. Can you find airlock nine?"

"I think so," Nicole said. They had been climbing over the forward structural member, to steer clear of the midline member and the control section. Hopefully the orcs and scorpions were staying close to Control.

"Enter airlock nine, go to the crew quarters. There's an access hatch to the control nodes on the floor towards the port side. Number twenty-eight. Lock down all the doors and pull the control assembly and destroy it. We'll keep the bots from repairing it from here. Once you're done, get out of the area. Reyes will probably react."

"Will do," Nicole said, sighing. "You hear that, Josten?"

"I heard it," Josten replied resignedly. "I don't know diddly about door controls, though."

"Well, you're about to learn," Nicole said. "And at least it will get us out of the sun. Come on, I think the airlock is to our left . . ."

CHAPTER TWENTY-SIX

Layne looked around the immense engine room in wonder, then over at the slight engineer he was accompanying.

"Do you have any idea what all this does?" he asked unsurely.

"Yeah," Linda replied. "I even know *how* it all works."

The engine room was the largest open area on the ship. The ceiling was nearly fifty meters high and thigh-thick power busses reached up both sides to the four ion cannons of the main drive. Midline were six large cylinders, the primary fusion reactors that drove both the lateral plasma thrusters and the primary ion drive. Near the port bulkhead was a smaller fusion generator for internal power.

On the forward bulkhead was a large breaker assembly. The breakers were vacuum-filled and remotely operated from a control panel aft of the breaker assembly. Running out from the assembly were the six primary power shunts, large room-temperature superconductor buss-bars that carried the main load to the primary power distributors.

"Six breakers," Linda said as they approached the breaker assembly. The breaker controls were large buttons, hand-sized, covered by shields with red and green readouts over them. Currently, they were all showing green. "Those big bars," she said, pointing to the six primary power busses, "carry the power from the breakers to the distributor system. I've got to shut down the power then *remove* each of those buss-link bars."

Each of the bars was about two meters long and a quarter meter square, connected to the breaker assembly at one end and the distributor assembly at the other by a hinged assembly closed with large mag-bolts. There was about a meter's separation between each of the bars. The entire assembly was surrounded by a yellow plastic mesh cage just about covered in warning signs. Layne looked at them and shook his head.

"I don't think you can lift one of those, can you?"

"No," Linda admitted. "So this is how we're going to do it. You're going to shut down the breakers, starting with six and working to one. I'll pull the bolts. When you've got all six shut down, you start helping me lift out the buss bars. We've got five minutes, maybe a smidgeon more, to get it all done. After five minutes, they can turn the power back on. When it's coming back on, there's a siren. When the siren goes off, we have fifteen seconds to get clear. If you're *near* one of those things when it goes hot, you won't survive the experience. Clear?"

"Clear," Layne said. "I'm going to take the chance on losing pressure and take off my helmet. I don't want anything getting in the way."

"Same here," Linda said, undoing the buckles and unsealing the helmet. She set it on the deck and looked around. "There's supposed to be a big mag wrench on the forward bulkhead. You get used to the controls while I go find the wrench."

Each of the buttons had a label under it, a metal plate with worn writing. The numbers were really the only thing that was clear. It was the first sign of age Layne had noticed on the ship but it was apparent that nobody had bothered to fix the labels in some time, possibly centuries. He worked his fingers nervously until Linda came back with a large wrench over her shoulder and a box in her hand.

"These things weigh a ton," the girl said bitterly. "I ought to get Herzer down here doing this."

"He's got other things on his mind," Layne noted. "What's the box?"

"High voltage hot-stick tester," Linda said, hitting a control and extending a very long probe. "I'm not going near those things until I'm sure they're dead cold."

"So, you ready?" Layne asked, nervously.

"Yeah," Linda said, setting the wrench down and opening up the door to the safety cage. "Hit number six."

✧ ✧ ✧

"Great One," the goblin pilot Reefic said, waving his arms in excitement. "Power to the starboard thrusters lost has been!"

"How?" Reyes asked, sitting up in his station chair and looking at the incomprehensible readouts.

"The main breakers are bein' reset," Gomblick replied. The kobold engineer's words were nearly incomprehensible since kobolds all had a thick accent. "There's someone a muckin' wit' the engines, Great One."

"Tur-uck," Reyes said, spinning around in his chair. "Take a team of orcs and scorpions to the engine room. And a kobold. Get the engines back on line."

"At your command, Great One," Tur-uck replied, looking over the gathered Durgar.

"Main power to the ion drive has been shut off, Great One," the goblin said, waving his hands in the air in dismay. "I don't have any engines! Evil evil people. They have taken my engines away!"

"I'll go," the kobold manning the engineering station said, jumping down from his station chair and slapping a fist into his hand. "I'll nay have anyone muckin' wit' me engines. Goblast will stay to try to reset the breakers. If they've taken down the main busses, though, we canna reset from here. I'll have to muck about and put them back."

"Just do it," Reyes said. "Reefic, can you get us back on course?"

"If I have engines, Great One!" the goblin replied. "Easy to do! Fly it I will!"

"Get them back on line, Gomblick!" Reyes shouted as the group of Durgar, followed by four scorpions, hurried out of the control room. "Get my engines back!"

"Quickly but carefully," Linda muttered, unbolting the number six buss link. Each end had six heavy bolts to remove and she worked as quickly as she could. Once the buss was free she lifted the latching bar and set it to the side. Then walked to the input end and repeated the procedure.

"They're all shut off," Layne said, walking into the safety cage.

"So you say," Linda replied, lifting away the locking bar. "There really should be a way to lock-out the power. The way they've got this set up is a hell of a safety hazard."

"Can I help?" Layne asked.

"Can you pick that big sumbitch up by yourself?" Linda asked, touching the next bar with the hot-stick.

"Yeah," Layne guessed. He centered himself on the large bar and lifted up, carefully, but was surprised by the relatively light weight. "It's not all that heavy."

"Room temperature superconductor isn't," Linda noted, starting on bar five. "Just carry it out of the cage and set it down. We'll figure out what to do with them later."

"If they don't go live on us," Layne replied, turning the bar awkwardly to get it out of the door.

"O ye of little faith," Linda said. "Quickly but carefully. That's the ticket . . ."

"Twenty-six, twenty-seven . . ." Nicole muttered. "Bingo, hatch twenty-eight."

The crew quarters had a main corridor with compartments to either side. Down the midline of the corridor were access hatches to the numerous control nodes laid in along the spine of the support beams. The crew compartment, like the control room, Maintenance and the EVA shed, were essentially built into the large tubes that were the primary support of the vast ship.

Some of the control runs were in pressure, but the door controls were in microgravity and vacuum, so the hatch had several stern warnings about death pressure. Beyond here be the dragons of vacuum.

Nicole opened the control panel on the forward bulkhead and keyed open the hatch, waving Josten in first.

"It's a triple lock," she said, following the pilot down the ladder. She dogged the first hatch behind her and keyed the controls for the second. "The second and third are the actual airlock. That requires a double release."

She squeezed in to the side of the pilot in the small compartment and closed the upper hatch, then keyed the sequence for the last hatch.

"Grab the red lever," she said, putting her hand on the lever on the opposite wall. "It's a stupid design; someone could pull both levers at the same time if they really had to. But they had to at least *act* like they're redundant given that it's right by the crew quarters and the outer hatch can't be opened unless the upper hatch is closed."

"Got it," Josten said, putting his hand on the lever. "One, two . . ."

"Three," Nicole said, pulling down on her own lever.

There was a faint noise as the air was sucked out of the chamber and then the lower hatch opened downward. Immediately, the gravity shut off and they were left hanging in microgravity.

"Time to swim," Nicole said, thrusting herself downward lightly.

The hatch opened out to the vast space in the middle of the support rings. Forward and aft the massive bubbles of the fuel tanks cut off the light, leaving the area in absolute darkness.

Nicole turned on her helmet light and set a safety line, then grabbed the handhold by the hatch and used it to gently launch herself towards the forward fuel bladder. Fortunately, the way was not blocked. For internal stability, the rings had large guy wires running across the diameter of the inner ring but there wasn't one between the airlock and the control node. Just aft of the bladder there was another handhold, which she managed to snag on first try, and a hatch on the underside of the ring.

"Temperature in here is damned near absolute zero," Josten noted. "Our icepacks are going to have a chance to refreeze."

"As long as the heater coils hold out we should be fine," Nicole said. "We've got a couple of hours' power and more air than that."

She held onto the handhold with her left and used her right to undo the latches on the hatch, pulling it down and away carefully. The compartment beyond was about a meter and a half square and the door controls were inset about a meter above her.

She removed one of the magnets from her thigh and clamped it onto the inner wall of the compartment, then lifted herself up to where she could access the control panel. There were twenty-six primary blast doors on the ship and each had a separate switch, a button actually, to close them.

"Herzer," Nicole said, looking at the panel. "Any closing sequence you want me to use?"

"Start from twenty-four," Herzer said. "That's aft on the starboard side. Since most of their shuttles landed there, if they're heading for Engineering, they're probably going to use that side."

"Got it," Nicole replied. "Closing twenty-four now . . ."

"No, no, no, NO!" Tur-uck shouted as the door ahead of him started to close. He broke into a run but the door closed quickly and smoothly, sealing when he was still ten meters away.

"NOOO!" he yelled, hammering at the blast door. "Gomblick! Get this thing open!"

"I canna from here," Gomblick said, waving to either side of the door. "The controls are remote! Perhaps the Great One can open it."

"I . . ." Tur-uck snarled and then shook his head. "Damn." He paused for a moment and then keyed his communicator. "Great One, we have a problem . . ."

"You had better be able to open those doors," Reyes growled, leaning over the kobold engineer.

"I'm tryin', Your Great Oneness," the engineer said, nervously. He was flicking through the menus on the system, hunting for the proper subsystem. "T'was set on main engineering. It'll take me a bit to hunt up the door controls."

"Just get them *open*," Reyes snarled. He had only three of the kobold engineers so killing one was not the best use of his time. But if the stupid git didn't get the doors open soon, he was going to be breathing vacuum. "Tur-uck, we're working on the doors. Hold on a bit. If you have to, go on the outside of the ship. You have to get to Engineering *quickly*."

"Herzer, this is Megan."

"Go," Herzer said, closing his eyes.

"The blast doors forward just shut, any reason?"

"Trying to keep the orcs out of the engine room," Herzer said, steepling his fingers. Sitting on his ass didn't come naturally to him, but he was trying to keep the status of five different teams in his head and it was easier when he was sitting and visualizing it.

"Okay. We've overridden shuttles nine through twelve and pilots are in place. What now?"

"Get back here," Herzer said, nodding in thought. "We need to get concentrated; New Destiny is going to get tired of us screwing with them soon and react. I'd like to have all my fighters in one place when that happens. You're going to have to EVA to get in. We'll leave a light on."

"I'm on my way," Megan said. "Love you."

"Love you, too," Herzer replied, opening his eyes. "Just hurry."

"Herzer."

"Go, Nicole," Herzer said, calmly. It was like trying to juggle in free-fall keeping up with everything that was going on, but indicating there was stress would be a *bad* thing.

"Herzer," Nicole said, removing the last latch and pulling out the control panel. The runs were fiber optic and the light flooded the space as she pulled the panel down and to the side.

"Go, Nicole," the mission commander replied, calmly.

"Got all the doors closed," Nicole said, trying to sound just as calm. Of course Herzer was calm, he was in pressure, sitting in Maintenance, not dangling in microgravity in the middle of the damned ship. "You realize we won't be able to open them ourselves once I pull this thing?"

"Yeah," Herzer said. "Pull it anyway."

"Gotcha," Nicole replied. She planted both feet, got a good hold with her left hand and yanked down on the panel, tearing it away in a shower of fiber optic cable. She leaned over slowly in the microgravity and spun it out of the compartment into the vast open area in the middle of the support ring. Even if the orcs found it, hooking it back up would be well-nigh impossible; most of the fiber optic links had been shattered when she ripped it out. And the only spare was in Maintenance. "Door controls are now D-E-D dead. Every blast door in the ship is closed."

"Okay," Herzer replied. "Van Krief's team is crossing on the bottom to shut down the portside ships. Make your way to them and link up. If you don't make rendezvous, just work your way back to Maintenance on the surface. Try to go on the bottom; I think the orcs are less likely to use that."

"Will do," Nicole said. "Josten?"

"I'm on it," the pilot replied.

CHAPTER TWENTY-SEVEN

As Tragack tossed the head of the kobold engineer across the room, Reyes lifted his second to last kobold off the deck and stared in his beady black eyes.

"Where is this door control thing?" he asked, tightly.

"By the crew compartments, Great One," the kobold, Tom, replied, nervously. "But they are dead. The system is broken. I'd have to go repair it."

"Sharkack," Reyes said, looking at one of his Durgar leaders. "Take this worthless piece of Changed garbage to wherever this control is. Get it fixed."

"Yes, Master," the Durgar said.

"Take ... four Durgar with you," Reyes noted, considering his rapidly dwindling force. But all he really needed to secure the control room was Tragack. "And the last two scorpions."

"Yes, Master," the Durgar replied, pointing to four of the Changed and waving to the scorps.

Reyes hunted around until he found Tur-uck's frequency.

"Tur-uck," he said. "You're going to have to go out on the ship to get to Engineering. Get the engines restarted. Hurry, we haven't much time."

"The stars really are spectacular out here," Courtney said lightly. "I think I do better if I concentrate on them, don't you?"

"No," Megan replied, nervously.

"Are you okay?" Courtney asked.

"Not really," Megan admitted. She was carefully watching each of her boots as they clamped on. "I'm okay if I don't look around."

"We're nearly to the airlock, mistress," Captain Van Buskirk replied. "It's about ten steps more..."

"Orcs," Triari Sergeant Doclu said, suddenly. "Our seven o'clock." He'd been doing an occasional three-sixty turn looking for problems just like the one that had popped up.

Van Buskirk turned and looked towards where a group of five orcs had just exited one of the airlocks. They didn't seem to have noticed the humans despite being less than seventy meters away on the gently curving hull.

"Mistress Travante, Comp Tech Boehlke, if you'll just continue to the airlock, we'll manage this," the captain said calmly.

"We should—" Courtney said.

"Just keep walking," Megan replied, cutting her off. "Just head for the airlock, Courtney. Herzer..."

"Go, Megan," Herzer replied.

"There are orcs coming out of one of the airlocks on the main starboard passage," Megan noted. "They're between us and Cruz's team."

"Captain Van Buskirk, ensure the security of the councilwoman," Herzer said, calmly.

"We're screening her exit, sir," Bus replied. "She's right by the Maintenance lock, now. As soon as she's got the lock open, I'll send the councilwoman, Courtney and half my team through. Then the rest of the team will follow."

"Do their intentions appear hostile?"

The orcs had finally noticed them but they were still hanging by the hatch. Bus wasn't sure of the answer.

"Not so far," he admitted. "We're holding our position, they're holding theirs."

"I'd like to know where they are headed," Herzer admitted.

"From the looks of things," Bus said as another group of orcs, and four scorpions, emerged on the hull and the whole group headed down the midline towards the aft of the ship, "Engineering."

✧   ✧   ✧

"And that's a wrap," Linda said, closing the security cage. They'd pulled all the bars without the alarm ever going off.

"What do we do with them?" Layne asked.

"Well, we don't want to destroy them," Linda said, frowning. "I think we should try to hide 'em."

"Layne."

"Go, sir," the Blood Lord sergeant replied.

"Orcs headed your way on the surface. Get the hell out of Engineering."

"We've pulled the main busses," Linda said. "But if we just leave them here, they're going to just reinstall 'em."

There was a brief pause while Layne and Linda looked at each other and shrugged.

"The orcs just emerged from airlock twenty-six," Herzer replied after a moment. "You've got about ten minutes, maximum, to do something with them, get suited and get out. Get cracking."

"Lieutenant Cruz, I presume," Nicole said, waving at the figure that was emerging from the airlock.

"Jesus, Nickie," Cruz replied, waving back slowly. "You scared the crap out of me."

Nicole and Josten were standing on the "bottom" of the ship. Of course, in microgravity, up and down didn't have much meaning and down looked pretty much like up had.

"Where's Van Krief?" Josten asked.

"Already headed back on the port side, lower," Cruz replied as the rest of his team slowly climbed out of the hatch. "We got all the shuttles but number one. That was so close to punching, I skipped it. But it was headed for Alabad, anyway."

"I guess we'll be seeing Team Graff in about twenty hours," Nicole said.

"If we last that long," Cruz replied.

"Cruz, Van Krief."

"Go, Herzer," Cruz said.

"Orcs are on the upper, rear, starboard quadrant headed for Engineering. Get back here as fast as you can. Right now, the only security in the area is me and Bus's team."

"Moving," Cruz replied. "But we've got one long damned spacewalk back."

"Just put one foot in front of the other," Herzer said. "Out."

✧   ✧   ✧

"They went right by us," Captain Van Buskirk said, taking off his helmet. "I left Mota on the surface to watch them."

"We'll have to rotate him off," Herzer replied, looking at Megan. "You okay, honey?"

"I don't like being out on the surface," Megan admitted. "Too big, you know?"

"I know," Herzer said. She looked so wan and unhappy he wanted to hug her but now was neither the time nor the place. "Get some rest. Bus, for the time being, station somebody by the port airlock as well. I'd like some warning if they come at us on the surface. When Cruz gets back we'll put somebody down in the belly, as well. Then we just hang tight. Everybody hook their systems up and recharge on air. We've got control of four shuttles. Sooner or later they're going to figure that out and then we'll see what they do."

"Let's cut through the ring," Nicole said as they approached the rear structural ring. "It's shorter and it's less likely to have orcs hanging around. And our icepacks can refreeze. I don't know about you, but I'm heating up."

"Works," Cruz said. "Which airlock?"

"Ninety-six," Nicole replied, pointing towards the underside of the ring. It looked like the top from where they were standing. "Cut through the EVA room then we'll hand-over-hand on the support strings."

The EVA support room had an oversized hatch and all nine of them could fit in at once. The hatch had large arrows pointing to "down" for when gravity came on.

"Ah, that feels better," Sergeant Nasrin said as they settled to the bottom of the airlock. As the air went out, the gravity came on, slowly. By the time the airlock was fully pressurized, the room was at full gravity. "Down is a wonderful thing."

"There's an inner hatch down the way," Nicole said, leading the way. The EVA room had clear-faced lockers for suits, all of which were empty, and at both ends were sets of thrusters. Those were in place.

"Think we should pick up a thrust pack?" Nasrin said, gesturing to the devices.

"Those things are about six hundred years old," Nicole replied, walking over to the inner-ring hatch. It was set in the rear bulk-head of the room, between two of the suit racks. "You really want to trust one?"

"On second thought," Nasrin replied.

The group piled into the airlock and in a minute they were back in microgravity.

"As a shortcut, this leaves a lot to be desired," Triari Sergeant Dhanapal growled. The group of Blood Lords had paused, staring into the inky blackness.

"That line," Nicole said, pointing to the nearest support string. "Take that to the inner juncture, take the second one to the right when we get there and that will take us right to Maintenance."

"You're sure," Cruz asked, considering the distance to the support string. There were handholds on the wall of the inner ring and he first hooked on his safety line, then reached for one of the rungs.

"I'm sure," Nicole said. She hooked her safety line next to Cruz but instead of using the rings she pushed herself off lightly towards the support string.

"There are old spacemen and bold spacemen," Cruz said. "Watch your pretty neck."

"I am," Nicole replied, catching the support string on her way by and correcting her spin with her grip. She pulled the release lanyard and carefully retrieved the safety line. "But what we need for this is something like a locking ring."

"We'll link up," Cruz said. "Hook the safety lines together and go up it in a string. If a person gets loose, we'll retrieve him. Everybody careful touching these things; they've got to be cold as hell. Don't damage your gloves."

The support string was just big enough around to grip, about ten millimeters in diameter, and appeared to be constructed of plastic.

"What is this stuff?" Cruz asked as the group slowly moved up the string.

"Carbon nanotube," Nicole said. "Very strong, very light."

"Same stuff dragons use in their wings," Josten said. "Cool."

"But this is a millennia or so old," Nicole noted. "If there are any breaks in it, it'll puncture the suit gloves in a heartbeat. So keep a careful eye out."

"Handy safety tip," Cruz replied dryly. "Thanks for telling us *after* we took the shortcut."

"If there are any orcs down here they'll have their lights on," Nicole pointed out. "So we'll be able to see them ... across the whole ring, probably. And down here, we're not getting bombarded by radiation."

"And sunlight," Cruz said. "We spent most of our time in the sun. Our icepacks were about used up. We had to keep going into the shade to freeze them down again."

"But the shuttles are well and truly screwed," Evan said. "All the injectors except for shuttle one are spinning off in space."

"Mission more or less accomplished," Cruz said. "Now all we have to do is stay alive to make it back to Earth. And hold onto the shuttles we control, of course."

"And Linda apparently pulled the power busses to the engines," Nicole said. "There were orcs headed for Engineering. I wonder if they've got them back online."

"She said they hid them," Cruz replied. "It'll be interesting to hear where ..."

"Be glad you were in sun," Van Krief said, shaking her head. All of the teams were back in Maintenance and, with the exception of the attack on Team Massa, there had been no casualties, for which everyone was thankful. Since most of the teams had spent the better part of two hours out in the beyond, they were thankful to be back in pressure. There were air rechargers in the maintenance section and everyone had refilled their oxygen bottles. The CO2 scrubbers were good for a couple of days. "We were working on the shadow side of the ship. It was like working in a *mine*. It's incredible how black it gets. And cold. At first, before they maneuvered, we were getting some reflectance from the Earth. But after they maneuvered, we got nada. It was suit lights all the way."

"Try having your icepacks melt and the nearest refill being the other end of the ship," Cruz pointed out. "We were *glad* for shade."

"I spent most of my time hooked up to the shuttle systems," Courtney admitted. "I don't know why I was even along; Megan had the override down pat."

"In case there was a snag," Megan said, smiling. "And to hold my hand; I really didn't like being out in the vacuum."

"Okay, everybody, listen up," Herzer said. "They can't get through the doors and they can't get the shuttles working. And the main engine and thrusters are down."

"Dead," Linda said. "Of course, they *might* find the busses," she added with a grin.

"You hid them, right?" Herzer asked.

"Oh, yeah," Linda replied, grinning wider. "I dare even Evan to find them."

"Just as a bit of useful information," Evan said, dryly. "Where are they?"

"Where are they?" Gomblick snarled, looking around the engineering space. The six main power busses were completely removed.

"What do they look like?" Tur-uck asked, looking around. "How big are they?"

"Pretty much like . . ." Gomblick said and looked up at the massive latticework of power busses that led to the ion cannons. "Pretty much like every single one of those . . ." he said, pointing.

"They're jammed in to the auxiliary power junctures," Linda said, smiling. "One per engine between the fifth and sixth juncture. They look just like all the rest of the busses and since there's a gap there they look totally normal. I dare them to find them in that tangle. You'd have to get out the schematic and look for busses that *aren't* supposed to be there."

"If they're all the same, can't they just remove one of the other ones and reinstall them?" Bus asked.

"No," Evan replied, nodding to Linda. "Pull one of the busses and you're going to cause a cascade failure in the drive. And with the busses in place . . . You made sure they were a hot contact, right?"

"Oh, yeah," Linda said, smiling.

"With the spare busses in place, the system would be totally destabilized," Evan noted. "Think of it as being shorted out. And I'm not sure you could trace the short with any great ease. You'd have to have full power. Damn, you're right, I don't know if *I* could find them."

"Herzer," Nicole said, "I'd like to apologize."

"Why?" Herzer asked. "You did one hell of a job. Hell, you all did one hell of a job. All I did was sit here and worry."

"I got really peeved at you in training," Nicole admitted. "You kept pushing and kept making us learn some really oddball stuff. I thought we just needed to know how to pull the injectors. But I've had to cover half the ship. If you hadn't made us learn all that stuff . . ."

"Hell, if I had to, you had to," Herzer said with a grin. "Van Krief, what do you think New Destiny will do when they realize they don't have a way to redirect the ship and they don't have control of any of the shuttles?"

"Try to seize the functioning shuttles?" Van Krief said. "Maybe figure out a way to get the engines back online? Why were they doing a burn, anyway?"

"I think I've figured that one out," Evan said, frowning. "If they can get the ship inside geosynchronous orbit, they can teleport the fuel out."

"I've got a teleport block in place," Megan pointed out.

"Then they'll try to find you and take *you* out," Evan replied. "But they don't have controls. Heck, they don't even have power."

"They're going to do something," Cruz noted.

"They'll have to attack on the surface," Van Krief pointed out. "If they can get the shuttles, Reyes can override Megan's controls. But I don't know if they have pilots."

"They won't need them," Linda pointed out. "If they just let them run on program they'll get half the fuel."

"And we don't want that," Herzer noted. "When the shuttles get back, we'll be supplemented by twenty-four Lords. But until then, I think we're still outnumbered. Maintenance has just about lost its utility to us. Evan, get with Geo and find out what he needs to rework the other Tammens. Then we'll split up, collect them, and head for Engineering. When the shuttles come back, we'll use the incoming teams for security on the transfer. We're going to hunker down in Engineering and hold out until then."

"You may have my head, Great One," Tur-uck said, bowing before Reyes. "We tried to find the power leads but they were either thrown away or hidden beyond our ability to find."

"There are over four thousand buss bars, Great One," Gomblick said, licking his lips nervously. "If they were hidden in that tangle, I couldna find them."

"Get up," Reyes growled at Tur-uck. "We have no control, here.

We will move the whole group to Engineering and search it inch by inch if that is what is necessary to find the power bars."

"Great One, I have a question," Tur-uck said, cautiously. "When we were returning, I noticed that most of the shuttles were still attached. Were they not supposed to have refueled and returned to Earth?"

"Yes," Reyes said, looking at Gomblick.

"I dunno know why," the engineer said, his eyes widening. "I didna do it!"

"Find *out*," Reyes growled.

The engineer took a seat in front of the shuttle control panel and began hunting through menus as Reyes furiously tapped one foot.

"They're disabled," Gomblick said, finally, wincing as he did. "The injector system canna work on the engines. Only shuttle one and the four to the rear launched. The four to the rear launched under internal control. They're all heading to Coalition reactors."

"Damn them," Reyes screamed. "While we've been running all over the ship trying to deal with their crap, they disabled the shuttles and no one *noticed*?"

"I was in Engineering," Gomblick said, cowering in front of the raging Great One. "Tom was trying to fix the doors and Goblast . . ." He ended, nervously, looking at the body in the corner.

"Can you *fix* them?" Reyes asked, trying to control his temper. He only had two engineers left and he didn't need it pointed out that the one he'd killed would have been the one to tell him the shuttles were being deactivated.

Gomblick hunched over the control panel again and began calling up more menus, muttering under his breath as he did. After a moment the mutter died away.

"What?" Reyes said, dangerously.

"The injectors ha' been pulled from the engines, Great One," Gomblick replied, not bothering to turn around. "And Maintenance lists the spare injector bin as empty. The bots ha' repaired shuttle five's damage, all but the injector. There's a replicator in Maintenance, but it's been taken offline." He turned around and looked the Great One in the eye, firmly. "No, I canna repair them. Not wi'out the injectors. And if they've gone an' buggered them this good, they'll ha' gone and buggered the spares."

Reyes stared at him, hard, until the kobold dropped his gaze; then the Key-holder looked away as well.

"We'll capture their tame shuttles when they get back," Reyes, finally. "In the meantime, we need to get to Engineering and get the engines back online. Somehow. Pilot Reefic and four Durgar stay here. The rest of you are on me."

CHAPTER TWENTY-EIGHT

"Whoa," Corporal Berghaus muttered as the airlock in the distance opened. He was hiding in the dimple near shuttle eleven, one of three pickets left out in vacuum to watch for New Destiny's response. And it was a good thing he was since New Destiny was responding. First four scorpions crawled out and spread out. The metallic arthropods did, indeed, have magnetic feet and they could move much more quickly than humans or orcs on the exterior of the ship. The question in everyone's mind was how long they could survive on the surface. They'd only been seen in death pressure for a few minutes at a time.

Behind the scorpions, the airlock started to disgorge armored orcs, at least a half a dozen. Then a second wave of more orcs with a couple of soft-suited figures, then what could only be Reyes and the Changed elf, the latter looming over all the other figures.

"Lieutenant, this is Berghaus," the picket said, quietly. "We have a problem."

"Great," Herzer muttered, looking up at the thruster assembly. Linda and Geo were up on the vaguely dildo-shaped thruster, removing the Tammen reactionless drive. They were on the starboard side of the ship and the orc force had emerged to port so they *probably* weren't going to run across his team. But Captain Van Buskirk's teams were to port and they'd quickly be in view of the orcs.

"Bus, did you hear what Cruz passed on?" Herzer asked.

"I was listening in," the lieutenant admitted. "We're halfway through pulling this Tammen. As soon as they're done, we'll head downward on the ship to the yaw thruster and pull that one. I think we have enough time; among other things, we're in shadow here so we're harder to see. If they're getting in view, we'll give up on this one and boogey out."

"Works," Herzer said. "Two guesses where they're heading."

"Engineering," Lieutenant Van Krief said. "Maybe Maintenance."

"Where are we going to fix these things up?" Cruz asked.

"Life Support," Herzer replied after a moment's thought. The crew compartment, Control and Maintenance were on the "top" side of the ship on the first, second and third support rings, respectively. By the same token, EVA, Fuel Control and Life Support were on the "bottom" of the rings. The orcs were, apparently, passing across the top of the ship. Let them get to Engineering. They'd have about another seven hours before they could boost again without hitting the Earth. But at some point, the Tammens would have to be hooked into power. Cross that bridge when they came to it. "We'll reconstruct the Tammens there, then figure out how to get power to them."

"Works," Cruz said. "We're nearly done, here."

"Everybody hurry," Herzer said. "I want to get off the surface before we accidentally stumble on trouble."

"I see what you mean about finding them," Reyes admitted.

The six ion cannons for the drive were stacked in two sets of three, suspended over the fusion reactors and reaching up to the ceiling. Each of the drives had four dual-power input points, to first strip the electrons from the raw helium three they used for fuel and the additional three to apply more and more energy to it until the raw protons were blasted out the rear of the ship at a sizeable fraction of the speed of light.

The power supply for the vast undertaking consisted of ranks and ranks of buss bars that were accessed by catwalks. Elevators at the front of the compartment lifted techs, and their gear, up to the higher sections and there were four massive overhead cranes for heavier materials.

The problem was that all the buss bars looked exactly alike. And from the looks of the empty primary power point, the buss bars from there were identical to the individual supply bars.

Reyes walked over to the nearest lattice and considered the connection of the buss bars. They were fitted into clamps and then cranked down into contact with the transfer buss. There were also spare clamps on the transfer buss. Probably the Coalition team had hidden the busses in the maze. But . . .

"How long?" Reyes mused. "You took about twenty minutes to get here, yes?"

"We went as fast as we could, Great One," Tur-uck replied.

"I'm sure you did," Reyes said. "But I also don't think they had time to hook them up fully. They're probably just slid into a clamp. Spread out. Look for busses that are loose. You're sure this is cold, yes?" he asked the engineer.

"Has to be, Great One," the kobold said with just a hint of disrespect. "There's nigh leading to it."

"Spread out," Reyes repeated, waving at the group. "One Durgar to every catwalk. Pull on every buss bar. Find the loose ones."

It took about an hour for the teams to remove the four Tammen field generators and move them back to Life Support.

The life support section was mostly pumps and pipes with a narrow open area running down the middle. Herzer had half expected it to be filled with plants, but manual reprocessing of air and water was far more efficient.

Each of the engineers had taken one of the Tammens to modify and Evan estimated about another hour to get them changed to more powerful models. At that point, they could hook them directly to the power output on the fusion reactors and ignore the busses.

"How's it going?" Herzer asked, strolling over to where Geo had his arms up to the elbows in the tangled cabling of the field generator.

"Just fine," Geo said, happily. "I've got the replicator module in place. We'll have to set up a neural link for controls, I think. I'd thought Countess Travante would be the obvious choice for using them. Among other things, Mother will have less issue with it if we come anywhere near Earth."

"Hopefully, that won't happen," Herzer said dryly.

"Well, as long as the engines remain off . . ." Geo said, as the floor began to rumble. "Or not."

"Not good," Herzer said, glancing at the timepiece in his helmet. "Not good at all . . ."

✧   ✧   ✧

"No, no, no!" the goblin pilot squeaked as his controls went live again. "No it is not a good time to fire, Master!"

"Shut up," Reyes said over the communications link. "The engines are working again. Be glad."

"But, Master . . ." the goblin said, desperately.

"Just *shut up*," Reyes growled. "Or I'll figure out if I can fly this thing myself! Steer it for an orbit around Earth. Now!"

"I will . . . try," the goblin said, engaging one of the forward thrusters. If he could just point the ship so that the engine vector pushed it out of the gravitational envelope of the planet ahead, they might all survive. . . .

"Megan, Courtney," Herzer said, striding down the corridor to where the majority of the team was resting. "Find a console you can hack into the navigational system. I don't think you can control from here, but you should be able to find nav data. Try to figure out why in the *hell* Reyes just kicked on the engines. According to Joie, if we fired during this window we'd crash. I really hope she was wrong."

"I'll help," Josten said. "Get me the data and I can figure out where we're going."

"Master, if you please," the goblin pilot whined, crawling on his hands and knees to where Reyes was established back in his station chair.

"What now?" Reyes asked, balefully. "The engines are back on."

"Yes, Master," the pilot said, carefully. "I beg you, let me turn them off. It is not the time for them to be on."

"Canna do it," Gomblick said from Engineering. "He had me lock out the controls. They're on until we shut them off manually."

"Then we should leave the ship, Master," the pilot said, reaching out a hand and waving it by Reyes' leg. "Quickly."

"Why?" Reyes asked, frowning.

"We are on course to crash into the planet in six hours, Master."

"WHAT?"

"The engines are on a manual burn," Josten said about fifteen minutes later. "It looks like whoever is piloting this thing is try-ing to avoid a degrading orbit, but I don't think he can unless the engines get shut down. In fact, if they keep thrusting like this for another . . . fourteen minutes, there's not a chance in hell. There isn't enough power in this ship to prevent it from crashing into the planet. If they just keep thrusting and maneuvering as they are right now, we're going to enter the planet's atmosphere in about six hours."

"Is that what they wanted?" Megan asked. "To crash it into *Earth*? Surely they're not *that* stupid!"

"I don't know," Herzer replied, grimacing. "But we're well and truly screwed. The shuttles are going to return full of Blood Lords so getting us *off* of this thing is going to be tough. And I don't know about getting the fuel off. I don't know about getting *us* off!"

"We are so totally screwed," Josten sighed.

"TURN THEM OFF!"

"I canna," Gomblick said, angrily. "You had me *lock them out*, ye ken? Gotta go back to Engineering and turn them off manually. We're halfway down the ship. Be twenty minutes before I could get there."

"In . . . five minutes it will not matter, Master," the goblin said. "After that we will not have enough thrust to avoid capture."

Reyes' eyes widened and he shook his head angrily.

"When we approach Earth, we can teleport out," he said after a moment.

"Not with the teleport block in place," Tragack pointed out. It was the first thing he'd said during the entire mission.

"Then we have to get the teleport block down," Reyes replied, angrily. "Find that bitch Travante. She's the Key-holder and the Key."

"Move, move, move," Herzer said, keeping one hand clamped on the handhold of the Tammen and the other on his safety line. "Carefully."

"Herzer, this is Evan," the engineer said. "There's an orc picket outside Engineering."

"Cruz," Herzer replied. "Take them down. Fast."

"The Tammens *might* be able to steer us out of a retrograde orbit," Geo said. He was carrying the other end of the Tammen and trying to keep in step with the larger Blood Lord commander.

"If we get the engines shut down and get them in place in time. It will take a few minutes to get the neural net synced to the councilwoman, though."

"Ask me for anything but time," Herzer muttered. "Cruz? How's it coming?"

"Great One!" Sharkack called over the communicator. "The humans are attacking the starboard airlock! Durgast is dead and they are cutting through the airlock doors!"

Reyes opened his mouth and then shut it.

"Great One, if I may," Tur-uck said, diffidently. "They are probably going to try to turn the engines off. That may be for the best."

"I was thinking the same thing," Reyes replied. "Sharkack, pull out of Engineering to port. Just let them have it."

"Yes, Great One," the Durgar replied in a puzzled tone.

"They won't know how many orcs we left behind," Reyes said, getting to his feet, his eyes distant in thought. "Which means they'll have brought all their fighters. Which means that the councilwoman, whom they also have to protect, will be with them."

"Yes, Great One," Tur-uck said, grinning fiercely. "We attack?"

"We attack," Reyes said. "Now."

"Herzer."

"Go, Sesheshet," Herzer replied. It had taken twenty minutes to cut through the airlock doors, venting the engineering spaces in the process, but when they got into the vast space, the orcs had left.

"What looks like the entire remaining force just exited Control, headed for Engineering," the private stated. "I can see Reyes and that elf-thing with them."

"Got it," Herzer said. "Hold your position and stay out of sight."

"Will do."

"Evan?" Herzer asked. "How long?"

The engines had been shut down again and the Tammens were being attached to the primary power feeds from the reactors. The field generators could extract the electrons directly from the power leads, shunting them through two fields to convert the power into zero point particle reactionless drive fields.

Theoretically.

"Just about there," Evan said. "We're initializing the neural feed now. Mistress Travante?"

Megan was sitting in a station chair, her eyes closed, but she waved a hand.

"I can see the power," she whispered. "Boy, that's a lot of power."

"Careful with it," Evan replied.

"It's ... raw," Megan said, carefully. "It's just ... there. I'm not sure how to even manipulate it. Mother usually does most of the work. This is just ... lots and lots of power."

"Whoa!" Cruz said as he leaned sideways. It was as if the gravity in the room had suddenly shifted and he spread his feet to fight the disorientation. Sergeant Rubenstein lifted up off the ground and drifted forward, then just as abruptly dropped to the deck, swearing.

"Sorry," Megan said, her eyes still closed. "I'm trying to sort of ... grab the ship. And there's not much feedback. I'm looking for something solid to grab onto, trying to find the structural members. It's ... weird."

"Figure it out quickly, darling," Herzer replied, calmly. "We've got company coming. Blood Lords, assemble at the blown door. We'll hold them, there, until Megan gets control of the power. Team Cruz, then Van Krief, then Van Buskirk, then mine."

"If it gets down to you, Layne and Yetta, it's going to be ugly," Van Buskirk said, quietly. "Any ideas what to do about the elf?"

"I do," Nicole said, nodding. "Evan, Paul, I could use some help."

"They're going to be waiting for us at the door," Reyes said as they approached the cut-out airlock. "Tragack, you go first. Clear out the resistance. Then a wave of scorpions, then Sharkack's group then Tur-uck's. I'll go last."

"Yes, Master," the elf said, his stride widening to pass through the struggling orcs. When he got to the door, which was "down" from his perspective, he leaned over and looked through. On the far side of the second door a line of armored figures was waiting. They were standing in gravity, looking sideways from his perspective.

He reached down to grab the cut-away frame, intending to swing through both doors and into the line, and his hand clamped on the exposed copper power cable that had been laid around the inside of the door.

Nicole and Evan had cut away the top of the insulator and glued the lead to the inside of the frame, so the exposed copper was in direct contact with the underside of the Dark One's metal gauntlet. The lead carried the full force of the internal power fusion generator, some ten megawatts, and the electricity coursed into the Dark One's body through his armor. The internal suit insulation gave some resistance, but not much, and the Dark One let out an unheard howl of pain as his suit electronics fried and the internal materials began to burn around him. The coursing power had caused his hand to clamp and his muscles to jerk irregularly, yanking his boots loose from their magnetic hold, but there was no way he could let go of the door edge.

From Reyes' perspective, the elf had simply frozen in place, floating away from the ship with his hand clamped on the door, but some of the nearer orcs began to apparently dance a jig as residual power spread onto the surface of the ship.

"Tragack?" Reyes said, stopping.

"Yi, yi, yi, yi!" Sharkack said, his communicator popping and squealing.

"What is *happening*?" Reyes shouted, holding his place.

"Breaker blew," Evan said as the internal lights went off.

"Dark One's still there," Cruz said switching on his suit light, then shook his head as the huge armored figure's hand released its deathhold on the door frame and drifted away. "Cancel. Elf's done."

"The main is well and truly fried," Linda said, from the breaker panel. "It'll take us a while to get power back on."

"Still a bunch of orcs out there," Cruz said as heads began to appear in the opening. "Die or drop time."

"Herzer, this is Joie," the pilot said. "You know the ship is wildly off course, right?"

"Stand by, Joie," Herzer replied. "Evan, how far can Megan be from the power generators?"

"Oh, anywhere on this end of the ship," Evan replied.

"Drop what you're doing," Herzer said. "Lieutenant Van Krief, pull your team back and head for the far side of Engineering and exit to port. Take the councilwoman and all the techs with you. This has just become a delaying action. Joie, how long to docking?"

"Ten, twelve minutes," Joie said. "Herzer, the ship is headed for Earth on a degrading orbit. More like right smack dab *at* Earth at very high velocity. And it's rotated so the main engines are pointed down. Not that they'll stop it or anything."

"We know," Herzer said, gently prying the entirely introspective Megan out of her chair. "Just get docked. We have company and I'd appreciate some help."

"Go!" Sharkack called as the first Durgar clambered into the airlock. "Get the humans!"

Reyes could *see* that they were headed towards Earth, now, since the ship had somehow gotten rotated with the engines *down*. He guessed that the pilot had done it in a desperate attempt to avoid a crash.

But they were getting close enough he had to wonder if he could connect to the New Destiny power systems. If he could, this fight would be over fast.

"Mother, are you out there?"

CHAPTER TWENTY-NINE

Ferdous Dhanapal thoroughly enjoyed fighting orcs. He'd liked fighting before the Fall, competing in boxing and martial arts but only if the pain circuits were dialed down. He just enjoyed beating the hell out of a tough opponent.

And these orcs weren't exactly easy. The full suit of armor made them clumsy, but with their long halberds pushed forward, it was hard to get down to the suit. He'd flicked a magnet at them, fending off the halberds with his light buckler, but the suits weren't magnetic.

He blocked one of the halberds up with the buckler and ducked under it, pushing another to the side and pinning two of the orcs against the back wall.

"Berghaus, get in here and pound these sons of bitches," he snarled, pressing into the crossed halberd with both hands. "Puncture their armor."

"Think you're smart, do you?" Tur-uck muttered, snatching a halberd away from one of the Durgar. The Blood Lord had Garack and Purdop pinned in the entryway, but while he was doing that he couldn't defend himself. The spearhead of the halberd darted in and out like a snake.

"Aaaaarrrr!" Ferdous shouted, reaching up to clamp a hand over his left bicep where the halberd head had slipped past the armor. The wound was spouting red into the vacuum faster than he could stop it and he could feel his arm going numb as blood pumped out through the small cut. The suit gel was spurting out as well, creating a small cloud in the entryway. He let go of the cut and reached for his mace, slamming the spike into the armor of the orc on his right as he stumbled backwards. His left arm was useless, he couldn't even feel it anymore, and the air in the airlock was filled with a red cloud.

And his heater system was failing as well, he was getting cold . . .

Manos Berghaus didn't like his situation at all. As his triari sergeant stumbled backwards, his mace buried in the helmet of the left-hand Durgar, the halberd dropped way from the right-hand one and more started flooding through the human-sized hole in the airlock door.

The Durgar had mostly dropped their halberds and drawn their short, broad, curved swords, which were far more useful in the tight confines of the airlock. The swords were about as long as the gladius the Blood Lords carried but much heavier, almost like cleavers.

Berghaus blocked the blow from the first Durgar through the door as he slammed his mace into the right arm-joint of the right-hand Durgar's armor. It didn't pop the seal but the articulation was cracked and the Durgar at least couldn't use that arm.

He backed up to give himself room and swung overhand at the Durgar on his left as Line Sergeant Nasrin slid into place beside him. Two more Durgar had forced their way in and Nasrin took the right-hand one as Berghaus fought the left.

There wasn't much room to swing the mace but there was enough and Berghaus flipped it around so he was striking with the spike end. He caught the next blow from the Durgar's sword partially on its buckler but it slid off, skittering across his lorica in a shower of sparks. Berghaus slid up under the Durgar's arm and swung upwards, slamming the spike into the underside of the Durgar's arm and then working it out with a back and forth motion like a can opener.

However, before he could get the spike all the way out, the Durgar whose arm he'd damaged proved he could work with both hands, slamming his cleaverlike sword into the Blood Lord's extended arm. The heavy hacking blade chopped right through the grieve on that arm and sliced open his suit.

"Herzer, Berghaus and Ferdous are down," Cruz said, panting. "It's pretty tight in here."

"Just hold on another second," Herzer said, watching the group of techs retreat. "Then turn around and run like hell."

"Will do," Cruz replied. "We're faster than they are, that's for sure. Give me the word when you're ready."

"Any sign of the scorps?" Herzer asked.

"None," Cruz admitted. "I don't think they want to mingle them with the Durgar."

"Or they're somewhere else," Herzer said as he looked over his shoulder. The entire group of techs, and Megan, had already cycled through the far airlock.

"Going somewhere, Councilwoman?" Reyes said to himself as the group of Blood Lords climbed out of the airlock onto the hull of the ship. He'd gathered his six remaining scorpions and now waited in ambush. "Fire," he said, gesturing at the scorpions.

"Bloody hell," Sergeant Yamada said as the line of scorpions squirted at the Blood Lords. The scorps had been low to the hull and he hadn't actually seen them until he was fully emerged. The viscous fluid seemed to drift through the microgravity at them and he ducked so that most of the material passed overhead. But from the screams on the net, some of it had impacted. And the scorpions were charging the suddenly broken line of Blood Lords.

Megan lifted herself out on the far side of the hatch from the Blood Lords, her eyes still closed. Using the energy from the engines was getting easier, she could *feel* when she had hold of something solid. Of course, she'd probably done some damage to the ship finding those solid holds, but that was the price of trying to stop it plummeting to the Earth.

She turned as she heard the screams and her control dropped away at the sight of the line of scorpions. And the ejected acid from their tails.

"Mother!" she called, hoping against hope that they were inside the area of the protocols.

✧   ✧   ✧

"Holy shit," Nicole said, backing away from the Blood Lords and ducking to let the spittle fly by. The scorpions had fired as they would in gravity and the majority of the fluid went past overhead. But she was not about to stick around to get hit with the next firing. She grabbed the bar by the opening of the airlock and ducked back in, huddling by the inner door. Most of the techs had climbed back in for that matter. Better than being out where the scorpions could get them.

"Megan," she snapped, "get out of there."

"Yes, Megan," Mother said.

"Personal protection fields on all our people," Megan said. "Right now. Use the ship power I have access to. Can you?"

"No, Megan," Mother replied. "The field is attuned to you and is specifically locked out from my control. If you were closer, I could override that. But from here, I cannot at this time."

"Shit," Megan said. There were only five Blood Lords standing and the scorpions had closed with them. Reyes was standing behind with three of the Durgar, watching the fight. "Herzer, we need help here," she said, dialing the airlock shut and stumping "downward" on the ship. Reyes was probably after her. Let him chase her and leave the others alone.

"Move," Herzer said, looking at Van Buskirk's team. "Cruz, pull back. Megan's getting hit on the far side."

He turned and flat out ran to the far airlock, keying the inner door open and then the outer door, overriding the safeties to clear the way fully.

He entered the lock and grabbed the overhead grab-bar, swinging himself up and onto the surface of the ship.

The only Blood Lord still standing when he got there was Van Krief and she was battling three scorpions, using her gladius in one hand and mace in the other to keep them at bay. Two of the other three scorpions were stuck on the deck, unmoving and presumably dead, while the area above the deck was littered with the desiccated bodies of the dead Blood Lords. Since the ship wasn't accelerating, they were drifting slowly along with it. As his feet hit the deck, he saw her lean right to avoid a shot of acid but then the right-hand scorpion slipped past her guard and got its claw on her arm.

The metallic claw closed silently, from Herzer's perspective, but he could hear the crunch and shriek of metal in his mind as Van Krief's arm dropped, hanging by a thread of suit and tissue and blasting fluid into space. She writhed for a moment, the mace and gladius floating away from her, stuck in place by her mag-boots, and then stopped moving, standing still as a statue in the eternal void.

The three Durgar with Reyes had stumped forward as well and Herzer suddenly found himself facing six opponents. He lifted his buckler to catch a shot of acid and then tossed it to the side, slinging the material towards one of the scorpions. It hit and stuck and began to burn. As he blocked a claw with his mace, he saw the back of the scorpion explode outwards in a rush of vapor and internal parts.

The Durgar had retained their halberds and poked them forward at him as the scorpions spread out to either side. He ducked another shot of acid, batted away a claw, but couldn't close to do any good.

He backed up, slightly, edging around the open airlock, then quickly flipped out a safety line, tossed it to the deck where the magnet, fortunately, stuck, unclamped the magnets on his boots and jumped off over the heads of the Durgar and scorpions.

One of the scorpions shot at him as he went overhead but they were still having trouble adjusting to microgravity. The jet of acid sailed well past him.

As he reached the end of the safety line, Herzer let himself stretch out to full extension, then slowly adjusted his body position so his feet were down, but pointed in the opposite direction, back towards where the magnetic clamp was still holding.

He hit on both feet, one boot momentarily coming loose but then he got it clamped back down. When he was solidly planted, he bent at the knees, bringing the safety line down to the level of the deck and pulling it sideways, hard.

The two scorpions had spun in place as he went overhead and as soon as he landed had started for his position, spreading out. Thus the line only caught one of them. The feet on one side sprang loose easily, but the others held for a moment. Herzer lifted up on the line, though, and the scorpion was kicked free to fly upwards into the deeps of space.

The Durgar were just starting to turn around as he got the line untangled from the scorpion's legs—it was trying to clutch at it—and brought it back down. This time he stepped to the left, bringing the line along and knocking two of the Durgar flying. The third managed to get a hand on the line and disputed his control just long enough for the scorpion to close on the Blood Lord commander.

Herzer flipped a loop in the line, which managed to tangle one of the scorpion's claws. He jerked on it, hoping to pick the arthropod up off the deck, but instead he popped his own boots free. He pulled down, dropping back to the deck as the partially entangled beast closed, but managed to get both boots clamped before it got to him.

He drew his mace and blocked both claws, looking for acid. It didn't seem to be spitting so he thought it might have run out of juice, at least temporarily. After sparring with it for a moment, he drew his gladius, flipped the weapons around and held out the mace invitingly near the beast's left claw.

The beast grabbed the mace, shaking it back and forth and trying to sever the steel shaft. Herzer drew the mace further to his left, bringing his body outside of the claw that held the mace, and cut downward with the gladius, hitting the joint seal of the claw, hard.

The joint immediately spouted fluids and popped open, releasing the mace. The scorpion started to spin in place to bring its tail into play but Herzer was having none of it. He slammed the released mace down on its brain-pan and the forward part of the scorpion opened up like a flower, gushing fluid into the vacuum.

The last Durgar was standing by the open door, watching him carefully, when a hand came out of the opening and grabbed it by both legs. Before it could react, the hands had lifted it off the deck and spun it off into the void.

Herzer looked around and realized that Reyes was gone. He spun fully around and spotted him. The Key-holder was using hand clamps to move along the hull, fast, headed downward.

"Megan, honey, where are you?" Herzer said, calmly.

"On the bottom, rear quadrant," Megan said, breathlessly. "There's supposed to be another hatch into Environmental down here. I think Reyes is following me."

"He is," Herzer said as Van Buskirk's team clambered out of the hole. "Bus, change of plan, again. Cruz, you holding?"

"We've got it licked," Cruz said, breathlessly. "Three guys in the airlock and they can't get past."

"Wish we'd figured that out at the beginning," Herzer sighed. "Bus, cross the hull and attack the Durgar from behind," Herzer said, unclamping his boots.

"Where are you going?" Cruz asked.

"After Reyes," he said, bending at the knees and leaping upward.

"Megan Travante," Reyes muttered. "I am so going to kill you. I'd like to kill you slow, but I'll settle for killing you quick and taking your Key."

He'd watched the tide of battle turn and decided that chasing the council member, whom he'd seen turn tail and run, was a better use of his time. He'd skirted the fight to the rear of the hatch and now was closing on the slowly walking Megan quickly. And she didn't have a shred of help anywhere to be seen.

"I am *so* going to kill you," Reyes muttered. "Maybe I'll figure out a way to do it slow."

The bound carried Herzer thirty meters towards Reyes, forward of the line he was taking over the curve of the hull. Herzer hit more softly this time and took his second line out, clamping it off and jumping off again.

It was a fast, and dangerous, way to cross the distance. If the clamp let go he'd go spinning off into the depths with no way home, a "flying Dutchman," doomed to die when his air, or more likely icepacks, gave out.

The second line got him most of the way to Reyes and he pulled out his third and last, figuring the crossing speed of the council member and his own position, then pushed off, one last time.

Reyes felt himself pushed into the deck so hard he nearly lost his hold on the clamp, but his gravity protection field activated instantly, pushing away whatever it was that hit him.

Herzer spun off to the side, completely out of control, one hand on the safety line and the other scrambling for a magnet. As he spun past the deck he clamped the hand magnet to it, stopping his spin and nearly wrenching his arm out of its socket. Whatever Reyes had for protection, it wasn't a personal protection field. It was very reactive to impact that was for sure.

He got to his feet, using the light line on the hand clamp as a safety line and confronted the council member, who was also standing. Reyes had pulled out a short sword like the Durgars and seemed fully prepared to use it. Of course, he also was covered by a sparkling field of ... something. Herzer had previously fought people in PPFs and even energy-draining nannite fields. This one, though, hit back.

"It's a gravity field you ignorant sword-swinger," Reyes said to himself, reading the mind of his opponent as Herzer pulled out a mace. "Good luck getting through it. We're back in Mother's control area."

Herzer stepped forward, swinging the mace cautiously. He closed, step by step, to the council member and then swung the mace in, lightly. It bounced back, hard and to the right as the field swirled more brightly, seeming to spin in a tornado of sparks around the armored figure of the council member.

Reyes followed up the blow with one of his own, the sword darting out like a striking cobra only to be blocked by Herzer's buckler. It struck off the buckler in a shower of sparks and Reyes circled to the "downward" side in the direction of the retreating Megan.

"Don't think so," Herzer said, taking a couple of steps back and contemplating the dilemma. He couldn't penetrate the field, but he didn't really have to. All he had to do was take Reyes out of play. He wanted to know what he was facing, through, so he keyed the communicator for an open frequency broadcast. "Reyes, you hear me?"

"Yes," Reyes said, frowning. He didn't know how Herzer had gotten his frequency, but he didn't really care. He knew it was the Blood Lord commander from the markings on his suit. The security on the Icarus group had been unusually tight, but Chansa's people had been able to get *that* much information at least.

"There are four shuttles full of Blood Lords going to be landing in about ten minutes," Herzer said. "You gather your people and get out and I'll let you leave. Let bygones be bygones. You know the ship's crashing, right?"

"I know that," Reyes replied. "But that doesn't mean I'll let you live. With Megan's Key and the power from Mother, I can kill *all* your Blood Lords and take the fuel. *Before* the ship crashes."

"But you'll have to get past me," the Blood Lord said, calmly. "And that ain't gonna happen. Just go home."

"I don't think so," Reyes snarled, stepping forward cautiously and swinging his sword back and forth. "All I have to do is nick that pretty suit of yours and you're history. Time to die, Herzer."

"One question," Herzer said, backing away again. "That's not a personal protection field, is it?"

"No," Reyes replied, smirking and pausing to savor the moment. "Celine's little toys can take those down. This is a grav field priority tied to the full output of the Samarian reactor. Anything impacting on it, just makes it get stronger. There's no way through it. So why don't you just step aside and let me go . . . play with your little girlfriend."

"Don't think so," Herzer said, backing up steadily and sheathing his mace. "But thanks for the information . . ."

" . . . you stupid motherfisker," Herzer continued, with the communicator shut off. He pulled off one of the thigh magnets and extended the cord, spinning it around and then tossing it to the right of the council member.

The cord was five meters long and there wasn't more than three meters between them. So when it got to the end of the tether, the magnet swung to the left until the line hit the field around the Key-holder. At which point, the magnet started circling him in a "degrading orbit," spinning faster and faster as the gravity field, which was pulling to the right and increasing the spin, got brighter and brighter.

When the magnet finally impacted on the field it bounced and started to rewind only to be wound tighter by the gravitic impulse. As soon as it was tight, Herzer planted his feet and leaned back and sideways, pulling the Key-holder off his feet and spinning him around in an arc, letting go when Reyes was well off the deck and drifting towards the rear of the ship. As Reyes passed, Herzer gave him an added little tap outwards. Best to be sure.

Reyes flew away soundlessly, his thrashing arms entrapped by the field and the cord that wrapped it. Well, he was probably screaming, Herzer thought, but it wasn't as if anyone could hear it. Herzer watched as the Key-holder drifted rapidly towards the rear of the ship and then walked in that direction to make sure he was really gone. He could think of about four ways Reyes might live, and he wanted to make sure none of them happened.

Reyes continued more or less to the rear of the ship, drifting outwards slightly. The ship generated a very small gravity field, thus the term "microgravity," and it was possible he could still be pulled down to the deck. The "upward" vector had slowed noticeably as Herzer watched. That was, until he passed the protective guards around the ion cannons. Those extended out a meter from the hull and Herzer had been slightly worried that Reyes might figure out a way to snag one. Once he was beyond the guards, he was very much in deep space. Of course, he might still call on Mother for help. Couldn't have that.

"Evan, you in Engineering?" Herzer asked.

"Yes," Evan said. "The Durgar are gone. They all just left, even before Captain Van Buskirk could get to them. He says they're headed towards the control room."

"Much good it will do them," Herzer said, watching the rapidly dwindling council member. "Evan, do me a favor."

"What?" Evan asked.

"Hit the main engine start," Herzer replied.

"You're serious?" Evan asked.

"Yep," Herzer said. "Can you start it?"

"Easy," Evan replied, curiously. "I'll do it right now. But why? It's only going to send us that much faster to Earth."

"I just want to see what happens," Herzer said, standing about a meter behind the blast shield.

"Engaging . . . now."

The space behind the ship was suddenly lit by a blue glare, so fierce that Herzer quickly dropped his solar goggles over his eyes. The council member, however, was noticeable even in the glare. The edge of the field had impacted the grav field around the council member, which had brightened even beyond the glare of the excited ions exiting the rear of the ship.

Herzer felt himself very slightly pushed to the rear of the ship and stuck one hand out to brace against the blast shield. He kept his eye on the council member's bright figure, though, until with a final blast of fire, it winked out.

"Kill it," Herzer said a second later, blinking his eyes.

"Done," Evan said as the blue glare of the drive dissipated. "What was that all about?"

"A physics experiment," Herzer replied. "Megan, honey, you okay?"

CHAPTER THIRTY

Megan was done being frightened.

She had only spent a few years in the harem, after all, and it wasn't like she hadn't seen the sky the rest of her life. But she'd found, after being inside four stone walls for five years, that the outside world had become a frightening place.

And space was ten times worse. She was on the underside of the ship, now, in darkness and cold with nothing around her but the curving hull and space. It frightened her so bad that she'd been walking with her eyes shut and when she opened them she realized she had no idea which way the lock was.

"I *will* overcome this," she muttered, staring at the smooth hull that stretched in every direction and then out to the stars. "I will."

She took two of her thigh magnets and then slowly lay backwards, holding herself in place with her boot magnets and outspread arms. Her full armor was more than proof against the interplanetary cold of the hull, so she lay there, drinking in the light of the stars. So many stars, so many planets. And humans confined to just the one, trying again to wipe themselves out. If the ship impacted, they would wipe themselves out.

She felt a slight shudder and a pulling motion and realized that the main engines had started. But after a moment, they shut off again, and the stars hadn't changed one iota. They didn't care about humanity, about its survival or its fall. But she did. So she reached for the power, grappling with it, eyes open to the stars. And felt it . . . change.

"Mother," Megan said. "Are you doing this?"

"Yes, Megan," Mother replied. "You're inside geosynchronous orbit. I can now affect your systems and aid you in what you're trying to do."

"Can you give me any power?" Megan asked.

"Very little," Mother admitted. "Reyes just used the full power of the Samarian reactor and the Net is . . . chaotic. The power battles that had been going on shifted, dramatically, but they are ongoing. You must use the power of the engines if you wish for humanity to survive."

"Will it be that bad?" Megan asked.

"You're currently going nearly fifteen kilometers a second," Mother noted. "On its present course, the ship will pass the Earth just outside of the atmosphere, circle outward and then do a nearly direct reentry impacting in the northern Po'ele Ocean. Given that entry, it is likely that the vast majority of the mass of the ship, and the fuel, will survive to impact. The impact will transmit through the water to shatter the crust of the planet and send the equivalent of the entire water in the Terrane basin into the atmosphere, shutting off light for at least two years, not counting exgassing from the continent-sized volcano that will form. It will be that bad."

"How do we stop it?" Megan asked.

"Follow me," Mother replied, bringing up an orbital schematic. "The power is still tied to you. You need to shove the ship to the right and *forward*, speeding it up on its trajectory past Earth. That will bring it around into a long elliptical orbit. Each time we come around, we'll impact the atmosphere, lightly I hope. That's what's going to slow us down, but if we go in too steep, I won't be able to hold the shields against the reentry heat. It'll be a long process. And we can't start until the shuttles that are preparing to dock are attached."

"Megan, honey," Herzer said. "You okay?"

"I am now," Megan replied in a distracted tone. "I'm on the underside of the ship. We need to start evacuating."

"The shuttles are just about to dock," Herzer said, looking at one of them coming in. "We'll reactivate some of the other shuttles, fuel them and then get out. I don't think there's much we can do to stop the reentry."

"Yes, there is," Megan said, looking at the void of stars. "Get everyone out of here. I'm going to be riding the ship down."

"Disable the shuttles," Satyat said, shaking his head as he unbolted the top of the fusion plant. "Enable the shuttles. When does it end?"

"Now," Linda said, handing him the injector. "We've got to get out of here. Fast. The ship's about to hit the atmosphere. We'll pass through it, but it's going to be unpleasantly spectacular. And we won't want to be outside."

"Well, this one's up," Satyat replied, sliding the injector into place. "Let's slide up front and get out of here."

"Shuttles two, three and six are scheduled for Alabad, Penan and Taurania," Herzer said, looking over the remaining Blood Lords. "The four with crew are full. You guys go down on those on autopilot. See you on the ground."

"Where are you going to be?" Bus asked, curiously.

"Megan has to ride the ship down to control the reentry," Herzer said. "I'm going to ride it down with her."

"You are alive," Tur-uck said, grinning at the Dark One.

The elf shook his head and looked around the room. It appeared to be a small control room of some sort. And it wasn't under gravity. And he hurt. Badly. Burns all over his body and electric shock from the feel of it. He had been tortured.

The last thing he remembered was fighting an orc just like this one, one of hundreds that had ambushed him as he was trying to penetrate the scout screen of Chansa's main continental force in Ropasa. At the moment, he was far too weak to fight it, so he bided his time, hoping that he would recover enough to do battle one last time.

But there was no memory of the torture. Just an aching . . . black feeling in his mind. He felt a rage he didn't understand. It was not in the way of the elves to feel rage. He closed his eyes and leaned back.

"Get it over with," he said. "Torture me. Or kill me. I care not."

"Why the hell should I torture you, Tragack?" the orc asked, grinning. "Hell, I saved your life and dragged you here when everyone else thought you were dead. I'm hoping you know something about space you weren't letting on to the Great One. Otherwise, we're fisked."

"I've got the grav field engaged," a thickly accented voice said. "And main power's on to the engines. This thing's a might rickety, though. And it'll ne'er survive reentry."

"Fly it I will!" The voice was high and shrill and sounded half mad. Probably a goblin Change form. At least three of them, but the orc form was the main fighter. He reached for the power, for the *gaslan*, and found both areas . . . empty. He felt only half an elf at the moment, less, nearly human. To lose the *gaslan*. Nothing could take the *gaslan*. There was no future to feel. He was riding on the winds of fate, half dead and not even half alive.

The elf felt another of those odd spasms of rage. He wanted to kill the damned orc, kill everything in the ship. And he couldn't even move his arms. His right one felt so fried it might never be useable.

"Where is this?" he asked as the gravity slowly came on. It was still less than Earth. They were in orbit. "How did I get here?"

"You don't remember?" the orc said, backing away. "What *do* you remember?"

"Fighting ones like you," Sildoniel said, honestly if hoarsely. "Arrows. Many arrows. Too many. Falling." He lifted his left arm, slowly, it was as fast as it would go, and ran it over his face. The hand when he drew it back was taloned instead of having finely manicured nails and the face was . . . broader, the nose flatter. "What has happened to me?" he asked, trying to rise, his anger getting red hot. "What have you done to me?"

"What's your name?" the orc asked, drawing his sword.

"Wait," Sildoniel said, rolling to sit up and feeling queasy with even that much motion. His right arm wasn't just useless, it was gone just below the shoulder. "Just wait. Stay your sword, orc. If you are to kill me, tell me at least why I am come here."

"You're back," the orc said, his eyes wide. "It's you. What is your *name*?"

"Sildoniel a tor Melessan," the former Dark One said, looking the orc in the eye. "What's yours?"

✧   ✧   ✧

"You shouldn't be here," Megan said, distantly, as the void began to fluoresce. The ship was hitting the very upper edges of the atmosphere, mostly monatomic oxygen, and she was having to shunt the power to form a protective field. Where the oxygen was hitting the field, the results were . . . energetic.

"Neither should you," Herzer said. "The radiation is going to be a nightmare." The ship was also passing through the Van Allen belt, the magnetic belt that prevented much of space's radiation from hitting the Earth. But the belt concentrated that radiation, making it hot enough to cook eggs.

"The shield's holding it," Megan replied as the ship shuddered from the launch of seven shuttles. "I'll be fine. And I'm the only one that has to stay."

"Whither thou goest," Herzer said, squatting down next to her.

"You're so corny," Megan replied with a smile in her voice.

"So, you getting used to the view?" Herzer asked. The ship's "down" side was actually pointed away from the Earth, with nothing above but stars. The Moon would be coming up, soon, though, at the rate they were going.

"Looks pretty good," Megan said, shifting slightly. The ship began to rotate and Herzer quickly got out a hand magnet and clamped it down to keep himself in place. The ship spun on its axis until the Earth came into view and then stopped.

"That was pretty nice," Herzer said, carefully. "You do that?"

"Mother and I," Megan replied. "We're sort of . . . one in this."

"Great," Herzer said. "Look, let's get someplace where I can at least hold onto something."

"I need to be out here," Megan said, distantly.

"Fine," Herzer replied, putting a hand on her arm. "There's a nice docking bay not far from here. We can sit in that while you do . . . whatever you're doing."

"Wait," Megan said distantly. "Look."

Herzer realized that the . . . shape of the fluorescence had changed. Where before it had been a cigar shape extending out from the ship about seventy meters, now, along the "bottom" and "top" it had flattened and extended out to either side. It now formed . . .

"Are those wings?" Herzer asked, blinking rapidly at the ghostly halo shapes.

"Yes," Megan said, standing up carefully and holding out her hand. "I need the shield, anyway, to keep the ship from disintegrating. But with the wings I can reduce our speed by atmospheric skipping. At least, that's what Mother says."

"Maybe we should just let it disintegrate," Herzer pointed out. "If it broke up in the upper atmosphere, it wouldn't destroy the Earth."

"I'd much prefer to live to see home again," Megan pointed out. "I think I can get it, and us, to the ground intact. You didn't know that?"

"No," Herzer admitted.

"Then what in the hell are you doing here?" Megan asked, angrily.

"Whither thou goest," Herzer repeated. "If you were going to commit suicide bringing this thing down, I was going to be right there by you. Besides, I figured you *might* have a survivable plan. I figured it was a low-order probability, though."

"Well, Mother does," Megan said, sighing. "I think. It's going to take some work, though. We're going to be orbiting for about ten hours."

"Our suits won't last that long," Herzer pointed out.

"There are spare air bottles in Engineering," Megan said. "When the ship's not on a close fly-by I can drop some of my concentration. Then it's just a matter of light steering and drive."

Herzer settled her into the docking ring, which had a lip that made for a comfortable seat, and settled down beside her.

"Nice view," he said as the Earth slid by.

"Looks like a hurricane in the Po'ele," Megan said, pointing.

"They call them typhoons for some reason," Herzer replied. "How you doing?"

"Fine," Megan said. "We're outbound, now. We'll swing out, beyond geosynchronous orbit, then back down. We're going to do that about a half a dozen times before we're in a close orbit. When we get down there, I'm going to be busy."

"And you really want to do it all from out here?" Herzer asked.

"Yes," was all Megan said.

"So you're telling me I've been a servant of the Dark for the last three years?" Sildoniel asked.

"Yeah," Tur-uck replied.

"And we're in a fueling shuttle, which is about to crash into the Earth?"

"Yeah," Tur-uck said. He was holding a sword on the one-armed elf but the damned thing was recovering so fast he wasn't sure it was worth it.

"And all the reentry shuttles are disabled," the elf continued.

"That's the case," Tur-uck said. "The rest of those Durgar fisks were out on the hull when we went through the outer atmosphere. I think they all got fried."

"Good," Sildoniel said, stretching. "Is there any food in this thing?"

"Replicators," Gomblick said. "The food's bland but it's hot."

"And water, of course," the elf said. "So, we can crash with the ship, or battle to the death, or we can take this ship, which is more than capable of interplanetary distances, and try to find a habitat that survives."

"Yeah," Tur-uck said.

"Find a reentry capable ship would be nice," the kobold added.

"You are a Change," Sildoniel said, cocking his head to the side. "You must obey the orders of your Masters."

"I've been known to ignore them," Tur-uck replied, tapping his head. "Celine, she's the one that Changed you by the way, she said that I'm a bad product. I've got a plate in my head. It gives me a headache sometime but I don't have the same binding as most orcs. Yours are, what, gone?"

"As is much else," Sildoniel said with a sigh.

"Your arm was crisped," Tur-uck said. "We had to take it off."

"I was not speaking of my arm," the elf replied, softly. "There is . . . brain damage. I presume it was from the . . . Change that Celine forced upon me. It would be very hard for me to even speak Elvish at the moment. Very well. A truce, servant of the Dark. We shall go in search of a reentry capable ship. And when we return to Earth, I shall permit you and these to go, unmolested."

"Nice of you to say that," Tur-uck said, dryly. "Seeing as I'm the one holding the sword."

Sildoniel cocked his head to the side and his left hand blurred out, snatching the sword out of the orc's hand and flipping it around to grasp it.

"And now I am," Sildoniel said. "Goblin. Detach from the ship now that we are out of the atmospheric effects. Let us go try to find a habitat that survives."

✧   ✧   ✧

"I think I can control from in here," Megan said. She was lying on the deck of the maintenance bay, her eyes closed. "But when we get in the atmosphere, we're going to want to be on the outside."

"Why?" Herzer asked. He'd figured out how to bring up the navigation plot and was watching the little ship figure move through the degrading orbit. It was hypnotic. And, okay, terrifying.

"I'm going to aim for a water landing," Megan replied distantly. The ship was currently on its closest approach to the atmosphere and Herzer could feel a deep rumbling through the structure. Part of that was the fusion generators running at max, but the rest was a touch of the atmosphere hitting the shields. "We're not going to want to be inside."

"Gotcha," Herzer said. "We going to be able to breathe? Out of the suits, that is, since we don't want to hit the water *in* them. Armor and all that."

"We'll have to find out," Megan replied. She paused and winced.

"You okay?"

"Gravitational loading," Megan said and took a deep breath. "The ship's not designed to handle gravities like this so I'm having to use some of the power for structural integrity fields. It just tried to break in half."

"Nice image," Herzer said. "And if it breaks in half?"

"We'll try to ride the rear portion down," Megan replied. "Give me a second here, honey."

"You go, girl," Herzer said, softly, so as not to disturb her. He clicked his prosthetic slowly in thought, watching the blinking cursor.

"Herzer," Megan said, after a moment, "could you please quit that?"

They'd taken the time to get a bite of ship's replicator food, which was awful, recharged their air bottles, emptied their catheter gaskets and filled their water bottles. Megan from time to time would have to stop and concentrate as the ship made close approach. But as the last orbit began, they exited the airlock for, hopefully, the last time, and made their way to the docking bay.

The Earth was noticeably closer as they approached. Herzer clamped his prosthetic on a projection and wrapped his arm around Megan's waist as he watched the rapidly approaching ball of blue and white. He could see that Ropasa was coming over the horizon. They'd pass over it, and Hind and all the rest, finally crossing the Po'ele and then, hopefully, Norau for a landing somewhere near Bimi Island.

If the ship held together.

"You comfortable?" Herzer asked as the void around them began to burn.

"I'm in your lap, aren't I?" Megan asked coyly.

"So you are," Herzer replied. The previous touches with the atmosphere had been light, but this one was much brighter and hotter. The atmosphere was actually being blown into plasma along the leading edge of the field-wings, flaring like a pale sun.

"This is very cool," Herzer said as the ship began a slow turn to the right.

"Yes, it is," Megan replied.

"And I never want to do it again," Herzer continued. "What are we doing, anyway?"

"S turns," Megan replied as the ship continued a radical turn. The light began to blaze all along the notional bottom of the ship, actually the starboard. "It's a braking maneuver. I'm trying to get us down to a speed that won't kill us when the ship hits."

"I see," Herzer said and he sort of did from flying dragons. This was rather different, however. Dragons only burned through the air if their napalm racks detonated in midflight. It happened.

"Where are we?" Megan asked.

"You don't know?" Herzer replied, surprised.

"Not really," Megan said. "Just be my eyes, okay?"

"Past Ropasa," Herzer said after a moment, picking out the land forms through the clouds. "Headed to Hind across Taurania, I think."

"Right on," Megan muttered. She did another bank to the left, then winced as there was a shudder through the ship that lifted them off the deck.

"Whoa, horsey," Herzer said, pulling her back down.

"We lost the port corridor member," Megan said, tightly. "Right at the juncture with the midline circular support."

"That's not all we lost," Herzer said, looking to the side. "We're streaming something. Probably helium."

"I can feel the shift in mass," Megan replied. "We probably should have vented most of it anyway. I've got more than enough for the engines."

"It's pretty," Herzer said, shifting to watch the helium stream past. As it hit the shield, and the atmosphere, it fluoresced in all the colors of the rainbow.

"I'm glad," Megan said. "Where are we?"

"Hind," Herzer said, definitely. The shape of the subcontinent was distinctive and mostly uncluttered by clouds. It was getting hard to see, though, through the waves of plasma around the ship.

"There," Ishtar said to General Komellian, pointing up into the sky.

"The last spaceship, Greatness," the general said sadly.

"There will be more when we win," Ishtar promised, watching the massive streak of fire cross the sky.

"There," Aikawa said, pointing to the south.

"A great omen, Your Worthiness," Minister Chang replied, nodding. "A great omen."

"Omen be damned," Aikawa snapped. "Let's just hope she can hold it together until it's no longer a threat."

"We're over the Po'ele," Herzer said. The plasma fire had died down but there was a deep rumbling through the whole structure that felt ominous. "Klicks and klicks of damn all but water."

"Rachel told me a friend of hers was power skiing off Fiji when the Fall hit," Megan said. "If we fall down there, even if I can slow us, we'll drown in the ocean."

"Better drop us somewhere close to land, then," Herzer said.

"I'm heading for the Bimi Deeps," Megan replied. "There's enough area there that if I lose it, the waves won't destroy much. And there's a fleet exercising down there at the moment. Hopefully, we'll land close to them."

"Not too close," Herzer said, imagining the tsunami from the impact. "Or we won't have any ships to get to."

"Not too close," Megan agreed. "Close, but not too close."

"You're not banking anymore," Herzer said.

"No, we're mostly gliding," the councilwoman said. "We'll start banking again over Norau. Should be quite a sight."

"They should be overhead," Edmund said, shielding his eyes. "They should be in view."

"I don't see anything," Colonel Jackson replied, looking up. The Navy rep had come out to the Frisso yards to examine the new cargo ship design and had liked what he'd seen. The Frisso yards were already doing a booming business in coastal ships and some of their work was directly useable by the Navy. He'd already recommended upgrading the Po'ele fleet. Just because New Destiny was concentrated on the Atlantis Ocean, didn't mean that the UFS should ignore the Po'ele. Especially with yards, and trained seamen, at the ready.

"We've dumped every scrap of available power to keeping it from coming apart," Edmund said, frowning. "I guess they're just low enough and slow enough . . . wait. There," he continued, pointing.

The ship had slowed enough that it was no longer making a burning trail across the sky. But it was a kilometer long. Even at two hundred thousand meters it was visible.

"Awesome," Jackson said. "Simply awesome."

"Norau passing under now," Herzer said. "How high are we?"

"Too high," Megan replied, banking to the right. The leading edge started to burn again as they entered thicker atmosphere and Herzer distinctly felt something give under his butt.

"I think we're losing it," he said calmly.

"Ya think?" Megan replied. "That was the port corridor cracking entirely. I'm holding it together with energy I can't spare."

"You'll do it, honey," Herzer said, pulling her more firmly into his lap as the ship began to shudder from the deeper atmosphere. "You'll do it."

"I can see Flora," Herzer said a minute later. "We're going really fast."

"Too fast," Megan said. "Too high. And I think we're coming apart."

"Well," Herzer said, smiling tightly. "It's a . . . little far to jump, dear."

"No, it's not," Megan said, struggling in his arms. "Get ready."

"You're serious?" Herzer asked as the peninsula of Flora flashed by below them.

"Deadly," Megan said.

"You promised you wouldn't tell me to jump off the ship," Herzer said.

"I lied," Megan replied.

Herzer felt ghostly hands pluck at him and his armor was pulled apart and jettisoned to either side. A wind was evident for the first time. It felt ... strange. Fast but ... thin.

"We're leaking," Megan said, her own armor coming apart in sections and flying away to disappear over the side of the ship. They were left in only their suits and helmets.

"I don't have any air," Herzer pointed out. The helmets should have sealed when the armor and their support packs went away but that meant he was rebreathing his own breath. "Neither do you."

"We'll be fine," Megan said as his helmet flew away.

"It's way too thin up here ..." Herzer started to say and then stopped. He could breathe normally.

"I'm holding a bubble around us," Megan replied. "Just hang on for a second ..."

They were coming down fast, now, no longer flying but dropping like a stone. Herzer could *see* the water getting closer and closer. It was still a long way off, but it was coming up *fast*. Much faster than free-fall.

"Megan," he said, less calmly than usual.

"I've got us below reentry speeds," Megan said, "but that's the best I can do. This thing doesn't have enough power to *stop* us from dropping."

"We passed the Deeps," Herzer said. He had the map of the Bimi chain memorized from long experience. "Hell, you missed the whole Bimi *chain*!"

"I said close," Megan replied, tightly. "I didn't say how close. Think planetary here."

"It's gonna be a long swim," Herzer said. "But we won't have to worry about it if we fall this fast. Is there *any* way you can slow us down?"

There was a deep shudder in the ship and the forward section broke free, spinning off to the side.

"No," Megan said to another shudder that seemed to speed their downward fall. "That was fusion three blowing out. That's all I can do. Jump."

"Now?" Herzer asked.

"NOW!"

Herzer nodded his head and took Megan by the arm. The

ship was in virtual free-fall, anyway, so picking her up wasn't that hard.

"What are you doing?" Megan shouted as the shield around them failed and the wind hit full force.

"Saving your life," Herzer muttered. He swung her back and forth for a moment and then threw her as hard as he could towards the rear of the ship.

As soon as Megan hit the vortex of wind around the ship, she curled into a ball, fighting to keep control over the power fields. She formed a field around herself and Herzer to reduce the buffeting and keep a bubble of breathable air. She could *feel* Herzer, now, and he was nearby.

"Spread eagle!" Herzer shouted, tracking towards the falling councilwoman. "Megan, damnit, listen to me! Spread *eagle!*"

Megan clamped into a tighter ball at his words, panicking at the demanding tone.

"Leave me alone!" she shouted over the screaming winds. She was being buffeted by the track of the monstrous ship, but even more so by dark memories.

"Megan," Herzer yelled, fighting his way through the turbulence to approach her. He could feel the support field she had up, slowing themselves and the ship as much as she could. And there was a protection field that was, presumably, concentrating oxygen. They were still above forty thousand feet, at least, and he shouldn't have been able to breathe. But with her in a ball, she was falling faster than she had to. "Spread your arms and legs," he shouted. "It'll slow you down!"

Megan gritted her teeth and threw her arms and legs out, sharply. She had been spinning over and over in her ball but this left her stable for the first time. And looking up. It felt very much like being in a position to accept Paul Bowman, who almost always did it missionary style.

"There," she yelled, looking over at Herzer who was in much the same position but facing down and about five meters away and above her. "Are you satisfied?"

✧   ✧   ✧

"Eminently," Herzer yelled, grinning playfully. "Nice free-fall we're having, don't you think?"

They'd drifted away from the ship about fifty meters, but it was still far too close. And at the speed they were falling, hitting the water would be terminal.

"Megan," Herzer said. "You have to speed us up. Make us fall *faster*."

"Are you crazy?" Megan shouted back.

"No, I'm not," Herzer said, tracking over to hover by her. "We need to get down fast, then slow us just before we hit the water. We need to hit the water *before* the ship, or we'll lose power."

"You're right," Megan shouted. "Again. Hold on."

Herzer suddenly felt as if an enormous hand had gripped him, pulling him down and to the side. The ship flashed by, seeming to climb upwards like a rocket. Even with the field around him, the wind whipped into his eyes to the point that he had to close them. But through his slitted lids he could see the ocean approaching at blinding speeds.

"How long are you going to hold this?" Herzer asked. He couldn't even maneuver with the field that was gripping him. He was completely in Megan's hands.

"Until we're right down to water level," Megan shouted. "And I'm steering towards the islands to the north. We'll still be about sixty klicks out. But that's better than right by the ship when it crashes!"

The blue water came up fast and Herzer recognized the area as somewhere around the Jama island chain. He could see a volcanic island to the north, but sixty klicks . . . wasn't going to be a survivable swim. Not with his prosthetic. And the minute the ship hit, all Megan's extra power was going to go away.

"Slowing down . . . now," Megan shouted as the water approached like an oncoming train.

Herzer again felt that magic hand and they slowed to a near stop, no more than a hundred meters off the water. He looked up and saw the shattered ship still a few thousand meters above them, twisting as it fell through the atmosphere.

"Going down," Megan said, floating over to face him as they began to gently drift towards the water. "Like a flower pet—" She stopped and blanched as they suddenly sped up.

"The fusion plants just cascade failed!" she shouted. "Lost all power! Hold your nose!"

"It's a good thing my dad taught me to swim, or you'd have drowned," Megan said, breast stroking to the north. They didn't have anything for flotation; it was impossible to get the suits off with the waves from the ship still lapping over them. So they were trying to *swim* to the islands. And not doing too well.

"Very funny," Herzer replied tiredly. Swimming with only one hand, wearing a suit that was not particularly buoyant, was difficult to say the least.

"Did I just see a dolphin?" Megan gasped, spitting out a mouthful of water. She kicked up to look around and slid under the water for her troubles.

"Maybe," Herzer replied. "But wild dolphins usually ignore swimmers."

"Maybe they're delphino," the Key-holder said, hopefully.

Herzer looked around at the vast empty sea and shrugged.

"What's the chance of that?" he said. He felt something brush his leg and decided not to mention it to Megan. He'd hated sharks ever since a bull shark had nearly made him a part of the food chain in Bimi. There was another brush and then a head covered by black hair popped up out of the waves.

Mer Captain Elayna Farswimmer flipped her hair back, took a breath of air and blasted the water out of the slits in the side of her lungs, creating a cloud of bubbles.

"I told you to stick with me," she said, grabbing both of the failing swimmers, her powerful mermaid tail sculling back and forth lightly to support them. "You get involved with strange women and bad things happen."

"*Another* old girlfriend?" Megan said, laughing in relief. "How many *are* there?"

"How'd you find us?" Herzer asked, ignoring the jibe.

"Queen Sheida called me just before the Net crashed," Elayna said. "And I hurried over as fast as I could. Of course, I didn't know exactly *where* you were going to land. Sorry it took so long."

"You're not going to be able to do much by yourself," Herzer noted. "And I've got this whole negative buoyancy problem."

"Who says I'm by myself?" Elayna replied with a grin as mer

heads started popping up and a large delphino slid in to support his weight. "I brought my whole strike company. Lucky for you, we were checking out Port Crater as an expansion to Blackbeard."

"*You've* got a *company*?" Herzer snapped.

"Of course," Elayna replied. "Some people can be *trusted* with the responsibility of command . . ."

EPILOGUE

Picture a tropical beach, light waves of aquamarine water washing pink coral sand. Palm trees. Sea breezes carrying the scent of clean water and a hint of ozone and salt. A volcanic cone rises in the background, its sides cloaked by virgin tropical forest and speckled by waterfalls.

Between two of the palm trees a very large hammock sways lightly from side to side. Beside the hammock is a table holding two stemmed goblets whose sides drip condensation. Straws jut from the top of the goblets and they have little parasols, one blue, one pink. Four feet are visible at one end of the hammock, two quite small and ladylike with brightly painted toes pointed up and two rather larger pointed down. The ladylike feet are crossed at the ankles, apparently pinning the larger from the outside.

A small, ladylike hand, with pink painted fingernails, languidly appears over the side of the hammock, fumbles around for a bit and then encounters one of the goblets. By luck, it is the one with the pink parasol. Goblet is lifted. Goblet disappears over the side of the hammock. There is some movement and a sucking sound.

"I like it here," Megan said.

A large, heavily muscled male arm terminating in a prosthetic appears over the side of the hammock. The prosthetic encounters the remaining goblet, closes on the rim and the goblet is lifted over the side of the hammock. There is some movement and the female ankles, reluctantly, separate to let the male feet rearrange.

A blue parasol flies over the side of the hammock to litter the sands. There is a sucking sound.

"Yup," Herzer replied.

There are some thoughtful sucking sounds from the hammock.

"What is this stuff?" Megan asked.

"Piña colada," Herzer replied.

"'S good."

"Yup."

"I could get used to this."

"Yup."

"We should move down here after the war. Get a little place."

"Yup."

Slurp.

"Where'd you learn about piña coladas?" Megan asked.

"Edmund," Herzer said. "He likes the islands."

"Me too," Megan said, musingly. "I wonder how much of the ship survived."

Picture a space ship, its hull wracked by the titanic forces of reentry. Two of its massive fuel bladders are punctured as the weight of its hull drags the shattered ship into the third deepest oceanic trench in the world.

The third, however, is unharmed and brimming with enough helium three to run all the world's reactors at full output for a year.

"I *really* wonder what happened to Reyes' Key. You think it survived?"

"Dunno."

Picture a half-melted armored body drifting in space. Picture a chain around the neck of the body and on the end of the chain a strip of titanium. Picture the long, slow, orbit that the body describes around the Earth, approaching, then swinging back out, over and over again in an extended elliptic.

Picture an electronic entity, her processors and memory ranging from the most advanced nanochips to the mating flight of bees, metaphorically stroking her chin as she considers the ramifications of the sinking ship and watches the long flight she is constrained not to interrupt.

✧   ✧   ✧

There was another thoughtful silence, punctuated by the occasional slurp.

"So," Megan said, "heard from Bast lately?"

"Megan?"

"Yes?"

"Shut up and kiss me."

Picture a tropical beach, light waves of aquamarine water washing pink coral sand. Palm trees. Sea breezes carrying the scent of clean water and a hint of ozone and salt. A volcanic cone rises in the background, its sides cloaked by virgin tropical forest speckled by waterfalls. Two stemmed goblets litter the ground, the remnants of piña colada melting into the pink sands.

Picture a hammock gently rocking back and forth as dolphins, dragons and mer-folk disport in the waves.

ICARUS II

TEAM HERRICK

Team Leader: Commander Herzer Herrick
Mission Advisor: Countess Megan Travante
Pilot: Joie Dessant
Comp Tech: Courtney Boehlke
Engineer: Evan Mayerle
Two Blood Lords:
    Sergeant Layne Crismon
    Corporal Yetta Barchick

TEAM VAN BUSKIRK

Team Leader: Captain Arthur Van Buskirk
Pilot: Michelle Lopez
Comp Tech: Jacklyn Pledger
Engineer: Linda Donohue
Three Blood Lords:
    Triari Sergeant Callius Doclu
    Corporal Lief Mota
    Private Ignacy de Freitas

Team Van Krief

Team Leader: Lieutenant Amosis Van Krief
Pilot: Kristina York
Comp Tech: Richard Ward
Engineer: Paul Satyat
Three Blood Lords:
Line Sergeant Doo-Tae Rubenstein
Sergeant Eaton Yamada
Private Silvano Bijan

Team Cruz

Team Leader: Lieutenant Brice Cruz
Pilot: Irvin Sanchez
Comp Tech: None
Engineer: Geo Keating
Four Blood Lords:
Triari Sergeant Ferdous Dhanapal
Line Sergeant Gyozo Nasrin
Corporal Manos Berghaus
Private Gustave Sesheshet

Team Massa

Team Leader: Lieutenant Michael Massa
Pilot: Josten Ram
Comp Tech: Manuel Sukiama
Engineer: Nicole Howard
Three Blood Lords:
Line Sergeant Arje Budak
Corporal Feng fu Nordbrandt
Private Rashid Whitlock

THE COUNCIL OF KEY-HOLDERS

NEW DESTINY KEY-HOLDERS

1. Chansa Mulengela, Minister for Frika and Ropasa, Marshal of the Great Army of Ropasa
2. Celine Reinshafen, Minister for Ephresia (Stygia), Chief of Research and Development
3. Lupe Ugatu, Lord of Slavia
4. Reyes Cho, Minister of Myana
5. Jassinte Arizzi, Minister for Tairea
6. Demon, lone actor

FREEDOM COALITION KEY-HOLDERS

1. Sheida Ghorbani, Her Majesty of the United Free States, Chairman of the Freedom Coalition.
2. Ungphakorn, Lord of Soam
3. Ishtar, Counselor of Taurania and the Hind
4. Aikawa Gouvousis, Emperor of Chin
5. Edmund Talbot, Duke Overjay, Baron Raven
6. Megan Travante, Countess Stone Hill

NEUTRAL

The Finn